"W
hu
ed
st
ne

"H
Pa
or

"Pi
ro

"H

repel and attract commands the reader's attention to the very end and will lure genre readers enamored of paranormal romance or mysteries." —*Booklist*

"Phenomenal...the story, characters and dialogue, and descriptive setting are perfect." —*Romance Reader at Heart*

"Keeps you guessing until the very end...I was awed." —*Fallen Angel Reviews*

"A great plot, wonderful characters, and a setting to die for. You gotta pick this one up." —*Fresh Fiction*

"Mmm...mmm...mmm! Get ready for the ride of your life...an intriguing eye-opener...Twists and turns, secrets and shadows, captivating characters, a well-written, well-developed plot, and a romance." —*Romance Reviews Today*

"*Rising Moon* is suspenseful, passionate, and edgy, but it's also a true feel-good read with a message of hope and redemption." —*Eternal Night Reviews*

CRESCENT MOON

"Strong heroines are a hallmark of Handeland's enormously popular werewolf series, and Diana is no exception. *Crescent Moon* delivers plenty of creepy danger and sensual thrills, which makes it a most satisfying treat." —*Romantic Times BOOKreviews*

"Handeland knows how to keep her novels fresh and scary, while keeping the heroes some of the best...pretty much perfect." —*Romance Reader at Heart*

"An enchanting and romantic love story...compelling characters and a gripping plot...This captivating tale is wrought with mystery, mayhem, and an electrifying passion hot enough to singe your fingers."

—*Romance Junkies*

"Enticing, provocative, and danger-filled."

—*Romance Reviews Today*

"Will appeal to readers on the most primal level. It effectively centers on the dark side of life, the forbidden temptations."

—*Curled Up With a Good Book*

DARK MOON

"A riveting continuation to Handeland's werewolf series...Handeland displays a talent for creating characters that are original and identifiable to the reader...her styling and creativity ensure that *Dark Moon*, though third in the series, can be read as a stand-alone work...Handeland has once again delivered a remarkable werewolf tale that is a superb addition to the genre. Fans of this genre won't want to miss out on this paranormal treat."

—*Fallen Angel Reviews*

"The end is a surprising, yet satisfying, conclusion to this series...another terrific story."

—*Fresh Fiction*

"The characters are intriguing and the romance is sexy and fun while at times heart-wrenching. The action is well written and thrilling, especially at the end...*Dark Moon* is another powerful tale with a strong heroine who is sure to please readers and a hero who is worth fighting

for. Handeland has proven with this trilogy that she has a bright future in the paranormal genre."

"Elise is Handeland's most appealing heroine yet...this tense, banter-filled tale provides a few hours of solid entertainment."

"Smart and often amusing dialogue, brisk pacing, plenty of action, and a generous helping of 'spookiness' add just the right tone...an engaging and enjoyable paranormal romance."

"A fantastic tale starring two strong likable protagonists... action-packed...a howling success."

"Handeland writes some of the most fascinating, creepy, and macabre stories I have ever read...exciting plot twists...new revelations, more emotional themes, and spiritual awakenings are prevalent here."

MARKED BY
THE MOON

Lori Handeland

St. Martin's Paperbacks

This is a work of fiction. All of the characters, organizations, and events portrayed in this novel are either products of the author's imagination or are used fictitiously.

MARKED BY THE MOON

Copyright © 2010 by Lori Handeland.
Excerpt from *Moon Cursed* copyright © 2010 by Lori Handeland.

All rights reserved.

For information address St. Martin's Press, 175 Fifth Avenue, New York, NY 10010.

ISBN: 978-0-312-38934-5

Printed in the United States of America

St. Martin's Paperbacks edition / November 2010

St. Martin's Paperbacks are published by St. Martin's Press, 175 Fifth Avenue, New York, NY 10010.

10 9 8 7 6 5 4 3 2 1

CHAPTER 1

She'd been following the man for a week. She'd been after him for a month. Werewolves weren't that easy to find.

They weren't that easy to kill, either, but she managed. Once upon a time Alexandra Trevalyn had been a member of an elite Special Forces monster-hunting unit known as the *Jäger-Suchers*. Then they'd gone soft, and she'd gone rogue.

Night had fallen over LA hours ago. Once she might have stared at the sky, dreaming about . . . Well, she really couldn't remember what she'd dreamed. Seeing her father die at fifteen had turned any dreams Alex had ever had into nightmares. Tonight she was just glad the moon was full and soon the guy would shape-shift. Then she'd shoot him.

But, as usual, nothing ever went according to plan.

Suddenly the man appeared before her. Her heart gave one quick, painful thud before she controlled the panic. Werewolves drank the smell of fear like vampires drank blood, gaining both pleasure and sustenance.

"Hey, Jorge," she said. *"¿Que pasa?"*

His eyes narrowed. "Why you followin' me, *puta*?"

"Nice. You kiss your mother with that mouth?"

"My mother is dead."

"Since you killed her, I guess you'd know."

"You a cop?"

"You wish."

Confusion flickered over his face. "Why would I wish that?"

"Because a cop wouldn't know how to kill a werewolf."

He growled, the sound no longer quite human. But instead of shifting into a wolf, he grabbed her, too intent on pawing her breasts, squeezing them as if he were checking for the best set of melons in the local produce section, to watch her hands.

"Little girls who come looking for the big bad wolf usually find him," he muttered in a voice that hovered between beast and man.

"I always do," she said, and fired the gun she'd slipped from the back of her pants while Jorge was squeezing the melons.

Fire shot from the wound, a common reaction whenever a werewolf met silver. Alex tore herself away from his still-clutching fingers and patted at the flecks of flame dotting her black blouse. Then she emptied the rest of her clip into his body, just to be sure, and watched him burn. It was her favorite part.

Luckily they were in a section of LA where gunshots didn't draw any notice. Jorge had led her here, and she'd followed gladly.

Still, she probably should have waited for the change before she'd shot him. The powers that be wrote off barbecued beast a whole lot easier than barbecued man. However, Jorge hadn't given her much choice. She certainly wasn't going to let him kill her. Or worse.

"You think shooting a dead man more than once will make him any more dead?"

Alex spun toward the voice, beneath which she could hear the familiar trill of an inhuman growl. A man lounged against the nearest abandoned building as if he'd been there for hours.

Except he hadn't been there a few minutes ago. No one had.

He was big—probably six-three, about 220, and dressed in loose black slacks, a black long-sleeved shirt, his hair covered with a dark knit cap. The outfit was a bit warm for the balmy California night, but then so was hers. The better to conceal guns and knives and other shiny things, the easier to slink with the shadows or even disappear into them.

Alex couldn't determine the color of his eyes beneath the moon and the smog-induced shadows, but she thought they might be light like hers, blue perhaps instead of green.

She'd never seen him before; she'd remember, but that didn't mean anything. There were werewolves all over the place.

He strolled toward her as if he had all the time in the world, as if he had no fear of the gun, and that made Alex twitchier than him being here in the first place.

What man didn't fear a gun? What beast didn't fear the silver inside it?

Then in a sudden flash that made her stomach drop and her head lighten, Alex remembered . . .

She'd used every last bullet on Jorge.

She went for a clip, and his arm shot forward, blurring with speed. She braced for the punch that could knock her ten yards. Instead he touched her with a metal object. She had one thought—*stun gun*—before she fell.

He leaned over her, and she knew she was dead. She waited for the violence, the pain, the blood. Instead there was a sharp prick; then everything went black.

She awoke to a small room lit by a single bare bulb. She ached everywhere, and her mouth was as dry as an August wind. Her clothes were still on, but she couldn't detect the weight of any weapons—no gun, no ammo, no silver stiletto blade. Without them, Alex felt naked anyway.

Her shoulder-length light brown hair had come loose from the tight twist she preferred when working and now covered her face. She moved only her eyes as she took stock of the surroundings—four walls, a door, and the man who'd done this to her seated at a rickety wooden table nearby.

Alex was tied to a cot, and though she wanted to yank at the bonds, see how strong they were, instead she lay still, breathing slowly and evenly, in and out. She knew better than to let on that she was awake before she figured out everything she could about where she was.

She studied her kidnapper through the curtain of her hair as he leaned his elbows on the table, staring at something between them. From the sag of his shoulders he seemed sad, almost devastated, but she'd never known a werewolf to feel bad about anything, unless it was missing a kill.

He'd removed the knit cap, and his golden hair shone beneath the light. He'd drawn the length away from his face with a rubber band to reveal sharp angles at cheek and chin, as well as the shadow of a beard across his jaw.

He turned his head. His eyes were the shade of the sky right after the sun has disappeared—cool and blue, dark with vanished warmth. For an instant Alex could have sworn she saw a flash of russet at the center, which made her think of the flames of hell that awaited him just as soon as she got her gun back.

Hey, everyone has their fantasies.

"Alexandra Trevalyn," he murmured, getting slowly to his feet. "I've been waiting for this a long time."

He crossed the short distance between them and pushed her hair out of her face, then grabbed her chin, holding on tightly when she struggled.

"Look at her," he said in a voice that chilled despite the heat in his eyes.

He dangled whatever he'd been peering at in front of her. One glance at the photograph—a woman, pretty and young, blond and laughing—and Alex closed her eyes.

Ah, hell.

"You know her?" His fingers clenched hard enough to bruise.

Alex knew her all right. She'd killed her.

Julian Barlow could barely stomach putting his hands on the murdering bitch. He was torn between an intense desire to release her and an equally strong urge to crush her face between his fingers, listen to the bones snap, hear her scream. But that would be too easy.

For her.

He had something much better planned.

She tried to jerk from his grasp, but he was too strong, and she only ended up hissing in a sharp, pained breath when he tightened his grip even more.

"Her name was Alana," he said, "and she was my wife."

Alexandra's nose wrinkled in distaste. "She was a werewolf."

"She was a person."

"No." Her eyes met his, and in them he saw her utter conviction. "She wasn't."

Just as all people weren't the same, all werewolves weren't, either. Some *were* evil, demonic, out-of-control beasts. But his wife—

Julian's throat closed, and he had to struggle against the

despair that haunted him. He'd do what he'd come to do; then maybe, just maybe, he'd be able to sleep.

Julian drew in a deep breath and frowned. He didn't smell fear. His eyes narrowed, but all he saw on Alexandra's face was a stoic resignation.

"Get it over with," she said.

"What is it you think I brought you here to do?"

"Die."

"You wish."

Alexandra's teeth ground together as he repeated the words she'd used to Jorge. He released her with a dismissive flick of the wrist. Best to get it over with as she'd said.

Lifting his fingers to the buttons of his shirt, Julian undid them one after the other, then let the dark garment slide to the floor. Her eyes widened, and she let her gaze wander over him. Wherever that gaze touched, gooseflesh rose. He didn't want her looking at him, but he didn't have much choice.

Julian lowered his hands to his trousers, and her eyes followed. But as soon as he unbuttoned the single button, they jerked up to meet his. The sound of the zipper shrieked through the heavy, waiting silence.

She started, paled, and it was then that he at last smelled her fear.

"Dying doesn't scare you," he murmured as he eased his thumb beneath the waistband of the black pants and drew them over his hips. "Let's see what does."

"You're going to have a mighty hard time raping me with that," she sneered, lifting her chin toward his limp member.

"Rape?" He yanked the tie from his ponytail and let his hair swirl loose. "Not my style."

Confusion flickered over her face. "Then what's with the striptease?"

Instead of answering, he threw back his head and howled.

The scent of her fear called to his beast. He'd dreamed of this, of her, planned it, lived for it. He wanted Alexandra Trevalyn to understand what she had done, suffer for it a very long time, and there was only one way that could happen.

Julian's body bowed as his spine altered. Bones crackled, joints popped; his nose and mouth lengthened into a snout. Hands and feet became paws, claws sprouted where finger and toenails had been. When he fell to the ground on all fours, golden hair shot from every pore. Last but not least a tail and ears appeared as he became a wolf in every way but two— human eyes in an inhuman face, human intelligence in the guise of an animal.

"No one can shift that fast." He swung his head toward the woman, who stared at him wide eyed.

Having once been a *Jäger-Sucher,* she had to know the basics. To paraphrase Shakespeare: There *were* more things in heaven and earth than could ever be dreamt of.

And Julian was one of them.

He had been born centuries ago, and with age comes not only wisdom but talent, at least to a werewolf. The older Julian got, the faster he changed.

He stalked toward her on stiff legs, ruff standing on end, upper lip pulled back. Her jaw tightened as she tried not to cringe, but her body wouldn't obey her mind's command. His hot breath cascaded over her arm, her neck, her face. She was helpless. He could do anything that he wanted. She knew it, and her fear whirled around him like a midsummer fog.

Had this been what Alana felt in the moments before she died? Or hadn't she had a chance to feel anything before this child had shot her with silver, then watched her burn. A growl rumbled in Julian's throat.

The girl tensed and shouted, "Do it!"

So Julian sank his teeth into her shoulder.

Alex refused to scream even though the pain was worse than anything she'd ever known. Multicolored dots danced before her eyes; then the world wavered, shimmered, and disappeared.

Hours, moments, seconds later, she came awake sputtering. Someone had thrown water into her face.

The werewolf, now in human form—he'd even gotten dressed—leaned over her, empty plastic bottle crunched in his huge hand. "Soon," he murmured, "you'll understand."

Her shoulder on fire, she was weak, dizzy, feverish, but she remembered everything, and the horror of it almost made her retch.

"You bastard!" Alex shouted, pulling at her bonds. "You bit me."

"You told me to," he said.

"I didn't. I'd never—"

"Did you or did you not shout, 'Do it!' "

"I meant tear out my throat. *Kill* me."

If a werewolf *bit* a human, the human become a werewolf. If the ravenous beast ate from its victim, blessed death was the result.

Her tormentor tilted his head, and his long hair slid across his neck, spreading outward like a golden fan. "You'd rather be dead," he murmured, "than a werewolf."

"Damn straight."

"And my wife would rather have been a werewolf than dead." He shrugged, unconcerned. "I guess you're even."

Frustration and fury welled within her. She yanked on her bonds again, and the cot rattled as she lifted first one side, then the other from the floor. She was already getting stronger.

"Let me go." He did nothing but laugh. "Why are you doing this?"

"I want you to understand what you've done."

"I killed monsters. Evil, demonic creatures that belonged in hell."

"You killed wives and husbands, mothers and fathers, someone's children. You think we don't love? You think we don't mourn?"

"Animals don't feel."

He grabbed her by the chin again. "You're wrong."

Alex should have a huge bruise from when he'd wolf-handled her before. His touch *should* hurt, but it didn't. She was already healing faster than humanly possible.

He let go of her with a flick of his wrist, as if he couldn't bear to have his skin in contact with hers for one second longer than necessary—she knew the feeling—and walked away. Alex had to crane her neck to watch him disappear out the door.

"Hey!" she shouted, then paused. Would she be better or worse off if he left her behind?

The question became moot when he reappeared carrying an inert body, which he placed on the floor.

"Don't worry." He walked to the door again, drawing it closed behind him. "He's a very bad man."

As soon as he was gone, Alex fought to get loose in earnest.

He'd bitten her instead of killing her, then tied her down and left her in a room with a helpless human being. She had to pull free and run, then find a silver . . . anything and kill herself before she changed. Because as soon as she did, she'd need human blood, and there was some right here.

Her struggles only served to make her sweat. The room had no air-conditioning, no window. She pulled on the restraints so hard her wrists bled. The scent of blood, of man made her stomach growl.

Once bitten, a human shifts within twenty-four hours. Traditionally werewolves can only change between dusk and dawn—except that first time. Then it doesn't matter—day or night, full moon or dark, new wolves become. They had no choice.

Suddenly the room vanished, and Alex ran through a dense forest. Warm sun cast dappled shadows through the branches. The cool air seemed to sparkle. The scent of pine surrounded her.

She burst from the trees onto a rolling plain. Here and there patches of snow shone electric white against just-sprung grass threaded with purple wildflowers. In the distance loomed piles of ice that appeared as high as a mountain.

A sense of freedom, of utter joy filled her. She wanted to run across this land forever. It was . . .

Home.

Except Alex had no home. She'd been born in Nebraska— not many mountains there, ice or any other. They were a little short on forests, too. And she hadn't lived in one place for longer than a month since she was five.

She caught the scent of warm blood, of tasty meat, and turned tail—she had one—to return to the forest. Something flashed up ahead, crashing through the brush in terror.

Wham!

Alex fell back into her body, still lying on the cot in the horrendously hot, horribly small room. She wasn't any closer to being released, but from the way her skin felt, too small to contain her, she was much closer to being inhuman.

"Collective consciousness," she muttered. "God."

Once a victim is infected, the lycanthropy virus changes him from human to beast. He begins to remember things that have happened to others—the thrill of the chase, the love of the kill, the taste of the blood.

"It's coming," Alex said in a voice that no longer resembled her own. Deeper, garbled, she'd heard the sound before.

From the mouths of the soon-to-be-furry.

The pain became more of an itch, a need to burst forth. Alex tried to fight that need but couldn't. Her dark jeans and black blouse tore with a rending screech; her boots seemed to explode as her feet turned to paws.

Her nose ached; her teeth were too big for her mouth. Then suddenly that mouth became part of the nose, and those teeth felt just right.

The bonds restraining her popped. She writhed, contorted, snarled, moaned, and when she at last rolled to the floor, she was no longer human but a wolf.

Alex stared at her paws, covered with fur the same shade as her hair; she didn't need a mirror to see that her own green eyes stared out of an animal's face.

The world expanded—sounds sharp as the blade of a knife, smells so intense her mouth watered with desire; she could see every mote of dust tumbling through the air like snowflakes of silver and gold.

Hunger blazed, a pounding pulse in her head. If she didn't eat soon, if she didn't kill something, she thought she might go mad.

Then she saw him—there on the floor, trussed up and still. What was his name?

Oh, yeah. Brunch.

Alex took one step forward, and the door crashed open. The silhouette of a man spread across the floor. She skittered back, startled, growling, then lifted her snout and sniffed. Recognition flickered, just out of reach. She knew him, yet still the hair on her neck lifted as the growl deepened to a snarl.

The urge to attack warred with the clawing hunger in her belly. Her head swung back and forth between the two men as her human intelligence weighed the possibilities.

The bound one could wait; he wasn't going anywhere. Once she took down the newcomer, there'd be twice as much to eat and a lot less to fear.

Her muscles bunched, and she leaped. Before her body began the downward arc that would send her sailing directly into the man in the doorway, a sharp pain bloomed in her chest. Her limbs felt weighted with sand but strangely her mind cleared, and as she tumbled to the ground, she remembered who he was.

Edward.

Now she was definitely dead.

CHAPTER 2

When Alex came around, she was no longer a wolf but a woman. Naked, she lay beneath a blanket on the cot where she'd so recently been tied. The trussed man was gone. Unfortunately, Edward wasn't.

Tall, thin, pale, Edward Mandenauer, the leader of the *Jäger-Suchers,* didn't appear concerned to be in a small room with a woman able to sprout fangs and a tail. Probably because such things had been happening to him for more than sixty years.

With the rifle slung over his back, a pistol in hand, and a bandolier of bullets across his cadaverous chest, Edward was, as usual, ready for Armageddon.

"It has been a long time," he murmured.

You'd think that after residing in the United States for better than half a century, his heavy German accent would have faded. Everything else about him had. His once-blond hair was now white, his eyes pale blue, his skin paper-fine. It never ceased to amaze Alex that the man's kill count was twice her own. Or at least it had been when she'd still been required to count.

She sat up, uncaring when the blanket pooled at her waist.

A few hours ago she would have been mortified, which only proved she'd changed in more ways than one.

She felt damn good. Any minor aches and pains were gone. Energy pulsed within her, the buzz reminiscent of the one time she'd tried to unplug a cheap motel hair dryer while still sopping wet from the shower. *Zap!* She'd never done that again.

The world seemed so much more *there*. Alex could feel the air on her skin, hear every breath Edward took; if she listened she could probably distinguish the dull thud of his ancient heart and the slow flow of blood through his veins. She bet she could smell it.

Lifting her nose, Alex sniffed, then licked her lips. Edward lifted his gun.

So it was going to be like that.

"Let's get this over with." Alex repeated the same words to Edward that she'd so recently used with the wolf man, even as her gaze slid to the left, the right, searching for a way out. Though her mind had accepted the inevitability of her death, her body quivered with the possibility of escape.

"Get what over with?" Edward asked.

"My unavoidable demise. I suppose you want me to grow pointy ears and a snout again so you have less to explain after you shoot me in the head." Although Edward never had much of a problem explaining anything—one of his many talents.

"I'm not going to shoot you in the head, Alex."

"Chest then. Whatever."

"If I was going to shoot you with silver, I wouldn't have bothered with the tranquilizer dart."

Then why had he?

For that matter, why had she shape-shifted again? A werewolf must ingest human blood under the full moon before morphing back into a person, and after the initial change only a kill would do. Otherwise madness was the result.

Alex ran her tongue around the inside of her mouth. She probably had a raging case of halitosis but no blood breath. She was also way too calm for a just-made wolf, and while she did feel different, she didn't feel crazy or evil. Sure, if she had a chance to get away, she'd take it, and if that meant going through Edward, she wouldn't cry about it. But that was simply survival.

Alex studied the old man, who lifted his bushy white brows as if waiting for her to catch up. Eventually, she did. "What did you do to me?"

He held up an empty syringe.

Ah-ha!

Edward had his very own Dr. Frankenstein on the payroll—a virologist who'd spent a lot of time trying to cure lycanthropy. The main reason Alex had left the *Jäger-Suchers* was their edict that agents give werewolves a choice of being cured or being killed. In her book they didn't deserve a second chance. Her father hadn't gotten one. Hell, her mother hadn't, either.

"You cured me?" she asked. Alex didn't feel cured; she felt a little wolfy.

Edward shook his head. "I gave you a serum that removes the bloodlust, at least for a little while."

"Handy. Why don't I feel possessed?"

"It takes time for the demon to awaken. At first a new werewolf is confused, crazed. Most do not have access to this." He lifted the syringe again. "The more you kill, the better you will like it. Soon there is no going back, and you do not want to."

He pocketed the syringe, then removed a sheet of paper from another pocket and laid it on the table. "You will look at this."

Though Edward giving her orders made Alex's teeth ache—or maybe that was just because she was grinding them together with so much more force than she used to have— nevertheless she stood and crossed the tiny room, leaving the blanket behind. She didn't like how it felt against her humming skin.

The sound that rumbled out of Alex's throat at the sight of the drawing wasn't even close to human. The man portrayed in the sketch wasn't, either. He'd been a werewolf when he bit her.

"Who is he?" she asked.

"Julian Barlow." Edward's thin lips tightened. "One of the oldest I've ever known."

Which explained why Edward had brought a drawing instead of a photograph. Werewolves didn't show up on film. Any photos would have to have been taken before the people became werewolves, which made Alex wonder about Alana.

"Barlow isn't one of Mengele's wolves," Alex concluded.

"No."

According to Edward, whom she was inclined to believe since he'd been a double agent during The Big One, Hitler had demanded a werewolf army. His equally psychotic pal, Mengele, gave him one.

When the Allies landed and began to sweep across France toward Germany, the evil doctor panicked and released everything he'd concocted in his secret laboratory deep in the Black Forest. Edward had been trying to rid the world of them ever since.

What Edward hadn't known then, but found out fairly

quickly, was that there had been werewolves long before Mengele. A lot of them.

"*What* is he?" Alex asked. "From where? When?"

"No one knows."

"*You* don't? How can that be?" Edward knew everything, or at least pretended to.

"Barlow has more powers than any werewolf I've ever encountered. He can change in an instant. He can run so fast he seems to disappear. He can make things happen just by thinking of them."

"He's more than a werewolf."

"I want you to find out what."

"I don't work for you anymore. And besides, I've got a little problem with my tail." Alex wiggled her ass. It was still naked, and she still didn't care.

"He could have killed you," Edward murmured, "but he didn't."

"Dying would be too easy. He wanted me to suffer."

Actually, he'd wanted her to understand, and she was starting to. She was still Alex but better—and that she believed she was better, not doomed, scared her.

"I know you can fix me," she blurted. She just wasn't sure how.

"Barlow has been following you," Edward continued as if she hadn't spoken. "He's had this planned for a while."

As the words sank in, fury rolled through her, a wave of ice just beneath the surface of her overheated skin. It felt . . . glorious. She wanted to leap across the table, grab Edward by the throat, and—

Alex rubbed a thumb between her eyes, where her pulse still throbbed. Allowing the anger in was letting the beast out. She had to take several deep breaths before she could speak again.

"You let him bite me."

He didn't deny it; she hadn't expected him to. Edward could be depended upon for one thing, and one thing only. He'd do whatever he had to do to defeat the monsters.

"We need someone on the inside of Barlow's pack," he said.

"I don't think so."

"He's up to something, Alex."

"Werewolves always are."

Edward's face tightened, the expression stretching pale skin over sharp bones, making him appear almost skeletal. "There are rumors of another army amassing, with Barlow at the helm."

"A werewolf army?" Alex clarified.

Edward dipped his chin. "Can you imagine one with him in the lead? They will march over the earth, leaving blood and death and fire behind."

For an instant Alex saw the world in flames, an army of werewolves on the rampage, and she ached to be one of them. She'd never be alone again. She'd never be afraid. No one could ever harm her. Then the image vanished, and she was left blinking in confusion, stunned at the duality raging within her.

"I don't want to stay like this," Alex said urgently. "Cure me. Then tell me where they are, and I'll turn them to ashes."

"We don't know where they are. Anyone who's ever followed Barlow hasn't come back."

She lifted her brows. If the British SAS were considered by many to be the best Special Forces in the world, and the US Special Forces were easily the best equipped, the *Jäger-Suchers* were both. Not only did Edward recruit those who were willing to give their lives, but he had them trained by agents who had seen everything, fought it all, and won. Like her father.

Edward also had a secret ops budget that would make Delta Force envious, if they knew about it, and an in with whatever weapons and technology experts were considered the boy and girl geniuses of the moment. Edward volunteered his elite group to test new toys, and if they lived, they got to keep them.

So if every J-S agent he'd sent after Barlow had failed to come back, Alex had to wonder what the wolf man was packing. The only thing more powerful than American weaponry was magic.

"We've never had a chance like this before," Edward continued. "You're one of his now. He'll take you with him."

"He hates my guts."

"Nevertheless, he has made you. If you're in danger, he cannot abandon you. He will teach you things. It is their way."

Huh, their way didn't sound half bad.

Alex smacked the heel of her hand against her forehead. She had to stop *thinking* like that.

"What if he takes one whiff of me and smells you?"

Edward narrowed his eyes, sensing an insult in there somewhere but not quite sure what it was. "You'll have to take that chance."

"Why should I?"

"Because someone in that pack killed your father."

Alex froze. "What?"

"You think I allow the monsters who murder my agents to run free? It may take time, Alex, but eventually I find them; then I make them pay."

She didn't need to ask how he'd discovered the information when she couldn't. She'd been traversing the country hunting on her own, taking odd jobs wherever she could find them just to have enough money to keep herself in ham sandwiches and silver bullets. Edward had access to resources she did not, and still it had taken him eight years.

"Are you in," Edward asked, "or are you out?"

"In," she said without a moment's hesitation.

Julian's plan had been to infect Alexandra Trevalyn with the lycanthropy virus, gift her with a man who deserved very much to die, then leave. She would shift; she would kill; she would have no choice. Then, when she changed back, maybe she would understand a little better what she had done when she had murdered his wife.

That was the part he would miss seeing. The ecstasy followed by the agony. The unbearable hunger, then the quenching of it. The inevitable realization of what had happened beneath the moon and the horror that would result from it.

Most werewolves *were* evil, but some were not, and all the wolves in Julian's pack were of the latter variety. He'd heard of others as well, though he'd never met them.

Julian was different, and because of that, those he made were different, too. Instead of being consumed by a demon that urged them to kill at every opportunity, Julian's wolves retained their humanity. They valued their lives and the lives of others. Certainly human blood was required beneath the full moon. But blood and death were two very different things.

Unfortunately a kill was still inevitable after the initial change. It was the only way to come back from the edge of insanity. After that, however, Julian's wolves were loath to kill again. The core of evil that characterized other were-wolves did not exist in his.

Once upon a time Julian had attempted to prevent his wolves from making that original kill—supplying them with fresh human blood instead as he did on all of the full moons that followed. But it didn't work. For reasons he couldn't fathom, *not* killing that first time turned them into killing machines ever after.

A fate he didn't want for Alexandra. No, he wanted her to regain her humanity and experience the anguish of being unable to stop herself from killing, then live with it as they all did. He wanted her to understand that once the initial change and kill were behind them, some werewolves were just like everyone else. When she'd shot Alana, she had murdered a person; she had not rid the world of a monster.

He could have stayed and watched but he hadn't survived for more than a thousand years by remaining at the scene of any one of his crimes. He did not plan to be at this one when all hell—now known as Alexandra Trevalyn—broke loose.

Julian had no doubt that a *Jäger-Sucher* would show up eventually and put her out of her misery. And while he'd *love* to see how she liked it, he had no desire to run into any of Edward Mandenauer's superior hunters again. He'd already had to dispose of far too many, and Edward was not a man who forgot such things. The old warrior would do his best to exact vengeance, but Julian did not plan to give him the opportunity.

After exiting the abandoned apartment building, Julian drew on his ability to move faster than the human eye could track—with age came many advantages, and this was one of them. He was several miles away when a strange, cold, somewhat sick feeling invaded his consciousness. He slowed and nearly knocked over a kid running in the other direction.

"Jeez, dude," the young man said.

"Pardon me," Julian muttered.

"Pardon?" The boy laughed. "Man, where you from?"

Julian didn't bother to answer. He was both history and legend, from a time and place so far away there was no one left of it but him.

And one other.

The kid eyed Julian's new clothes, clean hands, and expensive shoes. A spark of avarice lit his eyes, and his grubby paw disappeared into his pocket.

"You don't want to do that," Julian said.

The young man glanced up, and Julian let him see what lay beneath his smooth human veneer. Next thing he knew, the boy was scurrying back in the direction he'd just come, leaving Julian alone to examine what had caused him to stop running in the first place.

The sick sensation still lodged deep in his belly, and the breeze, which he knew to be hot, slid across his skin like an ice cube. He'd think he had a fever, the flu, except he didn't get sick. Not since he'd become a werewolf.

He'd learned to listen to his feelings. In wolf form they would be called instincts, and they were as reliable as the sun at dawn.

Julian continued to walk in the direction he'd been headed. Immediately he began to shiver, and his stomach cramped.

"Knull mæ i øret," he muttered. The only time his native language came naturally anymore was when he cursed.

Slowly he turned in the other direction and retraced his steps. As he did, the pain lessened. He was unable to move very quickly, but the closer he got to where he'd left Alexandra Trevalyn, the better he felt.

Which made no damn sense at all.

Julian sat on a crumbling cement stoop in front of a half-burned warehouse. He breathed in and out, ignoring the scent of soot as he calmed his roiling belly. He managed to get past the nausea, but he couldn't make himself stand up and go. Eventually he faced the truth.

He couldn't leave her here. She was pack now.

"Knull mæ i øret," he said again, then he laughed.

He'd made other wolves in his lifetime. But he'd never tried to leave any behind as soon as he'd made them. That would have been a recipe for disaster.

New wolves were . . . a problem. Until they became accustomed to the changes, Julian always remained close. Because of that, it had never occurred to him that he would be physically unable to let Alexandra fend for herself.

Julian sat on the stoop and tried to enjoy what he knew would probably be his last peaceful moments for a good long while. He was going to bring one of his most hated enemies into the heart of his existence.

Whose vengeance was this anyway?

Edward snapped his fingers, and a woman walked through the door.

"What is this, Grand Central?" Alex asked.

Edward, who'd always had a problem with sarcasm—probably because of his English-as-a-second-language issues—frowned. "This is Los Angeles. Grand Central is in New York, is it not?"

Alex rolled her eyes and caught the ghost of a smile on the newcomer's face.

The woman was tiny, and that wasn't just because Alex stood five-nine barefoot. She was petite, too, in a way Alex could never be, her youthful face framed by dark hair with a slash of white at the temple. Her eyes were clear blue, and held an honest, earnest expression Alex wanted very much to trust.

"I'm Cassandra," the woman said. "Your friendly New Orleans voodoo priestess."

Alex's desire to trust evaporated. "Sure you are."

Cassandra's only answer was a widening of her smile, which convinced Alex more than any bones in the nose would have.

"Voodoo?" Alex glanced at Edward. "You finally lost that last marble, didn't you?"

Cassandra choked.

The lines in Edward's forehead deepened. "I do not understand why everyone is always discussing my marbles, or lack of them. I have not had any marbles since I was a boy."

"Got that right," Alex muttered, and Cassandra began to cough.

Edward pounded her on the back, more in irritation than to be helpful. "Move along," he ordered. "Alex has been holding off the demon thus far, but I worry it will overtake her soon."

Alex worried about that, too. She could practically hear their human hearts beating; she sensed the swoosh of blood through their veins. The scent of warm flesh made her stomach cramp and her mouth water.

On top of that, her own skin felt too small, her teeth too big. She kept hearing howls and growls, but they weren't real; they were in her head. Every once in a while she flashed on a forest, on prey, and her pulse accelerated in anticipation of the kill.

And there would be a kill. There had to be.

"Do something," she managed.

Cassandra got down to business, pulling bottles and vials and bags of what appeared to be grass out of her backpack; then she removed a clay bowl and set it on the table.

Tossing in a little of this and a little of that, she sang a song Alex had never heard before in what seemed to be a combination of French and something else. As she did, the sounds in Alex's head faded.

"Come here," Cassandra said.

Alex cast a quick glance at Edward. He had his gun pointed at her head. "Touch her and I will shoot you."

"You're under the delusion that I care if I live or die." Alex strode closer to Cassandra.

"You might not care," Edward said, "but the demon does. It wants to kill. It will fight what we mean to do."

"Just say no," Cassandra quipped, then she lifted a dagger.

Alex took a quick step back, the scent of the silver burning her nostrils. But Cassandra slashed her own palm before grabbing Alex's. A jolt, reminiscent of the stun gun, went all the way through her.

Cassandra released Alex, and she fell to the ground, dizzy with the crackle, the scent, of flames that weren't, the raging of a battle that was going on inside. She felt like a cartoon, as if her skull should be shaping and reshaping while the demon within poked and kicked and battered to be free.

Edward was right. It wanted her to kill. Them. Now.

The change threatened. Her teeth itched; so did her skin. She stared at her fingernails, waiting for them to grow. Once she shifted, she would be unable to control herself. She'd listen to the urges within her, urges that were no longer voices but instincts; they would be impossible to ignore. She would kill whoever was the closest, and she would enjoy it.

"No," she said. *"No."*

Everything stilled.

Cassandra knelt on the floor next to her, gaze intent on Alex's face. "You okay?"

"Saying *no* actually worked."

Cassandra shrugged. "Figured it wouldn't hurt."

"Is she clean?" Edward asked.

"She's right here," Alex muttered. "And I wasn't dirty."

He sniffed. "That is a matter of opinion."

"She's cursed." Cassandra got to her feet. "Just like you wanted."

"You *cursed* me?"

Cassandra flushed. "Yes and no. I took away all evil desires—what we refer to as the demon—but not the necessity of shifting under the full moon."

"Gee, thanks," Alex muttered.

"You cannot be too different," Edward said, "or he will know. You must fake the demon somehow."

She could probably do that.

Alex glanced at Cassandra. "I still don't understand how this is a curse. More like a blessing."

"Yes and no," Cassandra repeated. "Once the demon is removed you remember what you've done; you understand how wrong it is. The spell gives those without conscience a conscience."

"Which, if I'd actually been eating people, would drive me kind of mad."

"Exactly." Cassandra dusted off her hands. "Well, my work here is done. Nice to meet you, but I really need to get back to New Orleans."

She tossed all the voodoo paraphernalia into her backpack and headed for the door. New Orleans was definitely the place for her.

"Use the exit we devised," Edward said.

Cassandra glanced over her shoulder. "I know better than to waltz out the front." She held up her hand before he could speak. "Or the back."

"Go," Edward ordered, and with a roll of her eyes, Cassandra did.

When she was gone, Alex asked, "What exit?"

"We came in through a hidden connection with the building next door," Edward said. "We don't want Barlow to realize you've been in contact with me."

"Does he know I once worked for you?"

Edward shrugged. "If he does, he also knows you don't anymore. And he'll have heard that I don't suffer rogues gladly."

"How do you suffer them?"

He lifted his brow. "If they step too far out of line, they do not step out again."

"You kill them?" she asked, not surprised, not really.

"Why would I do that?"

Edward had always had the annoying habit of answering questions with questions, which weren't really answers at all.

"You will report back to me in a month," the old man said. "With detailed directions to his lair."

Alex bristled. She couldn't help it. "And if I don't?"

"Until you give me what I want, I will not give you what you want." He shrugged. "Remain furry as long as you like."

He had her and he knew it. She would do his bidding as quickly as she could, if only to get rid of her tendency to grow a tail.

"How am I going to find this guy," Alex murmured, "if the great and powerful Mandenauer couldn't?"

Instead of responding, Edward shot her with the damn dart gun again. Alex wanted to grab the thing and shoot him, see how he liked it. But whatever was in those darts worked fast. Everything shimmied.

As she slid to the floor, Edward's voice seemed to come from a long way off. "Don't worry, Alex. He will find you."

CHAPTER 3

"Alexandra."

Something wailed in her ears, so shrill, so loud, she'd never be able to go back to sleep. But she couldn't seem to stay awake, either.

"Alexandra!" *Shake, shake.* "The police are coming."

Whoever was doing the shaking stopped and slapped her across the face. Alex's eyes snapped opened; Julian Barlow hovered over her.

"Wha—?"

She was confused, dopey, but things started to come back. The gun, the dart, Edward's words.

He will find you.

The old man had been right again.

She sat up, then clutched her head. What the hell had he shot her with that time? If she ever saw Edward again, she was going to—

Alex wasn't sure what. But something painful.

She glanced down and a low moan escaped. Not because she was still naked, but because she was still naked and covered in blood.

Her head cleared at the sight, and she peered around the

room, which appeared to have been prepped for a scene in *Texas Chainsaw Massacre: The Return*.

The trussed man lay on the floor. From the amount of blood on the guy, he was dead. From the amount on Alex, she'd killed him.

Or at least that was what Barlow was supposed to believe. Alex didn't remember doing it, and there was one thing that made her almost certain she hadn't—the voodoo curse that had removed the desire to commit evil acts.

But was killing a very bad man an evil act? Hard to say.

Someone had killed the guy. The situation smelled to high heaven of Edward—king of the setup. Except—

Would Edward murder a man just to cement Alex's cover? That she wasn't quite sure disturbed her. She was starting to wonder just who was possessed by a demon around here.

"Put this on." Barlow shoved a pair of sweats and a T-shirt into Alex's hands as she stood. Both read UCLA and looked much worse for someone else's wear. They didn't smell too bad, yet she hesitated. The thought of putting clothes over all the blood nauseated her, and besides—

There was another way to escape.

The change rippled beneath her skin, calling to her, tempting her with the promise of speed and power. She took a deep breath and caught the scent of trees; her eyes drifted closed and—

"We don't have time to shift," Barlow snapped. "Or at least you don't."

Her eyes opened. He was right. Damn him.

"Why do you care if I'm caught?" Stifling her disgust, Alex pulled on the clothes.

"I don't care if you die screaming in the electric chair. But if they keep you behind bars until the next full moon—" He glanced at the dead man. "—and I'm pretty sure they will, there'll be too many questions once they see what happens then."

"Again, what do you care?"

"I hate questions." His fingers dug into her arm as he dragged her toward the door.

"I hate *you*," she muttered.

"Aw, and here I was hoping you'd fall madly in love with me, just so I could spit in your face."

Oh, boy, this mission was going to be *so* much fun. Especially when she nailed him.

Suddenly Barlow stopped, tilted his head, listened. Footsteps clattered closer. The police had arrived.

Alex tensed. What if Barlow decided to kill the cops so the two of them could go on their merry way? What would she do?

An evil, satanic wolf bitch would jump right in and help. *Decisions, decisions.*

Luckily she didn't have to make one. Barlow tugged Alex into the corner, then closed his eyes. His face became intent, as if he was trying very hard to imagine unimaginable things. A rumble came from deep in his throat; a flush darkened his skin. She could have sworn she caught the scent of . . . anger. And that she could smell anger distracted her for all of an instant before something else captured her attention entirely.

A weird, shimmery glow drifted downward; crystal waves cascaded between them and the rest of the world. A pair of officers thundered down the hall and into the room without a glance in their direction.

"Shit!" said one.

The other gagged. *He must be a rookie.*

"Who called this in?" the first demanded, probably more to get his partner's mind off the mess than anything else.

"Dispatch said—" *Cough. Cough.* "Some old guy from the neighborhood."

Edward. Asshole. He'd meant for Alex to get caught, or nearly so, to draw Barlow out.

As she and Barlow waited for the officers to leave, they remained crushed together in a cocoon created by Barlow's magic, her nose pressed to his neck, his chin brushing the top of her head.

He smelled wild, but not in a feral, unpleasant way. Instead Alex caught the scent of evergreens, snow, and fresh air. The great outdoors.

She leaned in and caught again the drift of anger, like jalapeño peppers preserved in ice. How strange. That scent seemed to swirl both around, then through her. Her entire body tingled, nerves dancing, the hairs on her arms, her neck, everywhere, alight with sensation.

He pulled her closer. The movement caused her lips to brush his collarbone. The texture both smooth and hard, she was compelled to taste.

Her tongue darted out, and she relished the flavor of man. His blood sang, just below the surface, and she wanted it; she wanted him. Her moan was protest, or maybe arousal.

"What was that?"

Vaguely she heard one cop speak, another murmur; then the two of them stepped into the hall. Alex didn't care. Her body seemed to have a mind of its own, or perhaps no mind at all.

Her hands crept under Barlow's shirt, touching his skin, the hills and valleys of his rib cage, his abdomen; her teeth scraped the vein in his neck as her thumb traced below the waistband of his trousers and over the hard, smooth head of his shaft.

His breath caught; she glanced up. Fury suffused his face, flushing his skin, honing the fine bones beneath. He glanced over her shoulder as the two men came out of the room, then grabbed her hair and yanked her head back so hard her neck cracked. She figured he was going to kill her, or at least try. Instead he crushed his mouth to hers.

Their teeth clashed; she grunted. He caught her lip between his teeth and bit down. A warning. *Keep quiet.*

However, this time the officers did not hear them. She opened one eye. The shimmering glow that encapsulated them appeared to have thickened.

Barlow let go of her lip, hovering over her, hesitant, uncertain. Then, almost as if he couldn't help himself—hell, she couldn't—his tongue flicked out, laving the tiny hurt. The gentling of his mouth was followed by a roughening of his hands. He ran them over her, as if memorizing the length of her body, testing the shape of her backside; then he skimmed them up her ribs beneath the borrowed T-shirt, cupping and lifting her unbound breasts.

Both his palms and his fingertips were callused. They scraped her skin, made her shiver. She arched into his touch, spellbound by his kiss.

How could he make her wet with just the taste of his mouth? There was something here, something she craved more than blood. She wanted to wallow in the sensations, the stroke of his tongue, the nip of his teeth, the all-encompassing pleasure promised by his touch.

She didn't realize she was fondling him still, sliding her curved fingers along his length, rubbing her thumb over his tip. Stroking, squeezing, making him come.

Almost.

He swelled in her palm. She increased the speed, the

pressure, skated her teeth over his jaw, down his neck, contemplated sucking on the throbbing vein there, or maybe sliding to her knees and sucking on something else.

Then he grabbed her wrist, yanked it out of his pants, tightening his grip to the point of pain when she struggled. "They're gone."

He shoved Alex away, wiping the back of his hand across his mouth. He might as well have slapped her.

What had she been doing? Had she lost her mind as well as her humanity? She'd never behaved like that with any man, let alone with one who wasn't even a man.

But she wasn't a woman anymore, either.

"What the fuck was that?" she muttered.

He wouldn't meet her eyes. She didn't blame him. She'd just had her hand down his pants. Alex dropped her gaze. Not that he'd minded. If he hated her as much as he said, and she was certain he did, then why did the front of his pants still bulge? Why had it ever bulged at all?

"Nothing," he said quickly. "A—a typical reaction to danger when in close proximity to your maker."

She blinked. "That's going to happen again?"

"Not if I can help it."

What the fuck was that? Julian thought to himself.

He'd come up with a quick excuse of danger combined with a common reaction to one's maker, but it was BS. Their reaction to each other was far from common.

At the moment, Alexandra seemed to believe his explanation. However, if that happened again—and considering he had no idea why it had happened in the first place, maybe it would—she'd know he was lying.

More sirens wailed in the distance, pulling his attention from the problem of his hands on her breasts, hers on his—

"We have to go." Julian reached for her, and she took a step back. He didn't blame her.

"This is nuts," she murmured. "Werewolves can't touch in human form. We should both have big fat migraines."

Ordinary werewolves—how was that for a misnomer—had a little tic. If skin met skin while in human form, mind-numbing agony was the result.

"I've always been able to touch the wolves that I've made."

Being *able* to touch her didn't bother him. That he wanted to so badly did.

Alex stared at him, green eyes wide in her triangular face. With her blond-brown hair, he found himself wondering what she looked like in wolf form. Right now she resembled a startled Siamese cat.

"Who *are* you?" she whispered.

"Julian Barlow." He glanced down the corridor where the cops had disappeared.

"No, I mean *what* are you?"

He didn't have time to explain. They'd be back.

"Later," he said shortly.

This time when he reached for her he didn't allow her to step away. He grabbed her by the biceps and dragged her into the next room. A tepid breeze trickled through the open window.

"Where are we going?" she asked.

Instead of answering, Julian climbed over the splintered wood sill. He was so old that the scrapes and scratches he received on his palms healed before he'd dropped the few feet to the ground. Unless a wound was very deep, or made by silver, it might as well not exist.

Julian turned as Alex leaned out, her gaze tilted upward. Shadows flickered across her face, making her eyes appear silver instead of lime green. She was really quite pretty, if he could get past her being a murderer.

He couldn't, but it appeared his penis could. Just the sight of her caused it to stir, and he made himself count to ten in Norwegian in an attempt to distract himself.

Alexandra's attention remained on the full moon as if she was fascinated by it. He understood. The moon called to them, its waxing and waning marking time until the one night they all ran beneath it as one.

At times like this, when the moon was round and high and white, it seemed to whisper, to pull at them like a past lover who is gone but never quite forgotten. On every eve of every full moon, Julian always missed Alana so badly that each howl he uttered resembled her name.

He'd spent centuries without a wife. He hadn't been interested; he'd never once been tempted. Why have one woman when you could have a dozen?

Then one of Julian's people, Margaret Jones, had begged him to save her granddaughter. A young preschool teacher who had an incredible gift with children, Alana had been diagnosed with terminal breast cancer, and she was very near the end.

Julian had gone to the hospice, and he'd asked Alana—as he'd asked every one of his wolves—if she wanted to live or to die. He'd shown her what he was, and she'd agreed to become like him.

When he brought her home, Alana's gentle, sweet nature had captivated him. She'd been so damn young, and Julian—though he appeared exactly her age—had been so damn old. She'd made him remember things he'd long ago forgotten; she'd made him see the world as brand new. She'd looked at him as though he could do anything, probably because, at first, she'd believed that he could.

Tonight he felt Alana's loss as an unhealed wound. Or what he remembered an unhealed wound might feel like. So why had he been unable to keep himself from touching Alexandra?

Certainly he hadn't had sex for a good long while. He tried to recall how long and couldn't. He remembered the woman, her face but not her name. The interlude had meant nothing but a release. Every interlude had been nothing more than that since he'd gone searching for his wife and found nothing but ashes.

"Get down here," he ordered. "Now."

Alexandra lowered her gaze. He was her maker, the alpha, and she had little choice but to obey him. Once she realized that, she wouldn't like it. Not that there was anything she could do about it.

Julian's lips curved. He'd been wrong to leave her behind to fend for herself. He could exact a much better revenge by taking her with him. A woman like her, forced to do anything he wanted—

Torture.

Which was what he'd had in mind all along.

She blinked as if she'd just come out of a trance. Moon madness. Happened to the new ones. Sometimes they stared at the bright, shiny, exquisite moon until a *Jäger-Sucher* walked up and blew their brains out. Which was why new wolves were not supposed to be left alone. At least in his pack. Most werewolves couldn't have cared less.

"Why are you taking me with you?" she asked.

Julian growled, a deep rumble that made her eyes narrow. If she'd been in wolf form, he thought she'd have growled right back. He felt a twinge of interest. He hadn't had anyone rebel in centuries.

"Why are you coming?" he countered.

She glanced over her shoulder, then quickly climbed over the ledge, landing barefoot at his side. The street person who'd sold Julian the sweats and T-shirt had been wearing canvas sneakers so filthy, so full of holes, and so huge he'd refused them. It didn't really matter. Despite the area being littered with broken glass and sharp bits of metal, any injuries she might attain by running over them *would* heal.

Julian heard the police milling about inside. They'd be occupied for a few minutes dealing with the scene, but soon they'd start looking around.

He took her hand, and she let him. Then they ran until they were far enough away for their presence not to matter. When he slowed, he immediately dropped all contact. Together they wiped their palms against their pants.

"Why are you coming with me?" he repeated.

"I—" Her gaze dropped to her feet. "I don't know how to live like this."

"And you think I'll teach you?"

She met his eyes. "Won't you?"

Of course.

The words whispered through his brain. The combination of fear and hope in her eyes pulled at him. The scent of her enticed him.

"I *should* leave you here," he ground out. "Let you run wild until the cops lock you up. If you're lucky, Mandenauer will arrive before the next full moon."

She blinked. "Who?"

"I'm not a moron," Julian snapped. "I checked you out." Though he hadn't come up with much. "You were born. You lived for a while in Nebraska, even started kindergarten. Then your mother disappeared—"

He lifted a brow, waiting for her to explain, but she didn't.

He figured *disappeared* meant "death by monster," especially considering what happened next.

"You and your father fell off the grid. Since only Edward has the connections to make someone disappear like that, either one or both of you was a *Jäger-Sucher* once upon a time."

She shrugged, giving up the pretense. "I don't work for him anymore."

"I know."

The *Jäger-Suchers* had rules, and Alexandra Trevalyn did not follow them. One of those rules was: *Wait until they shift to shoot them.*

As Alex had proved with Jorge, she didn't believe in rules.

"What else do you know?" she asked. "About me? About them?"

"Not as much as I'd like," he murmured. He and his kind stayed isolated from the world. It was the only way to live the way that they wanted to. Which meant information was hard to come by. Not that he didn't come by it. It was just hard. And expensive.

"The *Jäger-Suchers* are in disarray," he continued. "There was a—" Julian paused, searching for the word. "A purge. Many of them died; the rest are in hiding."

Her brow creased. "When did this happen?"

"Nearly a year ago. The werewolves banded together and began hunting the hunters."

"They never cared before."

Most werewolves only cared about themselves, which was how the *Jäger-Suchers* had so much success.

"There were whispers of a cure," Julian continued. "But werewolves don't want to be cured. They like what they are."

"Do you?" she asked.

"Yes."

She appeared to think about that for a minute, then nodded. "So the werewolves went on the offensive."

"In more ways than one," Julian agreed. "Not only have they gone after the *Jäger-Suchers* instead of waiting for the *Jäger-Suchers* to come to them, but they've made a concerted effort to replace what's been lost and purposely increase the number fighting on their side."

"A werewolf army," Alex said faintly.

"It's happened before."

Barlow knew about the werewolf army. However, according to him, he wasn't the one behind it.

Except he was a werewolf. Killing? Lying? Both came as easily to him as eating.

Why hadn't Edward told her he'd been losing agents? That he was on the defensive rather than the offensive for the first time in more than half a century?

He was a big believer in imparting info on a need-to-know basis, and he'd no doubt say if questioned that Alex hadn't needed to know. She was no longer one of them.

Maybe Edward thought Barlow was behind the whole thing. Although if that was the case, it was something she definitely needed to know.

However, she'd learned in the few years she'd worked for the old man that he had his own way of doing things, and he was usually right.

As they walked along the deserted street, her shoulder brushed Barlow's and memories rushed in—the kiss, his scent, the bizarre fact that they could even touch.

He skittered as far away from her as he could get and still remain on the cracked, broken remnant of the sidewalk. The expression on his face brought back the image of him wiping her taste from his mouth, her touch from his hand, and fury sparked.

Which was stupid. She'd felt exactly the same way once she'd come to her senses. Disgust for her lack of control, nausea over the flash of lust, horror at what she'd already done and what she'd been willing to do with the slightest hint of encouragement.

Just thinking about the interlude brought back Alex's thirst for vengeance. She wanted to kill Barlow not only for what he'd done to her but for the way he'd made her feel.

If Edward had not said the werewolf that had killed her father was a member of Barlow's pack, she would have put a silver bullet through the guy's brain and disappeared into the sunset, the fate of humanity at the mercy of a new werewolf army be damned.

But Edward *had* said, and since the only thing that had kept Alex going for the past eight years was the possibility of revenge, she bit her tongue and kept going, silently assuring herself that once she got wherever Barlow was taking her, she'd blast her father's killer to hell, along with anyone else who got in her way. Right before she left, she'd give Julian Barlow a parting gift.

Kaboom.

The promise soothed her as little else could.

Not that she didn't understand the man's need for payback—even sympathize with it. Alex shook her head.

He wasn't a man. Alana hadn't been a woman. They were murdering beasts. They didn't feel love, or pain, or remorse.

Except Barlow did. The agony in his eyes, the gruffness in his voice told the tale. He mourned his wife with an intensity that matched Alex's own.

Unease flickered. She was a werewolf now, and yet she

still missed her father, ached with his loss and her love for him.

But there was a reason for that. She been injected with Edward's serum and cursed by a voodoo priestess. She was as close to human as a werewolf could get. That was the only reason she still felt any emotions at all.

So what was Julian Barlow's excuse?

"Where's your car?" he asked.

Alex glanced around. They'd run a long way, then walked some more. She wasn't familiar with the area, but she recognized a few of the buildings ahead as some of those she'd passed while trailing Jorge.

She pointed to the west. "About a mile."

Barlow began to jog and she did the same, just a young couple out for a little exercise. Except it was the middle of the night, they were white, and—with Alex's oversize, worn clothes, bloody arms and neck, and lack of shoes—she looked like a bag lady in a *Dawn of the Dead* remake.

"Now you understand how it is for most werewolves," he said.

"How *what* is?"

"You were changed against your will."

"So?"

He sighed as if she were incredibly dense and continued. "New wolves are like babies. They can't be blamed for what they do. Would you punish an infant for banging a toy against a wall and breaking it?"

"I hardly think the man you left behind for me to kill was a toy."

"No, he was a habitual child molester."

Alex's lips pulled into a grimace.

"Kind of leaves a bad taste in your mouth, doesn't he?"

Thanks to Edward's serum and Cassandra's spell, she

hadn't killed her toy. Right now, Alex was kind of sorry about that.

"I told you he was a very bad man," Barlow continued. "He deserved to die."

Alex had to agree, but— "Who made you judge and jury?"

"Me."

Huh. He sounded just like Edward.

"You felt the madness as soon as you awoke, didn't you?" he pressed.

Alex glanced at him and told the truth. "Yes."

He continued to stare straight ahead as they ran much faster than she ever had with much less huffing and puffing.

Certainly Alex had kept up with her training. If she wanted to best supernatural beings daily she didn't have much choice. She could run ten miles without collapsing, sprint one hundred meters in thirteen seconds; she'd had instruction in Judo, and she could fight with every kind of weapon. Her father had been very thorough.

However, she hadn't kept up *this* well. No human being could. The virus in her blood was obviously good for more than a full moon fur coat.

"Would you execute an insane person for listening to the voices in his head?" Barlow continued.

Alex didn't answer, because her answer would give her away. Despite her new abilities, her conflicting feelings, she still didn't consider a werewolf a person.

They came around the corner of yet another empty building and stopped. Five guys stood between them and Alex's cargo van.

Yesterday Alex would have run the other way. She was interested only in killing werewolves, not stupid kids trying to be tough. Today she wanted to fight, even before she saw that they'd managed to get inside and were using their switch-blades on what few clothes she owned.

A growl rumbled from Alex's throat. Barlow cast her a quick glance. "No," he said.

"That's all I've got in the world."

"You don't need it anymore."

"That isn't the point," she snapped.

"*Don't* shift."

Alex had been inching forward, longing to plant her fist in the face of a guy who was shredding her underwear. She paused though she wasn't sure why. Something in Barlow's voice, in the tone of his command, made it difficult for her to disobey.

"You're too new," Barlow explained. "I can hold them off while you change, but once they've seen us do that, we'll have no choice but to kill them all."

Alex frowned. Since when did a werewolf care if he had to kill people?

"What do you suggest?" she asked.

Barlow cracked his knuckles, and his smile gave Alex a shiver. He might wear a veneer of humanity. He might play at being calm, reasonable, in control. But that smile and the flash in his eyes revealed the truth.

He liked violence as much as the next werewolf.

"Let's kick their ass," he said.

CHAPTER 4

Alex moved into position with Barlow as if they'd been fighting together for years.

The five young men dropped everything but their knives and approached holding the weapons as if they knew exactly what to do with them. Alex wasn't worried. Knives were made of steel, not silver; any wound they might have the good fortune to land would heal.

The boys rushed forward, and Alex decked the guy who'd dared to finger her panties. He flew off his feet and smacked into another one. They hit the pavement; their knives clattered every which way, and they lay still.

Alex glanced at her fist. She could get used to this.

Hyped, she bounced on the balls of her feet, spinning toward a third guy. She caught the scent of steel and jerked away an instant before the knife slashed her cheek. Barlow tackled him, and the two went down in a tangle of arms and legs.

A wild punch caught Alex on the chin. Her head snapped back, but she didn't go down.

"What the hell?" the guy muttered; then his eyes widened as Alex started to laugh. The blow hadn't even hurt.

He turned to run, and Barlow kicked the kid in the chest. Alex sidestepped as the boy sailed five feet and landed in a heap. He didn't move, either.

The one Barlow had tackled lay immobile, the fifth—

"Watch out!" Alex shouted, and Barlow rammed his elbow backward, catching his attacker in the gut.

"Ooof," the kid said, then dropped to his knees. His eyes rolled back, and he toppled over like a well-hit bowling pin.

Alex's harsh, excited breathing was the only sound that broke the resulting silence. Barlow wasn't even winded.

"That was—" Alex clenched and unclenched her hands. "Freaking fabulous."

"Learn to pull your punches," Barlow said, refusing to look at her. "You could kill someone, even in this form."

He walked to the van, opening the driver's-side door and climbing inside. Alex stared after him and thought again: *Since when does killing bother a werewolf?* Right now, it didn't bother her. Right now, if someone came at her with the intent to turn her to ashes, she'd kill him with ease and probably dance a jig on his broken bones.

What was wrong with her? She was behaving more like a beast than the king beast.

The adrenaline rush faded, and Alex was left in a cold sweat, her hands lightly shaking.

"Alexandra!" Barlow roared from the van.

Alex glanced at the bodies flung all around; her heart slowed as she noted that each one was still breathing before she followed him.

"Keys," he snapped as soon as she climbed inside.

"What's your problem?" she asked. "You *said,* 'Let's kick their ass.'"

"Seemed like a good idea at the time."

It had. In fact, it had seemed like a fantastic idea right up until the time the stillness had descended, and she'd realized how much fun she'd had, how easy it had been to hurt people, and how much she'd wanted to keep doing it.

Alex was both energized by their success and seriously worried by it. What was the weird connection between them, and how could she break it?

"Alexandra," Barlow murmured.

"Alex," she returned. The last time someone had called her Alexandra, finger painting had been the most important thing on her schedule, followed by snack and an afternoon nap.

"Your keys?"

Her hand went to her pocket before she remembered this wasn't her pocket. "I think they're back in that room." She put her palm against the passenger window. One of the boys stirred. Another groaned. "With my clothes."

Barlow muttered a word in another language, and despite her not understanding it she knew it to be a curse. "We need to get out of LA," he said. "The cops are going to figure this out."

"Right. They'll decide the torn clothes are because someone shifted into a werewolf, and the keys on the floor belong to—" She paused. "How will they figure out who they belong to?"

"Your ID?" he suggested.

"I was a *Jäger-Sucher* once. That translates to 'hunter,' not moron. No ID."

He placed his hands on the steering column, closed his eyes, and . . . was that a growl? She wasn't sure since, seconds later, the van started like magic.

"You're some weird werewolf," she said.

He ignored her. "You don't have any ID?"

"I didn't say I had no ID, just that I had no ID on me."

Reaching forward, she tapped the side of her fist into a plastic square above the radio. Instead of popping open to reveal the secret compartment, the plastic shattered into a hundred charcoal-gray shards.

"Whoops," she muttered.

"What did I say about pulling your punches?" he asked.

"Only do it when I'm not punching you?"

He gave a short bark of laughter, and Alex nearly joined in. Would have if she hadn't already reached into the hole and pulled out her fake driver's license and the single photo she had of her father, Charlie.

The sight of his face brought everything back. The years they'd spent on the road, the closeness they'd shared after her mother had . . . died.

They'd been the perfect family. Father with a good job. Mother who stayed home. Cute little girl who adored them both.

Every night after work, Charlie would take Alex to the park while his wife, Janet, made supper. He had loved softball—both watching and playing it—and he'd imparted that love to Alex. Even at five, she'd had her own glove, and she'd been able to catch pretty darn well. But what she'd loved more than the game itself was the time with Daddy.

Until there'd come a night when they'd returned to their house not long after dark and instead of supper, they'd found a nightmare.

Charlie'd had a secret life, one he hadn't shared with Janet. He'd thought he left his *Jäger-Sucher* past behind him. He'd changed his name; he'd even changed his face. Unfortunately he hadn't changed his scent. He couldn't, and his past had sniffed him out.

One of the werewolves that had gotten away found him. Or rather, he found Janet. Then he killed her.

His mistake was in waiting for Charlie. Because even though Charlie worked in a hardware store now, even though he pretended to be just another guy, he still kept silver bullets in the gun he'd locked in the trunk of his car, and he could still shoot with the accuracy of the marine sniper who'd trained him.

Luckily her father had a sixth sense about danger, or maybe he'd just smelled the blood. He'd told Alex to run to the neighbor's and play with their new kitten. By the time he'd picked her up, he'd packed the essentials into their car and called Edward to clean up the mess.

Charlie had rejoined the *Jäger-Suchers*. He hadn't felt like he had any choice. He'd never be free of his past, and his daughter would never be safe unless he killed every last monster on earth.

He'd made a mistake keeping the secret. But he would rectify that by teaching Alex all that he knew so she could never be surprised as her mother had been.

It hadn't been easy, but they'd managed. Werewolves hunted at night, and Charlie did, too, long after Alex was asleep. She'd been old enough to understand that something bad had happened to her mommy in the dark, and she knew better than to venture into it alone.

As she got older, she saw things, things that made her desperate to learn all her father had to teach.

So Charlie taught, Alex learned—how to kill werewolves, how to add and subtract—and when they had a little downtime between assignments, they played catch, just like they had when they'd still had a home.

Alex's eyes suddenly burned with tears she could not shed. Because if Barlow saw her crying over Daddy and Mommy, he'd know something was wrong with her.

When people become werewolves, their humanity dies. They lose all allegiance to their family, their friends, to anyone or anything but themselves.

Alex glanced at Barlow out of the corner of her eye as she slid the photo of her father beneath the seat.

So what was wrong with him?

Julian was spooked, but he didn't let it show. He'd learned long ago—before he'd even become what he was—to keep his emotions in check. Emotions were a weakness he couldn't afford. Just look where his love for Alana had gotten him.

Here with this woman-wolf who was really freaking him out.

His lips twitched at the slang. It had taken him a few decades to figure out that the only way to fit in was to learn the local lingo and use it. Of course now that he no longer needed to fit in, he could probably do so without any problem at all.

He had no idea why he'd encouraged the fight. Perhaps to see what Alex could do in human form. He needed to know all he could about her before he brought her into his inner sanctum. He definitely hadn't beaten those boys senseless because of the hint of sadness that had billowed around her like fading perfume.

Julian's fingers clenched on the steering wheel. She was still sad. He could smell it.

It had taken him a few centuries to hone his human senses until they were nearly as sharp as his wolf's. Trust a Norseman to adapt. It was one of the many things they were good at.

Of course he'd never adapted this well. He could smell anger, violence, fear. That was easy. But he couldn't recall ever smelling sadness before. Even with Alana.

Julian drove to the crappy motel near LAX, parked around back, and got out.

Alex got out, too. "What gives?"

"You can't get on a plane like that," he said.

The blood on her body had seeped through the T-shirt and the sweatpants he'd given her, creating a gory polka-dot pattern. The fight had torn a few holes, added another level of dirt. She still wasn't wearing any shoes.

Alex followed him into the dingy, dank room he'd rented when he'd arrived only a few days ago. The place smelled of a hundred others. He couldn't wait to get home.

"Use the shower," he ordered.

"What if I don't want to?" she asked, but she was already headed that way.

As soon as the lock clicked on the bathroom door—foolish on her part, no door would keep him out if he truly wanted to get in—Julian pocketed the key and returned to her van.

He sat on the passenger side, slid his hand beneath the seat, pulled out the photo she'd hidden there. A man—same eyes, same smile, hair closer to chestnut than Alexandra's shade of light brown. He was of average height, thin and rangy, with gold-rimmed glasses and big, hard, capable hands.

Charlie Trevalyn—Alex's missing father.

Julian knew the man must have been killed, most likely by

werewolves considering Alex's loathing for them. Of course there was no record of such a thing. Just as there was none of what had happened to her mother. Why would there be?

Werewolf kills were sometimes written off as rabid animal attacks, but usually people just disappeared. When they did, Edward Mandenauer was often involved.

Julian put the photo of Charlie back where he'd found it and returned to the hotel room. He placed a call to the airport and let his pilot know when he wanted to leave. By the time he hung up, sweat had broken out on his brow, dampened the back of his shirt, and begun to run down his neck. Sometimes werewolf senses were a gift and other times, like now, a curse.

He heard every drop splashing against her body, swirling downward, cascading over her shoulders, her breasts, belly, thighs. He could smell the soap, the shampoo, hear the swish of her hands as she washed.

If he closed his eyes he could see the water, the bubbles, the stroke of fingers against skin. His tongue darted out to wet his lips, and he tasted her—that mouth, her neck, the blood.

"Shit. Fuck. Hell." Sometimes if he cursed in English he managed to draw his mind away from whatever he was cursing about. But not this time. He could still see her naked body, hear her rapid breathing, smell the soap mixing with her tangy scent.

He opened his eyes. Steam trailed out from beneath the door, snaking toward him like a magical mist, enticing him to do things he should not. He'd taken several steps forward before he stopped, turned, and forced himself to retreat, to stare out the window at the coming dawn and once again count to ten, then fifty, then a hundred in Norwegian, trying to shake the bizarre sense of destiny from his brain.

* * *

Alex had closed the door behind her—locked it, too—then turned on the shower. When she'd stepped beneath the water, she'd discovered that the usual just-short-of-scalding temperature she preferred was something she preferred no longer. Tepid was all she could stand against skin that felt like she'd been lying naked in the tropical sun for hours with no respite—or sunscreen.

She easily scrubbed off the blood and the dirt, but no matter how hard she tried, no matter how long she rubbed, she couldn't get rid of the scent of werewolf. That scent was part of her now.

She had a sudden flash of Barlow's hands on her breasts, his tongue in her mouth, and everything she'd felt in that small clip of time she'd spent in his arms rushed back. Despite her hatred of werewolves, and him in particular, she'd wanted the man more than she'd ever wanted anyone else.

There was definitely something hinky about Julian Barlow.

Mind control? Witchcraft? A magic spell? Maybe all three. She'd find out of course. Finding out was what she did best—along with killing.

His brush lay on the sink; Alex used it even though the mingling of his golden strands with her light brown made her edgy. After wrapping herself tightly in a scratchy hotel towel, Alex opened the door. A fresh set of clothes lay on the floor just outside.

She snatched them up without even looking around. The clothes, obviously his, fit badly. The jeans were huge—she threaded a length of what appeared to be telephone cord through the belt loops to hold them up—the tank top, too. She didn't really want to wear his boxers, but what choice did she have? The long-sleeved shirt, heavy socks, and bulky, tree-hugger sandals were also too large. She managed by pulling the straps as tight on her feet as they'd go.

When Alex stepped into the room again, the first thing she saw was Barlow staring out the window. The night had turned gray as dawn approached. In the distance she caught the twinkling lights of LAX, so numerous and bright they seemed like stars that had fallen to the earth.

The room smelled of smoke—but not cigarettes—reminding her of the small towns she and her father had passed through, places where they'd burned their garbage in the backyard. The scent made her ache with the echo of loneliness.

Every dusk had brought another monster; every dawn had brought another town. They never got friendly. It didn't pay. Who knew when the kid you'd struck up a friendship with might turn out to be the next werewolf victim, or perhaps the next werewolf.

"We should get to the airport," Barlow murmured without turning. "We leave in an hour."

Alex opened her mouth to question him, then thought better of it. She'd know soon enough where they were going. All she'd have to do was read her boarding pass.

Except they didn't fly commercial. Barlow had his very own plane.

They also didn't leave in an hour. Something needed to be adjusted, and when dealing with planes Alex was all for adjusting it, however long that might take. She sat in a hard plastic chair and watched Barlow pace. He seemed more like a wild animal now than when he'd been one.

At last the pilot motioned for them to board. Alex reached for her ID, then remembered she'd left her license on the table in the hotel when she'd gone into the shower, then she'd never seen it again. The scent of burning waste in the room suddenly made a lot more sense.

"You burned my ID?" she whispered furiously.

"You won't need it where we're going."

"Just because you have your own plane doesn't mean we don't have to show ID."

He smiled. "It does on my plane."

"But—"

"If you have enough money you can buy anything. Especially anonymity. I'd think you would have learned that from Mandenauer."

Barlow got on board, leaving Alex to follow or not. Though she had no doubt that if she chose *not,* he'd make her.

They flew away from the sun, out over the Pacific. Just when Alex had begun to obsess about landing in China or Russia or some Stan country with a lot of caves and disappearing forever, the pilot turned toward land, then tilted the nose north.

"You'll see Fairbanks before you know it," he announced through the headphones they'd all donned along with their seat belts.

Alaska?

No wonder Edward had never found them.

Several hours later they flew over Fairbanks. The pilot couldn't help playing tour guide.

"Fairbanks has one of the largest population centers this far north in the world. About thirty thousand in the town, and another eighty-four thousand in there." He pointed to the acres upon acres of trees. "Place is surrounded by hundreds of miles of subarctic bush."

"How cold does it get?" Alex asked.

The guy grinned, enjoying himself. "In January down to sixty-six below; in July it can hit ninety-nine."

"What about right now?"

"September is a strange one. We've had snow, temps in the teens. Today it's probably forty." He waved at the western horizon where the sun was falling down. "But it's gonna cool off soon."

"Kind of early to be getting dark."

"You're near the Arctic Circle. In December they only see the sun for a few hours."

Alex definitely needed to be out of here before December.

The plane banked over the city, which appeared fairly modern, full of paved streets, concrete and steel buildings. She even caught the bright flare of golden arches; then they sailed past, headed toward some pretty thick timber. The trees were so tall, the belly seemed to skim the branches.

"Where's the airport?" Alex asked, and her voice shook just a little.

Barlow lifted a brow and mouthed, *Scared?*

She turned away.

"I don't need no stinkin' airport," the pilot answered in a very bad Speedy Gonzales accent.

Alex almost panicked—until she remembered she couldn't die. Unless the vehicle was pure silver, and if so neither Barlow nor she would be flying in it. This damn-hard-to-kill thing was kind of liberating.

The pilot set the plane down on a gravel road that wound among towering pines. They climbed out; he waved and was gone.

"Now what?" Alex asked.

"Now we run."

"Run?" She turned in a circle. All she saw was trees. "Where?"

"Two hundred miles." Barlow pointed. "That way."

Alex followed his finger, which pointed north and a little west.

What was it about this place that was so familiar? She closed her eyes for a second. Trees. Earth. Sunshine and shadow. Ice on distant mountaintops. The very air smelled like him.

"This is home," she murmured.

When Alex opened her eyes, Barlow stared at her as if she'd just sprouted another head.

"What?" she asked.

He looked away. "The sun's nearly down."

"Great catch, Sherlock," she muttered.

The way he watched her, so intent one minute, then dismissive the next, grated on Alex's already taut nerves.

"I can't run two hundred miles."

"Yes." He began to unbutton his shirt. "You can."

"You mean—"

"Wolves can run forty miles per hour, cover a hundred and twenty-five miles in a day." He tossed his shirt into the trees. "Werewolves are wolves, only better."

Or worse, depending on your point of view.

The sun had slipped below the horizon, and soon the moon would appear. Round, seemingly full to the human eye, Alex still sensed the slight difference. She didn't *have* to change, but oh, how she wanted to.

The howl startled her so badly she jumped. Barlow had already shifted and paced back and forth at the edge of the wood. The urge to join him was impossible to ignore.

Alex threw off the shirts, the shoes, the jeans, and let the cool silver hum of the moon surrounded her. The power poured into her. She reached for the wolf; her body contorted. She writhed and wriggled, struggled and strained. It took her a lot longer than it had taken him, but eventually she succeeded.

Then together they ran into the night.

CHAPTER 5

Julian ran until the stench of the city no longer filled his nostrils. Then he lay on the pine-needle-strewn ground and rolled until his fur smelled again like Alaska.

God, he hated leaving home. Which was damn funny considering he'd once done nothing but.

Julian had been born in Norway so long ago, his memories should have been hazy. Yet some were so clear they could have occurred yesterday. Burning and pillaging appeared to stay with a man for centuries.

Once his name had been Jorund the Blund. Julian shook his golden fur. Pine needles flew every which way. His hair, nearly white in his youth, and his height, tall even among Vikings, had marked him as different.

In battle, his men could see his pale head far above those of their enemies. Because of that, and his prowess with a sword, they'd followed him to the ends of the earth.

Or what had been the ends at the time. They'd conquered parts of Scotland, England, and Iceland. They'd plundered their way up and down several coasts. They'd done things Julian wished he didn't remember.

He had an excuse. He'd been a *Viking*. What was he

supposed to do, refuse to plunder and pillage? That was a good way to meet the pointy end of a sword. Besides, the concept that taking whatever he wanted, whenever he wanted it, because he could was *wrong* had never even occurred to him.

Not then.

Paw-steps approached, the slash of a body through the trees. Alex was closing in. He'd run ahead, eager to immerse himself in home. He had no worries that he would lose her. He wouldn't be that lucky.

She burst through the branches, sending the fresh scent of pine into the air. They were going to have to talk about silence and stealth. Perhaps tomorrow when they could actually talk.

Alex, whose snout had been to the ground as she followed his scent, pulled up when she caught sight of him. Her lip lifted; a snarl rumbled.

Certainly werewolves could think like humans—reason, plan—they were faster, stronger, and they didn't die without a silver bullet, but for the most part when they were wolves, they were wolves. Speech was beyond them.

However, they got their message across. Right now Alex was saying she'd kill him if she could.

Julian lifted his lip and snarled back. The feeling was mutual.

In truth, werewolf murder was rare. He'd heard it described as a fail-safe in the virus. Werewolves were selfish and vicious, and many were not quite sane. Therefore, if two met, they would fight to the death. Which would leave very few werewolves around.

Julian and his wolves were different. Yes, they became werewolves because of a virus, but they weren't evil. They didn't kill for the sake of killing. Excluding the first kill, they rarely killed at all—especially one another.

But they could.

Suddenly Alex tilted her head; her tail stiffened, her snout lifted, and a light breeze ruffled her tawny fur. She quivered once; then she was gone, racing through the trees at a pace only a werewolf would love. If she took one wrong turn in this dense cover she would smash headfirst into an immovable object and break her neck.

Too bad that wouldn't kill her.

She disappeared into the distance, and Julian huffed an annoyed breath through his nose. Was she *trying* to step on every stick in the forest?

He followed, but at a more sedate pace. Julian had run snout-first into a tree before. He didn't plan to do so again.

He found her sitting in a patch of moonlight, head tipped upward, mouth lolling open to catch the fat snowflakes that had just begun to fall.

For an instant he wanted to join her, to tumble her to the ground and wrestle as wolves did. To run and play, to hunt together, then later—

Mounting her as a wolf, again as a man. Fur against fur. Skin upon skin. His breath and hers, coming fast and sharp. Panting. The slick slide, that welcoming heat. She'd be tight, tighter still when she clenched around him and he—

Julian yipped in surprise at the images that cascaded through his mind. Alex yipped, too, startled, then glanced over her shoulder and showed him her teeth.

If wolves could laugh, Julian would have. Even if he didn't despise her, she certainly despised him. He could fantasize all he wanted about fucking her, but it would never, ever happen.

* * *

Alex found herself dazzled by everything. The world, when viewed as a wolf, was completely new. Scents swirled around her, and they told her things—a rabbit ahead, a mouse just there, a moose had meandered through not long ago.

The snow pattered like rain upon the ground, upon her, so much louder than snow should be. The night was silver and blue, exquisite, a shadow land that existed only for her.

Then Barlow blundered in and wrecked everything.

She was staring at the moon, fighting the bizarre urge to howl, when he yipped from just behind her. She nearly jumped out of her fur. Where had he come from? He moved as quietly as a wolf as he had as a man.

She, however, was having a hard time staying silent—and right now she was so hungry, she was wondering how Barlow would taste raw.

Glancing over her shoulder, she caught sight of a similar expression in Barlow's too human eyes. He was wondering how she would taste also. But in a totally different way.

Barlow came toward her, and Alex scrambled to her feet, nearly collapsing when they tangled together. She could not get her mind around four feet, *not* two. By the time she righted herself he was gone, and she stood in the clearing alone with the moon.

Her stomach growled so loudly she started. Then she wasn't sure if the skittering sound on the snow had been her own claws or the claws of another.

Her ruff went up, her wary gaze flicked around the open space, and she caught the scent of something "other."

Scents in this form were so precise, yet she had nothing to connect them to. She knew that once she could put an image with that scent, she would never again forget it. But right now all she felt was an intense urge to run. So she did.

Alex loped alone for miles, and that was fine by her. The less she saw of Barlow, the better. He wasn't going to be able to ditch her. She could smell him on the breeze, the grass. Hell, even the snow—which had begun to swirl heavier and faster, obscuring the tops of the trees—smelled like him.

Then she caught a whiff of something else. Something that made her ruff go back up, along with her lip, and her snarl rumbled into the chill.

Blood.

It had a scent all its own.

Alex hunkered down, crept forward, belly to the ground. She tried to be quiet. But no matter what she did, one of her paws always landed on a stick or a stone—crack, clatter, *come and get me.*

She took another sniff. Not just blood but death. Dammit! She'd wanted to kill Barlow herself.

Strangely, the idea of him dead did not make her want to roll across the snow and yip with delight. Instead, panic caused her to pant. She turned a slow circle and saw nothing but trees.

A whimper escaped, and she swiped a paw at her snout in annoyance. Whining would get her nowhere.

She used her human mind, made herself see reason. Barlow couldn't be dead. She hadn't heard a shot. Not that a silver bullet was the only way to go.

Lighten up! she told herself. If Barlow were ashes she could go back to civilization, find Edward—yeah, right—and make him cure her.

Except no one made Edward do anything.

Alex was starting to catch a clue to something she hadn't considered before. Even if she succeeded at this mission, *would* Edward cure her?

Why, when she made such a perfect spy?

She discovered she was gnawing on her own foot, as if caught in a trap.

Because she was. Damn Edward Mandenauer to hell.

Ferocity boiled inside. Consumed with the need to run and growl and fight, Alex shot out of the undergrowth.

All she found was a freshly killed rabbit, its blood a scarlet splotch against the pristine snow.

She finished dinner in less time than it had taken to "make" it. Though the "Alex" inside of her was squirming, the wolf enjoyed the meal. Nothing like fresh meat on an empty stomach.

When she was done she looked around for another, but she wasn't the only one that had smelled blood and death on the breeze. It appeared every small, furry creature in the vicinity had turned tail and run. She didn't blame them.

Alex trotted after Barlow. Miles upon miles she traveled, and the moon began to fall. She didn't get tired, but she did get thirsty. Luckily there was plenty of snow, and in the distance she smelled water. A lot of it.

She increased her pace; the water was close, but she could already tell it wasn't meant for drinking. Her nose was an amazing tool.

The trees became less dense, and she stood at their edge, gazing across the flat land that led to the sea. The glow of the moon banking across the ice floes dazzled her. A soft breeze bristled off the water, frozen and salty, making her think of margaritas. All she needed was a really big lime and an oil tanker of tequila.

The ice lifted and lowered, crashed against other floes and made a strange rumble, the only sound in the desolate land. She skittered beneath the trees. Everything was so different here.

The sky began to lighten, but that only served to send dancing gray shadows everywhere. She turned, planning to scurry into the densest part of the forest, and caught a flash of something huge and white. She barely managed to duck the claws that swiped for her head, then she was running.

Being chased by a polar bear has that effect.

How long had the thing been stalking her? She remembered the scent of "other" that she hadn't been able to put a name to, the slight *scritch* of claws on snow that she'd written off as her own.

Hell, he'd been hunting her for hours.

Thank God in this form she was faster. He'd never catch her. *Never.*

She gave in to the power within; she ran as she'd never run before. Now that she'd seen what was behind her, her fear faded. The bear was a fool for even thinking it could track and kill her. She was more than a wolf, more than a woman. She was both; she was neither. She was better.

Alex hugged the edge of the trees just as dawn burst over the horizon, and as the sunlight touched her, she stumbled, falling head-over-paws, which became heels and feet and toes as she shifted.

CHAPTER 6

Naked and vulnerable, she scrambled upright. Just as the bear came out of the woods.

Goose bumps raced across her flesh, and not just because of the chill air across her skin. She might not die from the coming attack, but it was certainly going to hurt. And if there were pieces of her all over the place, would she really be able to heal? She just didn't know.

"Barlow!" Alex shouted.

The bear roared right in her face. Its breath smelled like . . . Blood and hunger. With a little rotten fish on the side.

"Shit," she muttered. Should she run, or shouldn't she?

Her wolf howled for fight not flight. Her human self knew better. Even if she *could* shift in the daylight, a wolf wasn't going to win a battle against a polar bear, and while human she wasn't going to be able to outrun this thing.

The polar bear leaned to the left to swipe at her with its right paw; the animal was pretty damn quick for its size.

Alex eluded the claws; she was faster, even in this form, but she would never be fast enough. Unable to stop herself, she took several steps back, and the polar bear roared again.

Which was all Alex needed to make up her mind. She wasn't going to stand there and let it slice her apart. She had to at least try to escape. Maybe she could get far enough ahead and make her way up a tree.

Polar bears couldn't climb trees. Could they?

Alex ran deeper into the forest, thinking that perhaps she'd find a place so dense that she could fit through but the great white beast could not.

The earth trembled beneath her feet; the animal's hot, stinky breath brushed her ass. What was a polar bear doing in the forest anyway? Didn't they live on the ice?

Alex bore down. She couldn't keep up this pace for long, but she had to put some distance between them.

Suddenly Barlow stepped from behind a tree. Alex was so startled she forgot if she had two feet or four and got them tangled, tripping, skidding, almost falling. She managed to right herself, but those few seconds cost her.

The bear slapped Alex with one massive paw.

She heard her ribs crack, felt her skin tear, smelled the blood as it splattered. The blow lifted and tossed her several yards, where she landed in a heap at Barlow's feet.

Alex glanced all the way up his tall, broad, naked body. Too bad she was in too much pain to enjoy the view.

Why had he bothered to reveal himself? Without weapons, in this form, Barlow could do no more than she against this massive foe. They'd both be torn to bits, and they wouldn't be able to heal wounds like that completely until night fell again, and they shifted.

Barlow's gaze flicked over her, and his blue eyes darkened to black; then he threw back his head and emitted a bellow of fury that seemed to shake the leaves upon the trees.

The sound caused the polar bear to pull up short. Barlow

threw out his arms, hands spread wide, and at the very edge of his fingertips something twinkled.

Then he was shifting in the blink of an eye, so fast Alex couldn't tell the exact instant he changed from man to beast.

Fury turned Julian into an animal. Rain or shine, sun or shadow, if he became enraged enough, he changed. That was how he'd become what he was in the first place.

He shot out his hands, reached for his magic, believed he could become a wolf in the sunlight, and he did.

As he leaped over Alex's inert body, the scent of fear that oozed from her pores only infuriated him more, made him stronger, faster, better. She was one of his now. She should be afraid of nothing, no one.

But him.

Julian stalked around the polar bear, which had the good sense to turn away from Alex and keep an eye on him. Unfortunately Alex didn't have the same good sense. Instead of running, she lay there and watched.

Against his better judgment, Julian took his gaze from the bear and met hers, lifting his lip, jerking his head. Her eyes widened; he thought she understood. He was wrong.

"Julian!" she shouted, an instant before the bear hit him broadside.

Flesh tore; bones broke. He might be magic, but he couldn't prevent that.

Julian hit the ground and rolled, stifling a whimper when his wounds howled at the impact and the movement. He whirled, teeth snapping, but his jaws closed upon empty air. The polar bear had reared up, roaring, taking wild swipes at Alex as she poked him in the chest with a stick.

What was she thinking? She could barely walk, hunched to the side and bleeding. She was doing nothing but infuriating the animal with the smell of her blood and the annoyance of that stick.

Julian hurried forward, crowding her back, meeting the beast with bared teeth.

"He'll kill you," she managed, pain in every word.

Doubtful, Julian thought, then wondered why she cared. Why hadn't she run off and left him to be torn to pieces, or perhaps climbed a tree and watched? He knew why *he* felt compelled to protect *her.* But why on earth would *she* protect *him*?

Alex stepped around Julian, then poked the bear again. The thing growled and swatted at her, giving Julian the opening he needed. He dived in and tore a chunk out of the soft underbelly. The animal cried out, then fell back onto all fours where Alex promptly poked it in the eye.

The bear tried to swipe, but its vision was compromised. Julian snarled; Alex poked at the other eye, and the polar bear ran.

"Woo-hoo!" Alex lifted her stick to the sky, pumping her arm once before she grabbed at her injured side with a hiss.

Julian snorted even as a small kernel of admiration bloomed. It had taken guts to face that beast with nothing but a stick.

Said stick landed on the ground in front of him with a thud. Julian glanced at Alex just in time to watch her eyes roll back. Then she tumbled to the ground, too, and without arms there was nothing he could do to stop it. Instead he watched, helpless, as her head bounced against the earth with a dull thump before she lay still.

He nosed her arm, but she was limp. Not dead. Not from this. But she was broken, bleeding. He needed to get her out of the open and let her rest until the sun went down. For that he needed arms, hands, feet, and a body that wasn't broken.

Unfortunately, he'd shifted too many times, too close to-gether. His head was fuzzy with exhaustion. He wanted to lie down and sleep until dusk.

But to heal completely and quickly he needed to shift from one form to another, so he stood over Alex and tried to get angry. It was the only way he knew to draw forth his magic. Closing his eyes, he thought of why she was here, what she'd done, how she'd ruined his life. He remembered how he'd found Alana—or rather hadn't found her. Nothing left but a pile of ashes.

Anger began to pulse; warmth flooded through him as magic skated across his back, lifting his ruff like a heated summer breeze. A growl rumbled in his chest, and he imag-ined himself human. The next instant, he was.

Julian lifted Alex's inert body, stifling the rumble of hun-ger when her blood spilled all over him.

She opened her eyes on a wince, blinked a few times, then let her head fall against his chest. "Wha—? Where?"

"There's a cave near here," he said, uncertain if she could still hear him but needing to talk, to feel human again so his wolf would quit hearing the siren call of blood. "We stay there during the daylight. Can't exactly run around bare-assed and barefoot."

Well, they could. But frostbite made it damn difficult to run, and even werewolves needed to rest.

Unfortunately, he'd been exaggerating when he said "near." The cave was a good five miles away, and carrying Alex, the trip took him longer than he wanted it to. Especially since the pretty snowflakes began to swirl more thickly and a storm blotted out the remains of the sun. By the time they reached shelter, a full-blown blizzard was in place; he could barely see, let alone run.

Things got worse from there.

Julian stumbled into the cave on frozen feet, fell to his knees, set Alex on the ground, and hurried to the far side of the cave for wood.

"What the *hell*?" he shouted, his voice echoing back at him from a nearly empty cave.

The wood was gone, as was the food they stored here, along with most of the blankets. The single mattress and a battery-operated lantern remained—the two no doubt too cumbersome to steal—along with a threadbare quilt, which must have been too old to warrant carrying away.

He snatched up the light, turned the switch, nodded once when the lamp began to glow, and brought it over to where Alex lay.

She had begun to shiver. Her lips had turned a lovely shade of lilac, and her skin had turned a putrid shade of gray. He had to get her warm and fast.

She was slick with blood. Under normal circumstances, it would have dried by now. Unfortunately, the blizzard had not only lowered her body temperature but made the blood on her skin into a slurpy, pasty mess.

Exhaustion caused Julian to stumble. He righted himself, shook his head to make the blinking black lights in front of his eyes go away, and tried to focus.

"Angry," he muttered. "I am *so* angry."

But he wasn't. He could barely work up the energy to stand. He wasn't certain he could bring forth enough anger to help.

Julian's powers were a mystery. He believed they had come with his shape-shifting since he'd never been magic before, but none of his wolves was so gifted. He had not discovered any limits to what he could do beyond an inability to heal humans. The only thing that saved them from death was his bite.

Julian glanced again at the wall where a stack of wood should be, then at the empty box where nonperishable food should rest and managed a stir of fury.

"Good," he said. "More."

Even if he accessed the rage necessary to perform magic, he didn't have enough energy left to heal Alex *and* start a fire from nothing.

What should he do? He couldn't decide.

Which was not like him. He was the alpha. Decisions were his business. Of course he could never remember being this depleted and alone in all his lifetimes.

Didn't it just figure that *she* was at the heart of it?

"Okay," he said. Talking out loud seemed to make him feel more awake, more focused. "If you build a fire, she'll only bleed worse once she's warm."

She wouldn't die, true, but what if the loss of blood damaged her brain? That would be all he'd need—a pissed-off, *crazy,* ex–*Jäger-Sucher* werewolf.

"I'll pass," he muttered, then laughed. The laughter scared him. He sounded a little crazy himself.

Julian snatched up the quilt, lifted her again, and marched into the storm. There he used the heat of his hands to melt snow and wash the bloody muck from her skin; then he wrapped her in the blanket and carried her inside.

Her lips were still blue, her face ice white. She shivered so violently, he was afraid she'd bite off her own tongue from the force of her chattering teeth. Although maybe that wouldn't be so bad. Without a tongue she'd have a helluva time talking.

Until it grew back.

Julian peeled away the quilt, gritting his teeth as her scent washed over him. She smelled like pack, with a hint of lemony woman and an enticing tinge of blood. The fine hairs on his arms lifted and goose bumps ran across his flesh.

The bruises along her ribs appeared black against the snowy shade of her skin. The snow bath and the extreme cold had slowed the bleeding from the slashes across her belly. They were deep—they would, if she'd still been human, need a helluva lot of stitches—but Julian couldn't see any of her insides peeking through to the outside.

"That has to be good," he murmured.

She moved, moaned, and fresh blood pimpled her flesh. Werewolves healed fast, even in human form, but she would not heal completely unless she shifted, or he helped her.

Julian placed his palm against the wounds, closed his eyes, thought of—

His fingers flexed. She was so soft, so smooth and supple and—

"Damn!" He snatched his hand away as his penis twitched. What the hell was wrong with him?

She had killed his wife. *That* should make him angry enough to do anything.

But it didn't.

Instead the thought of Alana only made him sad. And sad was not mad. No matter how much he might wish it to be.

Julian tried again, placing his hand to the bruise. She wiggled beneath his touch, rubbing her skin along his. His eyes slid closed, and his fingers stroked the curve of her ribs; the soft, slight swell of her breast brushed his knuckles. This felt so good, so right, so meant—

He lurched back, falling hard on his ass, then sat there breathing heavily, staring at her still, pale form. This was *not* right. For him, nothing would ever be right again. Especially with *her*.

At last the anger came, and his fingers began to warm.

He held them over her, remembering what he'd felt, what he'd thought, what he'd nearly done. His hands sparkled as if covered in dew beneath the morning sun, and he watched, still fascinated despite all the centuries of magic, as her skin knit together and the bruises began to fade.

He could not heal her completely. He didn't have it in him right now no matter how angry he became. She'd have to do that herself once darkness fell.

The wind howled, tossing icy specks of snow against his back. Though he'd much prefer to walk into the storm than stay in here, with her, he needed his strength to make his way home.

Julian gritted his teeth and lay down, pulling the quilt over them both.

CHAPTER 7

Alex had to be dreaming. She'd never slept with a man in her life.

Certainly she'd had sex. But that was always a quick one-hour stand; then either she would leave or he would. Alex had never trusted anyone enough to fall asleep with him.

Therefore, this had to be a dream.

But what a nice dream. She'd been so cold, in so much pain; then the pain went away, replaced by a soothing warmth that spread throughout her aching body. With the heat surrounding her, she slept better than she had since childhood.

She was safe. No one, nothing would hurt her. Not here. With him.

Warm breath, soft lips, his taste both fire and ice. Her hands fluttered over a flat stomach, tight pecs, hard biceps as callused fingertips sculpted her rib cage, the swell of her breasts, the taut, tingling peak of her nipples.

"Mmm," she murmured, the sound vibrating against those lips, creating another kind of tingle.

She was cocooned in warmth; a chill hovered all around but it could not reach her. The dangerous, deadly world was gone. She lived in a magical place where all that existed were tantalizing sensations.

A strong, slightly scruffy leg wrapped around hers. Hands cupped her from behind and pulled her ever closer. The smooth, round head of a penis slid along her belly, and she gasped as every last inch of her flamed.

She reached for him in the darkness, and he was there. A mystery, a man, his touch making her forget . . . something. Everything. Until she remembered only this.

One tug on those biceps and he was above her, an instant later within her. Firm and fast, he gave; she took. Again and again and again.

"Come with me," he growled.

"Yes," she answered. "Yes." The word a surrender she'd never given anyone else.

Her palms ran over his back, relishing the ripple of muscle, the sleek slide of skin. He smelled like the earth beneath the moon, the trees tipped with silver, a sky full of rain. She pressed her face into his neck, took a deep long whiff, then drew his flesh into her mouth and tasted. His flavor was salt and surf. She wanted to gobble him up, make him a part of her forever, and she knew just how.

Grasping his hips, she urged him on, until he swelled and stretched and—

"Now," she whispered.

"What?" he answered.

Alex opened her eyes, just as Barlow opened his.

He'd been dreaming, and while he should have been disturbed that he'd been dreaming of her, the sex had been so incredible he'd ignored the warning whisper.

What could he say? He was a guy.

Most of the time.

But her teeth, while arousing, had also roused him and that one word had rumbled along his skin, tickling and taunting him. He'd half awakened, realizing he was on the verge of coming like a teenager in his bed, only to discover he wasn't at home alone but on top of someone, penis surrounded by a slick, tight heat.

His eyes widened; so did hers. Her hands at his hips, clenched; he figured she'd shove him away, and he tensed, prepared to resist, until he remembered who she was and that he'd rather fuck a tiger than Alexandra Trevalyn.

Unfortunately, his body had other ideas.

She arched—most likely to buck him off—instead he slid in farther, the friction of skin along skin making him clench his jaw before he groaned aloud. It had been so long, and she was so damn tight. He felt like his cock was in a vise—a soft, damp, really *great* vise, one that could both caress him until he was mindless and squeeze him until he was dry.

Instead of shoving him away, her grip on his hips tightened. Her breath, fast and sharp, rubbed her peaked nipples against his chest in a tantalizing rhythm.

Julian stared into her flushed face, her dazed eyes, and understood. She was coming, too.

Oh, what the hell, he thought. Too late now to pretend this was a dream. Might as well make her scream. He wanted to.

He slowed his hips as he lengthened his thrusts. All the way out until she strained forward, all the way in until her breath caught at the back of her throat. Again and again, slowly increasing his speed, plunging ever deeper until neither of them could stop the inevitable.

She cried out. He took her mouth, drinking the sound, and at last she closed her eyes, releasing him to do the same.

He hoped he could now imagine she was someone else,

anyone else, even no one, hell his *hand* was better than *her*—but just because he wasn't seeing her didn't mean she wasn't there. The scent of her, the taste of her, the *feel* of her was all around him. And the orgasm . . . it went on and on and on.

He was still enjoying the final tremors—her, him, he didn't know and he didn't care—when her body, so warm and soft, turned cool and stiff. Before she could shove him off, he rolled away, staring at the roof of the cave as she sat up and rested her head upon her knees, curling into herself as if he'd just violated her.

Her thin back, the bones of her ribs standing out in sharp relief, that faint shadow of the bruise still upon them made her seem fragile, vulnerable, womanly. He didn't even realize what he was doing until he saw his hand reaching out to touch—

"Don't," she said. "Just . . . don't."

Her voice was full of disgust and because of that, when she muttered, "Fuck me," he dropped his hand and said, "I did."

She punched him. He couldn't say that he blamed her.

Alex didn't realize she'd rounded on Barlow until her fist connected with his face.

He could have stopped her. That he didn't confused her, and when she was confused, she lashed out. A lot of people did.

"What did you do to me?"

He rubbed his jaw as he looked her up and down. "Isn't that obvious?"

She'd been shaking her hand, trying to make the numbness fade. He had a hard head, no shock there. But his words made her fingers curl inward once again.

He noticed and lifted a brow. "I gave you a shot," he said. "I deserved it. But one's all you get."

She rolled her eyes. If she wanted to punch him again, she would. Alex let her fingers go limp. Right now she didn't want to.

Just to be pissy, Alex yanked the blanket off Barlow and around her. Unfortunately that left him naked when he sat up, resting a wrist on his knee, open to her gaze.

She yanked her eyes from what lay below his waist and focused on an area just below his face. She'd left a mark on his neck.

"God," she muttered, and ran a hand through her tangled hair. What the hell had happened?

Suddenly everything came back—the bear, the fight, then . . . everything went fuzzy.

Alex glanced down. The only remnants of the attack were some dried blood, a few bruises, and several scabbed-over claw marks. "What the—?" She ran her fingers over the wounds, wincing. They might be nearly healed but they still hurt.

Alex glanced up, but he was staring out the opening of the cave and not at her. "How?" she murmured.

He lifted one shoulder, lowered it. Alex had a flash of those muscles bunching beneath her palm as he thrust into her so deeply—

"Magic."

She blinked, and the memory went away. "Magic," she repeated. "Like shifting in the daytime." He nodded. "Putting an invisibility cloak around us in LA."

"A what?" he asked.

"Harry Potter." She'd done a lot of reading in those hotel rooms. Alex waved her hand. "Never mind. You know what I mean."

"Yes," he agreed. "Like that."

"You healed me by magic," she said slowly. "Then you made me do you."

"You think I used magic to make you—" His cool blue eyes blazed hot with fury. "I don't need sex that bad."

"Could have fooled me," she muttered.

Was she imagining things or did his cheeks flush just a little?

"Glass houses," he said.

"Huh?"

"From the way you were writhing and moaning and *coming,* you needed it, too."

She had. But she wasn't going to tell him that.

"What kind of man climbs into bed with an injured woman—"

"According to you, I'm not a man," he snapped. "And because of me, you weren't exactly injured. You were, however, blue with cold."

Alex glanced at the still-swirling snowstorm outside the cave. "You were just keeping me warm?"

"Someone had to."

Alex narrowed her eyes. "You didn't have to seduce me."

"Are you so sure it was *me* who seduced *you*?"

Alex opened her mouth, then shut it again. He was right. She wasn't sure.

"How about we just forget it ever happened?" Alex asked.

"If you can, I can." He lay down and yanked the quilt off her and onto him with one sharp tug.

"Hey!" She yanked it back.

He shrugged and let her, placing his arms behind his head and crossing his ankles. Unfortunately the sight of him— long and bronzed, legs and arms thick with muscle—made Alex consider throwing the quilt back over him again. Because for every inch of his skin she appeared to have a memory of touching, tasting—

"Stop it," she muttered.

He opened one eye. "Stop what?"

"Your hoodoo, voodoo, witchy crap."

"I didn't do anything."

"You made me want you."

His lips quirked. "You wanted me?"

"As much as you wanted me."

"Who said I did?"

Alex lowered her eyes to his now limp member; it twitched beneath her gaze. Alex smirked.

Barlow sat up, flicking the corner of the quilt over his lap. "I did not use magic on you."

"You said—"

"I healed you," he ground out between clenched teeth. "I did not have the anger for anything more."

"What the hell does that mean?"

"My magic is based in anger."

"What are you, some kind of witch?"

"Do I look like an old woman with a cauldron and a cat?"

She tilted her head, peered at him for several seconds. "If you put on a hat, scowled just like that—maybe."

He sighed, unamused. "I'm not a witch."

"Sorcerer? Wizard? Warlock?"

"I don't know what I am. I only know that when I get angry, what I want to happen, does."

"Seriously?"

He lifted one finger. "Invisibility cloak." A second finger. "Shifting in the sunlight." A third. "Healing you."

Alex lifted her thumb. "Doing me."

"That I didn't want."

"Felt like it."

He made an impatient sound. "I thought we were going to pretend that didn't happen."

"Right." She flashed her hand in front of her face. "Forgotten." If only it were that easy. "Tell me more about your anger magic."

"I guess we aren't going to sleep anymore."

"You're tired?"

"Guys usually fall asleep . . . after."

"After what?" Alex asked sweetly, and batted her eyelashes.

She could have sworn she heard him laugh, but when she stopped batting and peered into his face all she saw was the same sour expression he wore whenever she was near.

"I have no idea how I became magic," he said. "I only know that the first time I changed, I did so because of my fury."

"You weren't bitten?" she asked.

"Not all werewolves are bitten."

"True," she agreed. "There were the genetically engineered ones."

"Mengele."

Alex cast him a quick glance. "You know about that?"

"I've been around a very long time. I know about everything."

Not everything. He didn't know Alex had been engineered to spy. And he'd better not ever find out or she might end up magically dead.

"How old are you?" she asked.

"I was born in the year 836 in what is now called Norway."

Alex let her gaze wander over him from his big feet, to his big hands, to all the big parts in between. "You were a *Viking*?"

"To be correct, *Viking* was a verb. To go a Viking."

"The act of conquering wherever, whatever, and whomever you wished."

"Technically, yes."

"How did you become furry?"

"Have you ever heard the Norse legend of the berserker?"

"No," she lied. She wanted to hear his version.

Barlow lifted his brows, surprised. "Aren't all *Jäger-Suchers* supposed to learn as much as they can about as many different types of shape-shifters as possible?"

"Where did you hear that?" He appeared to know more about the *Jäger-Suchers* than they knew about him.

"I have my sources."

Edward had said every agent he'd sent after Barlow had never returned, so Alex could surmise just who those sources had been. She wondered how long they'd lasted under Barlow's torture before they'd told him everything.

She didn't plan to.

"A berserker," Barlow continued, "is a Norse warrior who, in the heat of battle, becomes an animal."

"Poof, he's a zebra?"

Barlow's lips twisted as if he wanted to laugh but would never allow it. At least not around her. "Legend said that there were Norse warriors who wore the skin of a wolf; then they became one."

"How?" she asked.

"No idea."

"Yet you're one of those who became?"

"As far as I know, I'm the only one."

"Say what?"

"I'm the only one who actually became a wolf. Others wore the skin, fought with trance-like fury, became known as berserkers—"

"Hold on," she interrupted. "You're telling me you *were* the legend?"

"Could be."

"Did you ever hear the legend *before* you shape-shifted?"

"No. But it wasn't as if we had cell phones back then. We barely had books."

"Did you ever hear it on your travels? Before your story spread to the masses?"

He peered at the ceiling, considering, before he said, "No."

"Fantastic," she muttered. "You can't just be a regular werewolf, you have to be a magical legend with anger management issues."

"Go figure," he said.

Alex squinted at him through the gloomy glow cast by the lantern. "You're awfully hip"—she snapped her fingers—"for a Viking."

"I learned to fit in."

She laughed. "Believe me. You do *not* fit in."

He stiffened. "Of course I do."

"Just because you talk like a human and sometimes walk like a human, that doesn't make you human."

His jaw tightened. "I am more human than many humans I've met."

"Sure you are."

He frowned and Alex stifled a smile. Good. She'd gotten to him. He was far too confident. Most werewolves were. They had reason to be. And Julian had more reason than most.

"Getting back to how you became furry," she said. "Explain."

"I just did."

"You don't think 'I got pissed and became a wolf' requires a tad more clarification?"

"There is no *clarification*," he said. "We were in battle—"

"Where?"

He said a word that sounded like guttural gibberish to Alex. Then his lips tightened and he spat out, "Scotland now. They are nasty fighters, the Scottish."

"So *Braveheart* wasn't all Hollywood hype?" He appeared confused again, and she rolled her eyes. "You may talk like you're from this century, but you need to watch a few movies if you ever want to fit in for real."

"I don't," he said sharply. "I plan to stay in my village from now until the day that I—"

"Die?" she murmured. "Right. What was different about the battle in Scotland that made you—" She waved her hand. "You know."

"Furry?" he supplied.

She shrugged. The quilt slipped, and his gaze went to her bare shoulder, heating before he tugged it away.

"I saw my brother fall." His face filled with such anguish Alex got a chill and pulled the blanket closer. "I howled to the night sky. Called upon Odin to give me strength and fought my way toward him, but . . ." He shook his head. "In the fury that followed, the skin of the wolf that I carried upon me became my skin, and I ran beneath the fullness of the moon as a beast."

"And then?" Alex prompted when his silence stretched too long.

He looked up, blinking as if he'd forgotten she was there. "Ever after I became a wolf when the moon was round. Or my anger made me so."

He'd begun to speak with the formal cadence of those who spoke English as a second language, his memories more real, it seemed, than her.

"I discovered as time went by that fury brought forth my magic."

"Magic in the blood," she murmured. "Perhaps in your past."

"Perhaps."

"But you can make other wolves," she said. "That's strange."

"Why?"

"Lycanthropy is a virus, passed through the saliva. If you became a wolf by magic, then how is it you can spread the virus through a bite?"

He turned his palms up. "All I know is that I can."

CHAPTER 8

Alex fell asleep again. Shape-shifting required voracious amounts of energy, and the one small rabbit Julian had left for her dinner would barely have taken the edge off her hunger. Combined with the adrenaline rush from being chased by a polar bear, then being severely injured, her becoming unconscious for several more hours had been a given.

Julian, however, was wide awake. He lay side by side with Alex, trying not to let their skin brush, but every once in a while it did. Then he would have a flash of them together, and the only way to make the images stop would be to think of Alana and how he had lost her.

This child—and Alex was a child, even without the nearly twelve centuries that separated them—had killed Alana in cold blood and without remorse. That he'd touched her, kissed her, been inside her, not only kept him awake but made him slightly ill. That his body kept responding as if it wanted to do so again eventually forced him to leave behind the warmth of the quilt and venture into the chill of the cave where he sat with his back against the hard, icy stone and stared at her sleeping face. She really was quite beautiful.

Julian growled a curse in Norwegian and banged his

head against the wall. The resulting thud echoed throughout the small space and caused Alex to murmur what sounded suspiciously like his name.

What in Thor's hammer had possessed him to bring her along? Besides the fact that he'd been physically unable to leave her behind.

By dusk the storm had petered out. The sun set in a clear sky, red and pink and orange rays spreading across a vista of ice and snow. Julian shape-shifted, relishing the brush of the wind in his fur and the drift of the last few snowflakes tumbling onto his face.

"Planning to leave without me?" Alex stood in the opening. The quilt around her shoulders only reached to the apex of her thighs.

Julian's gaze was drawn to the long, toned length of her legs, and he remembered how they'd felt clasped around his hips as he'd pounded into her again and again—

"Wake up on the wrong side of the cave?" she murmured.

Only then did he realize he'd been growling.

Annoyed with himself for the hard-on he couldn't seem to shake, and with her for giving it to him, Julian ran into the deepening gloom.

Once Barlow's tail disappeared over a near ridge, Alex dropped the blanket and changed.

She'd slept better than she could remember sleeping in years. Had that been because of the great sex or because for the first time since her father had died she hadn't felt alone?

Alex caught the flash of Julian's golden fur just ahead and increased her speed. How was it that a man she considered her enemy, an animal that had turned her into one, too, had made her feel secure enough in his presence to sleep peacefully for hours? Just because the man had made her come didn't mean he was anything less than a beast.

They continued on throughout the night, moving farther and farther north. Julian appeared and disappeared ahead, but he never allowed Alex close enough to actually run at his side, and that was fine by her. Despite being housed in a wolf's body, her woman's mind remained confused.

She saw nothing but snow and ice and trees, a few bunnies, which she managed to catch and eat. Her legs were working almost in tandem with her brain tonight. She only tangled them together and fell once or twice.

Not long after midnight, lights sparkled on the horizon. Alex blinked and they disappeared. She figured they'd been a mirage, especially when they reappeared several times over the next few hours, winking out again each time she tried to focus on them more clearly.

The air was so cold her eyeballs ached. Maybe that was why.

They'd left the trees behind. Eons of ice and snow spread to the sky. Alex began to worry about what would happen when the sun came up and she changed. Naked, without any kind of shelter, life would become extremely unpleasant.

However, in that time of eternal darkness, when the moon drops away and the sun is not yet born, a light twinkled to her left. For an instant she thought perhaps it was the aurora borealis—something she'd heard of, though she wasn't quite sure what it was.

She paused, snorting with surprise, the chill of the night and the warmth of her breath creating a cloud of mist about her head. When it cleared, she saw the lights hadn't come from the sky but a village.

More of a city really, with streets and electrical poles, houses and businesses. Cars. Trucks.

Her snout hung open. This place appeared as modern as any small town in America. Probably because it *was* a small town in America.

She took one step forward, and Barlow howled—much farther up the trail.

Not that there was a trail. They'd left the road a few miles back and begun to cut across the tundra. Ahead lay nothing but ice and snow—mountains of it.

She glanced at the smoke trailing lazily out of chimneys. Who would want to continue into that seemingly impassable wilderness when they could remain here?

However if this wasn't the werewolf village, and considering Barlow's skirting of it she didn't think so, she'd do better to stay away. She had a feeling that in these parts, people shot wolves on sight. They'd definitely blow her away if she loped into town. Wolves didn't do that unless they were starving or rabid—two things that often warranted an express bullet to the brain.

They'd need a *silver* bullet, but she wouldn't put it past the folks of Alaska to pack a few of those just in case.

Barlow howled again, and this time he was annoyed. That howl very clearly said: *Come.* With a side helping of: *Now!*

Alex snorted, pawing at the ice with her claws. She didn't want to go, but she didn't have much choice. Not only did his voice call to her, making her twitch with unease at the thought of disobeying him, but her human mind understood that to walk into that village—as either a wolf or a naked woman—was beyond her.

With a growl and grumble, Alex scrambled up a very tall, slippery embankment and tumbled down the other side. She shook the snow crust from her fur and continued on.

The going was rough. No human would be able to follow this trail without snowshoes and a lot of practice. Maybe a snowmobile, but it wouldn't be easy. Alex glanced at the night sky. Perhaps a helicopter.

Another huge mountain of ice rose ahead. Barlow stood at the precipice, glaring at Alex as if she was the lamest werewolf in the land. Annoyed, she clambered upward. Right before she got there, he threw back his head and howled so loudly she lost her footing and slid halfway back down. By the time she recovered, he was gone.

She was so annoyed she didn't at first see what lay on the other side. A second, much smaller village appeared to have popped free of the earth.

A single light in the town square created just enough glow to illuminate Barlow trotting down the street, and there was an odd humming, almost a buzzing, in the air.

Barlow turned and yipped. Alex took a step forward despite herself. She found Barlow's "orders" damn hard to resist—all that alpha wolf, I-am-your-maker shit—which only made her more determined to resist them.

She forced herself to remain where she was despite his call. She would join him eventually. She didn't have much choice. The werewolf that had murdered her father was part of Barlow's pack. Barlow's pack lived in this village. Therefore, she would enter.

When she was damn good and ready.

Barlow waited in the town square. The place was spooky silent. Businesses lined the street. But nowhere did she see a car or a truck. Of course she hadn't seen a road, either, since they'd left the first village behind.

Houses rose behind the commercial district, chimneys smoking. Lights flickered here and there, and she suddenly understood that the odd hum was the buzz of the generators that powered the place. Beyond that buzz she heard not a single rumble of a car, or even the bark of a dog.

In the space of a blink, Barlow changed from wolf to man. For an instant she envied him that power. She hated being vulnerable for the time it took her to morph into a woman.

"I want you to meet my people," he said.

Alex glanced around the deserted town pointedly. She had to wonder where he was hiding that werewolf army.

"Shape-shift," he ordered.

Alex stuck out her tongue. The long, languid, loose organ flopped free of her mouth and she drooled, which was not the effect she'd been hoping for.

"Suit yourself," he muttered, then he threw back his head and howled.

Alex skittered, startled by both the action and the sheer volume. Her ears, super-sensitive in this form, rang, and her throat ached with the desire to answer.

She could not drag her gaze from the man, big and bronzed and naked in the half-light, as the howl of an alpha wolf curled toward the slowly lightening sky. If she'd had human skin, it would have had goose bumps. As it was she shook herself vigorously to make the odd tingle go away.

Alex turned her gaze toward the buildings, expecting his people to answer that call, but no one opened the doors and stepped outside. No one walked in from the side streets. No headlights blazed in the distance.

She turned to Barlow, ready now to reach for her humanity, to shape-shift into herself if only to ask him *what the hell,* and she saw them.

Dozens of wolf-shaped shadows materialized from the gloom.

Alex glanced at the empty village, then back at the approaching cadre of wolves. Huh. It hadn't occurred to her that the whole town would spend the night hunting together. In her experience, werewolves were solitary. Of course she was starting to understand that Barlow and his wolves were nothing like the ones she'd known.

They loped across the expanse of snow and ice, even as the approaching dawn crept up behind them, sweeping down like a tidal wave. The instant the sun touched their tails, they changed, tumbling end over end just as Alex had yesterday. But unlike Alex, they gracefully gained their feet, continuing toward the village on two legs instead of four.

The sun moved inexorably forward, changing each and every werewolf from beast to man or woman. By the time the pack ran into town, they were human.

Their faces reflected joy—Alex thought because of the night they'd spent in the woods. She understood now the ecstasy of running, the cool wind in her fur, incredible speed at her beck and call, feeling at one with the earth, the trees, the land—at home in a way she'd never felt before.

Alex tensed. This wasn't home. What she had experienced was the collective consciousness of this pack. It would fade; it wasn't real, and she needed to remember that.

However, the joy of the others didn't appear to be residual spunkiness from their nightly frolic. Instead, their happiness stemmed from Julian's return. Every person came to him, and he set his hand upon them. A shoulder here, a cheek there, the top of a head, a pat on the back. Once he'd done so, they let out a sigh of utter peace and moved aside so the next supplicant could step forward.

Alex was so fascinated with their behavior and his, she neglected to keep her eye on the sun. Just as the last person

was blessed by Barlow, and everyone turned to her, the rays
of dawn cast over her face, and she shifted.

Julian waited for Alex to break and run—to burst into the
grocery store, the bank, the café and try to find something,
anything with which to cover herself.

But to her credit, she didn't. She straightened from four
legs to two, either refusing to be embarrassed by her naked-
ness or not embarrassed at all. If that was the case, she was
adapting to being a werewolf much quicker than most. Even
Alana—

Julian frowned. Alana had needed help to adjust; she
hadn't quite fit in. They'd fallen in love while Julian in-
structed the shy, sweet young woman in the ways of the werewolf world.

He pulled his attention from the past into the present where
his people stood naked in the dawn's hazy light. No one
cared. They were pack. They had nothing whatsoever to hide.

"I told you to shift," he murmured. "If you'd have listened, you could have grabbed some clothes before I called
them."

"I'll shift when I want to," she said. "Or when I have to.
Not when you tell me to."

He'd been right about her defying him. *And* about his
enjoying it.

"Besides," she continued. "They don't have clothes; you
don't have clothes. Why should I have clothes?"

"Frostbite?"

"I'll heal frostbite easier than I healed—" She glanced at
her ribs. The bruises and the scratches were gone. She met
his eyes and shrugged.

His people began to shuffle impatiently. The initial change
left them warm enough to withstand the extreme cold. But

the longer they were human, the more human they were, and while frostbite could be healed, it would have to wait until the moon rose to do so completely. A day of frostbite on tender extremities would not be a day full of sunshine.

"Everyone welcome Alexandra Trevalyn," he said. "Alex. She is one of us."

He felt her swift glance. Had she thought he would reveal her past? If his pack knew she was the hunter who had killed his wife, they would kill her.

If he'd wanted her dead, he would have ended her himself. *Before* he'd made her a werewolf.

Everyone moved closer, welcoming her. Pack members were touchy-feely, and that made Alex uncomfortable. Julian crossed his arms over his chest and watched as she tried not to squirm.

A sudden insight stunned him. He had not planned to bring her here. Therefore, he had not brought along the serum that would allow her to touch anyone but him in human form. Which meant she should now be writhing on the ground in agony along with everyone who had touched her.

"Enough," he barked.

His people turned to him in surprise. Welcoming a new pack member meant getting to know their scent, their touch, and letting the new member get to know yours. They believed Alex had taken her medicine, as they all had. So why was he stopping them?

Since he couldn't tell them that something very strange was going on, he chose to tell them nothing.

"Ella." Julian addressed the oldest female in the pack—a dark, thin Frenchwoman who appeared the same age as Alex but in truth had narrowly escaped the guillotine during *la révolution*. "See that she gets settled."

Ella moved forward, hand outstretched. Alex frowned,

staring at Ella's palm as if she had no idea what the woman wanted. She wasn't afraid; she must have come to the conclusion that since she could touch Julian, she could touch everyone.

Alex backed up a few steps. "I'll—uh—be right back." She moved out of the crowd and came to Julian. "Where will I stay?"

"With Ella."

"But I—" She broke off, biting her lip. "I just met her."

"You just met everyone."

"Not you."

Julian blinked. "You want to stay with me?"

"I don't *want* to," she said at the same time he said, "That wouldn't be smart."

"Because of yesterday?" she asked.

The instant the words left her mouth, Julian remembered the taste of that mouth, the feel of it on his body, the scent of her all around him, and his penis leaped.

"Faen," he muttered. *Shit!* He was naked. If he got a hard-on now—

He didn't want to think about that. In fact, he'd better *not* think about it or he'd definitely get one.

Her eyebrows lifted, and her lips twitched as if she knew his every thought. "What if I promise not to jump you?"

"You're admitting that you *did* jump me?"

"No."

Her defiance caused amusement to flicker, quickly followed by annoyance at both his reaction and the sight of her face. How could he be both attracted and repelled by her every minute of every day? He wanted to grab her by the shoulders and shake her, at the same time he wanted to throw her down on the ground and take her.

"Ella," Julian snapped, and strode away without bothering to reiterate his orders. It was a sign of weakness to repeat himself, and Julian could not afford to be weak.

Just because he was their leader, and had been for close to a century, did not mean a wolf wouldn't challenge him if given the opportunity. Julian had managed to keep the peace because he was the strongest, the biggest, the baddest when he chose to be. No one dared question him.

Except Alex.

He sighed, wondering if he might have to kill her after all.

CHAPTER 9

Following a long, hot shower where Julian both warmed his chilled skin and jacked off to ascertain he would not have any surprise erections later that day, Julian dressed, then checked his messages.

Between traveling, locating Alex, following her, and setting up his plan, he'd been away over a week. He had a lot to deal with. Julian was not only the mayor of what had come to be known as Barlowsville—a joke at first, but the name stuck—he was also the chief of police, the judge, and, when necessary, the executioner.

The latter was rare. For the most part they lived in harmony. But when dealing with nearly two hundred werewolves . . . well, shit happened.

Thankfully none of the messages awaiting him spoke of misbehavior so severe that capital punishment would be necessary. Just the usual minutiae of village life—boundary disputes, nonpayment for services or goods—and the minutiae of werewolf existence—the snatching of a rabbit from someone's very jaws, the taking of more than one's share of a larger kill—elk, deer, moose.

He put aside his duties until later. He had one duty he must attend to first.

His house, a two-story log cabin at the farthest edge of the village, backed a squat, white edifice that blended into the landscape during the majority of the year when snow covered the land.

Presently the snow reached Julian's knees, but the distance between the rear of Julian's house and the rear of the building was only a few hundred feet and wasn't that difficult to traverse, especially for someone with the strength of ten.

Inside, the air was cool—though not unpleasantly so. Silence reigned, broken every so often by the click of electricity or the whisper of the wind through the eaves.

"Cade?" Julian called, but no one answered.

Typical. His brother often became engrossed in his work to the detriment of all else. If it weren't for the full moon that forced the issue, Julian thought Cade might forget to shape-shift altogether.

Julian walked through the silent halls, ducked his head into Cade's empty living quarters, then followed his nose to the laboratory where he found his brother boiling what smelled like death over a tiny blue flame. For a few minutes Julian just watched him.

As a Viking, Cade had been a bust. Without Julian to protect him, he would have died long before that fateful day in Scotland.

Cade was a gentle soul, a healer by trade. He'd been indispensable when they'd gone a Viking, his knowledge of the human body and the herbs and potions necessary to mend it vast.

Whenever they'd invaded a new country, Cade spent his time talking to the local healers, gathering knowledge from every corner of the earth. He fought, but not eagerly or well, which meant Julian always fought at his side.

Except for that one time.

"Hey," Julian murmured, and Cade looked up, blue eyes widening when he discovered his brother in the room.

He frowned at the clock, then the calendar, then back at Julian. "What day is it?"

"Friday."

The frown deepened. "But you left on Thursday."

"I've been gone over a week, Cade."

Cade glanced at the calendar again, then shrugged and murmured, "Huh. Is it morning or is it night?"

"I told you to put a window in this place."

The laboratory was more like a fortress. The single window in the entire building existed in Cade's living quarters, and that only because Julian had gone behind his brother's back with the builders. He wasn't sure Cade had even noticed.

"It helps me to focus," Cade said. "If there are no windows, my only world is this."

"Your only world has always been this."

"True," Cade agreed, and returned to his work.

Julian's brother was shorter than he—though at six feet Cade was by no means short. He was also slim instead of muscular, pale instead of tan, and his hair, which had once been as blond as Julian's, had darkened to a dusty brown.

While Julian's brushed his shoulders, straight and smooth, Cade's reached halfway down his back, the length more because he forgot to cut it—hell, sometimes he forgot to wash it—than for any fashion statement. He'd attempted to confine it in a ponytail, but strands had come free and billowed, curling into his face.

"You never said where you were going or why," Cade murmured as he mixed a bit of this and a tad of that.

With good reason. Alana had not made friends easily, but she'd made friends with Cade. Her loss had hit him hard. If his brother had known why Julian was going, there would have been no leaving him behind, and Julian had needed to do this alone.

"I went to LA to follow a lead on Alana's killer."

Cade knocked one of the test tubes onto the floor as he spun. "Did you find anything?"

Julian stared Cade directly in the eye. "No," he said.

Cade sighed, then he began to clean up the mess on the floor.

"What did you drop?" Julian asked.

"Human blood derivative."

Julian straightened away from the counter. "You found it?"

"Not yet."

"You will."

"Sometimes I wonder."

The need for human blood on the night of the full moon necessitated some fancy planning on Julian's part. The amount of human blood necessary to satisfy the cravings of his entire village was copious, which was why Cade spent the majority of his time searching for a substitute. That and the fact that Alana had *hated* taking human blood. She'd said it made her feel *ew-ky*.

Julian smiled at the memory, but his smile faded as he recalled that her dislike of that basic need had eventually grown into a dislike of a whole lot more.

"You invented the serum that allows werewolves to touch in human form," Julian blurted, doing his best to make the unpleasant memories go away.

And speaking of unpleasant memories.

"I brought a woman back with me."

Cade, who had been choosing a new test tube from the

shiny selection near the sink, nearly bobbled and broke another. "You what?"

"She was . . . dying," Julian muttered.

Liar, liar, pants on fire, his mind taunted.

"What happened to the no-more-werewolves rule?"

"That isn't the rule," Julian said.

"Fine. You didn't ask *permission*." His voice twisted sarcastically on the final word.

"Since I'm the one who gives permission, I figured I'd save a step."

Cade rolled his eyes, and Julian stifled a smile. His brother was the only one who dared stand up to him—although not often or very well—the only one with whom Julian could be truly himself.

Alex's face flitted through his mind. She stood up to him. And if he wasn't being himself with her—evil, murderous beast that he was—then who was he being?

"You're growling," Cade observed.

Alex seemed to have that effect on him, even when she wasn't around.

"You said it's dangerous to create a new wolf," Cade pointed out. "That it should only be done by one who's done it before, for a damn good reason, with the new wolf's consent and preferably here." Cade jabbed a finger at the floor.

"I say a lot of things," Julian muttered.

"Besides, the village is packed. Where is this woman going to stay?" His eyes widened. "With you?"

"Hell no!" Julian erupted before he could stop himself.

His brother's expression became contemplative. "Who is she?"

"Just some woman." Julian put his hands in his pockets and became vastly interested in the ceiling. "She was lying there bleeding. What was I supposed to do?"

"You said yourself that we can't save everyone."

"I suppose, but there was something about her—"

That little matter of murdering my wife.

"Wait a second," Cade began. "You were in LA?"

"So?"

"You made a wolf in LA? A place with the population of mainland China shoved into a shoe box. You know how a new wolf is the first time they change." He walked away muttering. "Kill anything. Everything. Anywhere. Doesn't matter."

Cade booted up his laptop, typed a few quick commands, then peered at the screen. "No mass murders by unknown perpetrators. No wild dog packs loose in the suburbs. No rogue coyotes down from the hills munching on unsuspecting preschoolers."

Julian lifted his eyebrow and let his brother rant on. Sometimes that was best.

Cade continued to scroll and click, Google and search, his mutterings lapsing into Norwegian now and then.

"Ah-ha!" Cade pointed at the screen. "Known child molester found with his throat torn out in a nasty area of LA. No suspects." He cast Julian a glance. "That has you written all over it."

Julian didn't answer. Cade was right.

"Except . . ." Cade tapped his fingernail against the keyboard. "If you found this woman and she was dying, then you bit her and she shifted, she'd be ravenous. So how did you have time to find a child molester and take him for lunch?"

Good question.

Cade's eyes narrowed. "It's almost as if you'd planned it."

His brother was too smart for anyone's good. Especially Julian's.

"I didn't have to plan anything," Julian said. "I'm magic, remember?"

"You use that as an answer to everything."

"It's a pretty good answer."

Julian waited for Cade to call him a liar, but he didn't. He couldn't prove anything, and when it came right down to it, why would Julian lie?

"This woman," Julian said. "I didn't plan to make her."

Liar!

"So I didn't have any of your serum to give her." Julian spoke more loudly, trying to drown out the accusing voice in his head. Cade frowned. "Yet when we came into town just now, everyone welcomed her, and no one got a headache."

"That's impossible," his brother insisted.

"Since it happened, guess not."

"Who is this woman?"

"Name is Alexandra Trevalyn. Other than that . . ." Julian shrugged. "You've never heard of this happening before?"

"Never." Cade turned back to his computer, hit a few more commands, then began to type. "Bring her here. I'll need a sample of her blood."

Julian sighed. He'd hoped Cade would have a scientific explanation that would set Julian's mind at ease, or that his brother would at least say that while he didn't know the cause, he *had* heard of the phenomenon a hundred times before.

No such luck.

Ella took Alex's arm, ignoring her start of surprise. No one seemed to find it odd that they could touch, and since she'd been able to touch Julian, too, Alex guessed that this was just another of the many ways that Barlow's wolves were different.

Alex wasn't used to being touched so often and so easily. She'd lived alone for eight years. On the move. No friends, no family. Few reasons to touch anyone at all. Especially not a stark-naked woman she'd only just met.

"Welcome," Ella said. "We don't often have new arrivals."

As the others dispersed every which way, the woman led Alex across the square to a side street opposite the one down which Julian had disappeared. Had he chosen Ella simply because her home was the farthest from his?

"No?" Alex extricated her arm. "Why's that?"

Ella glanced at her. "Hasn't Julian explained about Barlowsville?"

"Barlowsville?" Alex repeated with a derisive snort. "What an ego."

Ella frowned, her dark eyes confused. "You sound like you hate him."

"Doesn't everyone?" Alex muttered.

"He is our leader, our maker."

Alex stopped walking. "He made *all* of you?"

"Yes."

Edward had been right. Barlow was amassing a werewolf army. Although . . . the army didn't appear to be very big or very vicious. But give them time.

Ella beckoned. "I have clothes for you. We seem about the same size."

And it was pretty easy to tell.

Alex followed the woman, who had the slightest of French accents, to a single-story house partway down a street filled with others just the same. They were so similar, they appeared to have all come from the same kit. Slanted roofs, boxy exterior, two windows at the front on either side of the door, each painted the same shade of white as the snow, with chimneys that spilled wood smoke into a sky of pristine blue.

Ella opened the door and walked inside. Alex was surprised the place hadn't been locked. Although where would Ella have carried the key?

She followed the woman into the house, eyes widening at the decor. She didn't know anything about furniture, but Ella's appeared both old and expensive.

"Nice," she ventured, nodding toward the living room.

Gilt mirrors graced the walls. Elaborately hand-carved tables flanked chairs of ruby-red velvet and a couch of burnished gold.

"Merci." Ella smiled. "It has taken many years but I've been able to reacquire most of my things."

"These were actually yours when you were . . ."

"Human?" Ella smiled. "Yes."

"How old are you?" Alex asked.

Ella put a hand on Alex's arm. "Much, *much* older than I look."

No shit, Alex thought.

"Come." Ella led her down a short hallway, pointing into one of the rooms. "Wear whatever you wish. I will make us some café."

When Alex hesitated, Ella gave her a little push, then closed the door behind her.

Here the decor was more modern: a bed that could have been purchased at Price Club—although Alex could not imagine Ella darkening their door—a nightstand of fake cherrywood, a lamp of false brass. However, upon the armoire—also fake cherry—sat several items that had definitely not been bought at a discount store.

A brilliantly painted china cup, a tiny vanity, small enough to fit into a doll's house, but with intricate carvings that must have driven the artist half mad, and a glass woman, dressed like Marie Antoinette.

Alex bent closer. Actually, the figure *was* Marie Antoinette. She was beginning to catch a clue as to how old Ella was.

Alex opened the armoire, afraid she'd discover frilly underwear, bras with enough lace to be at home on a Victoria's Secret catwalk, and silky stockings that would be useless in this climate. She was pleasantly surprised to be proven wrong.

Not that the undergarments weren't too frilly for her taste, but they weren't embarrassingly so. Not that anyone would see them.

An image of Julian came to mind but she thrust it resolutely away. She was here to spy on him. To kill him if she could. There would be no repeat boinking of the man no matter how fantastic it had been.

Alex discovered serviceable black socks, along with a black turtleneck made of cashmere so soft she rubbed her face against it with a sigh as she slid it over her head. She'd never owned anything so fine.

"And you still don't," she muttered, moving to the closet. Inside the clothes were arranged by color, and there was a whole lot of black.

She chose a pair of black wool slacks, and she had to admit the outfit suited her, although she felt a bit like a cat burglar.

Shoes lined the floor. Unfortunately, they weren't her size. Alex spent longer than she ever had in her life on her hair, which was tangled and littered with sticks. Since she had no comb or brush, she made do with her fingers, then quickly braided the length and secured it with an extra shoelace she found in a drawer. When she could avoid it no longer, Alex opened the door and went to the kitchen.

Ella sat on a tall chair at the center island, a tiny cup of very dark coffee in front of her. She was dressed in winter white. A bulky sweater with a cowl that dipped to the center of her chest, displaying a ruby in an elaborate filigree setting, and wool slacks similar but for the color to the ones Alex wore.

She glanced up from the magazine she was paging through with a smile that faded at the sight of Alex. "Oh, *non!*" She shook her head.

"Did I take something I shouldn't have? I'll change." Alex spun, but she'd only gone two steps when Ella was by her side. The speed in which the other woman had reached her caused Alex to start. Would she ever get used to the swiftness of the werewolf in human form?

"All that I have is yours for the asking, *mon amie.* But so much black." She made a *tsk*ing sound as she stepped past Alex and returned to the bedroom.

Alex followed, standing in the doorway as Ella rooted through the armoire.

"Ah-ha." The woman flipped up her arm, and a gorgeous silk scarf unraveled. In all the shades of autumn—gold, russet, amber, olive—it was not something Alex would ever have chosen for herself. She'd never understood silk scarves. They certainly couldn't keep you warm.

Ella crossed the short distance and draped it around Alex's neck. "Let it hang down, just so." She stepped back, gazing at Alex with a critical eye. Then she stepped forward and yanked the shoestring from Alex's hair, *tsk*ing again. *"Non."* She threw it into the trash and untangled the length from its braid.

"Oui." She gave a sharp, satisfied nod. "I knew this scarf would bring out the lights in your hair." She drew Alex to the full-length mirror attached to the back of the closet door. "Black is fine as a base, but add a flash of color and—" She

kissed the tips of her fingers, then released them to the sky with a smooching sound. "Very chic."

"Chic," Alex repeated. "Right."

She'd never been chic, would never be chic, did not know what chic meant. But Ella was right. The silly scarf did bring out highlights that Alex hadn't even known she had.

"Thanks." Alex's gaze met the woman's in the mirror. "It's nice of you to help me."

In her experience, people didn't just help strangers for the fun of it. There had to be something in it for them. She wondered what was in it for Ella.

"It's my pleasure," Ella replied, and her expression *was* pleased. Almost as if she enjoyed making Alex look as nice as she could, just *because* she could.

"You have a lot of beautiful things."

"Merci."

"I wouldn't think you could find all this way up here."

"Here?" Ella laughed, the sound throaty, sexy, very French. "Here we would find flannel shirts, Levi's, snow boots, and parkas. This—" She waved her hand at the full closet. "—is what the Internet is for."

"You use the Internet?"

"Most of us may be very old, but we have learned to leave our past behind." She glanced at the bric-a-brac on the armoire. "For the most part. We live in this world now."

"You call hiding away in the Arctic Circle living in the world?" Alex asked.

"It is the only choice that we have." Ella left the room, the downward slant of her shoulders making Alex want to slam her own head against the wall a few times until she knocked some sense into herself.

Alex had never had to watch what she said before. For the

most part, everything Alex thought came straight out of her mouth. But then she'd never had to interact in polite society. And who would have thought a werewolf village in the middle of the tundra would be considered polite society?

Alex followed Ella to the kitchen, where the woman wiped an already immaculate countertop with an equally pristine cloth.

"I was rude," Alex began.

"It's natural to wonder about your new home, but Julian must have told you why we live as we do."

"So he can be Lord of the Wolves?"

"He *is* lord of these wolves. And because of that, because of him, we live safely and well. There are hunters out there, Alex. They would shoot you with a silver bullet for no other reason than that you exist, then leave you to burn without a backward glance."

Alex had nothing to say to that since she had once been one of them.

CHAPTER 10

Julian tapped on Ella's door. When she didn't answer, he went inside.

He found the two women sitting next to each other, fine china espresso cups near at hand. If he wasn't mistaken, they were poring over French fashion magazines.

What the hell?

"Problem, Julian?" Ella didn't even look up from the magazine. She'd probably heard him come in the door. Hell, she'd probably heard him walking up the street.

Alex on the other hand, leaped off the chair so fast she set it rocking back and forth; it would have fallen if Ella hadn't reached out a slim, lovely hand to stop it.

"You—you just walk into anyone's house whenever you like?" she demanded.

"I knocked." Even to his ears, the words sounded defensive. "You were too busy with—" He waved his hand at the magazines, which *were* French and fashionable. Of all the things he might have expected Alex to be doing, this was not one of them.

"We were engrossed. Girl talk, Julian."

Ella gave his name a French twist on the *J*, turning it into something between a *Z* and a *G*. She only did that when she was irritated with him. What had he done? His eyes narrowed on Alex. What had she *said* he'd done?

"Unless there's something urgent," Ella continued, "I suggest you run along before we bore you to death."

"Yeah," Alex agreed. "Run along."

He lifted a brow. "Is there some reason you don't want me here?"

"How much time do you have?" she muttered.

Ella laughed, startling them both. Alex turned to her at the same time Julian did, and together they snapped, "What's so funny?"

Ella's smile widened. "You pretend to loathe each other, but you do not. As they say on TV: 'What is up with that?'"

"You're crazy," Julian said.

"So I have been told." She glanced back and forth between them. "Usually when I am right."

Julian had sent Alex with Ella because Ella was the most no-nonsense woman he knew. She had an uncanny knack of seeing the true person behind the facade. He trusted her opinion.

But seeing her with Alex, shoulder-to-shoulder like the best of friends, unnerved him. Didn't Ella smell the evil on her? He could.

To prove the theory, Julian sniffed—once, twice. Hell. All he could smell was *her*.

"What did you want, Julian?"

He'd come to bring Alex to Cade, but along the way he'd realized they needed to have a talk. She should keep her mouth shut about who she was, what she'd done, why she was here.

However, now he found himself wondering if he should

at least tell Ella the truth. It had not been fair of him to command the Frenchwoman to welcome the enemy into her home when she hadn't even known the enemy was here. Ella's sound judgment was obviously being clouded by—

What? He didn't think Alex had the ability to pretend to be something she was not. From what he'd observed, she was pretty damn honest about everything. For instance—how very much she wanted to kill him.

"Come with me," he ordered, and stalked toward the front door, expecting Alex to follow. He would speak with her on the way to the lab, where she would give blood to his brother. He really wanted to know why she was migraine-free after being touched by nearly two hundred werewolves.

He opened the door, stepping back to let Alex go first. Except she wasn't there. She was hovering in the entryway between the kitchen and the hall.

"I told you to come," he said.

"I told you to die," she returned. "But you're still breathing."

Quickly choked laughter drifted from behind her.

How could she deny his commands? No one else ever did.

However, when he observed more closely, he noticed that she would surreptitiously take two steps forward before clenching her hands, gritting her teeth, and taking a slow, difficult step back.

"Come," he said again.

She took three quick steps before she could stop herself. Then she punched her fist into the wall.

Actually she punched her fist *through* the wall.

Whoops.

Ella hurried into the hall, saw him standing by the door

scowling and Alex with her fist now stuck in the plaster. That was going to be a pain in the ass to fix, and it was going to leave a mark.

In the wall.

"Quit badgering her!" Ella ordered.

Julian's mouth hung open. "But she— Your wall. Big hole."

"I can see, Julian. Obviously you can't."

Alex yanked her fist free, sending plaster flying every which way. Some of it landed in Ella's hair, but she didn't seem to care. Which was strange considering he'd seen her throw the mother of all fits over a stray leaf in her fur.

"See?" he repeated, confused.

Ella pointed to the ground. "She can't go walking in the snow. She has no shoes. Bring some. Size nine." Then she took Alex by the arm and led her back into the kitchen.

"You don't know much about men, do you?" Ella asked.

"He's not a man."

Alex's knuckles stung on the outside, ached on the inside, but she wasn't really hurt, and they were already healing.

Her embarrassment, however, appeared there to stay. She'd behaved like the animal he'd made her. Every day, in so many ways, she was drifting farther from the Alex she knew in the direction of an Alex she did not want to become.

"He *is* a man," Ella said firmly. "And a good one."

Alex blew a derisive breath from between her lips.

"I can smell the desire between you."

Alex winced. Nothing wrong with Ella's nose.

"But you also seem to hate each other."

Or her intuition.

"Yet he gave you our gift and brought you home."

"This isn't a gift," Alex said, "and I'm not home."

"You could be," Ella murmured, but Alex pretended not to hear.

She sat at the island and finished her coffee. The jolt of caffeine gave her the guts to say, "I'm sorry about the wall."

"Walls can be fixed." Ella took a chair on the opposite side, wisely giving Alex her space. "I've never seen anyone deny him before. When he speaks, we listen. We *want* to. Don't you?"

"Hell, no. When he speaks I want to rip off his face."

"Interesting," Ella murmured, at the same time Julian tossed a pair of the ugliest boots ever invented onto the table between them.

Alex glanced up. Had he heard her say she wanted to rip off his face? If he had, he hid it well. Maybe he'd already surmised how she felt. He might be annoying, but he certainly wasn't stupid.

Instead of throwing the navy-blue rubber boots at his head, Alex put them on and followed him from the house. Perhaps if she fought him less, she'd feel like herself more. Couldn't hurt.

"We need to talk," he said.

"You couldn't just say that?" She fell into step beside him. "You had to order me to *come* like your dog?" His forehead creased as if he had no idea what she meant. "Let me clue you in—some folks don't like being told what to do as if they have no choice. However, if you ask nicely, at least pretend that they have the opportunity to refuse, they might agree with a lot less hassle."

"I'll keep that in mind."

Julian led her toward the center square, which now bustled with noise and activity. Snowmobiles rumbled—she'd yet to see any cars—store bells chimed, voices rose in greeting, to both Julian and Alex. Julian lifted a hand and returned every hello. Alex merely nodded. She wasn't used to so many people knowing her name. Hell, she wasn't used to *anyone* knowing her name.

They passed the café, which didn't appear to have a name beyond EAT—as evidenced by the neon sign in the window. A quick glance inside revealed every table full, with most of the patrons enjoying huge platters of steak and eggs.

"I guess the percentage of heart disease here is pretty damn low," she muttered.

"There *are* advantages, Alex."

"To being an evil killing machine?"

He let out a heavy sigh. "Does anyone you've met seem evil? Are there bloody body parts strewn all over? Do you see any intestines strung from the rooftops and severed heads on pikes in the town square?"

"That doesn't mean it can't happen."

"It won't. We're different."

"So *you* say."

"So you'll see."

As they continued to stroll across town Alex noted that most of the inhabitants made do with a hat, boots, and a flannel shirt against the elements. Alex wasn't wearing much more than that, either, and she didn't really mind.

"How cold is it?" she asked, wrapping Ella's scarf around her ears and neck.

"Not bad today. About five below."

"And that's 'not bad'?"

"It can get to minus fifty some nights."

She flicked a finger at him. "You wear a coat then?"

"Fur coat."

Figures.

"Why aren't I turning blue?" she wondered aloud.

"Another advantage. Increased metabolism, increased body heat. You don't want to leave your extremities out for too long in this cold, but you aren't going to need a coat unless the temperature drops another forty degrees."

"Where are you taking me?"

"There's someone I want you to meet," he said.

"I thought I met everyone when we were—" She waved at the town square. "You know."

His lips quirked. "Naked?"

She wasn't going to discuss naked with him. Not now. Not ever.

When she didn't take the bait, he shrugged and his smile faded. "Not everyone runs as a wolf every night."

"Why not if it's so fantabulous?" she muttered.

The sudden rev of a motor was followed by the overwhelming scent of exhaust. Julian paused and turned, calmly watching the snowmobile race up the street directly at them.

Alex fought the bizarre urge to step in front of him. Even if the machine hit Barlow head-on, he'd be fine. Since she'd prefer him dead, where on earth had the desire to protect him come from?

You'd think she'd put her *head* through Ella's wall instead of her fist the way she was acting.

She needn't have worried. Whoever was at the controls of the snowmobile stopped a safe distance away, then whipped off the helmet.

Long, flowing, inky black hair cascaded free. Alex couldn't take her eyes off it; the flow was like a river of ebony. So when the new arrival spoke, she started in surprise and yanked her gaze to the face.

Yep, it was a man all right.

"Ataniq," he began. "There is trouble in the village."

Alex wanted to glance at Barlow, but she couldn't take her eyes from the stranger. He was beautiful.

Obviously one of the original locals—were they still called Eskimos? She didn't think so, but *what* they were called she hadn't a clue—his skin was smooth and dark, that hair belonged on a supermodel, but his eyes—oh brother, those eyes.

They were Barlow's eyes.

She turned to him with a lifted brow, but he was already throwing his leg over the snowmobile.

"But—" Alex began, and Barlow's gaze flicked up. From his expression, he'd forgotten she was there.

He cursed, glancing at the sky as if asking for deliverance. What had *she* done?

Besides killing his wife?

For the first time Alex felt a hint of shame, but she thrust it resolutely away. She'd been a hunter, Alana the hunted. Alex had only done what she'd been told to do.

And, hey, wasn't that the excuse used at the Nuremberg trials?

Barlow beckoned, and her lips tightened mulishly. The young man's eyes widened, and his mouth fell open. She was getting really sick of everyone bowing and scraping to the wolf-god, then giving her grief when she wouldn't.

He pointed to the back of the snowmobile, then flicked his finger at the young man, who attempted to hand her his helmet so fast he dropped it. Alex snatched it out of the air and tried to give it back, but he merely held up his hands in a gesture of surrender and refused to take the thing.

Though the motor rumbled loudly, Alex knew Barlow, with his supersonic ears, would have no trouble hearing her. "Where are you going?"

He jerked his head at the youth. "George said there's trouble in the village."

"I thought this was the village."

"Didn't you see the other one when we ran past last night?"

Alex remembered the twinkling lights—first up ahead, then to the side as they skirted around it—the village that was more like a town.

"What business is it of yours if another village has trouble?"

Impatience crossed his face. "I don't have time to explain." He glanced around as if looking for someone to take her off his hands, then sighed and glanced back. "You'd better come along."

He shifted forward, making room for her as if her agreement was a given. Though she'd like to say no just to spite him, she *had* always wanted to ride on a snowmobile.

Alex wound Ella's scarf around her neck, tying it tightly in place so it wouldn't fly off; then she slipped the helmet quickly onto her head. Just the few seconds of exposure to the wind made her ears feel brittle enough to fall off. Although why she was worried, she had no idea. She'd just grow another set.

And she'd kind of like to see that—with someone *else's* ears.

The instant she was settled, Barlow took off, and Alex would have flipped backward and landed on her head if he hadn't grabbed her hand and pulled it around his waist.

His stomach muscles flexed, and she had to clench her fingers to keep from stroking them. Unfortunately, a clenched hand did not hold on very well, especially when they hit a rut.

The machine flew up, came down hard. Alex narrowly missed biting her tongue. She grabbed onto Julian's belt, her thumb sliding beneath his jeans and scraping skin. He straightened so fast his shoulder clocked her in the jaw. If she hadn't been wearing the helmet, she would have seen stars.

He reached for her other arm, yanked it forward with no small amount of force. "Use two hands!" he shouted.

His hair blew past her face, long and light, and when the sun hit the strands they turned every shade of gold. Even though the helmet had a visor, she could still smell him— that intoxicating scent of ice and snow and trees.

She should probably pull her thumb out of his pants, but he was so warm. She was tempted to slide the rest of her chilled appendage in to join it. And the allure of that thought made her yank the hand right out.

Instead she cupped her palms at his hips as lightly as she could and not be sent into outer space when they hit the next uneven patch.

The terrain was incredibly rough. Even the snowmobile had a hard time getting over some of it. Walking the distance between the two villages would be nearly impossible. Traversing it as a wolf had probably been the best way.

Despite the ridges and valleys, the bumps and thumps, Alex began to enjoy the ride. Her father had loved speed. You couldn't be a *Jäger-Sucher* and not be sort of a danger-junkie.

When they'd traveled the western highways, where there were no speed limits, he'd put his foot to the floor and taken them up and down hills and around curves with the skill and velocity of an Indy 500 driver.

The memory of those rides, combined with the rush of the wind and the flash of snow-covered terrain moving backward at an incredible rate, both thrilled and saddened Alex.

She loved the sensation of speed, but she really, really missed her father. Which made her wonder—

If he saw her now, would he shoot her in the head as he'd shot so many others?

CHAPTER 11

Julian clenched his jaw so tightly it began to ache. If he wasn't careful he'd crack a tooth. He'd done it before.

What *had* he been thinking to bring her along?

Well, he couldn't leave her in town until he'd spoken with her about keeping certain secrets, and he couldn't just order her not to tell anyone who she really was. Knowing Alex, that would be an open invitation to do just that, however if she did he'd have one less problem to deal with when he returned to Barlowsville.

But he wanted her to suffer, not to die. Although the way she was making him suffer right now had him rethinking the entire plan.

Sure, she was holding on to him so lightly, if he hit a particularly big rut she would go sailing. Regardless, he could still feel the warmth of her hands on his hips, which only made him think of the last time those hands had been in the same place, pulling him closer, urging him on—

"*Knull mæ i øret,*" he muttered.

"What?" Alex shouted, leaning closer, pressing her breasts into his back and her crotch more firmly against his ass.

Julian started to *look* for a huge dip in the snow so he

could send her flying far away before his hard-on became a reality instead of a threat. Thankfully, his searching eyes caught sight of the roofs of the Inuit village instead. He let off the throttle, and the snowmobile slowed noticeably.

"What's wrong?"

Julian lifted his chin toward the horizon as more and more roofs became visible, along with telephone and electrical poles, even a few flags. One of the villagers lumbered a hundred yards south of them carrying a string of fish in one hand and a spear in the other. Julian couldn't tell who it was since the hood of the man's fur-trimmed parka shaded his entire face.

"This is an Eskimo village?" Alex asked.

"Inuit," he corrected. "It means 'the real people.' The word *Eskimo* went the way of *savage, redskin, chief, squaw, papoose*—"

"I got it. Inuit," she repeated, leaning forward again as he reached the top of the swell that led down into the center of town.

"The village is called Awanitok."

"Which means?"

"Far away."

"Clever. But . . . I don't see any igloos."

He fought the urge to laugh. Certainly the Inuit had made use of igloos once upon a time—mostly as an emergency shelter for hunting expeditions—but now—

"This place seems more up-to-date than yours."

Exactly.

"The Inuit are mostly craftspeople these days. They need more contact with the outside world than we do."

"More contact?" She rolled her eyes. "From what I saw, Barlowsville doesn't have any."

He'd never said she wasn't smart. Just annoying.

"Your point?"

"What's up with the generators?"

"What do you think?"

Her lips curved. "Trying to avoid a *Jäger-Sucher* show-down?"

"Wouldn't you?"

She blinked as if he'd surprised her. He suspected she wasn't used to thinking of Edward as the enemy. She'd better *get* used to it. Mandenauer wouldn't care if she'd been changed against her will, he'd only care that she'd been changed at all.

"Barlowsville is off the grid," Julian said. "Anything that might alert the *Jäger-Suchers* to our existence is something we don't have."

She frowned. "Explain."

"If no invoices are generated for services, no mail, no phones—"

"It's as if you don't exist," she said softly.

"Voilà!"

"But—" She bit her lip. "Ella said she'd ordered all her clothes from the Internet."

"She did." He swept his hand out to indicate the Inuit settlement. "From here. Had it delivered here, too."

To power *his* laptop connection, Cade had done some fancy signal-bouncing, Internet-stealing mumbo-jumbo. According to him, a single bounce was undetectable. But a hundred wouldn't be.

"No one minds the lack of . . . amenities?" Alex asked.

Since most of the inhabitants had been born in another age—be it when Viking ships sailed the deep blue sea or the words *Vive la Révolution* rang free—no one did. Especially since all they had to do was make a short trip here to use anything that they wished.

"We don't need them."

"You've never had an emergency?"

"What kind of emergency would there be that we couldn't handle ourselves?"

Injuries healed. He was the law. In the past century nothing had ever happened to necessitate their breaking "radio silence," and he doubted it ever would.

"Huh," Alex said. "You wanna tell me why that kid had your eyes?"

Barlow gunned the engine, and the snowmobile tilted over the edge of the swell, then raced down the hill and into Awanitok. Guess he didn't want to answer her question.

If Barlow were anyone other than who he was—make that *what* he was—Alex wouldn't have even had to ask. She'd have known.

Hanky-panky with the Indian maiden. Except werewolves couldn't make babies. Or so she'd been told.

By Edward. Leader of the Liar's Club.

"Shit," Alex muttered. She'd only done Barlow once, but as she'd heard many times before . . .

Once was all it took.

She wanted to shout at him to *Stop this snowmobile!* And if he wouldn't, then dump them into a snowbank and make him face her, talk to her, tell her the truth. Unfortunately, if she did that now she'd be having the conversation in front of a village full of strangers.

Alex decided to pass. She could always beat the truth out of him later.

And wouldn't that be fun?

The machine coasted to a halt on what appeared to be the main street. Compared with Barlowsville, the place was huge. Twice as many commercial establishments, probably because there were at least three times as many houses on three times as many side streets.

Regardless of how large the town was, everyone seemed to be aware that they had arrived, because people began to exit the stores and restaurants; they hurried in from the residential avenues that led off the commercial area, and the air filled with the rumble of engines as those who lived on the outskirts started their cars or all-terrain vehicles.

Julian shrugged his shoulder and before she even realized that she'd understood what he wanted without benefit of speech, Alex climbed off the snowmobile, then stepped back so that he could as well.

Villagers approached, staring at Alex with open curiosity. She stared right back with increasing concern. They didn't *all* have Julian's eyes, but a damn good portion of them did.

How many Indian maidens had he boinked? Had every one he so much as glanced at produced offspring?

How long had he been here? There were people of all ages with those damnable blue eyes. They were *so* going to have a talk.

A rustle went through the growing crowd as Julian straightened to his full height. She had to admit he was impressive, and he stood out among the Inuit like a bright full moon in a cloudless night sky, his golden hair flaring in the sun, even as blue highlights gleamed in the ebony tresses of those that surrounded him.

"*Ataniq,*" they murmured, bowing their heads as if he were a god. Alex really wished she had a copy of *Inuit for Dummies* so she could look that up. Considering all the blue eyes she kind of thought it meant "Daddy"—and the more she thought that, the sicker she felt.

Alex was about to demand a translation when the entire group stilled, every gaze turning to the East. Alex turned, too.

"Is that a Smart Car?" she blurted.

The tiny vehicle chugged gamely down a snow-packed street lined with an assortment of SUVs and pickup trucks. As it passed the single Hummer—in an identical shade of black—Alex had the odd thought that the Hummer was big enough to have birthed the thing.

The baby car paused next to the snowmobile. No matter how hard she tried, Alex could distinguish nothing but a swaying shadow on the other side of the illegally tinted windows.

Perhaps a long, gray-haired woman wearing a multicolored skirt, clunky boots, and a T-shirt that read SAVE THE PLANET?

Or a teenager who liked to wear hemp pants, nose rings, and a baseball cap emblazoned with the logo GO GREEN?

Maybe a—

Alex's musings were cut short when the door opened and the last person in the world she would ever have imagined might drive a Smart Car stepped out.

Well, perhaps *stepped* wasn't the right word, since several of the Inuit men rushed forward and helped the skinny, stooped old man to his feet.

While most of the Inuit wore modern clothes—parkas from Land's End, Ugg boots, Levi's—the new arrival appeared to be dressed in traditional Inuit clothing. His parka, made of patched-together bits of black, brown, and white fur, reached to the knees of trousers the shade of a deerhide. Upon his feet he wore boots, also made of skin, though different in color and texture and therefore no doubt from a different dead animal.

One of those who'd rushed to assist him reached across the driver's seat and withdrew a heavy, carved cane, which he put into an outstretched, claw-like hand. However, when the ancient elder moved toward Barlow he had a spring in his step, and he barely used the cane at all.

"Taataruaba," he greeted, blue eyes shining in his dark and lined face. Though his voice wavered, nevertheless it carried over the assembled crowd. "Welcome home." He bowed his head.

"Tutaaluga," Julian returned, and touched that head as if in a blessing. "It is good to be home."

Alex moved closer. She wanted to hear what emergency could be so pressing that the young man had been sent across the tundra at top speed to retrieve Julian, yet everyone here appeared as calm as a Sunday afternoon.

The man Julian had called *Tutaaluga* glanced up, and Julian's face took on an expression of extreme fondness— although how Alex would know that she wasn't sure. She'd never seen such an expression when he was around her.

Barlow put out his hand, and the Inuit grasped it. For an instant Alex thought *Tutaaluga* might kiss Barlow's ring, if he was wearing one. Instead, Barlow drew the old man's brown, withered fingers through the crook of his arm, and they moved away from the ever-increasing crowd.

Alex took a step after them, then remembered . . . she didn't have to be nearby to hear everything that they said. Her ears were as good as CIA audio surveillance equipment. Especially since the gathered onlookers had gone as still as the sky right before a tornado hit.

"We are sorry to have to summon you, *Taataruba,*" the old man said.

"I know you wouldn't unless you needed me. What's happened?"

"I don't know how to tell you this."

Julian frowned. "I've never known you to have a problem speaking to me. I'm your *Taataruba*."

"You are also the *ataniq*."

"Which is why you called me." Julian let out his breath, then patted the man's hand. "What makes you nervous?"

"You are *qixa* and *amabuq*. Shaman and wolf."

Alex's eyebrows shot up. They knew?

"I would never hurt you," Barlow vowed; his voice but a whisper, it trilled over Alex's skin like a feather.

She could easily imagine him speaking like that in the depths of the night, and because she could—hell it appeared *most* of the women in town could—Alex battled the shudder of awareness until it went away.

"I would never hurt anyone here," Barlow continued.

"It is not you we are worried about."

Julian frowned. "Who?"

"If I knew that," the old man said, "I would not have needed you."

"Speak plainly," Julian ordered, and though *Tutaaluga* had to be his elder by decades, the old man rushed to comply as if ordered to do so by God himself.

"I apologize, *Taataruba*." He dipped his head.

Was *Taatarubu* Barlow's Inuit name? Maybe *Ataniq* was. Alex was confused. About a lot of things.

"Our wise woman was killed by a wolf last night."

They still have those? Alex thought.

"A real wolf?" Barlow asked.

"No, *Ataniq*."

"Are you sure?"

The old man cast Julian an impatient glance, though as soon as his eyes met Barlow's he immediately cast them down. "We know about werewolves, *Taataruba*."

"None of mine would do such a thing. They have no need."

"Need has little to do with it. There is craving. There is madness."

"Not for us."

"Are you sure?" *Tutaaluga* murmured, and it was Julian's turn to cast an impatient glance.

"Perhaps there is a rogue." At the word Alex started, and Julian turned his gaze in her direction.

The old man did, too. "Who is she?"

"She's new."

"You haven't brought a new wolf here since—"

"What did this killer wolf look like?" Julian interrupted.

"Brown." The elder's eyes passed over Alex's hair. "Light eyes. Blue or—" The man's gaze lifted to hers. "Perhaps green."

"It wasn't her," Barlow said.

His defense surprised Alex. She would have figured he would love to have her chased up and down the Arctic coast by a band of Inuit armed with silver harpoons. Although, considering the Smart Car and the Ugg boots, they probably had silver bullets and automatic weapons, too.

"No?" *Tutaaluga* murmured, still staring at Alex as if she were a bug on a pin. "New wolves are always the most vicious."

"She's only just arrived. With me."

"Hmm." The old man turned his gaze back to Julian. "You ran right past us in the depths of the night. Yet you saw no evil, heard no evil, *smelled* no evil?"

"Do you think it was her?" Julian's eyes flared. "Or do you think it was me?"

The old man shrugged. "I don't know what to think. There

is new wolf vicious and there is alpha wolf vicious. Sometimes they can be very much the same."

"The wolf is brown," Julian said. "I'm not."

"You are a shaman," the elder pointed out. "I think you could be anything that you wish."

CHAPTER 12

Julian sighed and lifted his face to the sky. The old man had a point. Julian probably could change the shade of his fur just by thinking of it.

But he hadn't. On the other hand . . .

He looked at Alex. She was staring at him, obviously wondering the same thing about him that he was wondering about her: What had she been doing during the time they'd been running separately last night? He doubted she'd been snacking on the local wise woman, but who knew?

Turning back to the elder, he murmured, "I swore to protect this village."

"For a price."

"There's always a price."

The Inuit inclined his head in agreement.

"I will discover who's done this, and I will make sure they never do it again."

Julian strode toward the snowmobile without another glance in Alex's direction. If she wanted to return with him, she could move her ass. If she didn't, he'd leave her behind.

He barely registered her climbing on as he started the

machine, barely felt her hands at his waist as he sped away. He was so damn mad.

His village had existed for over a century unharmed, undetected, because they had one simple rule and it was this: Never eat the people.

Now someone had broken it—at least once—and who was to say that someone hadn't ranged farther and wider and broken that rule again and again in a place over which Julian had little chance of damage control?

In no time there would be representatives of this or that government agency detached with guns and orders to kill the rabid wolf. They'd have a bit of trouble with that, of course—he doubted they'd bring silver bullets—which only meant that Edward would hear about it.

Edward would have no trouble at all.

Julian wasn't aware that he was driving faster and faster until Alex's fingers dug into his side as they bounced far too high over an incline, then came down far too hard on the other side.

"Brown wolf," Julian muttered. He should have asked what shade. Dark as mud at midnight? Or light as the sand beneath the dawn? That might narrow it down.

Anger flared, and Julian imagined himself as a wolf, chasing down another wolf—dark brown, light brown, didn't matter. He would leap; he would land on its back; they would roll over and over in the snow, but the golden wolf would come out on top; then he would grab the traitor by the throat and—

Julian jerked his head to the side with a ripping motion.

Ahhh. He could almost taste the blood.

His fury surged, and the next thing Julian knew both he and Alex were sailing through the air and skidding across the frozen tundra.

It wasn't until Julian slammed into a snowbank, the impact knocking the rage right out of him, that he understood what had happened. Then he lay there trying to breathe evenly so he could make the paws that existed where his hands and feet should have been disappear.

A boot heel scuffed against the snow; then a shadow was cast over his face. "That's a nice look for you."

"Mmm," Julian said noncommitally. He continued to concentrate on smooth, calm seas, balmy breezes, springtime. Anything that would calm him down. Alex's voice . . .

Just wasn't helping.

He breathed in and out, slow and steady. Which didn't help, either. The scent of her filled his nostrils, and when his body responded as if she were a bitch in heat he got all pissed off again.

"Hey," she said. "Your—uh—nose is growing."

"Back off," Julian snarled, the sound half man, half beast. To her credit, she did.

Once he no longer had to fight his anger and his lust, he managed to put all the pieces of himself back the way they belonged.

Julian sat up, flexed his fingers, then wiggled his toes. He'd burst out of his boots when he'd begun to change. Dammit. He'd liked those boots. Now they lay strewn in pieces across the snow-white ground.

Alex leaned against the snowmobile, which had a dent the size of an Easter ham in the fender. Hell. He'd have to buy George a new one, or at least fix this one.

Her eyes shone brilliant green in the morning sun, so bright they seemed to bore into his. She was as mad as he had been. Luckily his wolves didn't inherit his magic as well as his tendency to turn furry.

"Are you done with your temper tantrum?" she asked. "Did you put your tail back in your ass?"

He didn't bother to answer. She knew as well as he did that the tail always popped out last.

"I should be impressed." Alex pushed away from the machine and stalked slowly toward him, the rubber soles of her crappy boots making an annoying squelching noise in the snow. "I've never seen anyone change only their hands or their feet or their—" She wiggled her fingers at his face. "Snout. But I guess I've never met anyone as old or as powerful as you."

Julian got to his feet. "Don't you mean *killed*? You've never *killed* anyone as powerful as me?"

"Not yet," she muttered, then hauled back one foot and kicked what appeared to be half of a black, shiny basketball.

The thing sailed directly at Julian's face, and if he hadn't been what he was, it would have broken his nose. He snatched the object out of the air, then contemplated one portion of a cracked helmet.

"Sorry." He lifted his gaze to hers. "That must have hurt."

"I don't give a shit about hurt." She kicked the other half even harder. He managed to grab this one an instant before it slammed into his groin.

"When did you take up soccer?" he asked. "I thought softball was your game."

Her eyes widened. "How did you—?"

"I said I checked you out."

She frowned, obviously wondering how he'd discovered her talent. It hadn't been easy.

"Oh, yeah, I had *tons* of time to play games while I was being dragged around the country by my *Jäger-Sucher* father. Then once the werewolf ate him, it was directly into the pros for me."

"Sarcasm," he murmured. "My favorite."

Alex looked around, presumably for something else to kick. When she saw nothing, she just hauled off and went for his nuts with the toe of her boot. Once again, he managed to catch the projectile inches from his crotch. Without a second thought he heaved upward and sent her flipping heels-over-head to land on her face in the snow.

Unfortunately snow in the Arctic was more like ice. Her temple cracked against it with a sick thud, and she lay still.

"Faet!" Julian hurried to her side. Just as he began to kneel, her hand shot out, and she yanked his feet out from under him.

The back of Julian's head and the ice connected with the exact same thud. Then Alex landed on his chest, and he lost what was left of his air.

She leaned in close, seeming to press the boniest point of her knee into his very lungs, and blood dripped onto his face. Her eyes appeared a little crazy, and he wondered if getting knocked in the noggin twice in so short a time had unhinged her.

"Why did half that village have your eyes, Barlow?"

Now he knew she'd lost it. What kind of a question was that?

"Answer me," she said between her teeth, then rapped his head against the ground again.

"Long—" he managed, wheezing and coughing. She let up a bit on his chest, and the second word exploded, "—story."

"Then you'd better start talking."

He coughed again, right in her face, and she rolled her eyes as if he were the biggest crybaby ever, then got off him and stood.

Julian just lay there awhile and got used to his lungs again.

"Barlow . . ." she warned.

"Okay, hold on." He sat up, lifting a hand to stay her next attack. "What are you so mad about?"

"What—?" she sputtered. "You. Me. We." She clenched her hands, lifted her face to the sky, and screamed with fury. If Alexandra Trevalyn had been a Viking, Julian had no doubt she would have been a berserker, too.

When she stopped, she seemed calmer. He'd be the first to admit—sometimes screaming helped.

"You've told me over and over that your wolves are different," she began, voice a bit hoarse.

"They are."

"*How* different? Can you make little Barlows?" She took a step forward, and from the gleam in her eyes Julian could tell she wanted to kick him again. "Did you make one in me?"

He blinked. "No. Of course not. I—"

"Didn't use any protection." She gagged, bent over, and he feared for an instant she'd be sick right there on the snow.

"There was no need," he said. "My wolves aren't *that* different. We can't procreate."

He pushed aside the shimmy of memory his words brought forth. That fact had caused him no end of trouble already.

Alex took several deep, shaky breaths. When she straightened, she was pale but steady. "Explain the blue eyes. Even *Tutaaluga* had them."

Julian lifted a brow. "*Tutaaluga?*"

"The old guy. Which is kind of freaky considering how much younger you look than him."

"His name is Jorund."

Confusion spread over her face. "You called him *Tutaaluga*."

"*Tutaaluga* means 'my grandson.' "

"He's your *grandson*? But that's not possible if you can't impregnate the Indian maidens."

"The—" Laughter bubbled, but Julian refused to let it flow free. He had a feeling his testicles might get introduced to his throat if he did, and he liked them exactly where they were. "You thought I'd been . . ."

"Boinking the natives," she filled in. "Why not? They treat you like the local wolf-god."

Well . . . he kind of was.

"I wouldn't *boink* anyone."

She snorted.

Except you.

The thought floated through his head and nearly out of his mouth. He bit his lip. Hard.

"*Don't* say it." Alex narrowed her eyes. "Just don't."

Could she read his mind? Or merely his face?

"Explain how the old guy . . . Jorund?" Julian nodded. "Could be your grandson."

"He isn't. Not technically, as in son of my son, because—like you said—that's impossible. But he's a descendant."

"Of yours?"

"Yes."

"They're *all* descendants?"

"In a way."

Alex rubbed her head as if it ached. He had no doubt it did. Though her wound had begun to heal, her hand came away bloody. She scowled at the red slash, began to wipe her palm on Ella's pants, then thought better of it. Knowing Ella, the garment probably cost more than the snowmobile.

Instead she bent and picked up a loose handful of snow, held it between her palms until it melted, then rubbed them together until they were clean again.

She was adapting quicker and better than any of his others. But she'd had a lot of practice. Dragged from city to city all her life, blending in, making do, as she hunted monsters that would gladly kill her if they knew that she was there.

Sympathy sparked, but Julian squelched it. If she saw that expression on his face, he didn't want to think where she'd kick him next.

Alex waved a damp hand. "Go on."

Julian really wanted to get back to town and start questioning people. He needed to find out if anyone had gone crazy on him before another Inuit died. And if no one had, then he needed to find out how a rogue wolf had invaded his territory and no one had noticed. Had they lived safely for so long that they'd lost any sense of approaching danger?

First he should explain things to Alex. He didn't blame her for being worried. He should have considered what she might think before he'd brought her to a village where every third inhabitant had his eyes.

"I sailed here long ago. Back when I was called Jorund the Blund."

Her head came up. "Jorund? Like the old man?"

"Yes. Although he was named after me, not the other way around."

"How did that happen?"

"A lot of the Native American tribes believe that once a person dies, their name must never be uttered again for fear their spirit will haunt the speaker. But the Inuit believe that the good aspects of the dead will inhabit those who are given the same name."

"But you aren't dead."

"They didn't know that when they started naming a child in every generation Jorund." Julian shrugged. "It's become a tradition."

"So you sailed here back in what . . . 8000 BC?"

"The Viking era was a thousand years ago." He tilted his head, wondering what he could get her to tell him if he played dumb. "Didn't you study that in school?"

She looked away, across the wide expanse of tundra that rolled on and on, acres of snow that resembled a perfectly white sea. "When would I have gone to school, Barlow? Maybe after we chased down that nahual in Mexico. Or while we were hunting the Scottish wulver in the Blue Ridge Mountains."

"I don't know what those are," he admitted.

She laughed, though the sound held the whisper of a sob. "I learned to shoot a gun at the age of eight. By the time I was ten I could make my own silver bullets. Every night before bed I was drilled in the different categories of monsters. Nahual—" She lifted a finger. "—Mexican werewolf-wizard." She lifted another. "Wulver. A Scottish fiend with the body of a man and the head of a wolf."

"Alex," he began, but she kept talking.

"My quizzes consisted of ways to kill each one. And I got one hundred percent on them, because if I didn't, I knew I'd die."

The flash of sympathy threatened again. Again he squelched it unmercifully. So she'd had a rough childhood. A lot of people did, yet they didn't go around murdering innocent wives.

"Isn't it illegal not to go to school?" he asked.

"Call a cop." Her lips twisted wryly. "We never stayed in one place long enough for anyone to notice."

Julian frowned. "Wouldn't child services have come searching for you eventually?"

Now she laughed with true mirth. "You said you knew Edward."

"We all know Edward."

"Apparently not well."

"If I knew him well, I'd be ashes."

"Good point." She drew in a breath and as she let it out, her smile faded. "Edward has J-S agents everywhere. Social services. Child services. FBI. How do you think he knows every damn thing?"

"He doesn't know where I am."

"Give him time," she said.

A flicker of unease trickled across the back of Julian's neck. "What do you mean by that?"

She threw up her hands. "Edward's been at this since the Second World War. He's got funding up the wazoo. You think you can hide from him forever?"

"I've been at this longer than that. So yes, I think I can."

"Okay." Alex nodded, staring at the ground. When she lifted her hand to shove her hair out of her face, her fingers trembled. Maybe she was cold, but he didn't think so.

Alex knew Edward. She understood, perhaps better than anyone here, how dangerous he was, how far reaching his influence, of what he might be capable. And he'd made her into the very thing Edward excelled at killing. He couldn't blame her for being a little scared.

"You're safe here, Alex. I promise."

Her gaze flicked up. "You can't promise that."

"I've been promising it for a century. We're still here, and he isn't."

"Yet," she muttered.

"Yet," he agreed, and she shivered. "Let's continue this conversation back in town."

"I'm all right," she said.

"I'm not." He pointed at his stocking feet. "Come on."

Julian climbed on the snowmobile, and Alex joined him without further argument.

Which proved more than anything else just how *not* all right she was.

Barlow thought she was worried that Edward might show up and shoot her with silver along with the rest of them. She had to make sure he kept thinking that, which meant she had to behave like a frightened girl.

Too bad she had no idea how.

She hadn't stepped foot in a traditional school since kindergarten—except that time when there'd been the were-wolf massacre at Graystone Middle School—

Alex shuddered, and Julian shouted, "Almost home."

The word *home* made her start. This wasn't her home, and it never could be.

Edward had manipulated the media, and everyone else involved, into believing that the twelve dead at Graystone were the result of a school shooting. Edward manipulated a lot. Manipulation was what Edward did best. How else had he convinced her to do this?

Alex yanked her mind from her memories and Mande-nauer. While she was here she had to think like a werewolf, not like a *Jäger-Sucher*. If Julian discovered that she was working for Edward—

Alex shuddered again, and Barlow pulled her arms more firmly around his waist so that the entire front of her was pressed to the back of him. He gave off heat like a furnace, and before she could stop herself she actually cuddled.

Alex did *not* cuddle. Especially with werewolves.

But *she* was a werewolf.

"Fuck," she muttered, her own thoughts making her dizzy.

Barlowsville appeared on the horizon, and Alex was damn glad to see it. Which only confused her more.

They roared into town, straight past the square and down

a street Alex had never been down before. She'd figured Barlow would take her straight to Ella's and leave her there so he could discover the traitor in their midst. She certainly wouldn't want to be *that* wolf.

But what if . . .

She'd heard the old man point out that Barlow was a sorcerer; he could be anything. Even a brown wolf when his hair was gold. However, according to the wolf man he didn't kill for sport. No one here did.

So then who had eaten the wise woman?

Barlow stopped in front of a two-story log structure at the very end of the street. Behind it she could see a long, white, really ugly warehouse-type building. What the hell did he keep in there?

Alex heaved a silent sigh. She was going to have to find out. That and a whole lot more.

Barlow shut off the motor, slid free of the seat and trotted up the steps, then into the house. Alex sat on the snowmobile, uncertain what she should do. Did he already know who the rogue was, and he'd come directly to the wolf's house to kill it?

However Barlow reappeared with the Inuit kid. He saw her still sitting there and frowned. "George has to go home now," he said. "Come inside."

Alex glanced at the rustic home. "This is *your* place?"

"What's wrong with it?"

"Nothing." She climbed off the machine. In truth, she wanted it with a longing that embarrassed her. Whenever she'd dreamed of a house of her own—not often, it was never going to happen—she'd dreamed of a log cabin very similar to this. "Where are the white pillars, golden window frames, marble steps, and neon sign that flashes HOME OF THE WOLF-GOD KING OF BARLOWSVILLE?"

George's blue eyes widened, and he glanced at Barlow as if he expected him to . . . what? Kill her now?

Instead Barlow's lips twitched. He appeared to be finding her funnier and funnier as time went on.

Huh. Usually people found her less and less funny the more she hung around. Then again, Barlow wasn't most people. Hell, he wasn't even *a* people.

"I left it in my other suit," he said. Which made no sense. So why, then, did Alex laugh?

George glanced back and forth between the two of them, his expression of concern fading to one of confusion. He didn't get the joke, either.

"I'm afraid we had a bit of an accident." Barlow pointed to the dent. "And your helmet is—" His eyes met hers, and he smiled.

"Toast," Alex said. "Your helmet is toast."

"I'll buy you a new one." Barlow continued to hold Alex's gaze, and something flickered just below her breastbone— a trickle of heat that both intrigued and disturbed her.

"It's all right, *Ataniq.*" George came down the steps. "I have other helmets."

"I meant the snowmobile," Barlow said drily.

"Oh!" The boy glanced at Alex, and his cheeks reddened. She wasn't sure why.

He smiled at her shyly, and she smiled back, which only made him blush all the more.

Barlow cleared his throat, and George's clear blue gaze flicked from Alex to Barlow; then he straightened as if he might click his heels together and bow.

The incongruity of that image—the Indian boy with the long flowing hair, bowing like a European underling to a lord—almost made Alex laugh again, but she managed not to. Poor George would think she was laughing at him.

"There's no need, *Ataniq*. I can fix it."

"You've always been good at that." Barlow beckoned Alex, and with a small shrug in lieu of good-bye, she moved toward the house.

Barlow's eyes suddenly narrowed, and Alex glanced behind her, concerned, only to find George's gaze on her ass.

"Go," Barlow ordered in a voice so icy she got shivers. Then he watched until the snowmobile had left town as quickly as it had entered.

"You scared him," Alex said.

"Good." He flicked her an unreadable gaze and disappeared inside.

Alex followed, shutting the door behind her. "He's just a kid."

Barlow, who'd sat in what appeared to be a hand-carved wooden chair in the hall and begun to pull off his wet socks, tilted his head to look at her. "Are you a kid?"

"What? No." She didn't think she'd ever been a kid.

"He's your age, Alex." He stood and carried the dripping socks into the kitchen. "Or close enough."

Alex remained in the hall. He was probably right. George was her age, maybe even a year older. But he'd seemed so damn young.

"Hey!" she called, striding down the hall, then pausing when her ridiculous rubber boots slid as the ice on the bottoms melted all over the polished wood floor. Alex cursed, yanked them off, and left them on the mat near the door. "You got any paper—" She stopped just inside the entryway, mouth half open as she stared at the most gorgeous kitchen she'd ever seen.

The sun spilled through a skylight, illuminating the honey shade of the wooden beams and walls. The countertops were blinding white and the appliances chrome. But what she really liked were the huge natural stones that decorated both the center island and the fireplace in the attached dining area.

"Got any paper what?" Julian asked as he came out of a tiny room to the rear. Alex caught a glimpse of a washing machine before he shut the door.

"Towels," she managed, still staring.

Julian noticed and glanced around. "What?"

"It's beautiful."

"Thanks. I—uh—" He shrugged. "Like to cook."

Alex's eyes widened. "Really?"

"Why not?"

"I just, well I never . . . have."

"I suppose not," he said quietly, and for an instant she could have sworn she heard sympathy, or pity, in his voice. Which made her anger flare and she lashed out.

"I figured you'd eat everything raw. Like the wise woman."

She'd been staring at his face, waiting for a flicker of . . . what? Guilt? Could a werewolf feel guilt?

But he merely lifted a brow. "You think I killed her?"

"Someone did."

"Maybe it was you."

"I don't kill people."

"You keep on believing that." He yanked a huge handful of paper towels off the roll and handed them to her without even asking what she wanted them for. She guessed it was obvious when he followed her into the hall and leaned in the doorway while she wiped up her mess.

"I didn't kill the wise woman," he said quietly.

"Neither did I."

Silence settled between them. Did he believe her? Did she believe him? She wasn't sure.

Alex straightened and handed him the sopped towels. "I guess we'll have to reserve judgment until we have proof."

"Like catching each other red-pawed?" He returned to the kitchen and threw the towels into the trash.

"Mmm," Alex said noncommitally. They had been separated for short periods last night, but would he have had time to wash the blood from his fur before she saw him again?

Probably not. Then again—magic man. How hard would it be for him to abracadabra away the stains?

Barlow motioned for Alex to sit at a table of white tile and sandy-shaded wood. She couldn't help herself. She ran her palm over it like a lover. How was it that everything in his house was exactly what she would have chosen herself?

Barlow sat on the other side of the table, remaining silent until she met his gaze. "You want to tell me about it?"

"I didn't kill the wise woman," she said.

"Not that. The *Jäger-Suchers*."

"You want me to tell you about the *Jäger-Suchers*?" Alex snorted. "So when Edward shows up he kills me first? No thanks."

"Alex." Julian reached across the table and laid his hand over hers. She frowned at it, and at her own because even though her head was telling her to break his fingers, her hand wanted to curl around his and hold on. "You're one of us now."

"I didn't choose to be."

"This is what I've been telling you. Most werewolves are made against their will. But the *Jäger-Suchers* don't care. They kill them anyway."

"They don't have much choice," she said. "Teeth and claws, blood and death. *You* try and reason with that."

Julian sighed and leaned back, taking his hand with him. "You don't understand—"

Because she missed his hand and she wanted it back, she

snapped, "I've been there. I *know*. Werewolves are serial killers in a fur coat. They don't change. They don't want to. And the only way to stop them is with silver. Period."

"You'll discover differently here. I promise."

"Considering what we heard from your grandson, there's at least one wolf in this village that proves me right." She smirked, feeling some of her old self shine through. "How long until there are more?"

"There won't be."

"Just because I didn't get past kindergarten doesn't mean I didn't read and research and learn. I particularly enjoyed history, and one thing history's good for is revealing patterns of behavior."

"You lost me."

"The more you hold these wolves under your thumb, the more you make them behave in a way that's not natural, the more they're going to want to break free, and the more violent they'll be once they do."

"This werewolf is a rogue," he insisted. "Probably isn't even from here."

"You keep on believing that," she said.

CHAPTER 13

A few moments ago, Julian had felt sorry for her. A few moments after that he'd touched her, and it had felt so . . . perfect, he'd kept his hand right where it was.

Now he wanted to take that hand and wrap it around her throat until her smirk died, and she did, too.

Of course she wouldn't stay dead—and he had only himself to blame for that.

"Why don't you finish telling me why, if you can't make baby Barlows, there are all sorts of people with your eyes running around calling you Daddy."

"Grandfather," he corrected.

"Whatever." She tilted her head. "George called you *Ataniq*. Sounds a little like asshole, but I doubt he'd have the balls."

"Unlike you," Julian returned.

Alex spread her hands and shrugged.

"*Ataniq* means—" He paused, realizing that once he told her she'd only smirk again.

"You may as well spill it. I can borrow the Internet as well as the next werewolf."

"Boss, president, king, master," he blurted.

She stared at him for several seconds, while he discovered he'd been wrong. The smirk didn't come back; instead a look of incredulity spread over her face. "You raped and pillaged your way through that village and now they call you grandfather and master?"

"No."

"You just said—"

"We didn't. I mean I didn't—"

"You were a Viking, *Jorund*. You didn't sail here to teach the natives about Jesus."

No, they'd come here at Julian's insistence. He'd had a sudden urge to sail west, though very few ships did. Such a trip had been a danger at the time considering the belief in sea monsters and a flat, flat world. The waters were uncharted, the land beyond the horizon a mystery. Naturally, he couldn't resist.

Julian had always remembered the beauty of the place they had found. The ice, the snow, the freedom that swirled in the air. He'd wanted badly to come back. About a hundred years ago, he had.

"There weren't any sea monsters," he said. Alex blinked, then frowned. "They said there'd be sea monsters, and I wanted to find one."

"Were you twelve?" she asked.

"Twenty." And in command of his own vessel. "I think the sea monsters they spoke of were actually whales. Great beasts that rose up from the ocean, blowing huge gusts of water out of their heads."

She was beginning to stare at him as if he'd lost his mind. "The sea monsters were whales. Check. And you sailed past them, landed . . ." She wiggled her fingers in the general direction of the ocean. "Then marched into Awanitok and took whatever the hell, and whoever the hell, you wanted."

"No."

She sighed impatiently. "Barlow, your eyes don't lie. Well, *your* eyes do. But all the eyes, in all the faces, all over that village don't."

"I led a raiding party," he began, then went silent, remembering.

It had been summer. If it hadn't they'd never have been able to sail near the land since the water in the Arctic froze solid.

The Inuit village had been small at the time, perhaps sixty people. They'd lived in homes dug into the ground, the earth providing natural insulation. Anything aboveground was fashioned with sod over wood or whalebone frames. Julian had thought the method ingenious.

He'd had ten men with him. Plenty to pillage the natives. Unfortunately they'd been too poor to pillage.

"They offered a sacrifice if we left them alone."

Alex lifted a brow. "Indian maidens?"

Julian shrugged. "They didn't have anything else."

"You took them. In more ways than one."

"As you pointed out, we were *Vikings,* and we'd been on that ship for a very long time."

Alex glanced out the floor-length sliding glass door to her right. "Then *all* the blue eyes aren't descended from you."

"Most of my men were related to me in some way." It made for less hassle on the high seas. If everyone was related, there was a slimmer chance of not only mutiny, but wholesale slaughter as well.

"Go on," Alex said.

"I just told you everything."

"Not everything. Why does an entire Inuit village in the twenty-first century call one man master? Not very PC."

"PC," he repeated, his mind churning to find a meaning.

"Yeah, you really fit in," she muttered. "Politically correct. We did away with *master* in this country about a hundred and fifty years ago."

"I didn't tell them to call me that."

"You didn't stop them, either."

"It's a courtesy title. It doesn't have the connotations you're giving it."

"They still consider you the boss of them, and I want to know why."

Julian took a deep breath and continued. "I returned a century ago."

"Scene of the crime," she murmured, but he ignored her.

"I brought my wolves. We wanted to live at peace."

"Alaska is huge. You had to build in their backyard?"

At first Julian had come merely to see the place he'd idealized in his mind, one he'd visited while he was still human. But then he'd caught a glimpse of all the blue-eyed Inuit . . .

"Family is important." Especially since he'd thought the only family he had left was Cade. Especially since he'd never have any children, any descendants but the ones he'd found here.

Something flickered in Alex's eyes. Sadness? Anger? Guilt? He couldn't say. The expression was there and gone so fast, and he didn't really know her that well at all.

Not that he wanted to. Not that he *would*. Once they finished this discussion, he'd leave her to Ella and interact with her as little as possible. Because every time he saw Alex, he remembered Alana.

Eventually.

"I protect them," he said.

"From what?"

"Everything. Anything."

"Wow! How did they survive a thousand years without you, Jorund?"

Pretty well. Until he'd set up a werewolf village right next door.

"You're protecting them from you," Alex said slowly. Could she read his face, or just his mind? "From the city of monsters you plopped down right next to them. Talk about extortion!"

"I do more for them than just ascertain none of my people . . ." He waved his hand in the general direction of Awanitok.

"Snack?" she supplied.

He ignored her. "They live in the way that they wish. No interference from the government."

"How do you manage that?" she asked, but before she even finished the last word, her face lit with understanding. "Magic."

He shrugged. "How else do you deal with the government?"

She tilted her head. "Go on."

"My Inuit have no trouble hunting. Their crafts are the most coveted in tourist centers everywhere."

"You bribe them."

"An ancient method," he agreed. "But it works."

"And in return they give you . . ." He watched comprehension dawn in her eyes, quickly followed by condemnation. "Oh, you suck!"

"I'm sorry?"

"They give you a sacrifice, but this time it isn't boinking the Indian maiden. This time it's blood."

"A fair exchange."

Fury suffused her face. She pushed back from the table and stood over him, fists clenched. "I should know better."

Her jaw was tight; he could practically hear her back teeth grinding together. "You say you're different, but you aren't. You're just like every other werewolf in the world; you have no respect for human life."

"I have more respect than you do."

"She wasn't human."

And they were back to that again. Julian had hoped Alex would begin to understand once she was here, once she could see. But it had only been a day and—

"Wait a second." He grabbed one arm, and she took a swing at him with the other. He caught her wrist before it smashed into his face, then he shook her just once. "What's human life got to do with anything?"

Her eyes widened, and the angry color drained from her cheeks. "They're your family, yet you chase them through the woods beneath the full moon, and you tear them into pieces."

"What?" he shouted, releasing her as he straightened to his full height.

Barlow towered over her, and for an instant Alex was reminded of the polar bear, roaring and posturing. She half expected him to shape-shift into one. She'd studied berserkers, and in the legends many could turn into both a wolf *and* a bear. She wouldn't put it past Barlow to have left that part out.

But he didn't shift, not even his paws. Instead, he closed his eyes, and his lips moved silently, as if in prayer.

"How do you pray and not burst into flames?" she wondered aloud.

He opened one eye, which was all he needed to give her a very impressive glare before he snarled, "Explain why you think I'm accepting human sacrifices."

The rumble beneath the surface revealed just how close the beast within him had come. Oddly, Alex wasn't scared. Considering what she'd just learned, she wasn't sure why.

"Werewolves must kill, then consume fresh human blood on the night of the full moon," Alex said. "I knew that even before I became one."

"We require blood, yes." He opened both eyes, and though the blue had hardened to the color of ice beneath a clear, summer sky, they still bored into hers with such heat she was surprised her corneas didn't explode. "But blood and death are two very different things."

"How would you—? Can you—?" She leaned back. "Wait. What?"

"I have told you over and over that my wolves are different. Our full moon craving can be satisfied with blood. No death involved."

"The Inuit give you blood," Alex clarified. "Like some full moon communion?"

"If you like." His lips tightened. "You really thought I'd let my wolves kill one person a month?"

"You let *me* kill someone," Alex said softly.

He looked away. "That was different."

"Oh, right. I needed to *understand*." Alex allowed the full weight of her sarcasm to fall on the last word.

"Yes," he agreed. "But I didn't have much choice once I'd made you."

"You could have *not* made me," Alex muttered.

Barlow ignored her. "Every new wolf must kill the first time or embrace madness. Even my wolves, if that initial kill isn't accomplished, become killing machines ever after."

"You think that's what happened to the wolf that's stalking the Inuit?"

"No. All of the wolves here were made by me and brought into this life with their consent."

"Not all," she said.

"All the ones that count."

Well, she'd asked for that. "Were every one of your wolves given a very bad man as their first meal?"

"Not every one."

"When did you grow a conscience?"

His eyes narrowed. "I became a werewolf in the ninth century. Conscience was a little different back then."

"I suppose you just tossed them a conquered captive and called it a day."

When he didn't answer, she knew she was right. She also knew that living for eons meant that a lot of things had changed, including how people viewed right and wrong. Judging a Viking with the mores of the twenty-first century was as backward as he had once been.

She didn't like cutting Barlow any slack, but to be fair she had to.

"You're certain none of your wolves might have made another and let him or her run wild, so to speak?"

"They wouldn't dare."

Alex snorted. She couldn't help it. "Not everyone is as beta as you think."

She could tell by the way he went silent and still that she'd gotten him thinking. She decided to leave him to it.

"I'm going back to Ella's," Alex said. If she didn't sleep soon, she just might fall on her face.

Julian glanced up. "Don't tell anyone who you are."

She'd been headed for the door but turned at his arrogant command. "I think that ship has sailed."

His eyes flared. "Why would you do that?"

"*I* didn't. You introduced me the instant we got into town."

"Oh." He let out a quick, sharp breath that blew a stray strand of golden hair away from his face. "Your name. That's all right. But don't tell anyone *why* you're here."

"You think your people would mutiny if they discovered you hadn't followed your own rules? That you *made* someone against their will?" Alex's lips curved. "That might be fun to watch."

He rubbed his forehead. "Do not tell anyone you're a hunter. Do not tell anyone you know Edward. Specifically do not tell anyone you murdered my wife." He dropped his hand and looked into her face. "Werewolves *can* die, Alex, and mine will kill you."

"They can't. There's a fail-safe in the lycanthropy virus that keeps werewolves from killing one another."

"Not around here."

Alex stilled. "What?"

"Because I'm different, my virus is different, and so are my wolves. No demon. Also no fail-safe."

Her eyes widened. "Then how can there be any of you left at all? Why haven't you torn one another to shreds? Why isn't there only one wolf left standing?"

"Because we don't kill for sport. We don't enjoy it. And while we *can* kill one another, we don't want to."

"But sometimes," she murmured, staring into his face as she heard what he'd left unsaid, "you have to."

"It's the only thing werewolves understand."

Barlow offered to take her back to Ella's, but Alex refused.

"Even if I didn't know the way, I could follow my nose," she said. An appendage that was becoming increasingly useful with each passing day.

During the return trip, which took her along one street, through the square, and halfway down the avenue on the opposite side of town, no less than a dozen villagers greeted Alex.

The place was a hodgepodge of accents and nationalities, races and ages. But one thing she didn't see were any children.

"Guess that makes sense," she murmured, considering the conversation she and Barlow'd had earlier.

They all seemed damn glad to see her. Ecstatic almost. Like she was the best thing to happen to Barlowsville in years.

But they wouldn't be happy, or welcoming, or even civil if they discovered who she was, why she was here—be it Barlow's reason . . . or Edward's.

That knowledge, combined with the town's excessive friendliness, made Alex feel like the lowest of lying scum. She had to remind herself that this was a town of *werewolves,* the lowest, lying scum on the planet.

And she was one, too.

Yet she still didn't want to eviscerate small children. She wasn't consumed by the urge to rip off the faces of everyone she met—except Barlow. She didn't feel evil. She felt like . . . herself. Which went against everything she'd ever believed about werewolves. Sure, Cassandra had said she'd removed "the demon," but maybe there hadn't been one there to remove.

Alex reached Ella's house, climbed the steps, then hesitated. Should she knock? She wasn't sure. If the door was locked she'd have to.

It wasn't. Did anyone lock their doors in Barlowsville? Knowing Barlow, the punishment for theft was the removal of a paw with a silver axe. Which should be enough to deter any werewolf with kleptomaniac tendencies.

"Hello?" she called, thrilled when no one answered. Alex had done all the talking she could stand for one day.

She searched through the armoire for pajamas, sweat-pants, scrubs, anything to wear to bed that wasn't the gorgeous cream silk peignoir she found.

No such luck. Since Alex would rather sleep in nothing than that, she did.

The bedroom came equipped with custom shades that blocked the sunlight, or what there was of it, no doubt very handy for those mornings after an all-night run through the woods as a wolf.

Alex planned to sleep away what remained of the day and maybe even the night. What she hadn't planned on was the dream.

She hadn't had it for a very long time. She'd begun to hope it was gone. Then she'd begun to fear that it was.

Though the dream always ended badly—because it was a memory as well as a dream—it began with Alex and her father together as they could never be again. And for the short time before the werewolf came, Alex could exist in a world where he was still alive.

Wasn't that what dreams were for?

They're having breakfast in a small mountain town in Tennessee when the call comes. The previous night had been busy, and they hadn't yet gone to bed.

A rash of drownings in the area, combined with tales of a really big snake and a mysterious, decrepit old woman, had precipitated their visit. Sure enough they'd found, then dispatched, a nasnas.

Every culture has a shape-shifter legend. What the common folk don't know is that those legends are true. For a *Jäger-Sucher,* legends are the stock of their trade.

A nasnas is an Arabian shifter, which takes the form of an old man or woman and begs for help crossing bodies of water. Once in the water, the nasnas changes into a sea serpent and drags its victim beneath the surface to feed.

To kill one, the victim must yank the head of the nasnas below the water first, then hold it there. Which had proved damn difficult despite the old lady weighing about eighty pounds soaking wet and possessing the bony fingers of a baby bird.

Still, Alex managed. They celebrated with pancakes.

"Full moon tonight," her father observes, pouring half the syrup in the pitcher atop his Paul Bunyan–size stack.

Alex, being fifteen, widens her eyes. "You think?" She counts the nights between full moons, and so does he.

Charlie doesn't tell her to behave, be respectful, watch her mouth, or anything of the sort. Charlie pretty much lets her be. He knows the only thing that might save Alex in the long run is being tough, smart, and really, really bitchy.

"Where to?" she asks, carefully pouring syrup on only a portion of her cakes. She doesn't like them soggy.

"Haven't heard." Her father speaks around a mouthful of food, and as he does, his cell phone rings. He pulls it out, glances at the display, lifts it like a toast, and greets the caller with, "Elise."

Elise Hanover is Edward's right hand. Alex has never met her, never spoken to her, doesn't know all that much about her. Elise lives at the *Jäger-Sucher* headquarters, wherever that is, and spends what time she has that isn't taken up coordinating the agents and their assignments trying to discover a cure for lycanthropy. Alex has always figured the best cure is to wipe every werewolf from the face of the earth. If there aren't any left, they can't make any more.

Of course that hadn't stopped Hitler.

"Will do." Charlie shuts his phone and goes back to eating pancakes.

"We'll do what?" Alex asks.

"Not we'll," he corrects. "Will."

Alex doesn't think Elise knows that she's been hunting with her father for two years. Although maybe Edward's told her. According to her father, Edward knows everything.

"What *will* we do?"

Charlie smiles, though since the day he went looking for Alex's mother and came back alone, that smile no longer reaches his eyes. Alex knows he feels guilty, that he believes her mother would be alive today if he'd never been a *Jäger-Sucher.*

But the monsters are out there, and without people like Alex and her father, every person on the earth will eventually be a victim. Charlie's mistake wasn't made when he *became* a *Jäger-Sucher.* His mistake was in believing he could ever *not* be one.

"Rogue black bear a few hours from here," Charlie answers. "Northern Alabama."

"Is it really a bear?" Alex lays down her fork. Her father is already pulling out his wallet to pay the bill. When Elise calls, they move, because if they don't, people die.

Charlie merely lifts a brow. Elise wouldn't have called if it were really a bear.

"I meant, is it a bear *shifter* or code for werewolf?"

"Guess we'll find out." Charlie tosses some money onto the table.

Ten hours later, they do. The hard way.

They perform their recon same as always. Head into town and split up, Charlie to the police station, followed by the hospital and the newspaper office, where he learns all he can with a little help from his *Jäger-Sucher*–supplied fake IDs.

His favorites, which label him a warden for various Departments of Natural Resources, usually get him access to just about everything.

Alex works the locals, hanging out in the coffee shop, the diner, the pharmacy, the gas station—anyplace where people might discuss what's going on in their town. They're often more willing to talk to a kid than the hunting and fishing police.

Go figure.

When each has discovered all he or she needs to know, they meet at the local ball field, where they play catch and share info. It's what they do, what they've always done, the single connection they've kept to the life that died with Janet.

By the time Alex and Charlie head into the hills that night, they believe they are on the trail of a standard werewolf. Stronger, faster, better than the average wolf, with human-level intelligence, but nothing unexpected. Nothing that will prevent them from killing it with the silver bullets they keep in their guns.

In her sleep, Alex stirred, hoping to wake up before the bad thing happened. She even heard herself whimpering, the way she'd whimpered when the night had gone still, and she'd realized she was alone and would be for the rest of her life.

It happens so fast. One minute they are moving through the trees, confident, sure, their rifles ready, their pistols, too, the next a figure steps out of the trees. That it *steps,* as in on two feet, causes her father, causes Alex, to hesitate, and that is their fatal mistake.

The werewolf takes Charlie down with one swipe of its massive paw. The claws, razor-sharp, slice through his jugular with the ease of a sword through whipped cream. The spray of blood arches like a glistening black fountain across the silver moonlight, plopping against last year's leaves like rain.

The monster shoves Charlie Trevalyn aside as if he is nothing more than a gnat in the way of a windshield wiper, before falling onto all fours and moving toward Alex with the flash of speed common to the breed.

CHAPTER 14

Julian had plenty of work to catch up on, but the moon called, and he was helpless to resist.

Not that he wanted to. The instant he stepped beneath the cool, silvery glow, he felt calmer. Since Alex had left, he'd felt anything but.

Hell. Since Alex had become like him, he'd been feeling a lot of things and calm wasn't one of them. He was starting to believe that his plan for her might not have been one of his brighter ideas.

Gee, ya think?

Considering he continued to hear her mocking commentary in his head even when she wasn't around . . . yeah, he thought.

Julian drew off his shirt, shucked his pants and everything beneath. Shadows flitted through the streets—woman-shaped, man-shaped, wolf-shaped; his people had been marked by the moon just like him.

He jogged toward the tundra, the change rippling along his skin, warming him, soothing him. Often, when he had a seemingly unsolvable problem, clearing his mind and giving in to the wolf helped. By the time he came back from an all-night romp across this icy land with nothing in his head but the concerns of an animal, the answers to his all-too-human problems would be clear.

He raced through town; the buildings on either side of him became a blur as he gained superhuman speed. He would leap from the streets of Barlowsville as a man and land in the wilderness as a wolf.

Julian gathered his power, pushing off with his feet, reaching for his beast, and he heard a soft, heart-wrenching whimper.

He came down hard but not on his paws; he ignored the burn of ice across his bare skin as he turned toward the sound. His gaze zeroed in on Ella's house—dark, seemingly deserted, yet he knew it had been her.

The thought of what might make Alexandra Trevalyn whimper had Julian heading with equal speed back in the direction he'd come. Dozens of figures, in various stages of shape-shifting, brushed past him—a bizarre Wild Hunt beneath the Arctic night.

He was halfway up the front steps when he paused, tilted his head, and listened. Alex had come out the rear door, and from the sound of things, she was running for her life.

Julian leaped off the porch and sprinted for the back of the house, everything around him blurring in a pulse of panicked speed. They came around the corner at the exact same time and slammed into each other. Julian snatched Alex before she could fly backward and smash into the ground.

She fought, cursing and kicking, and he shook her. "It's me, Alex."

"I know," she said, and slugged him.

He should have dropped her right then—on her head—but he couldn't. Something was wrong.

She'd left the house unclothed, and it wasn't because she

wanted to join the village wolves for a nice, long lope. Her skin beneath his hands was like ice, not the usual fiery temperature that preceded the change. Instead she'd dashed out in a panic, forgetting her bra and panties, let alone a pair of shoes.

She continued to fight him, even though she couldn't win. But naked, sweating despite the chill of the air and her skin, she was slippery. He lost his grip, and she tried to dart around him. He snatched her back and pressed her body between his and the house.

"What happened?" he asked. When one of her arms slithered free, and she raked her nails down his side, he took both wrists and yanked them above her head, pinning them to the wall along with the rest of her.

She stilled then, thank God. All that wriggling and squirming and struggling was exhausting.

"What happened?" he repeated, more gently than before.

Her chest heaved; her breasts rubbed against him in a manner that would have been provocative if she hadn't been so obviously distressed.

"He's dead." Her hair hung over her face in damp hanks that had begun to freeze into extremely messy dreads.

Ah, hell, Julian thought. Who had she killed now?

He used his free hand to cup her chin, to tilt her face so that her hair slid out of the way. "Who's dead?"

Her eyes wide and unfocused, she murmured "Charlie" in a voice that, despite his attempts to steel himself against it, tore at his heart.

Julian let his forehead meet hers, and his hair cast over her cheeks, creating a golden curtain between them and the night. "Who's Charlie?" he asked.

He knew, but he wanted her to talk, to come back from

the dream, the memory, whatever had caught her in a grip so deep she seemed frozen by it.

A bank of clouds slid over the moon, painting them in darkness. He could smell her, that scent of sun-ripened lemons that was completely hers. For the rest of his very long life he would be able to pick her out of a crowd by that scent alone.

"Alex?" he murmured. "What's wrong?"

She moved beneath him, and her nipples, hard and cold as marbles left out in the snow, rolled along his chest. He grit his teeth and waited for an answer. But he didn't get the one that he expected.

Instead she arched her neck and let her scalding tongue—startling amid so much cold—lick the line of his mouth.

He gasped, jerked back, and she nipped, catching his lip between her teeth and holding on.

The damnable cloud stayed over the moon. He could only see the outline of her face, which served to make every other sense he possessed stronger.

Her scent mixed with the ice and the snow and the smell of the moon—sweet like blue snow cones. The bones of her wrists beneath his palm shifted like sticks trapped in a bag of the most delicate material ever made. Her skin, so cold, refreshed his, which felt like a blistering fever had broken free when he'd viciously put a stop to his change. Her mouth, soft as rain in the precious spring, opened and welcomed him within.

He shouldn't. He couldn't. He wouldn't.

He did.

That taste—both familiar yet still so new—called. The sex they'd already had, forbidden, dangerous, half remembered with the mind, was fully remembered by the body.

With her wrists trapped above her head, she lay open to him, like the sacrificial maidens of long ago. She could do nothing but accept—his kiss, his touch, him—and the idea made him so hard he wondered momentarily if his dick had frozen solid.

Except his dick wasn't cold but fiery hot, and she was rubbing her chilled belly against it as if the friction alone would warm her, the murmurs in her throat rolling along her lips and his like a low-level earthquake across the land.

His free hand cupped her hip, his thumb sliding across the bone, his fingernail scraping just a little because when he did that she arched, pressing her breasts with those fantastic marble nipples into his chest and shifting—back and forth, back and forth—until the rasp nearly made him insane.

He waited as long as he could to touch, palm itching, fingers twitching, and when he could wait no longer he swept his hand up, from hip to breast, sliding along the still-cool length of her waist until he could cup the glorious weight and roll that nipple beneath his thumb.

She cried out, and he drank the sound with his mouth, desperate to remain undetected, uninterrupted. Except . . .

Beneath the moon, they were the only souls left in town.

God. He thought he might explode before he even buried himself inside her.

Then he tasted her tears, salt and heat amid the cool and sweet, reminding him of the first blood he'd ever known.

It had been so damn good.

Julian released her and backed away. She was right. There would always be a beast inside him, one step from escaping and crushing everything.

The moon sprang free, cascading from the sky like a waterfall of ice, turning the tracks of her tears molten silver.

Julian lifted a hand—shaking, he saw—and ran a thumb across her cheek.

Her eyes snapped open, seeped of color in the night, their brilliant green now a shade identical to the moon. She looked like a painting, an ice goddess, sparkling white and pewter, her hair tumbling like tousled midnight across her pearly breasts. He ached to lick those tears from her face as he plunged into her over and over again.

"Faet," he muttered, and began to withdraw his hand.

Her fingers closed around his wrist. "No," she said, the rumble of her beast rippling near, calling wildly to his own.

"Sorry." He tugged on his hand, trying again to get away. "I—"

She growled, low, vicious, and his skin rippled. She let go of his hand, then reached forward with blurring speed to tangle her fingers in his hair. He had no choice but to come where she led, or lose big chunks from his scalp.

She pulled him back where he'd been, hip-to-hip, chest-to-chest, holding him still inches from her face; then she leaned her forehead against his, her silvery green eyes so close, the sheen of the tear tracks nearly blinding him.

"When you touch me," she whispered, "I forget. I need, *Julian*"—her fingers clenched on his name, drawing him ever closer, giving him just a hint of pleasurable pain—"to forget."

Had she ever called him Julian? He couldn't recall, but considering the way his name sounded in that voice—part woman, part wolf—the way it made him harden and pulse, he didn't think so.

Yet still he hesitated. The first time had been a dream, or so they'd thought, easily passed off as a mistake. This would be a choice, and there would be no denying it.

For either one of them.

She closed her eyes, perhaps to get herself under control, or let him do the same, and as she did a single, silver droplet fell.

Time slowed. Julian could see the tear plummeting, could hear the whoosh of it through the air; he caught the scent of the sea, could almost taste again the flavorful brine.

The tear splashed against his chest, and he hissed in a breath. How could it be so cold?

The sound caused Alex's eyes to flare open, and they traced the track of the tear across his nipple, then she leaned forward and did the same with her tongue.

How could he have been so wrong? Choice had nothing to do with it.

She suckled him hard and he cursed—Norwegian. English. A little Inuit thrown in—but when she would have lifted her head, he cupped his hand around her neck and pulled her back.

Her lips curved against his skin; then her tongue curled around his nipple, laving, tickling before her teeth grazed the flat disk until he pearled as hard as she had.

She slid downward, mouth busy on his ribs, his belly, his—

"Whoa!" He tried to lift her—if she got busy there, this would be over before it began—but she grabbed his penis in her ice-cold hand and he jerked. Maybe he *could* last a while longer.

Her breath was warm, her mouth even warmer. It had been so damn long. He'd had sex, sure, but this to him had always been the height of intimacy. You had to trust someone to put your "jewels" in a place where they kept all those teeth.

Julian stiffened. He had a lot of feelings about Alex, but trust wasn't one of them.

Struggling for control, at first Julian didn't realize that

Alex had gone to her knees. He looked down just as she leaned forward and licked him, quick as a cat, along his tip.

He cursed, reaching for her, but she struck away his hands, then with agonizing slowness she rose.

Her breath drifted over his belly, and the muscles beneath the skin fluttered. Moist heat curled across his chest, his neck and mouth. She lifted her gaze to his, tilting her chin just enough so their lips brushed.

"What kind of man *are* you?" she asked.

"Not a man," he said, and pushed her once more against the wall.

He could only take so much and he'd already taken it. Hell, he'd refused a blow job. He deserved a fucking medal. Instead, he'd take this.

He cupped her buttocks, sliding his fingers across the soft, virgin skin where thighs became ass. His biceps flexed to lift her, but she already had her arms around his neck, using the house to brace herself so she could hook her knees over his hips, cross her ankles at the small of his back, and pull him home.

He thrust, sliding within, relishing her heat—that soft, tight, moist heat. He'd meant to finish quick—he didn't have much finesse left—but instead, the instant she surrounded him, he stilled, then lowered his forehead to hers.

She wanted to forget; he could understand that. Some nights he would have given the soul she didn't think he had for just an hour's sweet peace.

"Barlow," she muttered, and wriggled, trying to arch but he had her pinned too tightly.

"Don't move," he managed. If she moved right now, if he did, this would be over far too soon; then they would both remember all that they wished to forget. He wanted to avoid that for as long as he could.

She said something that sound a lot like *Knull mæ i øret,* but in English, and he smiled, closing his eyes, reaching for the strength on which he prided himself.

"Be still," he murmured, and placed his palm on her belly, letting his thumb slide lower, delving into her tight curls. She was slick, swollen, perhaps as close now as he. He began to move just a little, in and out, flicking his thumb up and down.

"Yes," she murmured. "Yes."

And that single word, uttered in a voice he could only describe as *woman,* made him remember instead of forget.

His hand on another woman's stomach as they lay in their bed, all tangled in the sheets and each other. Her dreams, his hopes, the argument that had torn them apart, then sent her away.

To her death.

Julian yanked his hand back, and the chill night air burned across his fingers. Yet he could still feel her skin against his palm, and her body drawing from him his seed.

"I can't," he croaked.

"You are," she responded, "and so—" She thrust against him, hard and sure. "—am I."

Fury flashed, like lightning through the sky above, and in the distance he thought there was thunder. Why wouldn't the earth shake; why wouldn't the skies open up and rain down fire? He was fucking another woman, and not just any woman, but *the* woman.

The one who had killed his wife.

Of course if it hadn't been for him, Alana would never have been out there alone.

He threw back his head, roaring his fury to the heavens, and she clenched around him, the pulse of her orgasm fueling his own. But in that instant before he spilled everything, a memory sparked.

A boy with his golden hair. A girl with her green eyes. A dream that had become a nightmare through a bizarre combination of love and lies and impossibility.

The thoughts were agony, and Julian snarled again, his beast rumbling so close.

Alex drew his mouth to hers, and right before their lips met, she whispered, "Julian."

He came in a rush so strong, if he hadn't had the wall for support he would have fallen. As it was, he lost his grip on sanity, plunging into her, the thud of her spine against the house only fueling the violence within him.

She didn't seem to mind, clasping him to her, arms wrapped around his back as she took all that he gave, gave all that he took, gasping in his ear, "Again. Again. Again," to the rhythm of his thrusts.

When he was spent, when she was, he pulled out of her body without meeting her eyes. His hands and feet became paws a mere instant before they hit the ground running as some of the last words his wife had ever said to him rang in his shaggy wolf's ears requesting the one thing he could never, ever give her.

A child.

"Just like a man," Alex murmured as Julian's bushy golden tail disappeared into the darkness. "Get what you want, then shift into a wolf and run away."

She shook her head as she went inside. Talk about irrational, but then she was. What on earth had possessed her to let Julian Barlow do her against the side of the house?

"I didn't 'let' him do anything." She sighed as she turned

the shower to a temperature just short of scalding. "I begged him to."

Alex sat on the edge of the tub and took inventory. Bruised ass? Check. Scraped back? Check. Burning, slightly blue feet? Check. Self-esteem at an all-time low?

"Double check."

She'd never begged for sex in her life; she hadn't begged for anything except—

"Hell," Alex muttered, and let her chin fall down to her chest. She was right back where she'd started. Not wanting to remember, but unable to forget that night in Alabama.

The werewolf had come right at her. How she had missed killing it, Alex would never know. The whole night had been a disaster from the instant the beast first appeared. Charlie hesitating, when Charlie never did, and because he did, Alex had done the same.

She'd never made that mistake again.

The water was hot; so Alex climbed in and let the beat of it on her face wash away the grainy tracks of her tears. But the memories would never wash away.

The wolf had rushed forward; Alex had fired. But she thought maybe—*probably*—her hands had begun to shake, and the bullet went wide, catching something—an ear perhaps—because flames shot into the night. However, she hadn't hit anything vital since the beast kept coming. She'd known she was dead and—

"That was all right," Alex whispered, as the steam rose all around her.

But instead of slashing her to shreds, the werewolf had knocked her aside, too, and disappeared into the hills. She should have followed; she should have finished him off. Instead she'd dropped to her knees at her father's side, and as his blood seeped into her jeans, she'd begged him not to die.

Unfortunately, he was already dead.

When the sun rose, so did she. Leaving Charlie's body behind, she'd gathered his weapons with hers; then she'd called Edward.

He'd arrived within twenty-four hours, and he'd taken care of everything, including her. Alex had become a *Jäger-Sucher* in more than name that night. She'd been fifteen years old.

Alex gasped, realizing she'd nearly fallen asleep standing up, with the shower still beating on her face, and she felt a little sick. She shut off the water, ignoring the jitter in her stomach, and went in search of clothes.

She settled on another pair of black slacks and a bulky cable-knit sweater, also black. She didn't bother with a colorful scarf this time. She just didn't care.

Alex really needed to get to a store and find something that was more "her." Not that she had any money. Or that there was a Walmart anywhere nearby.

The idea of a Walmart in the middle of the Arctic, servicing werewolves and the occasional Inuit, made her laugh. Which felt really good until she started to cry. What was *wrong* with her?

She did *not* cry. What was the point? Crying wouldn't bring Charlie back any more than begging had. The only thing crying was good for was making her feel weak, alone, and sadder than she'd been before she started.

Her body languid—great sex appeared to have that effect—she decided to just lie down for a minute. The next thing she knew, she awoke—ears straining for . . . something.

Then, from the depths of the darkness, the scrape of claws across ice echoed. Alex was drawn to the window at the front of the silent house where she peered out upon an equally silent town.

Except for that *click, click, click*. It was going to drive her mad.

She shoved her bare feet into the horrible boots, which smelled like the burning remains of an old tire factory, and stepped outside.

The moon fell toward the horizon, throwing strange, elongated shadows across the snow. The village looked like a geometrically challenged children's game—one where colorful plastic squares, rectangles, and the like needed to be shoved into their matching holes before the timer went off and popped them all back out.

The sound of those claws was like the tick of that clock, creating a sense of urgency that caused Alex to head down the steps and into the street.

Alex had thought herself the only one left in Barlowsville after Julian loped off. Just like the previous night, all the werewolves were running beneath the moon.

Alex reached the end of the street that spilled into the town square and caught sight of a tail disappearing around an ATV parked at the edge. She hurried after, wincing as her boots crunched in the snow like newspaper crushed in her hands.

She paused in case she had to duck around the side of the ice cream shop—who ate ice cream in the Arctic?—to avoid being seen. Why she wanted to avoid that, she wasn't sure, but she did.

However, the animal kept going. With his super-duper ears he had to have heard her, but he didn't even glance back.

Who was this wolf? Why was it here? What did it want?

Alex had already rushed through the common and followed the four-legged shadow across the street before her brain caught up to her questions.

"Rogue," she whispered, then she cursed.

Why hadn't she brought a gun?

Oh, right. She no longer *had* a gun.

For an instant, Alex could barely think past the thunder of her heart in her head. Then she realized she had a better weapon within.

She'd just begun to slide Ella's slacks from her hips when she caught sight of the wolf again. Though the moon leached the color from everything, it couldn't change the shape of the body, the particular shagginess of the coat, the size of the paws, or the arrogant tilt of the head.

"Barlow," she muttered.

She nearly turned away and went back to Ella's. But then the wolf trotted right past Barlow's house and headed for the white monstrosity to the rear.

Alex followed. She couldn't help it. She wanted to know what that place was, and now seemed like a very good time.

She reached Julian's backyard just as the wolf turned into a man. Then she stood there frowning as the man opened the door and went inside.

She knew Barlow's backside better than she knew her own.

That hadn't been it.

CHAPTER 15

Julian ran through the night, attempting to make the memories fade. Not surprisingly, running didn't help any more than fucking had.

He avoided his wolves. Right now he wasn't fit company for man or beast.

He heard them in the distance, their howls lifting in a joyous serenade to the moon. If he was with them, he would do the same. The moon had marked them, it called, it soothed and invigorated. For werewolves, the moon was everything.

Julian ran until his stomach jittered and his head ached, and it became clear that he hadn't become ill in LA because he'd left Alex too soon, he'd become ill because he'd left her at all.

And wasn't that just fantastic?

Julian pushed that problem aside, dug a hollow in the snow, crawled in, tucked his tail atop his nose, and gave in to what was haunting him.

The memory of his wife.

I want your child, Julian.

She'd whispered the words into his ear as they lay side by

side in their bed, and her hand drifted over him. He smiled, rolling on top of her, hardening even as he slipped within. Then he heard what she'd said, and he slipped right back out again.

She reached for him, but he stilled her hand. "Alana, I thought you understood."

Sitting up, she pulled the sheet to her chin. "Understood what?"

"The limits of our existence."

"There are no limits. We're *werewolves,* Julian."

As if he didn't know.

Julian climbed out of bed and began to pace. "Your grandmother told me she explained things."

"She did. She said I'd have a second chance at the life I wanted."

"What was the life you wanted?"

"A dozen children." She laughed. The sound, which usually made Julian's heart flutter, suddenly made it stutter painfully. "Well, maybe not that many. But I love them so much. That's why I kept teaching preschool even though the money was crap. Kids make life worth living."

"Alana," he began, and her smile faded. "There'll be no children. Werewolves can't have them. It's impossible."

"That's . . . crazy," she said.

"Is it?" Julian came around to her side of the bed, refusing to be hurt when she scooted away as if she'd just seen him for the monster he was. "Why would you think a werewolf could procreate?"

"Because— Because Gran *said* so!" Her eyes darkened with shock. "She promised me. Do you think I would have agreed to become like this—" Her lip curled. "—otherwise?"

"You'd have been dead otherwise."

"Better dead than craving blood, being ruled by the

moon, living in the middle of nowhere, with a town full of freaks."

Julian jerked as if she'd slapped him. He'd known she didn't care for the blood; she rarely ran beneath the moon unless she had to. And she really hadn't made many friends beyond Cade and her gran. But he hadn't realized she felt like this.

"Better dead," she continued softly, "than an eternity of life without a family."

"You have a family!" Julian shouted, frightened by her still, white face. "You have me. You have Cade. You have Margaret." Although after the lie the old woman had told, she might not have her for very long. "You've got the whole damn town, Alana."

Instead of fighting back—something she never did; he wasn't certain she knew how—Alana had gotten out of their bed, dressed, and left the house.

Julian had let her go, figuring she'd gone to her gran. She'd come back; they'd talk, and everything would be all right.

But nothing was ever all right again.

Alex glanced at Barlow's house, which remained pitch dark and still; then she crossed the distance between his place and the mysterious white complex.

The door had closed, but she figured she could probably break any lock known to man. Her strength in human form increased daily, along with her senses.

But in keeping with the theme around here, the door wasn't locked. As she pulled it open, that lack suddenly made sense. What was the point to a dead bolt when everyone in town had the power to tear a door from its hinges? If anyone wandered in who wasn't a werewolf—and considering the terrain, that was unlikely—they'd be damn sorry, and really surprised, if they tried to steal a single thing.

Inside, the building was like a fortress. Brick walls, cement floors, gray and white everything. Perhaps she'd stumbled into the prison, although she doubted they'd leave *that* door open.

She also doubted they had one. Knowing Barlow, he treated misbehavior the same way Edward did. Follow the rules or die.

The place felt deserted, yet she'd seen the man enter. Who was he? Why did he resemble Barlow, then again not? Why was he running through the night alone? Did he *want* to be taken for the rogue?

She opened her mouth to call out, then thought better of it when she smelled the blood.

Alex hurried down the hall, following her nose. Which was the only reason she didn't see the man swinging the great big sword.

Luckily she *heard* it. A slight whistling whine coming toward her way too fast. Her instincts kicked in. She wasn't sure if they were hunter or werewolf and she didn't care when the sword clashed against the brick wall where her head had just been.

Alex, who had dropped to a crouch, kicked out, connecting with one of the man's naked knees. All he wore were a pair of boxer shorts and a snarl. Something crunched, and he collapsed. The sword just missed braining her on the way down.

Alex snatched it out of the man's hand and threw it as far as she could. The weapon slid along the floor, leaving a trail of sparks in its wake, then bounced against the door she'd just come through and lay still.

She turned to her attacker just as he reached for her

throat with both hands and caught him by the wrists, then yanked his arms wide. This brought his face in close to hers, and she saw that he had Barlow's eyes.

"Sheesh," Alex muttered, "who hasn't he banged?"

With the crumpled knee he had very little leverage, and she was able to topple him onto his back with a simple shove. Then she got to her feet and planted an ugly rubber boot on his chest. "Who the hell are you?" she demanded.

"Who the hell are *you*?" he returned.

Now that she got a good look, she wasn't sure why she'd ever mistaken him for Barlow. The eyes aside—which she hadn't seen until just now—his hair was darker, longer, messier. Besides being shorter, he was also vampire-pale and kind of weak looking. She was surprised he'd been able to lift that huge sword, let alone swing it.

Of course, he was a werewolf. He could bench-press a car if he wanted to.

"I asked you first." Alex pressed her boot into his chest, and he coughed. She let up a little. These days she wasn't sure of her own strength.

"You're in *my* home. Get out."

Alex laughed. "I don't think you're in any position to order me around. And if this is a home, you need a new architect. Badly."

"Why are you here?" he asked.

Why *was* she here? She'd seen him, followed him, kicked the crap out of him, and now—

She sniffed, and the hair at the back of her neck ruffled as if a chill breeze had just swirled past. She could still smell the blood.

"What is this place?" she asked. "It's not a home." She shoved at his chest again with her foot. "Don't bullshit me. I can smell the blood."

His eyebrows lifted, then his eyes slowly narrowed. "You're Alex," he said.

She stiffened. "How do you know?"

"You should have just told me. I can take care of this quickly. You'll be out of here in no time."

With a speed that blurred, even to her eyes, he snatched her foot and pushed it aside, coming nimbly to his feet, still favoring the knee she'd wrecked.

Alex brought up her hands, already clenched into fists, but he turned away, moving back into the room he'd just come out of.

"I'm going to grab some pants." He vanished through a doorway at the far end, and his next words were muffled. "Probably a shirt."

She'd taken one step forward, wondering if there was an escape route and he was using it, when he returned, pulling a geeky white lab coat over a pair of wrinkled black trousers.

The pronounced limp with which he'd walked away was already fading to a small hitch in his giddy-up. He was healing damn fast. Which meant he was a helluva lot older than he looked.

Around here, everyone was.

"Follow me." He strode past her and into the hall.

"Why?"

He disappeared around the corner just ahead without answering.

Alex glanced at the door that led outside, caught sight of the sword, and picked it up. The weapon was heavy, obviously very old, with an intricately carved but well-worn grip. She took it with her. She didn't plan on being surprised again.

But she was. How could she not be when she turned the

same corner he had and found herself in a huge, glaringly bright laboratory?

"Hello, Dr. Frankenstein," she murmured, gaze touching on the bottles and beakers, the test tubes and Bunsen burners, many of them sporting a liquid that shone scarlet beneath the fluorescent lights and explained why the place smelled like a slaughterhouse. She wondered if Elise knew about this.

Or if *he* knew about *her*.

"Cade," the man said, his back to her as he messed with something atop a long, shiny black table to the rear.

"Huh?"

"Not Frankenstein." He turned, a large needle in his hand. "Not yet."

Alex brought the sword up. "What do you plan to do with that?"

Confusion dropped over his face. "Draw your blood. What else?"

"Take your own. I'm not sharing."

"But—" The creases in his forehead deepened. "Didn't Julian tell you?"

Barlow had told her a lot of things. None of them had involved giving Herr Doctor her blood.

"No," she said, figuring that answered his question *and* told him what she thought of his poking her with that needle. But she waved his sword back and forth just in case he didn't get the message.

Cade—was that his first name or his last?—sighed. "He forgot again. He has a lot on his mind."

Alex lifted a brow. No doubt.

He motioned for her to come closer. "Just a little prick—"

"Don't sell yourself short, pal. I'm sure it's not that little."

He blinked, clearly not getting the joke. Then shook his head dismissing it. "No, really." He stepped forward. "I promise. It'll be over before you know it."

Alex waved the sword in a faster, wider arc. "Since it ain't happening, you're right."

"Don't you want to know why you're different?"

The sword stopped mid-arc. "What?"

"Julian said that you could touch the others and they could touch you."

"So?"

"Unless you were inoculated with my serum, your head should threaten to split open if you do that."

"But he said—" Alex paused. Barlow had said that he could touch the wolves he'd made and they could touch him. He'd never said that they could all play patty-cake together. "What else did Barlow say?"

"That he wanted me to find out why."

"And you always do what he says?"

"Doesn't everyone?"

"Not me."

Cade tilted his head. "I should probably find out why that is, too."

"Because I'm a bitch, he's an ass, and I don't wanna?"

Cade choked; then his laughter spilled free. "This is going to be so much fun to watch. No one's defied him in centuries. I think the last wolf that did woke up one day without a throat."

"I see now where the fun comes in," Alex said drily.

Cade, who'd finally stopped laughing, snorted. "If he hasn't killed you yet, he isn't going to."

"I wouldn't count on that."

The sword was getting heavy. Not that she couldn't

manage it but Alex saw no reason to continue holding the thing in front of her as if she were auditioning for the movie version of *Xena: Warrior Werewolf*. So she set the weapon on the nearest tabletop that wasn't cluttered with books and papers and glass, but she kept her hand on the hilt.

"How do you resist his . . . ?" Cade made a circle in the air with the needle.

Alex's mouth tightened. She hadn't resisted him very well at all—at least when it came to sex. She could tell Barlow to blow off, but when it came right down to it, all she really wanted to do was blow him.

"Commands," Cade finished.

Alex had to scramble for the question. Resisting his commands? It wasn't easy. But the more she did it, the easier it got. Maybe if she refrained from doing him a few times, she'd be able to resist him for good.

And why did the thought of never feeling his skin beneath her palms, his mouth on hers, his body deep within make her twitchy? She didn't know, and she didn't want to.

"I just say nuh-uh," Alex answered. "You should try it sometime."

"I have. It makes me . . ." Cade shifted his thin shoulders beneath the starched white coat. "Squirrelly."

Alex nodded. That was as good a word as any. "Me too. But I'd rather feel squirrelly than . . . owned."

"He doesn't own us."

"Close enough," Alex muttered. Then, since she didn't want to argue a point she wouldn't win—not with one of the ownees—Alex moved on. "Why were you out alone in the night?" she asked.

"Alone?" he repeated.

"There's a rogue wolf picking off the Inuit villagers one by one."

"Wasn't me," he said with the quickness of a seven-year-old accused of breaking into the cookie jar. "And no one from our village would ever hurt anyone from theirs."

"Because of the agreement."

Cade bobbled the needle, barely managing to keep from sticking himself or dropping it. "Julian's been chatty."

"Barlow's a lot of things. Chatty isn't one of them."

"Yet you know about Awanitok and our agreement with them after being in town for barely a day."

"I'm easy to talk to." And a really good liar. "If no one here would dare defy him . . ." Except Alex, and she hadn't eaten anyone lately. ". . . then whatever's doing it is a rogue."

"Must be."

"But a rogue, by definition, is . . ." Alex cast about for a word.

"A scoundrel?"

"If you live in the seventeenth century." Alex narrowed her eyes. "*Did* you live in the seventeenth century?"

"Among others."

"Where were you born?" she asked, suddenly curious.

"Norse land."

"Never heard of it."

"The land of the Vikings."

Alex looked him up and down. "*You* were a Viking?"

His face became distant. "I wasn't a very good one."

"Let me guess. You were from Norway. Like him." Cade nodded, and Alex flicked a finger to indicate his eyes. "Did he boink your mama, too?"

Cade jerked, mouth pulling into an expression of horror. "Why would you say such a disgusting thing?"

"Your eyes," Alex said. "They're like his."

The scuff of a shoe had them both glancing toward the doorway where Barlow leaned, the nonchalance of his posture belied by the flare of fury in his all-too-familiar blue gaze.

CHAPTER 16

"He's my brother," Julian said, and stalked across the room.

Alex's hand tightened around the hilt of Cade's sword, but she didn't take it up. Smart move. He'd disarm her quicker than she could say *boink your mama*.

How had she gotten the weapon away from Cade in the first place? His brother might have been a bad Viking, but he was a *Viking*. You'd think that would be good for something.

"Your brother," Alex murmured. "The dead one?"

Julian swung his gaze in her direction. "As you can see, he's not dead."

"You said he fell in battle, and that in your fury you shifted into a wolf."

"I did."

"Fell means died."

"In what dictionary?" he asked.

She made an impatient sound. "If he wasn't dead, then what pissed you off enough to make you furry?"

Julian was becoming pissed off enough right now to become furry. What was it about the woman that both infuriated and aroused him? Or was it only that her arousing him, infuriated him?

He pulled his eyes from the lips he'd so recently kissed, and pathetically wanted to kiss again, only to meet his brother's considering gaze. "What *didn't* you tell her, Julian?"

"Bite me," Julian growled, and Cade's lips twitched. Despite all the centuries of their existence, his little brother still enjoyed baiting him.

Cade glanced back and forth between Julian and Alex, then murmured, "Ah."

Both Alex and Julian snapped, "Ah, what?"

Cade lifted his hands in surrender. "Nothing," he said, but inside he was laughing.

Julian didn't find any of this funny. He'd just spent hours agonizing over the past, over the reason Alex was here, what she had *done.* Then a single instant in her presence and all he could think of was the texture of her skin, the smell of it, that taste.

"Knull mæ i øret," he cursed.

"You keep saying that," Alex murmured. "What does it mean?"

"Fuck my ear," Cade supplied helpfully, the laughter still bubbling in his voice.

Julian shot him a look, but while Cade did as he was told just like everyone else in town, he wasn't afraid of Julian. Never had been, never would be. Cade knew his big brother would never hurt him.

"I think I'll pass," Alex said.

"It's a Norwegian curse," Cade continued. "The Norse version of 'fuck me.'"

Alex studiously avoided glancing at Julian. Nevertheless he knew exactly what she was thinking.

Already did.

"What are you doing here?" he demanded.

"According to Cade, you promised him my blood." Alex indicated the needle and vial his brother still held in his hand. "Why didn't you tell me I'm not only a werewolf freak but, apparently, a freaky werewolf?"

Julian slapped himself in the forehead. He'd completely forgotten to bring her here. "Give him your arm."

"No," she said, then grabbed her own wrist, which had begun to lift in response to the order, and held it down. "Answer my question."

His teeth ground together so loudly, it sounded as if he had gravel in his mouth. "I planned to tell you when I brought you to have the blood drawn." He frowned, glancing between her and Cade. "Why did you come here if not for that?"

"I didn't know about that. Or him. I followed a lone wolf through town."

Julian tensed. The rogue had dared to walk into his domain? He'd tear the beast into pieces. "Where did it go?"

She lifted her chin in Cade's direction. "Right there."

Julian let out the breath he'd taken. Not the rogue. Just Cade. Cade liked to run alone. He always had.

"And when he came inside, you decided to come in for . . ." Julian waited.

"I decided to come in and ask, *What the hell?*" Alex said. "But he took a swing at my head with his Viking sword—"

"You did?" Julian glanced at his brother in surprise, squelching the desire to mutter *too bad you missed,* which would only arouse more suspicion. The wolves in Barlowsville were family. One didn't wish any of them dead.

Cade shrugged. "I didn't know who she was. I thought everyone was out with you."

Julian let Cade believe he'd been running with the others. He certainly didn't want to discuss why he hadn't been.

"You wanna explain this, too, while you're at it?" Alex stood next to Cade's laptop. "Thought you were off the grid."

"We are." Cade crossed over, picked up the computer, and brought it back to the center island where he stood within arm's reach of his toy. He never had liked anyone else touching it.

Cade quickly gave Alex a rundown on how he had Internet when no one else did. She didn't appear to understand the explanation any better than Julian did. She opened her mouth, no doubt to spew forth more questions, and the back door banged—open, then shut. Footsteps hurried down the hall.

George burst in, face flushed, chest heaving.

"Ah, hell," Julian muttered an instant before the boy announced, "We found another body."

"One a night," Alex drawled. "Someone's hungry."

Julian ignored her. "Who was it?"

"Dr. Cosgrove."

"Doctor?" Alex asked.

"Veterinarian."

"Maybe someone didn't care for the way he was sticking *them* with needles," she muttered.

"We don't see the veterinarian," he snapped. "We don't see any doctor at all. We don't get sick."

"Except in the head."

He shot her a glare.

"What?" She rounded her eyes with false innocence. "You don't think someone in the village has snapped?"

George was listening wide-eyed. He'd no doubt report every word to Jorund as soon as he got back.

"I'll come within the hour," Julian said.

The boy nodded and went out the way he'd come in. Silence settled over them. It didn't last long.

"Aren't you going to ask your brother what he's been doing out there alone in the night?" Alex demanded.

"Why?"

Alex rubbed her nose as if she had a sudden headache. "Rogue wolf killing Inuit nightly. Remember?"

"You think Cade is a murdering, rogue werewolf?" Julian asked. "Look at him."

"Hey!" Cade exclaimed. "I'm right here."

"And your sword is right there." Julian pointed at the weapon on the table. "You let a *girl* take it from you."

"Right here," Alex murmured. "And I'm not just any girl."

Julian spoke before his brother could question that comment. "Cade's a loner. Always has been."

"*Loner*," Alex repeated. "Isn't that another word for 'rogue'?"

"What are you?" Cade asked. "A cop?"

"Yes," Julian said, at the same time Alex said, "No."

"She was," Julian blurted. "Obviously she isn't anymore."

"I could be," she said.

"I'm all the cop we need around here."

"Yeah, you're doin' a great job so far. How many are dead?"

"I'll take care of it."

"Start with him. Can't you touch him and . . ." She wiggled her fingers like a sitcom witch performing a spell. "Voodoo the truth free?"

"It wasn't him," Julian said.

"Just because he's your brother doesn't mean he couldn't have killed someone."

"That *is* what it means. Exactly."

Alex threw up her hands. "He's a werewolf."

"What is there about this town that you don't understand?" Julian snapped. "We don't kill people."

She stared him right in the eye as she said with utter conviction, "One of you does."

Barlow wanted to smack her. Alex could see it on his face. But he didn't want to do it in front of his brother. Which meant he hadn't told Cade who she really was.

Interesting.

The two had been together for centuries. They appeared very close. Yet Barlow was keeping secrets. Was Cade keeping secrets, too?

"No one here would dare hurt anyone from there," Julian said.

"I think you're wrong."

"I don't care what you think. I know. Whoever's killing the Inuit does not live here."

"You'd rather believe a lone werewolf wandered out in the middle of nowhere and started snacking on the pets," Alex said. "Instead of the logical answer that someone from a village *full* of werewolves has decided you aren't the boss of them?"

Doubt flickered over Julian's face, there, then gone the next instant. "Yeah," he said. "That's what I believe."

But she'd gotten him thinking. Which was good enough for her.

Alex had also started to think. She'd come here to find the werewolf that had murdered her father, only to discover a werewolf murdering villagers. What were the chances they were one and the same?

Pretty damn high.

Especially if she bought into the theory that Barlow's wolves were different—and considering their seeming lack of a desire to kill everyone they met, she kind of did—then it would follow that the one wolf that had murdered before was now doing so again.

She was going to have to start meeting people, giving them a good, long look-see. She'd winged—or eared—the werewolf that had murdered her father with a silver bullet, and silver left a mark—in both forms.

However, cheerily chatting up the populace when she was supposed to loathe them was going to arouse Barlow's suspicions. She'd just have to do it when he wasn't around.

"Don't you have somewhere to be?" she asked.

Barlow lifted a brow. "Trying to get rid of me?"

"Always."

Cade laughed. She was really starting to like the guy.

"Before you go." Cade lifted the needle. "You mind?"

"I prefer my blood inside instead of outside." Alex turned toward the exit.

Barlow snatched her by the elbow, and she froze as his touch seemed to flow through her like another virus, this one making her want him, need him. Now.

She yanked her arm free, and he let her, dropping his hand to his thigh and rubbing the palm against his jeans as if his skin was buzzing, too.

"Don't you want to know why you're different from all the others?"

Yeah, she kinda did.

"Cade can help."

Alex turned to him. "Can you?"

Cade shrugged. "I'll try."

"What else have you been up to?" She waved her hand to indicate the room and all its contents.

Cade glanced at Julian, who nodded, making Alex grind her teeth. Did everyone have to ask him everything?

"I invented the serum so that we can touch in human form."

"And here I'd thought that was just another handy-dandy gift from Big Daddy."

Cade appeared about to laugh, but he coughed instead before giving her an answer. "I've been attempting to isolate what it is in the virus Julian passes on that keeps us from becoming—" Cade broke off, lips pressed together, forehead creased.

"Psychotic, evil killing machines?" Alex supplied.

"Sheesh," Julian muttered.

Oh, yeah. She wasn't supposed to hate them so much.

"For want of a better description," Cade agreed, but he glanced back and forth between Alex and Julian, waiting for an explanation that wasn't ever going to come.

"How's that working out for you?" Alex asked.

"I'm getting there."

"I've told you before that my wolves aren't possessed by evil." Barlow tilted his head, and his hair swung like a golden pendulum beneath the bright fluorescent lights.

"Except for that inevitable first kill," she pointed out.

"Except for that."

"Maybe some of your wolves like the first one so much they keep right on doing it."

"They don't," he said with conviction. "They don't have the taste for it."

"So you say. But what's truth and what's lies?"

"If you were evil, wouldn't you want to kill everything that crossed your path?"

She looked him up and down. "Who says I haven't?"

His lips twitched. "You've resisted. A werewolf not made by me wouldn't be able to."

"What good is that serum if you were all *born* demon-free?"

"It's not for us," Cade said. "It's for every poor human being who's been changed against their will."

"But—" Alex began, then paused.

Cade didn't appear to know about Edward's cure. Or maybe he just didn't care. According to Julian, being one of his wolves was *super*-cool. None of them wanted to go back.

In her experience, no werewolf wanted to. The ones that were possessed by the demon liked what they were. As the virus strangled the person they'd been before they were bitten, they embraced the evil. She had to wonder if, even after Edward's cure, that person ever found their way back.

"But what?" Julian prompted.

"Nothing." Alex was supposed to keep her secret *Jäger-Sucher* past a secret, which meant she wouldn't know about a cure, either. She stuck out her arm toward Cade. "Do me."

Julian choked. Cade fumbled the needle again.

At least she'd distracted them from further questions, and she *did* want to know why she could touch the other wolves without the serum. Or why she wanted to touch Barlow at all.

Alex watched the tube fill rapidly with her blood. Strange. It didn't seem any different now than when she'd been human.

Cade removed the needle and turned away.

"Aren't you gonna swab me with alcohol or anything?" Now that she thought about it, he hadn't swabbed her arm *before* he'd stuck her, either.

"You aren't going to get an infection," Barlow said.

"Right." A single drop of blood welled from the tiny pinprick before it healed over.

Cade capped the tube and began to write something on a label. Alex moved closer, fascinated despite herself. "Why don't you try and *cure* lycanthropy?" she asked.

"Why would I do that?" His voice was absent, his eyes focused on her blood and the mysteries it might solve.

"Wouldn't it be more productive to cure the disease itself and not just one symptom of it?"

Cade glanced up, and his gaze had gone shrewd. "You sound like you don't want to be a werewolf, Alex."

"I d—"

Julian's hand twitched. Several empty beakers flew off the table and crashed onto the floor. Cade's attention turned to the mess. Alex glanced at Julian, who drew his finger across his throat. Dramatic, but it got the point across.

"Do," she said. "I do want to be a werewolf."

Her mind mocked, *I do. I do. I dooo!* in the voice of the Cowardly Lion.

"Mmm," Cade said noncommittally. "From what I hear I don't need to waste my time. The *Jäger-Suchers* have a cure."

So he did know. Since Julian had, she shouldn't be surprised.

"Not sure what it is, though." Cade swept the glass into a dustpan with a tiny, handheld broom, then straightened and dumped the mess into the trash. The tinkling of the broken pieces sounded like distant church bells.

"If it were a serum or a pill, there'd be a lot less werewolves. Makes me think it's some kind of spell that only one person can do. It takes a long time to rid the world of werewolves if you have to visit each and every one in order to do it."

"What's a *Jäger-Sucher*?" Alex asked.

Cade sighed and let his head drop between his shoulders. Which was good since Julian rolled his eyes, along with his head, to indicate his total disbelief at her gall. But Cade was suspicious, and if she wanted to prove she was here because she wanted to be, not because she had to be—for more reasons than one—Alex thought she should at least pretend to be as much of a nube as Julian said she was.

"Julian." Cade's voice was exasperated. "If you're going to make a new wolf, the least you can do is be certain she's prepared."

"He isn't going to come here," Julian said.

Cade lifted his gaze. "She needs to know."

"Know what?" she asked. "And he, who?"

Cade put his arm around her shoulders and pulled her against his side. Alex was so startled she let him. Then it felt so nice, she didn't move away. She couldn't remember the last time anyone had touched her with anything but violence or lust.

Or in the case of Barlow—violence *and* lust.

"There's a secret society," he began.

"That's enough."

Alex glanced over her shoulder. Barlow's nostrils flared, his eyes, fixed on Cade's arm, blazed. What was he so mad about?

"I'll tell her," he said.

"I don't mind." Cade smiled, and Alex smiled back. She felt so much more at ease with Cade than she could ever feel with his brother. "Besides, you've got places to go, Inuit to see."

"Just find out what's wrong with her." Julian plucked his brother's arm off Alex's shoulder, snatched her by the wrist, and yanked her with him toward the door.

"Keep your skin on!" she said, hanging back.

Fury flashed, and for an instant she thought he might grab her by the throat. Instead, he bent, hitting her in the gut with his shoulder and effectively stifling any further protest before he lifted her over his back and headed down the corridor.

By the time she recovered her breath, he'd kicked open the rear door and fresh air wafted across her overheated face. "What is *wrong* with you?"

He unceremoniously dumped her to the ground. The only reason she didn't land on her ass in the snow was that she was getting more lithe on her feet with each passing hour.

His eyes still blazed; his voice now rumbled between wolf and man. "What we're concerned with here is what's wrong with you."

"There's nothing wrong with me that you didn't *make* wrong with me."

Barlow turned away, presenting her with his back as he leaned against the white building. "You need to leave Cade alone," he said. "He has work to do. You can't . . . fuck with him like you fuck with me."

Alex stiffened. "Excuse me?"

Obviously Barlow didn't hear the danger in her voice, because he just kept talking.

"He's innocent. A bit of a doofus. He's spent his life trying to heal people. All he cares about is helping others."

"I bet I could make him care about me."

Barlow spun so fast she didn't have time to move away. Not that she would have. She'd meant to poke the beast. He'd poked her.

"Leave him alone." His skin rippled. He was losing control.

Good. So was she.

Alex stepped in close; then she lowered her voice so that even super-wolf had to lean in to hear what she said. "You think I just bang anyone who comes along?" She lifted her eyes and showed him her fury. "Like you?"

He snapped, grabbing her by the shoulders and dragging

her against him. Despite her sweater and his flannel shirt, she could feel the heat wafting off him like the waves of the sun across the asphalt in August.

"You'll bang no one," he said between gritted teeth. "Except me."

CHAPTER 17

Julian wanted to kiss her. He wanted to throw her on the ground and do a helluva lot more than kiss. Ever since he'd walked into his brother's lab and seen them together, so comfortable, so at ease, he'd been itching to remind her to whom she belonged.

He shook his head. What was he thinking? She didn't belong to him. He didn't want her to.

As if she'd read his mind, Alex snapped, "You don't own me, Barlow."

"No?" he murmured, and lowered his mouth to the pale skin visible above the sweater and below her ear.

She stiffened, straining to get away, but he was stronger than she was; he always would be. She kicked him; he barely felt it, the scent of her calling him home.

He took a fold into his mouth and suckled, tongue pressing against the pulsing vein, and she stilled, going pliant in his arms. His hands slid around her back, then down her pants. He cupped her cheeks, warming himself before he slid his thumb along the crevice.

"Ahem."

Julian registered the sound of throat clearing like the buzz of a fly—annoying but it could be ignored.

"Ahem!"

Or not.

He kept his hands right where they were and raised his head. The mark left by his mouth resembled a full moon. Even as he admired it, the hickey began to fade. He grit his teeth against the nearly overwhelming urge to put it there again.

Julian lifted his gaze a bit more and met his brother's.

"I wanted to talk to Alex," Cade said. "I'll come back when you're finished."

Alex tensed as if to pull away, but with his palms still cupping her ass . . . wasn't happening.

"Shh," Julian murmured, tugging her closer, pressing a kiss to her brow.

She jerked away. "What are you *doing*?"

He blinked. What had he been doing? Comforting her, cuddling her, as if what he felt for her was more than lust, as if what he felt for her was—

Julian yanked his hands out of her pants and took one giant step backward, even as she tried to move away, snagged her clumpy rubber heel on the snow, and began to windmill her arms so she wouldn't fall.

Cade smoothly stepped up, caught her around the waist, and set her on her feet. Alex peered over her shoulder and smiled at him in a way she'd never once smiled at Julian.

"Stop growling," she said without even glancing in Julian's direction. Then she covered Cade's hands, which still rested on her hips, with her own. "Thanks."

Julian had never seen her behave so gently, or speak the same. He hadn't believed that she could. What he really couldn't believe was that he yearned to have her speak like that to him.

And because he did, Julian turned and walked away.

Barlow disappeared into his house. The slam of the door echoed in the still morning air. Alex understood the sentiment. Anger, hatred, lust—that she could get behind. But when he'd gone gentle on her, kissing her forehead, murmuring into her hair . . .

What the hell had just happened?

"He was marking you," Cade murmured.

Alex turned her attention from Barlow's house to his brother, who seemed far more amused than he should be.

"There's a mark?"

Cade lifted his hand, and his fingers brushed the place on her neck that still burned from Julian's mouth. "Not anymore."

Cade's touch was all business—like a physician during an exam. Nevertheless, Alex stepped out of his reach, suddenly uncomfortable. "Why would he do that?"

"You're his. He wanted me to know it."

Alex didn't bother to correct him. Right now, she *felt* his—chosen, branded . . . marked.

"It's a wolf thing," Cade continued. "Sometimes we pee on trees."

"I guess I should be glad he wasn't a wolf when he decided to mark me."

Cade's lips quirked. "I guess."

"Is everyone in town going to think I'm—"

"His?" Cade's smile deepened. "They already do."

"What?"

The word erupted, loud and confrontational, causing a middle-aged man who'd just come out of his house to glance across the street in their direction.

"Morning, Barry!" Cade lifted a hand, and after a few more seconds' contemplation Barry bent, picked up his newspaper—*The Werewolf Gazette*?—and went inside.

Cade tilted his head and observed Alex as if she were a fascinating new specimen. "Julian hasn't brought a new wolf to town since—" He paused and unease flickered over his face.

"Since Alana?" Alex asked.

Cade's eyes widened. "He told you about her?"

Alex shrugged. He had; then again he hadn't.

"If he didn't bring you here for himself," Cade murmured, "then why did he bring you?"

She wasn't going to touch *that* question with a ten-foot pole.

"You'll have to ask him," she said. "You wanted to talk to me?"

"I heard they were looking for a waitress at the coffee shop."

"And this is something I need to know why?"

"Thought you might want a job. I know you said you weren't a cop—" His forehead creased. "But Julian said you were."

"PI," Alex supplied. God, she was so good at lying it was kind of embarrassing. "Not really a cop, but close."

"Well, we don't need a cop or a PI in Marlowoville, but we do need a waitress at the coffee shop. I bet you could handle it."

"Maybe," she allowed.

"It's a great job for someone who's new to town," Cade continued. "Everyone drops by eventually. And once they know you're working there, they'll drop by even quicker."

"Why's that?"

"They'll want to talk to you. Get to know you and let you

get to know them." Cade opened the door, taking a step inside before glancing back. "If you're interested, just ask for Rose."

Alex had considered going door-to-door, or accosting people in the streets for answers. She could have made the case that she just wanted to get to know everyone, but she figured that would sound fishy. The coffee shop was the perfect cover. She could talk to people and get a peek at them. See if they had any telltale burn marks.

The owner, Rose Bianchi—not a mark on her that Alex could see—was so thrilled to have an applicant that Alex feared the woman might hug her.

"You can start today?" she asked, her fluffy, white halo of hair bobbing above cheeks the same shade as her name. "Right now?"

"I don't know anything about being a waitress," Alex lied. It wasn't as if she could mention all the towns where she'd picked up a few days' work for tips just so she could buy another box of silver bullets.

"What's to know?" Rose asked, handing her an apron, and her own pencil and pad. "You write down what they want; then you bring it to them."

The place smelled like every diner Alex had ever been in. Coffee and fried eggs, bacon and toast. What had she thought they'd serve? People burgers?

"What happened to your last waitress?" Alex asked.

"She's working at the bookstore now." Rose shrugged. "Folks switch around. After a few decades, even a job like this gets boring."

"Even a job like this?" Alex repeated.

"We're always busy. Got something new on the menu every day."

She indicated the chalkboard where the specials had

been written in a precise, curving hand. Today's omelet contained apples, spinach, and bacon, while the pancake of the day was cranberry nut. Alex realized she hadn't eaten since yesterday. Luckily free food came with the job. She wondered if they'd care if she ordered *all* the specials at once.

"Always someone to talk to. Stories to hear," Rose continued, patting Alex's arm with a surprisingly soft, supple palm. Didn't waitresses usually have rough skin? Although anyone that could heal a knife to the throat was going to heal dishpan hands in a jiffy. "You're gonna love it."

"Thanks," she said.

Rose grinned, exposing slightly crooked but very white teeth. "I'll be right there." She pointed at the ancient cash register near the front.

Sometimes this town seemed like the land that time forgot. Then someone would wheel in on a snowmobile, or turn up the sound on their iPod, earbuds trailing into the pocket of their plaid flannel shirt, or share the latest *Saturday Night Live* skit, as the guys at the corner table appeared to be doing.

"That's Joe behind the grill." Rose lifted her chin to indicate the equally white-haired man flipping pancakes as he sang a song about the moon, and an eye, and a big pizza pie. He saluted them both with his spatula, but the look he leveled at Rose was pure devotion.

"Husband?" Alex guessed.

"Nearly a hundred and eighty years now." Rose winked and headed for the register.

"A hundred and eighty years," Alex echoed. She couldn't imagine. She'd kill Barlow before the first year was through.

Alex jolted at her thoughts. She wasn't going to marry Barlow. She wasn't going to marry anyone. She was going to find the werewolf she'd come here to find, kill it, then run.

Once she got to work, Alex discovered that Rose was right. The job wasn't hard. For a werewolf.

Alex had superior strength and amazing stamina, even in this form, so being on her feet for hours, carrying heavy trays loaded with equally heavy plates, setting them down, picking them up, and running, running, running . . .

Not a problem.

However, if she'd been human she'd have washed out in an hour. The place was unbelievably busy, with wave after wave of customers filling the seats. Did anyone in the entire village eat breakfast at home?

A second waitress, who introduced herself as Cyn—short for Cynthia—and appeared to have been a waitress since the dawn of time, or perhaps the mid-1950s considering her red beehive and tendency to crack gum at the end of every sentence, handled most of the booths, leaving Alex the counter.

"That way you've only gotta deal with one person's order at a time," she said as she hurried by with a tray of coffee, juice, and tea for the local bridge club.

Alex couldn't help but stare at the table full of elderly ladies, who twittered and laughed and discussed rubbers, slams, and dummies with great animation. She had to remind herself that they were *werewolves*.

Then she got a flash of the same ladies sitting around the table in wolf form, pearls still encircling their hairy necks, earrings swaying from their pointy ears, tasteful pink nail polish adorning their claws as they finished a hand of duplicate.

"I bet if I painted that on velvet, it would be a surefire hit," Alex murmured. "Bigger even than the poker-playing dogs."

"Order up!" Joe sang.

Joe sang everything. Alex had yet to hear him simply speak, and whenever his wheel was empty, he performed songs by someone he referred to as Dino. Everyone in the restaurant went silent when that happened. Joe had a fantastic voice.

He also had both his ears and no visible scars, as did Cyn and everyone else Alex had encountered so far.

The order, for the dapper gentleman at the end of the counter, consisted of three eggs poached, sausage, bacon, cakes, *and* toast, as well as home fries with onions and mushrooms. Everyone at the EAT Café consumed enough food for a ravenous wolf.

Har-har.

The metabolism of a werewolf was much faster than that of a human, and without the concern of cholesterol poisoning and a nasty dose of heart disease, the possibilities were endless.

Four cheeseburgers with a side of onion rings, fries, *and* cheese curds? Two steaks, baked potato with melted butter and bacon, broccoli with cheese sauce? Go nuts.

Why would anyone want to go back to the way that they'd been?

Alex bobbled the tray but managed to keep all the food from sliding onto her customer's head. Her thoughts these days didn't seem like her own.

"Breakfast is served," she said brightly. It hadn't taken her long to remember that the more chirpy she was, the more tip she got. Since she'd come here with nothing but fur, Alex needed all the money she could get.

She barely managed to fit all the plates on her tray in front of her customer, considering the guy next to him had ordered an equal amount of food and had five or six plates of his own.

"Anything else I can get for you, Daniel?"

Daniel Finnegan appeared to be in his midfifties, with salt-and-pepper hair and a nearly white mustache. He wore a gray tweed suit from an era long past, though Alex wasn't sure which one, complete with a hat and shiny black dress shoes.

He'd introduced himself as soon as he'd taken his seat, refusing to allow Alex to call him by anything but his first name. "We're all family here," he'd said when she tried to call him Mr. Finnegan.

Everyone had the same attitude, introducing themselves as if they were sitting at Alex's kitchen table instead of her station at the EAT.

They talked to her as if they were sitting in her home, too, as if they were lifelong friends. She should feel bad about that, but every time she started to she merely brought up the memory of her father's last night in the mountains and all the guilt went away.

"I'll take a bit more coffee when you get a chance," Daniel said, tucking into his meal with a gusto at odds with his demeanor.

Alex made the rounds with the coffeepot, topping off the cups of all her customers and Cyn's, too. She'd discovered years ago that to walk by someone who had only half a cup of coffee while you were carrying a full pot and not offer them any was a good way to get snarled at—and that was *before* she'd started waiting on werewolves.

Conversations ebbed and flowed. Alex learned quite a bit just by wandering past the tables filling those empty cups. Of course no one admitted to killing a *Jäger-Sucher* or snacking on an Inuit. Had she really thought they would?

"No," she muttered.

"No, what, dear?"

Alex had made her way back to Daniel and poured him a refill. "Just thinking aloud," she said. "So, how long have you been a werewolf?"

Daniel, who had just taken a persnickety bite of bacon, choked. Then he began to cough. Alex began to worry, until the rest of the room's lack of interest reminded her that while Daniel might be choking, he couldn't choke *to death*.

Alex handed him a glass of water.

"Why would you ask that?" he managed eventually.

"Shouldn't I?" Alex leaned over the divider that hid the workings of the restaurant from the dining room and set the pot on a burner. "Is that 'not done'?" She made quotation marks in the air around the last two words.

Daniel sighed and took another sip of water, his sober chocolate-brown gaze contemplating her over the rim before he set it down. "All of us agreed to become like this, which meant we had one thing in common."

"What's that?"

"Either imminent death, or a very shitty life."

Alex was glad she'd set the coffeepot down or she just might have dropped it. Hearing *shitty* come out of Daniel Finnegan's prim mouth was both shocking and slightly hilarious.

This time Alex choked, and Daniel offered her his water. She took it—no worries anymore in sharing cups, utensils, spit; germs wouldn't hurt her—and took a swallow.

"Better?" Daniel dabbed at the pristine corners of his mouth with a napkin that did not appear to have been used at all. When Alex nodded, he went on. "We don't ask one another how we came to be like this because we don't want to remember what made us choose to leave behind our humanity. It's never a pretty story." His gentle gaze became shrewd. "Is yours?"

"No," she said before she even thought about it.

Her life hadn't been anything to write home about. Because she'd had no home to write to. No mother, no father, no family left at all. Her life had been death, or the distribution of it, with the certain knowledge that one day she'd find herself bleeding out from a werewolf attack just like her father.

If she'd been asked at that point—death or lycanthropy— would she have chosen this?

No. She knew what lay on the other side. Or at least she'd thought she knew.

Until she'd come here.

"You're telling me no one chooses this life unless their other one sucks so badly they can't wait to leave it?"

"Yes," Daniel said.

"But . . . you like being a werewolf, don't you?"

"I do." He straightened his tie, adjusted his hat.

"Then why wouldn't someone prefer to be one without the motivation of death or a really shitty life?"

He smiled at her as if she were a foolish child. To him, she probably was. "Humanity isn't something to toss off lightly, Alex, there are things you give up that you can never get back. I hope Julian made that clear."

Not so much, she thought.

"What things?" she asked.

Daniel contemplated Alex for several seconds, and she feared he might press her on the issue of what Julian had made clear and what he had not. She really didn't want to lie to Daniel anymore, but she couldn't exactly tell him that Julian had not only neglected to give her instructions, he'd neglected to give her a choice.

Eventually Daniel glanced away with a sigh. "Pets."

Alex blinked. "Did you say pets?"

"Dogs are afraid of us. Cats hate us."

"Cats hate everyone," she said.

"Not the person with the can opener," he muttered. "Unless he isn't a person."

Huh. Alex never would have taken Daniel for a cat lover.

"I think I can live without pets." She'd done just fine so far.

"Children."

What on earth would she do with one of those?

"Next," she said.

Daniel turned to her and frowned. "I have to believe that whatever you left behind was sufficiently horrible that you chose to forfeit any chance of having a child in order to escape it."

"Okay," Alex said agreeably. So far she hadn't heard anything she'd given up on this side of furry that she'd wanted in the first place.

"Peace of mind," he said. "A pristine soul."

Except, maybe, for that.

"You better explain, Daniel."

"You killed someone after you changed, yes?"

Alex didn't think so, but still she nodded.

"It's the price we pay for immortality." Daniel laid his hand atop hers, and Alex's throat went thick. She must not be as over the choking fit as she'd thought. "It's a very high price."

"What if the guy—" Daniel lifted a brow. "—or girl you killed deserved to be dead?" A thousand times over.

"Ah, Julian's method," he murmured. "A very—"

Together they said, "—bad man."

"You still killed a human being," Daniel continued. "Your soul is no longer white."

"It ain't black, either."

"Perhaps," he said, though he didn't sound convinced.

"You agonize over who you killed," Alex murmured. "So you have no peace of mind." If that was the case, it was going to be a very long eternity for Daniel.

"No," he said. "Well, yes. I do agonize over the person who ensured my immortality, and I always will. But that isn't the loss of peace I'm talking about."

"What is?"

His eyes met hers and within them she saw a stark fear that gave her an unpleasant little jolt. "We're hunted, Alex."

"The *Jäger-Suchers*."

"We can never be completely at peace because there is always someone—" He took a breath. "—many, many someones, and they aren't all *Jäger-Suchers*, who live and breathe to kill us."

You'd think Alex would be happy to know that she'd struck fear into the hearts of werewolves everywhere. Strangely, she wasn't. She felt like Godzilla, stomping on all the little racing ant-people.

"You're safe here," she said soothingly.

His dark gaze seemed to bore into hers. "Are we?"

CHAPTER 18

Did he know?

That was impossible. If Daniel thought she was working for Edward, he certainly wouldn't be this nice to her. No one would be.

The reminder of the second reason that she was here, and what she was supposed to do once she had what she'd come for, made Alex's stomach pitch and her skin crawl.

She had a sudden image of Edward Mandenauer and a posse of J-S agents descending on Barlowsville, shooting wolves like fish in a barrel.

Alex gave a mental wince. She should probably stop being so buddy buddy with the enemy.

"You don't think you're safe?" she asked.

Daniel shrugged. "I know Edward."

"Personally?" Alex's voice lifted with surprise, and the older man smiled.

"Unfortunately, yes."

Alex opened her mouth to ask for this story, forgetting her resolve to stop befriending every werewolf that sat in her station, and Daniel's smile bloomed, happiness lighting his eyes and causing his slightly slumped shoulders to straighten. However, the expression wasn't for Alex but for the young man who'd just walked through the door.

"Wow" was all Alex could manage before the new arrival's gaze went to the counter, zeroed in on Daniel, and the same smile blossomed all over his face.

The guy was Calvin Klein model handsome—with feathered black hair, deep blue eyes, chiseled cheekbones, and a body that would make a werewolf jealous. Hell, she was.

He wore a blue, white, and black plaid flannel shirt over what appeared to be an extremely tight white wife beater. She had time to wish it was warm enough in here to take off the flannel before she was distracted by how he filled out his jeans.

He strode straight for Daniel, and the older man stood, waiting for him with obvious pleasure. Alex figured he was Daniel's son, or maybe his grandson, produced before whatever tragedy had made Daniel choose to become a werewolf. Though what could have induced this specimen to become one, too—and hide himself away here in the Arctic when he could be strutting shirtless on a catwalk somewhere—Alex probably didn't want to know. Then Hot Guy reached them, cupped Daniel's jaw, and planted one right on his lips.

Alex blinked. Then she blinked again. Then she glanced around the coffee shop, but no one appeared as shocked by this as she was. She suspected they'd seen it before.

Eventually the new arrival stopped giving Daniel the tongue and lifted his head, meeting Alex's eyes and winking. "Probably want to close that mouth, ma'am, 'fore you catch flies."

He had the most gorgeous southern accent, incongruous with the flannel shirt and heavy boots he wore, and the land of ice he'd just walked in from.

"I—uh—yeah," Alex returned. Why she'd thought all werewolves were straight she had no idea. In truth, she'd never thought much about werewolves beyond how she could kill them.

Daniel turned, stars in his eyes, goofy smile on his lips, and the young man reached for Daniel's hand with a gesture Alex found very sweet. They stood there, the tall, muscular, youthful demigod and the short, skinny, dapper old gentleman, both grinning like idiots. Alex just hoped Daniel didn't get his heart broken anytime soon. She didn't want to be here to see it. She liked Daniel.

And since when did she like a werewolf?

"This is Josh," Daniel said.

"Hi." Alex offered her hand. "I'm—"

"Alex." Josh placed his palm against hers. His was toasty warm, despite having just come in from the cold without gloves. "I know." He shrugged, and his lips quirked engagingly. "We all do."

"Right." She'd met them in the town square while naked. That should bother her, but it didn't. There were a lot of things that used to bother Alex that didn't any longer.

"We're off to the market," Daniel said.

"We need to get some hamburger," Josh informed him.

Alex hoped hamburger was actually hamburger around here.

"Don't you have a job?" she blurted.

Daniel cast her a quick glance, and she realized she might as well have asked: *Is he your boy toy?*

But Josh just laughed. "We own the movie theater. Don't have to go in until later."

"There's a movie theater?"

"It's a town. Why wouldn't there be?"

Considering that the inhabitants of this town liked to

spend their evenings running on four paws beneath the light of the moon, Alex didn't figure a theater would get much business.

"What do you show?" she asked. "*Wild Kingdom* kind of stuff?"

Josh's forehead creased. "What?"

"Caribou? Rabbits? Whitetail? Maybe some zebra and antelope to jazz things up?"

Josh glanced at Daniel, who shrugged. "She thinks we show films of prey."

Understanding spread over Josh's face, quickly followed by confusion again. "Why?"

"She's still new." Daniel patted Josh's arm. "She'll catch up."

"Catch up?" Alex echoed. "To the caribou?"

But the two were already headed for the door.

"See you tomorrow!" Daniel called as they left.

"You seem worried." Rose had left her perch at the cash register to join Alex behind the counter.

"I hope he doesn't get hurt."

"Hurt?" Rose repeated, appearing genuinely puzzled.

"Young guy, older man. Usually doesn't last."

Rose laughed. "They've been together since 1783."

"They— What?"

"You thought they met here?"

Alex wasn't sure what she'd thought.

"You know," Rose said quietly. "We're people most of the time."

Alex tilted her head, studying Rose's serene face. "I don't understand what you're trying to say."

"You think we're different than other people? We really aren't."

"You turn into wolves beneath the moon, Rose. How different can you get?"

"But when the moon is down, we're just like everyone else."

"Order!" Joe sang.

Alex began to load her tray. "You sure don't eat like everyone else."

Rose laughed. "Barlowsville is the same as any other city in the Arctic. Coffee shop that serves the same food as a thousand other coffee shops. Movie theater that shows the same movies they show at any other theater in Alaska. Bookstore with the same books. Shoe shop. Grocery store."

"Big white laboratory with your own resident Dr. Frankenstein," Alex continued. "Lord of the Wolves telling everyone where to go and what to do. And your own personal blood bank of Inuit."

Rose's eyes widened. Alex wanted to bite off her tongue. Why not? It would grow back.

"Julian really must trust you," she said.

Alex moved back to the counter and began to unload her very full tray in front of the single customer that remained from the breakfast rush. She glanced at the clock. She had maybe half an hour before the lunch crowd descended.

She smiled at the young woman, who could have been the local schoolteacher if there'd been a school. "Anything else?"

Mouth already full of scrambled eggs, she shook her head, and Alex turned back to Rose. "Why would you say that?"

"You've been here what? A day? And you've already met Cade; you know what he does. Not to mention the village." Rose peered into her face as if she might discover all of Alex's secrets. "New wolves don't usually learn about the Inuit until *after* the first full moon."

Alex wasn't going to admit how she'd discovered Cade,

or why Julian had taken her to Awanitok. But she wasn't sure what she should say instead, so she said nothing.

"And now with all the trouble over there—"

"You know about that?"

"Not much stays secret around here."

Alex hoped that wasn't true.

"Any idea who's gone rogue?" Alex asked.

"No one in this village!" Rose put her hand over her ample bosom. "We would never hurt anyone."

Rose obviously believed that, as did the rest of the café. Everyone in the restaurant was bobbing their head in agreement. They'd been listening in. Considering their werewolf ears, it was hard not to.

Rose nibbled her lower lip. "Julian hasn't brought home a new wolf since—" She broke off.

"Alana. I know."

Rose's eyes widened even farther. "You won't hurt him, will you?"

"Hurt? Him?" Alex thought he'd be more likely to *kill* her. But she decided to keep that to herself.

Rose lifted one shoulder. "He's our alpha. I don't know what we'd do without him."

"Anything you wanted," Alex muttered.

Rose tilted her head. "You don't seem to like him."

"What's to like? He's an arrogant, domineering control freak."

Rose's lips curved. "We are what we were when we were made." At Alex's confused expression, she continued, "He was a Viking. Becoming a werewolf didn't change that."

"Becoming a werewolf changes everything," Alex said.

"Yes and no. At least for wolves like us. Certainly there

are lifestyle changes." She tapped one ear. "No more silver hoops. Can't make any plans for one night out of twenty-eight. But when we become one of Julian's wolves, we retain who we were. Haven't you?"

Alex nodded absently. She had. She couldn't argue. But Rose's explanation had given her an idea.

"So Barlow is a dick because he was a Viking, and Daniel was, is, and always will be gay, just like Josh."

"And Joe will always love music and people and food, and I will always love Joe," Rose said.

"What if you were a killer when you were made?" Alex asked. "What then?"

Rose, who'd been smiling at Alex as if she were the smartest kid in this year's kindergarten class, froze. "I—uh—what?"

"If fabulous human beings become fan-damn-tastic were-wolves, then it follows that a psychotic killer as a human would become an equally psychotic killer as a werewolf."

"I suppose," Rose agreed. "But Julian would never allow someone like that to become one of us."

Alex glanced out the front window as a cloud danced over the sun. "What if he didn't know?"

Julian was so furious when he came into the house that he took one look at the empty fireplace, absently thought about building a fire, and kaboom—he had one.

Flames shot up the chimney with such force he was concerned he might set the roof ablaze. As it was he singed the arm of a chair that he'd placed a little too close to survive spontaneous combustion.

"*Faet!*" he muttered, then closed his eyes and recalled how he'd pressed a kiss to Alex's head and murmured *shh.*

The image caused a fresh burst of fury, allowing him to put out the fire without having to climb onto the roof or even step a single foot into the living room.

Then he strode through his house, tossed off his clothes, turned the shower to Arctic, and stepped right in. He hadn't made a mistake like that with his magic since . . .

Julian yanked his head from beneath the frigid stream. He hadn't made a mistake like that with his magic since he'd discovered it.

Alex took over his mind, his body, his emotions. He had a hard time controlling himself in any way when she was near. Which, if he wasn't careful, was going to lead to a lot more serious mistakes than starting a wildfire in his fireplace.

How long was he going to be able to stand having her in town? How long before he did something he really regretted like—

"Like what?" he muttered. "You've already slept with her. What else is there?"

Shh. His own voice drifted through his mind, followed by that image of himself kissing her hair, holding her close.

The jittery roll in his gut reminded him that there were a lot worse things than *sleeping* with the enemy.

Julian shut off the water and heaved a relieved sigh. He might live in the Arctic, he might be a Viking by birth, but no man enjoyed ice on his genitals for very long.

Julian donned a fresh pair of jeans and a MINNESOTA VI-KINGS sweatshirt that someone had given him for Christmas as a joke—really, who wore purple and yellow on purpose—and stepped onto the porch.

His snowmobile sat at the north end of the house. Minutes later he raced toward Awanitok where Jorund the younger told him what had happened to Dr. Cosgrove.

"When he didn't come to work, his assistant went to the

house. She found him—" The old man sighed. "—or what was left of him in the backyard."

"The first body was discovered several yards *outside* of town," Julian clarified, and Jorund nodded.

Which meant the rogue was becoming bolder.

"No one saw anything this time?"

"No, *Ataniq*."

The two of them stared down at the bloody blotch in the snow. There were no tracks. The snow was like ice. A common problem around here.

"Order everyone to stay inside after dark," Julian said.

"There is a lot of dark at this time of year."

"Then there will be a lot of staying inside until this is over," Julian snapped, and went home.

Ella stood on his porch wearing a concerned expression. "Have you seen Alex?" she asked.

He'd thought she would go back to Ella's that morning, but if she hadn't . . . maybe she'd stayed with Cade just to piss him off.

Julian's blood pressure rose at the idea of what else she could do with Cade that would piss him off. "She wouldn't dare," he muttered.

"Dare what?" Ella tilted her head. "Your face is getting red."

Julian imagined steam coming out of his ears. Big mistake because the next thing Ella said was: "There's steam coming out of your ears."

If he wasn't careful he was going to melt his brain into gruel.

"*Faet!*" Julian said. "*Faet. Faet. Faet.*" Anything to keep himself from imagining something he might not be able to recover from.

"Calm down." Ella opened the door to his house and

stepped inside, drawing him along with cool, slim fingers on his arm. "I'm sure she's around here somewhere."

Julian was sure she was, too. Because if she'd gone too far he'd be gripping his gut and wishing for a basketball-size Tums.

And that thought had him sitting in the nearest chair and putting his head between his knees. *Idiot.* How was he ever going to get rid of her?

Ella bent down, put a hand on his leg, and peered into his face. "Maybe you should tell me what's going on."

"I wish I knew."

"She bothers you."

"Bother." He laughed. "Yeah. That's what she does."

"She seems angry. Like she doesn't want to be here. Like she despises you. I can't believe—" She paused. "You wouldn't—I mean you didn't—"

Julian's patience snapped. "Just ask me what you want to know, Ella."

"Tell me that you didn't make her like us against her will, Julian."

He remained silent. She *had* said not to tell her.

"How could you?" Ella straightened and stepped back, as if she could no longer stand to be near him. "The poor thing."

Poor thing? Alexandra Trevalyn was *not* a poor thing.

"There are countless women in this village who would be happy if you looked their way. Women in Awanitok as well. You didn't have to—"

"Hold on." Julian lifted his head. "Why do you think I brought her here?" His eyes widened as her cheeks flushed and she glanced down. "You thought I saw her, wanted her, and took her?"

"You're a Viking," she said simply.

"I haven't raped or pillaged in at least a decade."

Ella gave him a look that only a true Frenchwoman could give—one that made Julian want to apologize not only for being sarcastic, but for every transgression he'd ever made in all his lifetimes.

Julian sighed. "You know why I went to LA." Ella was the only one he'd told.

"You had a lead on Alana's killer. But you came back with—" Ella's mouth continued to open and close, but no sound came out for several seconds. "Julian," she finally managed. "What did you do?"

"Isn't it obvious?"

She smacked him in the back of the head as if he were a recalcitrant student and she a teaching nun from the Dark Ages. "Why would you make the woman who killed your heart, your soul, your *wife* like us? That's a gift."

"She'd consider it a curse. She *does* consider it a curse. Which is the whole point."

"You had better explain your point, because I am not seeing it."

"She believes she killed a monster."

"But she did not."

"She'll never understand that until she understands   "

"Us," Ella finished, comprehension dawning in her eyes. "You made her like us so she could see what she'd done and agonize about it forever."

Julian spread his hands and shrugged.

"Fool," she snapped.

Julian pulled back quickly before she smacked him again. But Ella was so furious, she began to pace like a caged . . . wolf.

"You brought the enemy into our midst. You think she won't tell Edward where we are and how to get here." Ella stood and turned toward the door. "She's probably halfway to Juneau already."

Julian caught her hand, holding on when she tugged and snarled. "When I get too far away from her I get physically sick."

She stopped struggling, and her frown returned. "Why?"

"She was the first one of my wolves I ever tried to leave behind before she was able to fend for herself."

Ella gave him another look that would have melted metal and muttered a word that sounded suspiciously like "Ass" before continuing: "You believe the same thing would have happened if you'd left any of us too soon?"

"I did, until I went running the other night and had to stop because of the pain." He took a deep breath, then let it out. "I think it's only her."

"There's something different about Alex," Ella murmured. "You need to find out what it is."

Julian was already on top of that. He stifled a wince at the innuendo and the predictable image it brought to mind.

He'd meant to tell Cade about this development when the two of them were alone—call him foolish, but he hadn't wanted Alex to know that the absence of her company turned him into a weak, writhing wimp—but he hadn't done so yet. Now would be a good time.

Julian stood. "Alex may be at the lab. You want to come along?"

"I need to get back to work." Ella ran their version of a post office, routing all deliveries through the Inuit village. "If she isn't with Cade, let me know. Otherwise I'll see her when I get home tonight."

"You don't want her out of your house?"

"What?" Ella had been heading for the door, but now she turned. "Why?"

"You said she was the enemy."

"I've changed my mind. Edward would kill her just as quickly as he'd kill any one of us. He'd think she was the enemy, too." Her lips curved. "The enemy of my enemy is my friend."

"Alex is a killer."

"We're all killers, Julian."

"That's the wolf; it's instinct. We don't—"

"We *do*," she interrupted. "Only once, *oui,* for most of us, but we kill. It's instinct, as you say. At the time we do not know any better. But wasn't it instinct for Alex to shoot a werewolf? At the time, did she not know any better?"

"I—" Julian paused, uncertain. "I still wouldn't think you'd want her in your house."

Ella stared at him as if he'd lost his mind, then muttered something in French, ending with a word that sounded like an epithet: *"Hommes!"*

Translation: *Men!*

"What did I do?" Julian asked.

"I would not throw that poor girl from my home. She is the victim here."

Julian snorted, then backed up with his hands raised when Ella's eyes narrowed. He might be the alpha, but that also meant he had the brains to know when his interests were best served by shutting up.

"You said you had not raped and pillaged in decades, but making someone a werewolf against their will *is* rape."

He opened his mouth, but she made a sharp gesture and he shut it again.

"She has had her very self stripped away." Ella walked to the front door, opened it, then glanced back. "You need to think about that, Julian."

Her anger caused Ella's accent to deepen, and his name came out sounding very French indeed.

CHAPTER 19

Alex was ankle-deep in the lunch rush when Ella walked by the front window. She opened her mouth to call out, then shut it again when Ella backtracked, peered in through the glass, then made use of the door.

Alex had one seat left at the counter, and Ella took it. "You're here," she said.

"Where did you think I was?"

Ella glanced around, then lowered her voice. "Halfway to Juneau."

Alex had leaned in so she could catch the words and in doing so caught a whiff of—

"Julian," she murmured.

Ella's gaze lifted, and for an instant guilt flickered in her eyes. But guilt for what? Did Ella and Julian have a thing going on? Did she think Alex would care?

Strangely, Alex did. The thought of Julian in bed with this gorgeously exotic Frenchwoman, touching her the way he'd touched Alex, made her so angry she thought she might actually shift in the daylight, too.

The thick plastic glass Alex had been holding in preparation for filling it with Pepsi for the young, Hispanic man on the other end of the counter erupted into several dozen shards. Everyone in the restaurant glanced her way.

"Alex?" Ella murmured. "Are you all right?"

"Uh—yeah." Alex dumped the pieces into the trash. Her palm appeared no worse for the explosion, so she filled another glass and set it carefully in front of her customer before returning to Ella.

By then, she was calmer, though she wouldn't say exactly calm. The scent of Julian that wafted her way every time the door opened and sent a gust of air across Ella made Alex both furious and nostalgic. She missed him.

And wasn't that just the most pathetic thing ever?

"Why would I be halfway to Juneau?" she asked.

"If he'd done to me what he did to you, I would be."

"He told you?" This, after he'd insisted Alex keep who she was a secret, that if anyone in Barlowsville discovered the truth, they'd want her dead. Was Ella an exception to the rule? Or did Barlow just want Ella to have first crack at her head?

Alex glanced around the restaurant to make sure no one was listening. However, considering they were all werewolves, a private conversation . . . just wasn't happening.

"What the hell?" Alex whispered.

"He's searching for you."

Alex's eyes narrowed. "And now I'm searching for him, too."

She had to wait until the wave of customers receded. She couldn't just up and leave Cyn and Rose snowed under, and it wasn't as though Barlow was going anywhere. According to Ella, he'd already been to Awanitok and was headed to see Cade. He'd probably still be there when she got through.

As she stepped out of the café, Ella zoomed by on a

snowmobile, disappearing into the steadily descending gloom in the direction of the Inuit village.

Alex went to the house to change clothes. The ones she wore now smelled like bacon grease and bleach. While there, she took a shower to get the scent out of her hair.

Alex had never minded working as a waitress, but she'd never cared for how she smelled afterward. Now that her nose was ultra-sensitive, she cared for it even less.

She set the cash she'd made that day on top of the nightstand. Tomorrow she'd buy some jeans and T-shirts for work. Ella was never going to get the scent of hash browns out of those wool slacks.

Alex strolled from her end of the village in the direction of Barlow's place. People continued to greet her as if she was one of them. No one looked at her like she was a serial killer. Although, now that she thought about it, Ella hadn't looked at her that way, either. Ella had looked at her as if she wanted to pat Alex on the hand and give her a hug.

Alex opened the rear door of the laboratory. She heard their voices right away.

"I can't get more than a few miles from her and I become physically ill."

Alex crept closer, frowning. That was Barlow.

"I've never heard of such a thing before." Cade.

"Find out why. Make it stop. She can't stay here forever."

"Why not?" Cade sounded very confused.

"Yeah." Alex stepped into the room. "Why not?"

It was a testament to how engrossed they'd been in whatever they were discussing that they hadn't heard her come in. Both men started, then spun—Julian snarling, Cade wide-eyed.

"Where have you been?" Julian demanded.

"Halfway to Juneau."

"Huh?" Cade glanced at Julian, "I thought you couldn't be separated."

Julian's gaze held hers as he answered his brother. "She wasn't halfway to Juneau."

"What's going on?" Alex asked.

"Nothing for you to worry about," Julian said, at the same time Cade answered, "He gets sick if you're too far away from him."

Julian glared at Cade, who spread his hands. "How could she not know this?"

"She doesn't get sick," Julian said between clenched teeth. "I do."

"You sure?" Cade asked, turning to Alex. "Any desire to throw up? Headaches, dizziness?"

Alex shook her head. "I thought that being a werewolf cured all ills."

"For him," Cade grabbed a pencil and scribbled on a yellow pad. "Apparently not."

Julian crossed to Alex. "Where were you?"

"Didn't Cade tell you? He sent me to Rose for a job."

"You're working?"

"I can't wear Ella's clothes forever."

"Of course you can." He waved his hand regally, dismissing Ella's charity as only a man could. "There's no reason for you to get a job. You're not—"

"Staying? From what I heard, you'd better hope that I am. Unless you're a big fan of puking." Alex squinted. "Is that steam coming out of your ears?"

He glanced over his shoulder at his brother, who was busy talking to himself and making notes on his yellow pad, then grabbed her elbow and half dragged, half led her down the hall and out the back door.

"Why are you here?" he asked.

"Two reasons." Alex yanked her arm from his grasp. "Why did you tell Ella about me?"

"I didn't." Alex raised her eyebrows, and he shrugged. "She figured it out. The way you behave, as if you hate me—"

"I do," she said, but there was no heat behind the words.

"She figured that I'd made you against your will; then she added the fact that I'd gone to LA to look for Alana's killer, and come back with you and—" He shrugged. "She's pretty damn mad about it."

"Why didn't she kill me before I knew that she knew? I'm going to be ready for it now."

"Ready for what?" Julian asked, even as understanding spread across his face. "She isn't going to kill you. She was mad at me. She called you 'poor thing.'" He made a face that revealed what he thought of that statement.

Alex had to agree. She did not much care for being called "poor thing."

"You said two." Alex glanced up. Barlow leaned against the building watching her. "You came here for two reasons."

"Oh." For an instant Alex couldn't remember what the other one had been. Discovering her secret revealed, yet still being alive to worry about it despite Barlow's threats to the contrary, had thrown her off her game. "We are what we were when we were made, right?"

"Yes," he said slowly. "That's what this—" He waved a hand at her, then himself. "—is all about. You're still you, despite being marked by the moon."

"Marked by you," she muttered.

"Same thing."

"There's a rogue wolf." He seemed startled by the change in subject, but he nodded. "If I'm the same at heart when woman and wolf, then so's this rogue."

"I'm not following."

"A psychotic killer in *both* forms."

Julian straightened so abruptly, Alex had to force herself not to back away. "I don't make wolves lightly, Alex."

"Except for me."

His teeth ground together, the sound reminiscent of a bulldozer rolling over gravel. "That was hardly done lightly. And I knew all about you before I did it."

Not all, Alex thought.

"Who's the most likely candidate for psychotic killer of the week?" she asked.

"You," he muttered.

Alex didn't bother to comment. She could claim she didn't kill *people*. He'd swear she did. They'd start to argue and blah, blah, blah.

"Think back on who you've made," she said. "Did you know all of them as well as you knew me?" *Or thought you did.*

"None of my wolves were killers when I made them," he insisted. "Why do you care? It's my Indian village that's being targeted, my people who are being accused."

She couldn't tell him the truth—that she believed his rogue and her father's killer were one and the same—so she told him a different truth instead.

"I'm good at finding murderous werewolves. It's kind of what I do."

"Did," he muttered.

"Just because you made me one, too, doesn't mean I lost the ability to track them. You should let me help."

"Help?" he echoed as if he didn't know the word.

"I'll find the rogue for you, Barlow. You can count on it."

She sounded sincere, and for an instant Julian felt something like hope. She was one of the best hunters Edward had ever had, second only to the man himself now that Leigh Tyler had gotten pregnant and retired. Although that rumor was so bizarre Julian had a hard time believing it. Still, there'd been no whispers lately of Leigh blasting her way through more than her share of werewolves. So something strange had definitely happened.

Julian had never understood why Edward allowed Alex to leave his agency and run rogue. He thought the old man was up to something there; he just couldn't figure out what.

"You never answered my question," Julian said. "Why do you care?"

"I live here now. Sounds like I could be living here for the foreseeable future."

Julian stifled a growl. Not if he could help it.

"I don't want to find myself in the middle of a Barlow family civil war."

Might it come to that? Would his Inuit relatives begin to hunt his werewolf offspring? Could the peace he'd found here deteriorate into another war?

Julian sighed. *Yeah.*

Despite her obvious skill at the job, and his need for it, Julian just couldn't set Alex loose on his people. There was no telling what she might do to get her answers.

"We'll search together," he said.

"What?" The slight smile on her lips froze. "No. I work alone."

"Not anymore."

Julian nearly laughed as Alex sputtered and stomped. She couldn't seem to find her words, and that suited him just fine. He liked her best when she wasn't talking.

An image of what she was usually doing when she wasn't talking—*him*—flitted through his mind, and for the first time that he could remember, it didn't make him angry and horny. It just made him horny.

The woman was the best lay he'd ever had.

Julian's heart seemed to stop as he heard his own thoughts. What was the matter with him?

He took several deep gulps of the clear, icy air. Unfortunately, the air didn't smell clear—it smelled like her.

"He's really your brother, right?" Alex murmured.

Julian, whose face had been tilted to the graying sky, now glared down at her. "What the hell kind of question is that?"

"You don't look that much alike." She lifted a brow. "You certainly don't share a personality."

"What's your point?"

"When you call him your brother do you mean brother in arms, blood brother—" She made a strange gesture with her hands that reminded him of something done by an LA gang member on the only episode of *Cops* he'd ever seen, and muttered, "Bro!" in a voice that was very LA. "My brotha from anotha motha."

At his continuing blank expression she sighed, dropped her arms and continued, "Did you have the same mother, the same father? Did you grow up together? Is he really your brother or is it some kind of honorary title?"

"He's my brother," Julian said. They had not had the same mother, but back in the days of the Vikings, that wasn't uncommon. Life was hard, and women did not live long, which meant Vikings often had more than one wife.

"You still think he's the rogue?" Julian laughed. "All Cade ever cared about was healing. He wouldn't hurt anyone—then or now. He definitely couldn't kill them."

Alex's gaze went to the door that separated them from Cade. "I'll have to take your word for it since I wasn't around when he was completely human."

"You weren't around when any of us were completely human," Julian pointed out.

Which was going to make it damn difficult for her to discover who'd enjoyed spilling human blood even before he'd grown fangs.

"If someone were a crazed killer," Barlow continued, "wouldn't he have killed before now?"

"You'd think," Alex agreed. "Maybe he went somewhere else to do his dirty deeds. Anyone leave the village periodically?"

"Everyone leaves now and then. They aren't prisoners."

"*They* aren't," she muttered.

Julian sighed. "If that were the case, why start killing the Inuit when they were doing just fine somewhere else?"

"Yeah, why?"

"You're the expert."

"I don't deal in theories, I deal in . . ." Alex's voice trailed off and she frowned, seeming to search for a word.

Julian supplied one. "Death?"

Her eyes narrowed; then she shrugged. "Okay. I deal in death. I find them; then I kill them."

"Find *us*," he corrected. "Kill *us*."

"Whatever. Do you want me to help you or not?"

Julian was very tempted to say *not*. But he wasn't stupid. The quicker they discovered, then eliminated, the rogue, the fewer people would die. If it meant sleeping with the enemy, literally and figuratively, then . . .

"So be it."

CHAPTER 20

"We need bait," Alex muttered.

"Like . . ." Barlow's brow creased. "Meat?"

Meat. Wasn't that just like a werewolf?

"You call them meat," she said. "I call them people."

"You want to use a person as bait?"

"What would you suggest? We're talking *were,* not wolf."

"That would mean sacrificing at least one more life."

"I didn't say we were going to let them get killed for the greater good. I'm not you."

His teeth ground together again, and Alex resisted the urge to smirk. Why did she enjoy annoying him so much?

"Maybe you'd better tell me exactly what you have planned," Barlow said.

"Person strolling in the moonlight." Alex walked the fingers of one hand through the air. "Rogue werewolf." She used her other hand to mimic creeping behind. Then she flipped both palms up. "Voilà!"

"Dead person."

Alex rubbed her eyes. *Amateur.*

"It takes a wolf to catch a wolf. Luckily we have two."

Understanding bloomed across his face. "What do you want me to do?"

They met in the village square, seemingly by accident.

Julian grabbed her arm, holding tight when she struggled. "Where have you been?"

"None of your business." Alex managed to pull free, but only because he let her.

"Everyone here is my business."

"Not me." She turned away.

He growled and snatched her hand, twirling her back and into his arms. "Anyone watching?" he whispered.

"Anyone not?" she returned, then kicked him in the shin.

He was so surprised he let her go, then had to scramble to catch her again. Wary of her boots, he hoisted her over his shoulder without further ado and headed for his house.

"Already?" she murmured, flailing both arms and legs.

He didn't answer, just carted her out of the square—ignoring the knowing grins of three-quarters of the village—down the street and into his house, where he dumped her onto her feet in front of the large picture window.

"You told me to make it believable." He ducked when she took a swing at him.

"By arguing in front of everyone!" She threw up her hands, as if they really were arguing. Julian wasn't certain they weren't. His blood pressure was definitely on the rise. "That wasn't much of an argument."

"I'm the alpha." He took a determined step closer, smirking when she took a quick step back. "There's never much of an argument with me."

She snorted, but when he took another step in her direction—a big one that nearly brushed them together—

the laughter died, and she shoved at his chest. "You manhandle everyone who defies you?"

"Only you."

"I'm the only one who defies you, or I'm the only one you manhandle?"

"Yes," he answered.

Did she even realize that her fingertips had crept beneath the collar of his flannel shirt and were running lightly across his collarbone? Probably not since he'd just discovered that his hands had reached out to steady her hips and stayed there.

"Anyone watching?" she murmured as he continued to crowd her and she continued to retreat.

"Anyone not?" he answered, his mouth a breath from hers.

The plan was simple. The two of them would make a huge show of arguing in the village square. He would drag her bodily to his house, where they would stand in plain sight, kiss, then turn off the lights.

Once the entire village believed they were doing the horizontal mambo—again—they'd sneak out a window, shapeshift, and hie away to Awanitok. There, George would be out strolling, seemingly clueless and just waiting to be eaten.

However, the plan went slightly awry when Alex's shoulders met the window with a muffled thud. Instead of hitting the lights, Julian captured her mouth with his.

She'd told him to make it believable.

Her lips parted—on a sigh or a curse, he wasn't sure. With Alex sometimes they were the same. Her fingers clutched at his shirt even as his hands tightened on her hips. They were plastered together, her back against the window, as their tongues met and did the dance of the ages.

Then she was sliding downward, drawing him down as well. They hit the floor, their mouths still melded, their bodies, too. He braced himself, hands on either side of her. He was so much bigger than she was. Not that he could hurt her—not permanently. But he didn't want this to end. Not yet.

She nipped his lip; he sucked on hers. The combination of sharp teeth and soft tongue was, as always, seductive. He lowered his body, the erection he'd gotten the instant he'd tossed her over his shoulder landing safe in the cradle of her thighs.

She gasped, arched, the movement pressing them together in both new and familiar ways. Her neck, so long and slim and white, slid along his mouth, and he remembered taking her skin, marking her, and he wanted to do it again. Since he'd never been one to deny himself—*Viking*—he did.

She tasted like fury—heat and blood—everything that had made him what he was, everything he both loved and loathed in this world.

Her hands beneath his shirt were cool. They felt like heaven against his flushed skin. Her hair brushed his cheek, sending her scent—lemon ice—across his face. The flavor of her mouth made him desperate to plunge within.

Their clothes fell away—boots, shirts, jeans—and in moments they lay naked on his living room floor.

He lifted his head, shifted his body, and she put her palm against his chest, staying him. Confused, he glanced into her eyes. "This is supposed to be pretend," she said.

He froze as reality tumbled in. The argument. The stakeout. The rogue. Damn.

"I've never been very good at it." He rolled off her, his erection dying in an instant.

She came up on one elbow. "Don't sell yourself short," she said. "You're very good at it."

The twist she put on the final word left no doubt the *it* she was talking about. The mark on her neck was already fading, and he wanted to put it there again. He wanted to mark her in such a way that everyone in this town and every other would know that she was his.

He sighed and laid his arm over his face. What was wrong with him?

She wasn't his. He didn't want her to be. But tell that to his treacherous body.

"You think we've been down here long enough for everyone to believe we're . . . you know?"

"Yeah," he said. "I'm sure everyone believes we're *you knowing* our brains out."

She laughed, and he was so surprised, he dropped his arm and got an eyeful of her bare-naked ass as she crawled away from him.

"Hey!" He wrapped his fingers around her ankle.

She paused and glanced back. The sight of her on her knees, her hair swaying in time with the light sway of her breasts, made his penis consider a repeat erection.

"We need to get to the village before the rogue really does eat George," she said.

He let go of her ankle, rolling onto his feet.

She tackled him before he could stand, throwing her body atop his. "We're supposed to be doing the horizontal bop, Barlow. Don't stand up and show everyone that we're not."

He really *was* no good at pretending. Which was proved when his semi-erect penis poked her in the belly.

"Maybe later." She leaned down and kissed him, quick

and hard, before she came again to her knees and crawled out of the living room, smacking her hand against the light switch, plunging the room into darkness as she stood.

Julian continued to lie on the floor, willing his erection to wither—hey, there was a first time for everything—and not having much luck.

Maybe later?

How on earth did she expect him to function with those words echoing in his ears?

The sound of a window being opened at the back of the house was followed by a series of moans and grunts that did nothing to aid in his withering.

Shape-shifting wasn't easy. Unless you were him.

Julian closed his eyes, breathed in, breathed out, and eventually managed to stop imagining Alex naked on her knees. By the time he made his way to the bedroom, she was a wolf—sleek and soft, her green eyes shining from her tawny wolf face. She leaped onto the sill and disappeared through the opening, the crunch of her paws on the snow outside a siren call to the wolf awakening within him.

Then he was running, springing from the floor as a man, going through the window as a wolf, landing next to her mid-lope as together they welcomed the night.

Alex felt the pull of the moon, a shimmer like lust deep within. She wanted to tilt her muzzle to the sky and howl. She wanted to roll in the snow; she wanted to tumble, snout-over-paws, across the ground. She wanted to get all tangled up.

With him.

She could no longer deny that something in Julian Barlow called to something in her—and not just when they were wolves.

The silver orb seemed to whisper her name. The moon knew her, and she knew it. When the moon called, Alex would answer. It had marked her as one of the children of the night.

Running beneath the shimmery glow both soothed and energized. She was wolf and woman, strength and intelligence in perfect form.

The dark side beckoned. She knew she should resist, but she was helpless against it. She couldn't leave until she had what she'd come here for. But the longer she remained, the more she became one with the moon, with this other half of herself, the less chance she had of finding the woman she'd been before he had changed her. When she was like this she didn't want to.

Barlow ran at her side, his golden fur spiked by the shimmering sheen. Their claws clicked against the ice-soaked land in perfect syncopation. She could swear his heart and hers beat in the rhythm of time.

Then he swerved, bumping into her, sending her tumbling across the ground. Before she could right herself, he pounced and together they frolicked, like puppies, cubs, kittens—something young and furry—beneath the smiling, brilliant moon.

They wrestled and rolled, striving for dominance—a game and a gamble she lost. He pinned her to the ground, her underside exposed, his mouth at her neck, teeth just pricking the skin beneath her fur. And as before, his penis pressed against her belly—hard and pulsing—calling to the lust that lived within her for both him and the night.

They stayed like that, him above and in control, her on her back barely breathing, and she began to imagine his mounting her, her letting him. He'd ride her from behind, perhaps even bite her as he came, then she did.

He let go, and the sudden release of her throat from captivity had Alex spinning from back to front—the instinct of an animal to protect its soft side—where she met him face-to-face as he hunkered shoulders low, tail end high, wiggling in anticipation of play.

He feinted; she parried; then he was running, she was chasing. They went skidding across the ice. She felt like a kid again, until she remembered that she'd never *been* a kid.

Had he?

The distant howl of a wolf had them both pausing mid-wiggle. Alex knew with an instinct she hadn't realized she possessed that the howl had been that of an actual wolf. But the call reminded them both of why they were here and sent them trotting briskly in the direction of where they needed to be. Clouds danced over the moon; then snow began to tumble down.

Barlow had taken a quick trip to Awanitok that afternoon and had an equally quick chat with George. The young man was supposed to wait until he heard Barlow's howl before walking about in the night like the foolish boy he wasn't.

The Inuit settlement was quiet and dark as they approached, until something moved on the outskirts.

The ruff on Alex's neck went up. She lifted her nose.

George.

The kid had heard the call of the wolf, but, unlike them, he'd been unable to distinguish wolf from werewolf, so he'd exited his home and begun his stroll. He was already leaving the boundaries of the village.

Barlow jerked his head, indicating Alex should go in one direction; he would go in the other. They needed to be closer to George, and they needed to stay downwind.

Alex stalked the boy as he clumped along, making as

much noise as he could, whistling, too. If the rogue was out there, it couldn't help but hear him.

The snow had thickened, the wind had come up. At times the flakes became so frenzied, Alex had a hard time seeing.

Her gaze scanned the area. Flat in some places, there were also mounds of snow and chunks of ice big enough to hide a wolf. Combined with all the nooks and crannies within the town itself plus the damnable snowstorm, the rogue could be anywhere.

Then something moved, a shadow just there, low to the ground and very quick. Alex looked for Barlow, didn't see him, which didn't mean he wasn't there. Considering who— make that *what*—he was, he might be invisible. He'd been so before.

Regardless, she needed to get closer to George. If the rogue attacked, someone had to stop it.

She slunk from behind a building, slithered along its edge, blending into the swirling shadows as best she could as she kept her gaze on the lump of snow and ice where she'd seen the movement.

It hadn't been wolf-like. Then again it hadn't really been human. Alex tilted her head, considering. Maybe the movement had been Barlow.

She blew air out her nose, pawed the snow a little, confused. She wanted to charge over there and discover what was going on. But she couldn't reveal her presence and perhaps let the rogue get away for good.

Almost as if he'd heard her thoughts, or perhaps merely seen the shadow, George ventured closer to the suspicious pile of snow. Alex whined, just a little, hoping he would hear her and hesitate.

Instead George walked nearer and nearer the place where

danger might lie, and Alex couldn't stay in the shadows any longer. If the rogue crouched behind that glistening white mound, it would kill the boy before she could stop it.

As there was no cover once she left the protection of the buildings, Alex didn't even try to be subtle. She shot across the distance separating them, headed straight for George.

A loud *crack* split the night an instant before a wolf erupted straight through the snowbank. Covered in white, she couldn't see the true shade of its coat, and the animal was moving too fast to catch a glimpse of its eyes or anything else. The beast ran straight for George.

Alex leaped at the boy, knocking him to the ground, then rolling to her feet, trying to put herself between the downed kid and the second wolf.

Before she could gain her balance, the animal hit her broadside, and she flew off her paws, slamming into the ice hard enough to stun.

At the same time she heard another crack, wondered distantly what it had been, even as she waited for the wolf to tear at her throat or her belly.

And by the way—where in hell was Barlow?

Then he landed next to her in a heap. It took an instant before she understood that this wolf *was* Barlow. But why had he been chasing George? Why had he knocked her down?

And what was that smell?

Alex rolled onto her belly just as George came to his knees. "Someone's shooting at us," he said.

Alex glanced at Barlow. Flames sputtered in the center of his chest.

"Or maybe just at you two," George murmured.

Alex threw her body atop Julian's. Her fur caught fire.

George tried to help by scooping snow in his hands and tossing it on top of them both. He managed to put out Alex, but Barlow was another story.

Because once a silver bullet pierced a werewolf somewhere vital, they were done for.

CHAPTER 21

"Ooooooo!"

The howl rose through the sifting snow toward the grainy, hidden moon.

Alex wished she had a gun, and fingers, so she could end Barlow's torment. Her throat ached to join him as he howled out the remaining seconds of his life.

George had run back to town, presumably to find water—a bucket, a hose, a fire hydrant. It wouldn't do any good, but it gave the boy something to do.

Her eyes prickled—the smoke, the stinging snow, that was all—as Alex fought the wolf's urge to run away. Barlow might be the bane of her existence, but she wasn't going to let him die alone.

"Ooooo—whooo!"

The shift in the howl from mindless pain and fury to a distinguishable word had Alex tilting her head, stepping closer. The snow had become a blizzard, and she could just discern the outline of Barlow shimmering—there, and then gone and then there again. Was he getting taller as he died?

"Whooooooooo dares?"

The words echoed across the night as Barlow, naked and man-size, his chest a bloody mess, burst from the swirling blanket of white.

His arms stretched outward, muscles flexing, fingertips twinkling, as his head tilted back and the cords in his neck tightened. A sound of pure, animalistic rage lifted toward the moon and the silver bullet popped out of his chest, arcing through the chilly air and plopping into the snow with a wet *thunk*.

Alex stood there, mouth hanging open, tongue lolling free as the hole in his skin knit together and the burn marks faded away.

No wonder Edward wanted this guy dead.

George returned with a pail in one hand and a down quilt in the other. The snow had thickened considerably and Barlow had become a shadow again an instant before George tossed the quilt at Alex, then hauled back to toss the water in his direction.

Barlow stepped out of the snow and, shocked, George let go of the pail, which flew several feet in the other direction. From the sloshing sounds, it landed upside down.

"What?" the boy began. Then, "How?" He finished with, "Huh?"

"Did you tell anyone what happened?" Barlow asked.

George shook his head. "I didn't know if whoever shot you was still here or if the rogue was, too. I didn't want them hurt."

Barlow grunted, peering into the storm. "Get us some clothes," he ordered.

The kid ran. Alex didn't blame him. She wanted to.

Alex imagined herself, herself and began the annoyingly

slow process of becoming human again. She had a few things to ask the wolf-god.

"I am still so *pissed*!" Barlow muttered, then he stomped closer, knelt, and set his hand on her back, which was contorting this way and that as it went from wolf to woman.

As soon as he touched her, the world spun, and by the time Alex opened her eyes, she had legs, fingers, skin. She lay in the snow, dizzy and freezing, doing her best to catch up.

"What can't you do?" she muttered.

Barlow, who'd straightened and returned to staring at the swirling white, glanced over his shoulder. "What?"

"You can move at the speed of sound." He snorted. "Almost. You can become invisible." He shrugged. "Change the shade of your fur."

"Not sure about that." He turned again to the storm.

"Well, since you can heal silver, I'm betting turning from a golden wolf to a purple one wouldn't be any trouble for you at all."

"Mmm," he murmured.

"That's all you can say? Mmm?" She got to her feet, ignoring the burn of the ice against her soles. "You just popped a silver bullet out of your chest, Julian." Alex threw up her hands. "What the fuck?"

For an instant she considered that Barlow himself could be the werewolf that had murdered her father. He could heal silver; there wouldn't be a mark on him from the bullet she'd fired on that long-ago night. But if Barlow were the culprit, wouldn't Edward have mentioned that?

No, whispered a little voice. Because if he had, Alex would have shot Barlow the next time she saw him rather than allowing him to lead her to the werewolf village. And

the village was what Edward was after—that and the army
Barlow didn't appear to have.

Alex's mind whirled. Who was the bad guy? Who was
manipulating whom? Who could she trust?

"I don't know what I can do," Julian murmured, still facing away from her. "Most everything I've ever tried, I've
done."

"Maybe that's why someone tried to kill you."

Barlow turned then, eyebrows lifted. "They weren't trying to kill me, Alex, they were trying to kill you."

"Me? What did I do?"

If possible, Barlow's eyebrows went higher.

"Lately," she muttered.

Alex considered what had happened. She'd left the safety
of the village; there'd been a sharp crack, which she'd ignored in her concern for George. Barlow had burst *through*
the snowbank, knocked her aside, and then—

Crack!

"You pushed me out of the way," she said.

Barlow shrugged and didn't comment.

Why would anyone want to kill her? No one knew her
well enough yet to hate her.

It suddenly occurred to Alex that while she had not gotten
a good look at her father's killer, her father's killer might have
gotten a pretty good look at her. But if that was the case, why
hadn't the culprit outed her as a *Jäger-Sucher* to the others the
instant she'd loped into town?

Because to do that would be to admit that he or she had
not been the good little Barlow-escue werewolf he or she was
supposed to be but had instead been out killing *people*.

Alex thought it far more likely that the wolf, if it had recognized her—and maybe it hadn't, she'd been fifteen at the
time—would try to kill her. Now someone had.

Which meant her father's killer *was* here. Perhaps Edward hadn't been manipulating her—much—after all.

"Aren't you the slightest bit concerned?" Barlow asked. "I just told you someone tried to put a silver bullet into you, and you stand there staring into space."

"Werewolves try to kill me every damn day," Alex said. "It's when they try to be my friend that I get a little freaked out."

"Who said it was a werewolf?"

Alex scowled. "Who the hell else would it be?"

"Let's find out."

George appeared out of the ever-thickening snow, his arms full of clothing and boots. He dumped them onto the ground between Alex and Julian.

"Thanks," Julian said. "Now get inside and stay there."

The boy opened his mouth to argue. Julian narrowed his eyes, and George snapped it shut again, then spun on his heel and marched away.

Alex snorted and muttered something that sounded a lot like *wolf-god*. As if that were some kind of insult.

Julian wasn't sure where George had found the clothes, but he'd done a good job. Certainly everything was a bit tight on him, but Alex's apparel appeared just her size. Probably because he'd caught the kid staring at her ass on more than one occasion.

And why wouldn't he? It was a damn good ass.

Julian coughed to cover the growl that rumbled in his chest, then winced and put his hand over the shooting pain. He might have popped out a silver bullet, then healed the wound, but it still hurt and probably would for a good long while. He wasn't sure. He'd never healed silver before.

Had anyone?

Alex stomped her foot into a second boot and straightened. "Now what?"

Julian lifted his chin, indicating the ice mound where the shots had originated. "Now we see if there are any tracks worth tracking."

"But the ice—" she began, hurrying to keep up as he strode in that direction.

Julian kicked at the fluffy layer of white. "Snow," he said.

She smacked herself in the forehead. "Duh."

Julian had to stifle a smile. Sometimes she amused him.

Alex stopped abruptly and laid a hand on his arm. Julian paused and gazed at her quizzically.

"What if they're still there?" she murmured.

Julian started walking again. "If they were still there they'd have shot you while I was burning."

His amusement faded with those words. He might have angered out the bullet; he might have magically healed. But while the silver had been in his chest, while his skin had been sizzling and his hair had been frying, the agony had been beyond anything he'd ever known.

It had made him so mad.

When he'd seen the first shot kick up the snow a few inches from Alex's paws, rage had sparked, allowing him to burst through the icy bank that had concealed him. Then, when the bullet had slammed into him, his fury had exploded along with the flames.

They reached the looming hill of ice and stepped gingerly around its edge. Then together they stared at the rifle half covered with snow.

"Why would an Inuit shoot me?" Alex asked.

"True. They barely know you."

She laughed. Julian's smile broke free, but it faded as he continued to peer at the ground.

"Look."

He pointed at the tracks—first feet, but then several yards away from the village, out where the snow would have masked everything, the feet became paws. A few yards farther, the wind across the tundra had erased them completely.

"The rogue is both human and wolf," Julian said.

"Needed fingers to pull the trigger," Alex murmured. "And paws to get the hell gone. But how did he know what we were planning?"

Julian cut her a quick, curious glance, and she explained. "He—or she—knew we were coming. He brought a rifle loaded with silver. If he was here to eat another villager, no need for a gun."

Julian stared into the wall of swirling white. She was right.

"There's nothing else to see here," he said. "Let's go."

But Alex was staring into the storm now, too. "Shh," she whispered, head tilting, eyes narrowing.

Julian listened, detected nothing, held his breath and tried again. Somewhere out in that swirling white he heard the patter of paws.

He glanced at Alex. She lifted her chin, sniffed. So did he. Definitely a werewolf. But who? The snow, the wind, all the people who lived nearby were throwing off his nose.

Julian stepped forward, and Alex touched his arm, shook her head; then her gaze tracked to the right and she slowly lifted her arm, pointing to the glistening black wolf that burst from the night.

"Ella," he whispered.

They followed her back toward Awanitok. Julian bent and grabbed the discarded rifle as they hurried past. He didn't bother to check if there were any bullets left. He could smell them.

Ella appeared on her way somewhere, trotting purposefully through town as if she hadn't a care in the world.

"Just because she's here," Alex said, "doesn't mean she's evil."

"This from the woman who thinks that just because we breathe we're evil."

Alex didn't have a snappy comeback for that, and Julian would have asked why if Ella hadn't chosen that moment to turn into Jorund's backyard.

"Faet!" Julian spat, and began to run.

He came around the corner as the wolf gracefully leaped onto the back porch. Sliding glass doors reflected the swirling snow and the foggy sheen of the moon. Julian feared Ella would crash right through them.

Was Jorund sitting at his kitchen table, peacefully drinking tea? Did he have his aching feet propped up on an ottoman, glasses settled on his determined blade of a nose, a science-fiction novel—his favorite—open on his quilt-covered lap?

When the werewolf burst through his window would the old man spring up, tangle his feet in the quilt, and fall down? Break a hip? An arm? Have a heart attack? Any of those would be preferable to the alternative—bloody, painful death by rogue werewolf.

Julian couldn't let that happen. He lifted the rifle to his shoulder and sighted on Ella's flank.

"Wait," Alex whispered.

"No."

"Look."

Something in her voice stopped him. Perhaps that she'd tried *to* stop him. Alex would be the first person to let him shoot a werewolf—unless she had a very good reason not to.

The glass doors slid open. Jorund appeared in a wash of yellow light from his kitchen. He wore a black silk robe adorned with golden dragons and tied loosely with a matching sash. His hair flowed in a river of silver-threaded black past his shoulders, and he held a glass of red wine in one hand. Behind him, on the table, sat the bottle and a second, empty glass.

The old man stood to the side, and the wolf trotted in. Jorund let his free hand trail over her back, on his face an expression Julian had never seen there before.

"Maybe we'd better go," Alex said.

"Put down the gun, *Ataniq*." Jorund turned away, leaving the door open. "And come inside."

By the time Julian and Alex got there, Jorund had pulled out two more glasses and poured them each some wine. Ella was nowhere to be found, though Julian heard someone moving about in one of the bedrooms.

Jorund sat at the table. From the way he carefully adjusted his knee-length robe to avoid flashing them, he wore nothing beneath the silk. Julian was becoming more uncomfortable by the second. He downed his wine in a single swallow.

"George told me what you had planned."

Julian scowled. "He was supposed to tell no one."

"I'm the leader of this village, not you."

Annoyed, Julian snapped, "Yet you call me master."

"Courtesy title," the old man murmured.

"Then why did you send George to bring me here each time you found someone dead?"

"You promised to protect us from your wolves. You aren't living up to your end of the agreement. Why wouldn't I call you?"

"We haven't established that one of my wolves is *the* wolf."

The elder lifted his brows but didn't comment.

"Who else did George tell?" Alex asked. She had yet to touch her wine; she merely kept toying with the stem of the glass.

Jorund's gaze flicked to her, then back to Julian. "No one."

"Who did you tell?" Julian demanded.

"Just me," Ella said.

She'd donned a robe that matched Jorund's, and her pale skin held a flush across the cheeks.

"What's going on here?" Julian asked.

Ella's lips curved, and she entwined her fingers with Jorund's. The contrast of her youthful hand and his ancient, gnarled appendage was like a monkey's paw and a baby's fist. "I love him," she said. "And he loves me."

"Since when?"

"Twenty years now," Ella answered.

"Give or take," Jorund added.

"He's old enough to be your great-grandfather," Julian pointed out.

"I'm two hundred and forty-six years old, Julian."

"Got you there," Alex said.

Julian ignored her. "He's going to die, Ella, and you're not."

"Barring a silver bullet."

Julian took a second to scowl at Alex. He did *not* need any help. From her smirk, she was enjoying this.

"We wanted to talk to you about that."

Ella's comment brought Julian's attention back to them just as Jorund's hand jerked. "Not now," the old man murmured.

"Yes." Ella's grip tightened on his. "Now."

For an instant Julian wondered if Ella *had* been behind that shot. He really had no idea who to trust anymore. Everything he'd thought to be true was not.

He lifted his gaze from their linked fingers to Ella's dark eyes. "Talk to me about what?"

"I want you to make Jorund like us."

CHAPTER 22

Alex's amusement with Julian's obvious discomfort at the sexual activity of his "grandson" faded with Ella's words.

"Why?" she blurted.

Julian gave her another dirty look—he was getting very good at them—then glanced back at the Frenchwoman. "Why now?" he amended.

"Jorund's fading," she said simply.

Julian let his gaze wander over the old man. "He seems to be doing all right to me."

Jorund's lips twitched, but he didn't take the bait.

"Julian," Ella snapped, her impatience evident in her Frenchifying of his name. "If you do not do it, I will."

"Told you they all weren't as beta as you thought," Alex murmured, which earned her another evil glare from the wolf-god.

Alex was beginning to wonder about Ella. Although in the robe, she could see the woman's neck for the first time and it was unscarred, she'd never gotten a decent peek at Ella's ears since she always wore her hair down.

Alex would not have considered the Frenchwoman a good candidate for rogue werewolf killer of the month—until she'd trotted out of the snowstorm right after the rogue had trotted into it. What better way to remove suspicion than to appear as if you hadn't just disappeared?

Ella had obviously been sneaking away and coming here for a long time. The Inuit would think nothing of her hanging around, and she could therefore eat whomever she liked and lope off with no one the wiser.

Except if she was an evil killing machine, why hadn't she started evilly killing before now?

Julian pushed back his chair and stood, towering over them all. "We have rules about new wolves."

Ella glanced pointedly at Alex. "You mean like asking them if they want to become one?"

"I told you that was going to bite you on the butt," Alex muttered. "So to speak."

Ella's comment reminded Alex that the Frenchwoman knew who she really was. Sure, Ella had taken Alex's side; she'd called her "poor thing," but if she was a rogue werewolf, lying was the least of her sins. Wouldn't a rogue be first in line to kill the person most qualified to kill them?

"If Jorund wanted to become a werewolf, why didn't he do it before he was eight thousand years old?" Julian asked.

"I wasn't . . . certain." The old man sighed. "I'm still not."

"Then I can't turn you. You have to be sure."

"Alex wasn't," Ella said flatly.

"Dammit, Ella," Julian erupted. "That was different."

"I agree. This is about love. That was about hate."

Alex winced, even though she was right.

Julian pressed his lips together. The table began to shimmy as if there were an earthquake, though nothing else in the house moved.

"I told you not to upset him," Jorund said.

Ella kept her gaze on Julian's face. "I'm not afraid of him."

The wine in Alex's glass began to bubble and boil. She stood up, moved back. "Maybe you should be."

Suddenly the table stilled, the wine calmed, and Julian sat back down. "Is it because of the initial kill?"

The old man shrugged. "I don't like the idea of taking a life to ensure my immortality." He lifted one hand as Ella leaned forward to speak. "*But* I also believe that there are some humans who should be removed from this earth. I'm just not sure we should be choosing who they are."

"*We* aren't," Julian said. "I am."

Jorund's lips twitched. But he didn't comment.

Julian's gaze narrowed. "What else?"

"It's not that I don't want to be with her forever." Jorund lifted his gaze to Ella's, and his eyes reflected his devotion. "But I can't leave my people now."

"Because of the rogue?" Julian asked, and Jorund nodded.

"He'll take care of it," Ella said.

"I promised to protect my people," the old man said. "How would it look if I suddenly became the creature that was killing them?"

Ella stood, throwing up her hands and making a very French sound of aggravation deep in her throat. "You would not *be* that creature. You would be you. You would never hurt a living soul now, and therefore you would not hurt a living soul after."

"So you say," Jorund returned.

"Once you die," Ella murmured, "it is too late."

The Inuit ignored her. "If my people are safe, then I can be sure."

"Okay," Julian said. "Okay."

Julian released the throttle of the snowmobile and coasted to a stop in front of Ella's. Alex climbed off immediately.

They'd been silent all the way back. He didn't know about her, but he'd been fighting the response he seemed unable to stifle whenever she was near. She touched him, even without meaning to, and he was lost.

Alex rubbed her hands against her pants as if she was trying to rub the sting from her palms. He knew the feeling.

Julian lifted his chin to indicate the dark and quiet house. "Will you be all right?"

"Why? You think Ella tried to kill me?"

"No." He frowned. "Do you?"

She spread her hands. "Someone did. Right now, the only one off the hook for it is you."

"And George."

"And George," she agreed.

"If Ella wanted you dead," Julian began, "she could have killed you in your bed."

"A little obvious."

"I doubt anyone would have been calling for her blood once she told them who you really were. In fact, if she wanted you dead, all she would have had to do was tell the truth, then stand back and watch."

"Maybe it wasn't Ella." Alex smiled. "I'm glad."

"*Someone* tried to kill you, Alex."

She shrugged. "I'm used to it."

Her nonchalant attitude about that situation made Julian twitchy, anxious. He wanted to stay and protect her. But he knew what would happen if he did.

"No one should want to kill you at all," he said.

"Don't you?" she asked, then she strode up the steps and into the house.

Julian was left staring after her, wondering when in hell the answer had become no.

He parked the snowmobile at the back of Ella's house, covered it with a tarp, then went searching for his brother.

Dawn was fast approaching. Cade would either be hard at work in the lab or—

Julian frowned and glanced into the night. Out there somewhere, like the others.

If he was honest, any one of his people could have taken those shots at Alex. But why would they? The only ones who knew who she really was, what she'd done, were Julian and Ella. And probably Jorund now, too.

They'd already established that Ella didn't need to shoot Alex. There were easier, less dangerous ways to get rid of her.

Besides, Ella thought Alex was the victim. She'd be more likely to take a shot at Julian.

Jorund hadn't done it. He'd been channeling Hugh Hefner at the time.

Julian hadn't done it, so—

He opened the door to the lab and stepped inside, pausing to rub at his eyes. None of this made any sort of sense.

Julian glanced into Cade's room. He wasn't in bed.

He wasn't in the lab, either, and he wasn't in the bathroom that Julian checked on his way out.

Julian stood in the yard between his building and his brother's, watching the moon die. Then he walked to Ella's, and he sat on the porch until the murky light of the sun tinted the sky and his werewolves began to trickle into town.

"I've been looking for you."

Julian blinked. Where had his brother come from?

Cade was dressed. So either he hadn't been out running, or he'd already gone home to change.

"She kick you out?" Cade jerked his head at the house.

"Ella?"

Cade rolled his eyes. "Ella's taken."

Was Julian the only one who hadn't known about Ella and Jorund? What else was going on in his village that he didn't know about?

"I was looking for you, too." Julian stood. "Where'd you go?"

"There's something you need to see."

Julian opened his mouth to point out that Cade hadn't answered the question, then paused. His brother was—

Julian wasn't sure. He'd never seen that expression on Cade's face. He didn't like it.

"Okay." He stood. "Show me."

"Back at the lab." Cade glanced at Ella's house. "You'd better bring her along too."

Alex had known the exact moment Julian arrived. The connection between them appeared to be getting worse.

She'd been in bed, sound asleep; then suddenly she was wide awake and smelling him. She'd trailed through the house, gone to the window, then lost several minutes watching the silver rays of the moon play over his face.

How could she have smelled him? The doors and windows were tightly shut against the bitter cold. Yet his distinct scent of fresh snow on evergreens was everywhere. It had followed her back to sleep, playing across her dreams, making her yearn.

When the sun's muted rays had just begun to lighten the Arctic skies, his voice had drawn her awake. She'd thrown on more of Ella's clothes—she still hadn't managed to buy any of her own—and gone to ask him in for coffee. She opened the door just as he was lifting his hand to knock.

"Morning."

"Uh," he returned.

"Morning!" Cade stood at the bottom of the steps.

"Come on in," she said. "You want coffee?"

But as she turned, Julian caught her hand. Suddenly Alex couldn't breathe. Her fingers clenched around his; she stared into his face. He didn't appear to be breathing, either.

"Are you going to bring her along or aren't you?" Cade asked.

He sounded like a petulant little brother, and Alex laughed, which allowed her to breathe again.

"Where are we going?"

"The lab." Julian was staring at her as if she'd just sprouted horns; then he dropped her hand and spun away.

Why did she feel as if she'd done something wrong?

She glanced at Cade, who shrugged as Julian pushed past and left them behind. "You need more blood?" she asked.

His face took on a strange expression, and suddenly Alex was worried. What had he found in the last batch?

She put on her boots and followed. Julian stalked ahead, refusing to look back. He knew they were coming.

Alex felt a strange urge to hurry after him, almost as if he'd ordered her to, except he hadn't.

She'd been doing so well ignoring his alpha orders. The more she did so, the easier it got. But this morning she felt connected to him in a way she never had before. Was it because Julian had saved her life last night? And was he behaving strangely because he was sorry that he had?

He entered the building ahead of them, not pausing to hold the door, instead letting it slap closed. Annoyance flared, and Alex relished it. When she was annoyed with him, she wasn't in lust with him.

Much.

Julian waited in the main room. His hair was a mess and

the dark circles under his eyes made him seem very pale. He still wore the same clothes George had given him last night.

"You never went to bed," she said.

He flicked her a glance before switching his gaze to Cade. "Show us what was so important."

Cade beckoned them to join him at one of the high-topped tables where he had several petri dishes spread out. "I was trying to discover why Alex could touch the others without the serum, and I got nowhere. So I thought about the other—" He glanced up and caught Julian's scowl. "—problem," he finished.

"You mean the one where he pukes if he gets too far away from me?"

"Uh, yeah," Cade said. "That problem I thought I wouldn't mention since it makes the alpha a little—" He wiggled his hands next to his head.

"Ape-shit?" Alex murmured.

Cade choked. Barlow growled. Alex grinned. When she poked him with the proverbial stick she felt so much more like herself.

"What did you find?" Julian demanded.

"I . . . Well, it's . . ." Cade took a deep breath, let it out, then reached for two clean petri dishes. "I'd better show you."

He set the glass circlets next to each other, then went to the refrigerator in the corner and returned with two font tubes of blood. Alex read her name on one and Barlow's on the other.

Her chest hurt, and she realized she was holding her breath. She wasn't going to like this.

Cade set the tubes in a stand, uncorked them, then took an eyedropper in each hand and filled it with blood. He dripped a few drops of hers into the petri dish on the right; then he met her gaze and Julian's. "Ready?"

Neither of them answered.

Cade sighed and squeezed the rubber on the other eye-dropper. A bead of Julian's blood seemed to fall in slow motion toward the petri dish on the left. Alex had enough time to wonder what experiment Cade could possibly have done with their blood in *different* dishes; then the drop hit the glass.

And immediately *leaped* into the other one.

Utter silence reigned. Alex glanced at the left dish. Not a mark on it. The right dish held a tiny puddle of blood, all the drops merged into one.

Maybe she'd been mistaken. Maybe Cade had dropped Julian's blood into the right petri dish and not the left at all. Her eyes deceiving her made a lot more sense than blood hopping through the air.

"Do it again," Julian said.

Cade nodded and pressed his first finger and his thumb together around the rubber bulb. This time, two drops of blood fell.

And two drops of blood arced from one petri dish to another.

"That's impossible," Alex said.

"I thought so, too," Cade replied. "Until it happened."

"What does it mean?" Barlow asked.

"I'm not sure. But—"

"You'd damn straight better find out," Barlow snapped.

Cade's eyes narrowed. "What do you think I've been doing?"

"Not confiding in me, obviously."

"You weren't *here*," Cade ground out. "Or if you were, you weren't answering your door."

"Why didn't you walk right in? It's always open."

"After the two of you were doing your mating dance in the center square, then making out in the front window? I draw the line at walking in on that."

At least their plan had worked. Everyone thought they'd been horizontal bopping all night.

Except for the rogue. Who'd somehow known they'd be in Awanitok.

"One problem at a time," she murmured.

Cade and Julian ignored her. They were too busy staring into each other's eyes like alpha wolves ready to fight.

"Hey!" She grabbed their shoulders. They both jerked away and snarled at her. She let them go, holding her hands up in surrender. "We all want the same thing." She pointed to the petri dish. "An explanation for that."

Julian rubbed a hand over his face. He seemed so tired. Cade went back to the table and pulled out two more clean glass dishes.

"I got to thinking that I'd never compared anyone's blood before I compared yours. And that maybe this reaction was common." He lifted one shoulder. "Maybe it has to do with the fact that Julian made us all."

"That would make sense," Alex agreed.

"You'd think." Cade went to the refrigerator and brought back several more test tubes filled with blood. He dropped the blood of someone named Barclay into the right dish and Julian's into the left.

Nothing happened.

"*Faet!*" Julian said without any real heat.

"Yeah," Alex agreed.

Cade looked at them both and lifted a brow before he reached for two more dishes and shoved the others out of the way. He dropped the blood of another werewolf onto the right and the blood from a completely different test tube than Julian's into the left.

The one on the left boogied through the air and splashed on top of the quivering drop on the right, turning the two separate droplets into a puddle of one. Cade lifted the two mystery donors and turned the labels front and center.

"I thought you'd want to talk to them yourself," he said.

"You thought right," Julian agreed.

CHAPTER 23

Julian didn't wait for Alex to join him. He knew that she would. Cade came along, too. Julian didn't try to stop him.

They made their way to the EAT Café. The place was already packed with customers.

"You," he pointed to Rose. "And you." He pointed to Joe. "Come with me."

Julian tramped up the steps that led to the apartment over the café, going through the unlocked door in front of Alex and Cade. The three of them waited in silence for Rose and Joe to turn over the register and grill to their employees, then join them.

They appeared scared witless. Julian had been a little harsh. Before Alex had shown up he never would have noticed.

"Sit," he ordered.

Alex made an impatient noise to accompany the scowl she aimed in his direction. "Don't worry," she said to the older couple. "He won't bite you. Again."

Rose smiled without her usual spark. Joe didn't bother.

"What have we done?" Rose asked.

Julian opened his mouth, then shut it again. How was he

supposed to explain this? He glanced at Cade, but his brother had never been very good at explaining things so anyone could understand them.

"If one of you goes on a trip," Alex began. "Does the other one feel . . . strange?"

The worried expressions on both their faces smoothed out. Rose laughed a little. "Oh, that," she said.

"What?" Julian said between clenched teeth. The worried expressions returned.

"Quit scaring them!" Alex ordered.

If possible, Rose and Joe appeared more concerned. Rose put her hand on Alex's arm. "Don't yell at the alpha, child."

"Yeah," Julian said. "Don't yell at the alpha."

"Bite me," she muttered.

"Again?" Julian drawled.

"Oh!" Rose lifted her hands to her cheeks, then stared back and forth between Julian and Alex. "I see."

"See what?" Alex and Julian demanded at the same time. Cade had retreated to the window, staring out at the street, and while he was obviously listening, he was pretending not to.

"You're mates," Rose said, then turned her adoring gaze to Joe. "Like us."

Alex stiffened. Julian did the same. Each studiously avoided looking in the other's direction.

"Explain," Julian demanded.

"You know, Julian." Rose patted his hand fondly. "You were there."

"He was where?" Alex asked.

"He was there when Joe almost died."

Now Alex did glance at him, but Julian refused to return the favor. Mates? This sounded bad.

"Go on," Alex said.

"Joe volunteered for the army. He was a bit old, but he felt like he should serve his adopted country." She paused and beamed at her husband. "He loves America so much."

"I do," Joe said in a thick Italian accent. "It's-a true."

Alex's eyes widened. She'd probably never heard Joe speak, only sing, and when he sang, not much of an accent.

"He was hit at Gettysburg—"

"Whoa!" Alex held up a hand. "He was a soldier in the *Civil* War?"

Rose shrugged and spread her hands.

Alex turned to Julian. "What in hell were you doing there?"

"I'm a warrior," he said. "It's the only thing I've ever been good at."

She opened her mouth, then snapped it shut again and stared at the floor as her cheeks flushed.

Well, he *was* good at that, too.

Rose gave a strangled cough that sounded very much like a stifled laugh, and Alex's head came up, eyes snapping. "What did you do, Barlow? Hire yourself out to the highest bidder?"

"I don't fight for money."

"Then what do you fight for?"

"Whatever is *worth* fighting for." Julian glanced at Rose, needing to shift the subject back to what they'd come here to learn. "I'm not seeing how my saving Joe from dying on the battlefield leads to—" He couldn't say it, so he just twirled a finger to indicate that she should go on.

"Joe was dying and you—"

"Why Joe?" Alex interrupted. "Why not one of the thousands of other guys who died there? Or why not *thousands* of the guys who died there?"

"What would I do with a thousand werewolves?" Julian muttered.

"Make an army."

He narrowed his eyes. "And what would I do with an army?"

"Rule more than Barlowsville. You could rule the whole damn world."

"Ruling the world is highly overrated," he said. "All I've ever wanted is my own little corner." He turned again to Rose. "Continue."

"You saved him; then you came to see me."

Julian's mind drifted to that long-ago day. The heat. The blood and smoke. The scent of gunpowder and death. Why had he volunteered to fight again?

Oh, yeah, because he was good at it. And he hadn't wanted to see the Union die. Before Gettysburg, it had been.

He could have told the Yankees that when you invaded someone's homeland, the invadees fought so much harder than the invaders. Unless you were a Viking. They just kicked ass all over the place.

The Yankees definitely weren't Vikings—except for him and Knut. Speaking of which—

"Has anyone seen Neil?" The name Knut was using these days.

Rose and Alex stared at him as if he'd lost his mind. Joe, who had met Neil the same day he'd met Julian and Cade, understood the connection.

"He's fishing," Joe said. "Or maybe it was hunting."

"Has been for a few weeks now," Cade murmured.

The question was: Had Neil been hunting elk? Or Inuit?

It hadn't occurred to Julian to tally the village and discover who was missing. Werewolves came and went. They weren't prisoners. But he didn't like it that Neil was away. He didn't like it at all.

"I took Joe to see Cade first," Julian said.

"But gut-shot is no good." Joe shook his head sadly as if he was talking about someone else's gut and not his own.

"Cade was there, too?" Alex glanced at Julian's brother, who nodded but continued to stare out the window.

"Neil also," Joe said.

"Who in hell is Neil?"

"The only other Viking, besides Cade, that I made like us."

Neil and Julian had joined the Northern forces to fight. Cade had joined to heal.

"Cade was an army doctor," Julian said. "That day he'd just gotten back from visiting an Iroquois woman. He always talked to the healers in every culture we . . . visited."

"Sometimes it helped," Cade said. "They knew local herbs. Back then, that was all we had."

Julian waited for Cade to take over the tale, but when he turned again to his window—what was so blasted interesting out there anyway?—Julian continued. He felt better when he was talking. When he was talking about the past he wasn't thinking about the present.

"Like Joe said, gut-shot is gut-shot."

"Why didn't you magic him back to health?"

"The only way I can heal a human is with a bite."

"So you bit him."

"He wanted me to."

Julian had liked Joe. Hell, he still did. He'd never regretted saving the man's life, and he couldn't say that about every werewolf he'd made. Anyone could become damn annoying after a few centuries.

"I don't see how this is explaining . . ." Alex moved her hands in a semicircle to indicate Joe and Rose, her and him.

Julian didn't, either. He wasn't sure he wanted it to.

"Once Julian saved Joe's life," Rose continued, "Joe brought him to me."

"Why?" Alex asked.

"We're soul mates. Joe wasn't going to leave me behind."

Alex's eyes widened. "You made her a werewolf so they could be together?"

Julian shrugged. "Why not?"

"I insisted," Rose said. "So did Joe. Without each other eternal life would have been hell."

"It didn't bother you that another human being would give their life for your immortality?"

Rose frowned. "Of course it bothered me. But Julian took care of that. He found a very—"

"Bad man," Alex finished, staring at Julian all the while.

"Yes!" Rose agreed. "I'll always be grateful to him for assuring that Joe and I would be together forever." She grasped Julian's hand and squeezed it. "But we discovered that being soul mates as humans meant we were mates as werewolves."

"What does that *mean*?" Alex asked, her voice a little louder than necessary. Neither Joe nor Rose had ever been deaf, and they certainly wouldn't be anymore.

"Wolves mate for life, child. Some humans do, too. And when you have humans that are soul mates and werewolves that are mates, you have the strongest bond of all."

"I tried once to leave her," Joe said. "Just-a to go to wine country and choose a few places to do business with. Before I even reached the cave where we rest, my stomach cramped. I could-a not move. I thought that I would die of the pain." He gazed at Rose, everything he felt evident on his face. "I have never tried to leave her again."

"Why would you want to?" Rose murmured, and kissed him.

"This is nuts," Alex murmured. "I don't even *like* you."

Rose *tsk*ed. "That's not true!"

Alex stood so close to Julian he could touch her, yet his

stomach roiled and his head ached. That he *wanted* to touch her, would apparently always want to, was no doubt the cause.

"How did you know you were soul mates?" he asked.

"From the first moment we met, we knew there was something special between us," Rose said.

"Love at first sight?" Alex let out a relieved breath. "That definitely wasn't us."

"No." Joe laughed, the sound as joyous as his songs. "Not love at first sight. At first sight we fought like cats in a sack."

"But the passion," Rose murmured, staring into Joe's eyes. "Whenever we touched . . ."

"Sex happened," Alex finished.

"That's *amore*." Joe spread his arms wide, and Rose walked into them.

"Faet!" Julian said.

"Got that right," Alex agreed.

After a brief hug, Rose faced them. "What brought this up?"

Julian glanced at Cade, but his brother still didn't appear inclined to speak. "Cade did an experiment. Trying to figure out why Alex and I are so—" He searched for a word.

"Fucked," Alex muttered, and he scowled.

Rose did, too, or at least her face creased into an expression that was the closest she ever came to one. "I don't understand, child. The mate bond is a gift even greater than the one Julian's already given you."

"Given." She snorted. "Yeah."

Rose's frown deepened. "A love like this will never go away."

"That's what I'm afraid of." Alex straightened her shoulders. "And it isn't love."

"It will be," Rose said.

They weren't getting anywhere, and there were still a few

things Julian needed to know. "You're saying that if Alex and I were human we'd be soul mates?" Rose and Joe both nodded like bobble-headed dolls. "But what if we never met?"

"Soul mates always meet. It's fate."

Considering that Julian had been a Viking while human—centuries ago, before Alex had even been born—he had a problem with that theory.

"What if he'd never made her a wolf?" Cade asked.

Everyone glanced in his direction as if they'd forgotten he was there.

"Becoming werewolves allowed the mate connection to be born." Rose beamed at Julian like he'd done it on purpose.

Julian's stomach began to burn as if he'd suddenly sprung a very bad ulcer. "So if I'd left her human, there'd have been no connection?"

"Why-a do you think I insisted on making Rose like me?" Joe asked.

Julian could have sworn the ulcer began to bleed.

"With me human," Rose said, "and Joe a werewolf, the connection began to fade almost immediately."

"How do you know this stuff?" Alex demanded.

Joe shrugged and looked at Rose. Rose shrugged and looked at Julian. "Doesn't everyone?"

Julian growled, causing the older woman's eyes to widen. "Sorry," he said. "But I've never heard of this. And Cade's never seen a reaction like he saw with us—" He flicked his finger between Alex and himself before setting his hand on his aching gut. "And you two."

"What reaction?"

Quickly Julian explained what had happened with the blood hopping.

"I'd like-a to see that!" Joe exclaimed.

"No, you wouldn't," Alex muttered. "It was creepy."

"If you think about it," Rose said, "that makes sense. The mate bond is part of what we are. It's a connection in the blood."

"So there's no way that Cade can cure it?" Alex asked.

Rose and Joe frowned. "Why would he want to?"

Alex opened her mouth to recite a laundry list of reasons, but snapped it shut again when Cade turned from the window, one brow lifted as he waited on her reaction. She decided to save comments of a more personal nature until she had Barlow alone.

"Why didn't you know this?" she asked instead. "You and Alana—"

Rose and Joe gasped. Cade winced. Julian's upper lip lifted in a snarl, and he bolted from the room.

Whoops.

"What'd I say?"

"When Alana left," Cade murmured, "he didn't know she was gone for days."

"What? How could that be?"

"They had a fight. He thought she went to her grandmother's. By the time he checked on her, she was dead."

Now Alex winced. Luckily the others believed it was in sympathy and not guilt.

Guilt? Since when?

"I don't understand," Alex said. "If Alana left the village, why didn't Julian know it in his gut?"

"Because Alana wasn't his mate." Rose stared at the open door through which Barlow had disappeared. "You are."

"Oh, that's gonna go over really well," Alex muttered.

Silence settled over the room. No one seemed to know what to say or do.

"We should get back to the café," Rose murmured. "If that's okay?"

It took Alex a moment to realize that Rose had directed the question at her. "I—uh— Sure." She shrugged and looked at Cade.

He waited until the older couple left before answering. "You're the alpha's mate."

"So I hear. Why are they asking me if they can leave the room?"

"That makes you the second in command."

"Fan-tabulous," she muttered.

Cade's gaze went distant. "It explains why you could resist his commands. Mates are equals."

Alex didn't feel equal. She felt cursed.

"And also why you could touch Julian's wolves and they could touch you without the inevitable headache."

"Why?"

Alex wasn't sure she cared, but listening to Cade was better than listening to the voice in her head, which kept screaming that she was in *big* trouble.

"The mate bond must have given you the same link to Julian's wolves that he has. Like Rose said, a connection in the blood. It's the only explanation."

"Glad we got that sorted out." Alex's stomach was starting to roll. She felt a little dizzy. "Is it hot in here?"

Her forehead had gone clammy. She stepped onto the landing and took several gulps of the chill Arctic wind.

Cade came up behind her. "Julian must have run pretty far this time."

"What?" Alex wiped the back of her hand across her mouth. "Why?"

"You're getting sick." He stared at her as if he'd like to

open her up and see what lay inside. "Fascinating. We don't *get* sick."

"Speak for yourself," Alex said, and puked over the railing.

Since she hadn't eaten since yesterday, she didn't puke much. Which only made things worse.

"You'd better come back to the lab." Cade helped her down the stairs. Alex felt so shitty she let him.

She tried to walk as if she weren't drunk off her ass, but it wasn't easy. Several of the locals gave her strange looks as she and Cade weaved past.

Ella was just pulling up in front of her house on what appeared to be, considering the dent in the fender, George's snowmobile. She took one look at Alex and cried out, "What's the matter?"

"That bad, huh?"

"I'll take her." Ella reached for Alex.

Cade didn't let go. "She can stay with me."

"She *lives* with me." Ella pulled on Alex's arm.

"Not a wishbone," Alex murmured, and tugged free. "What are you doing here?"

Ella's face was a mask of concern and at first she only stared blankly at Alex. Then Alex snapped her fingers in front of Ella's nose. "I didn't think you'd come home until to-night." She'd said as much when they'd left her at Jorund's yesterday.

"Oh!" Understanding filled Ella's dark eyes. "There was another murder."

Alex cursed. "We're gonna run out of villagers."

"Not a villager. A deliveryman I expected from Juneau. When he didn't show this morning, I went searching for him and—" Ella winced. "I found him."

"A dead deliveryman is going to raise a few questions."

"You think?" Ella muttered, and Alex would have smiled if she weren't afraid that would set off another bout of puking. The more Alex was around Ella, the better she liked her.

"We're going to have to camp out in the Inuit village," Alex said.

"I can do that," Ella murmured.

Alex managed to navigate Ella's porch steps. She used the door to steady herself as she turned. "Thanks, Cade. Maybe you'd better find Julian."

He didn't appear happy to let her go, but he nodded. "I'll drag him back here; then you'll feel fine."

Alex didn't think she'd ever feel fine again, but she did her best to smile before she went inside.

She barely made it to the bathroom before she tossed her cookies again. Too bad she didn't have any cookies to toss. She'd never been a big fan of the dry heaves.

Ella came in behind her, leaning over and pulling Alex's hair up and out of the way. Then she turned on the water in the sink. An instant later a cold cloth pressed onto the back of Alex's neck. Nothing had ever felt so good.

"What's going on?" Ella asked.

Alex flushed the toilet, stepped past Ella, who shuffled into the hall to give her room, then washed her face and rinsed with mouthwash. When her gaze met Ella's in the mirror, the Frenchwoman arched a brow, and Alex told her everything.

"Mates," Ella murmured. "Hmm."

"That's all you can say? I'm stuck here forever, unless I want to throw up until my insides are on my outside. Talk about a curse and a prison."

"Calm yourself, *mon amie*. Is it so bad to have a man like Julian as your mate?"

In truth, Alex wasn't that upset. She wondered if being sick until she had no sick left to be had put her in a state of shock—or perhaps just the news had.

"A love like that is not something that comes along every day."

"It isn't love," Alex said, although what love *was* she couldn't quite say.

"Are you sure?" Ella asked. "Didn't you find it odd that you felt ill every time he went too far away? Considering that we don't *get* ill?"

"I didn't," Alex said. "Until today."

"Not even when he left you the first time, after he made you?"

It appeared that Ella not only knew the truth about Alex, but the truth about every damn thing.

"He left you when we are like babies, and we should *never* be left." From Ella's expression she wished Julian were there right now so she could kick him. Alex wished he were there right now so she could see it.

"I was busy shape-shifting," Alex said. "I felt like my skin was going to explode."

"Then it did," Ella murmured.

"My stomach was the least of my worries."

"Come." Ella beckoned. "You need to lie down."

Since Alex *did* need to, she followed the Frenchwoman into the bedroom where she tossed her clothes and crawled beneath the quilt.

"You should sleep now." Ella sat on the side of the bed and brushed Alex's hair away from her face with a cool, gentle hand, and Alex felt a flicker of memory. Someone sitting on her bed, touching her face—a cool hand against her fevered brow.

Mama?

The childish voice—hers—made Alex blink. She had few memories of her mother. She'd been so young when Janet died; then Charlie had packed Alex up and taken her away, leaving every memento behind. Once in a while, she got flashes—like now—but in truth they were becoming more rare as time went on. She wondered if the same thing would happen to her memories of Charlie. God, she hoped not. If she lost those, she'd be completely alone.

"You feel any better?" Ella asked.

Alex nodded. Maybe Barlow was back.

And the rush of warmth that followed that thought made her dizzy again. She closed her eyes as Ella slipped out.

She hated this. Alex had rarely been sick in her life, and she wasn't supposed to be sick at all while a werewolf.

"Call it a perk," she murmured.

What was she going to do about this bizarre development? How could she ever leave Barlowsville if leaving made her so sick she couldn't move?

Although . . . If she could make it to Edward and partake of the *Jäger-Sucher* cure, wouldn't that make this all go away?

Or she could man up, stick to her original plan, and kill him, though that option was becoming less and less appealing.

How did you put a bullet into the brain of someone you'd slept with? It couldn't be that easy.

Hell, it *shouldn't* be that easy.

CHAPTER 24

Despite her roiling mind and equally roiling stomach, Alex fell into a deep, dreamless sleep. The last time she'd slept like that, she'd been in Julian's arms.

Eventually, the nagging thought that there was something she needed to do, somewhere she needed to be, someone she needed to see, penetrated, and Alex fought her way to the surface. She'd never been so bone-deep tired.

Ebony velvet darkness floated around her. She had no idea what time it was, even what day it was. Her mind was fuzzy; her mouth tasted like dirt, and her stomach was so damn empty. She lifted her head, and the darkness spun.

"Bad idea," she said, reaching out to touch the bedside lamp.

Light flooded the room, revealing a sliver of gray at the edge of the curtains, which, around here in the land of eternal twilight, did nothing to help her figure out how long she'd been asleep.

She caught the scent of salt and flour, and her stomach rumbled. When she turned her head, she discovered that someone—Ella—had left her a package of saltines and a note.

Eat these BEFORE you get out of bed.

Considering the state of her belly, who was she to argue? Alex devoured the entire package without dropping a single crumb. Amazingly, when she lifted her head this time, the world stayed right where it belonged.

"Ella, you're a genius," she muttered, dragging herself to the shower.

Twenty minutes and a cup of tea—the idea of coffee brought the nausea back—later, Alex was dressed and out the door. She'd stop by Julian's house, see if he was there. Though if he was, would she have awoken so dizzy?

"I'm fine now," she said. If talking to herself was fine.

The clock in Ella's kitchen had read just after noon, which meant Alex had slept for two hours. Unless she'd slept for twenty-six.

The sky was cloudy. Since the sun made an appearance only a few hours each day, cloudy just wasn't fair. But the moon would rise in another few, and perhaps by then the clouds would be gone. The thought that she and Julian might run together beneath those silver rays brought a lightness to her heart that Alex didn't want to examine. She had enough to worry about.

Alex knocked on Barlow's door. Several minutes later she knocked again. She was deliberating moving on to Cade's place—maybe his brother had found him and taken him there instead—when she lifted her nose and sniffed.

Snow and trees, his distinctive scent, and it was coming from inside. Too strong to be anything but Barlow. Without a second thought, Alex turned the knob and went in.

She searched the entire house without finding him. But every time she walked past the living room, the smell became sharper. Finally, she just followed her nose.

The scent intensified near the large leather chair. Right next to it stood a squat, glass-topped end table, in the center a picture frame that hadn't been there before. Alex didn't need to turn on the lamp to see that the picture in the frame was of Alana. She turned the lamp on anyway. All the gloom was starting to get to her.

"I know you're here," she said to the empty room.

The room stayed empty.

"I'll stay until you have a brain aneurysm from the anger it takes to keep that invisibility bubble up and running." Nothing. "Come on, Julian," she said softly. "Talk to me."

Slowly he materialized. First a mere shadow—there, gone, there again—then more and more solid until he was so close she could reach out and touch. But she didn't.

His back to her, his gaze remained on Alana's face. "I didn't know she left," he said. "If I'd gone after her right away, I could have stopped her."

The pain in his voice made Alex's throat tighten, but she made herself ask. She needed to know. "Why did she leave?"

He reached out and ran a fingertip down the glass, right over the smiling woman's cheek. "She needed something from me that I couldn't give her."

"What is there on this earth that *you* couldn't give?" And what fool of a woman turned her back on a love as deep as Julian's?

All the breath seemed to go out of him, and his shoulders slouched as his head sagged. "A child," he said. "All she ever wanted in this world was a child.

"But— Wait. What? You obviously asked *her* if she wanted to be a werewolf."

"Of course," he said, in a weary, haunted voice.

"And she agreed." He made a noise that she took to mean *yes*. "Was Alana—" Alex paused, not wanting to use the word *stupid,* but hey, if the shoe fit—

"I thought her grandmother had told her," he continued.

"I mean, if a child were so damn important, then why wouldn't she have told her?"

"Yeah, why?" Alex murmured, pulled toward him despite herself by the agony in his voice. She wanted to hold him and comfort him and make it better—three things Alexandra Trevalyn had never wanted before. That she wanted them with a desperation she could barely control scared her.

She just *might* have to kill him after all.

"Her gran knew Alana wouldn't agree to becoming a werewolf if it meant giving up her dream of a big family, and Alana had to agree or she would have died. So Margaret lied." He laughed, but the sound was more of a cough. "Told Alana that of *course* werewolves could have kids. When I found out I—" He paused. "Well, let's say Margaret won't be lying again anytime soon."

Alex frowned. Did that mean he'd scared the old lady speechless? Or something else?

"But when Alana asked me," he continued in that same voice that pulled at a part of Alex she'd never known she had, "and I told her the truth, she looked at me as if I were a monster." He gave that short, sharp, un-funny laugh again. "I thought she'd get over it. That I would be enough. That *we* would be enough. I mean . . . what choice did she have? She was a werewolf, for better or for worse. Forever." He shook his head. "Or not."

Alex had always wondered about that beautiful blond wolf in northern Minnesota. Either the woman had been dumb as a rock, or she'd wanted to die.

Alana had breezed into town, and people had started disappearing. That always got Edward's attention.

He'd sent Alex; she'd done her job. But she'd always wondered. Alana had shown up first, then—*bing, bing, bing*—several other strangers followed. Folks left town, and they didn't come back, and there were whispers of a wolf pack with a sleek, golden she-wolf in the lead.

Alana had been sloppy. She hadn't tried to hide their tracks. But it had always bothered Alex that she'd caught the other werewolves red-pawed, one with his snout buried in the local sheriff. But Alana . . .

She'd never attributed a single death to Alana.

Then came that fateful night. All of the other wolves were dead, and Alana had loped right into town. Strange behavior for a real wolf, kind of typical for a were.

She'd crashed through the picture window in the lobby of the hotel where Alex had been staying. That sound, followed by the screams, drew Alex out of her room and down the hall.

A wolf the shade of sunlight had backed the clerk—a teenage kid with a nametag that read HOLLY—into a corner. The beast had glanced once at Alex, as if making sure she was there and that she was armed; then she'd lunged at the girl, teeth snapping.

Ka-bam!

That had been the end of Alana Barlow.

Alex lifted her gaze to Julian, but he was still captivated by the photo. Alex couldn't tell him that his wife had committed suicide by *Jäger-Sucher,* that Alana would rather be dead than live a childless life with a man who adored her. She just couldn't.

Besides, it would sound like an excuse, and she wasn't going to make one. It didn't matter if Alana had wanted to get shot or not, Alex would have obliged her either way. If Alana hadn't been killing people in that town herself, she'd been leading a pack of monsters that had.

In Alex's opinion, Alana was as much of a psycho as the next werewolf. Obsessed by a child instead of blood, willing to give up her life rather than live it, screwing up Alex's future, thank you very much, by getting herself killed, thus causing her husband to agonize over her loss and eventually come gunning—so to speak—for the hunter who had ended her.

"You deserved better," she murmured.

He spun away from the photo. Alex hadn't realized she'd crept so close until his chest brushed hers. Together they gasped, their eyes widening, nostrils flaring as the awareness that had always been between them ignited.

Then he was dragging her against him, and she was letting him. As his mouth hovered, and his fingers clenched, and their breath mingled, he whispered, "Then there was you."

Julian believed in fate. And this was his.

He had loved Alana with all that he'd had. But she'd left him and gone away to die.

Though he'd suspected it he hadn't wanted to believe it, had refused to, until he'd heard the truth in Alex's voice, saw it in her face.

Suicide by *Jäger-Sucher*. What a way to go.

But Alana *was* gone, and Alex was here, and through some bizarre twist of that fate he believed in, she was his mate. At least he understood now why he couldn't keep his hands off her.

He was tired of fighting—her, himself, Edward, the rogue—all he wanted was to sink into the strange peace he found in the circle of Alex's arms and forget.

Still he would have let her go if she'd asked, if she'd made even a single movement toward freedom. Instead, she knotted her fingers in his shirt, pulling him close; then she closed the distance between their lips.

And he was lost.

Her taste was home, she smelled like . . . here. When had that started?

Mine, whispered his mind.

Mate, growled his beast.

He nipped at her lip, drank her sweet gasp, ran his mouth over the curve of her jaw. The line of her throat beckoned, the scent of her skin, the pulse of the blood that called to his, that made them one even when they weren't.

He marked her again, taking a fold of her flesh between his teeth and worrying it. She lifted her hand, cupped his head, tangled her fingers in his hair, and urged him on.

As he trailed his tongue over her collarbone, then followed the slight swell of her breast, he thanked all the gods he'd ever known that she'd found a blouse with buttons somewhere in Ella's closet.

He opened them, muttering hallelujahs that she hadn't bothered with a bra when she'd come looking for him.

Her skin held the flavor of cinnamon atop a cake of spice, her nipples swollen, hard, luscious as a cherry to his lips. When he suckled she cried out, arching, straining, and when he bit, just a little, her gasp whispered, *yes*.

Her knees were weak, or maybe just his. Nevertheless, they couldn't continue to stand in the living room, especially when anyone could walk in. So he carried her up the stairs.

He'd burned everything Alana had touched. All of his furniture was new. He'd never been more glad of it.

He laid her on the bed, straightened to take off his clothes, then became captivated with the picture she made there. Her hair matched the southwestern copper of his quilt. Her eyes, open a mere slit, gleamed like slices of limes against the honey shade of her skin sparkling in the half-light that spilled from the hall.

Her shirt fell open, one side covering a breast, the other revealing it. Ella's black pants gaped at the waist, exposing her navel, a round, perfect well, and the stepping-stones of her ribs drew his gaze to the smooth curve of her waist. He wanted to lick her from the tips of her toes to the top of her head, then start over again.

She lifted her hand. Her long, clever fingers furled back toward her palm.

Come to me, they said, echoing the invitation in her eyes.

He tossed shirt and jeans into a corner, then knelt, removing her boots—God they were ugly—her socks, the rest. He placed his mouth to her arch, running his tongue along her sole, nibbling at the fine bones of her ankle.

He touched her as if she were spun crystal, tasted her as if she were the finest of wines. She shivered when he skimmed his palms over her; she shuddered with his every breath.

Her legs were long, the muscles hard beneath the softest of skin. Her inner thighs trembled when he kissed them, as did her fingers in his hair.

The bones of her hips were like blades in a sheath. He tested them with his thumbs, ran his nails down her flanks, cupped her buttocks, then he feasted. By the time he moved on, his name on her lips had gone from curse to caress and back again.

He couldn't wait; he didn't want to, rising up, then sliding home. Her arms came around his shoulders, her legs around his hips; she held him close, she welcomed him in, yet still he didn't feel their connection.

He perched on the edge; she did, too. Deep within, he felt her tremble. He clenched his jaw to keep from coming.

It wasn't right. Not yet.

Please, not *yet.*

Sweat broke out on his brow as he tried to think what was missing, what he needed, what she did.

She clenched, clamping down on him, squeezing him from within, and her hand drifted across his chest, meandering right and left, thumb scraping one nipple, then the other, before coming to rest at his waist.

She stroked the sensitive flesh where his thigh became his hip, and he tensed. "Alex," he growled, both a wish and a warning.

Her eyes opened, and something caught in his chest when she whispered, "Julian."

He thrust one final time; then he was coming; then she was.

Two simple words. Her name and his. A recognition. An admission.

A vow.

It was enough.

CHAPTER 25

Alex waited until Julian slept; then she crept from his arms, his bed, his house.

What had she done?

Sex was one thing . . . This—

She glanced up at the window of his room. This had been another.

He'd touched her with such gentleness. He'd gazed into her eyes with—

"Faet!" she muttered, clattering down the steps and striding around the side of the house.

He'd gazed at her with love. And what had she done?

Loved him right back.

Alex stepped into Julian's yard and had a little talk with herself.

She did *not* love Barlow; he did not love her. They barely knew each other, and what they knew they did not like.

Just because their blood couldn't stay in separate petri dishes, and their hands couldn't keep to themselves, didn't mean they were meant for each other.

Then again, maybe it did.

She'd thought him a monster; he'd thought her one. Had

they learned differently, or merely come to accept that beneath the surface, everyone had a little monster inside?

"No one's perfect," she whispered. Especially Alexandra Trevalyn.

Julian had never lied about who he was, about what he was, about what he planned to do.

Unlike her.

She was a spy; she'd come here to kill—both him and one of his wolves. While she might not kill Julian—

"Won't," Alex said to the night, and sighed. "I won't."

She *would* kill the werewolf that had killed her father. As soon as she found it.

Once she did that, she would not be able to stay. However, when she left this place, Edward would find her, and he'd insist she reveal the location of Barlowsville.

Could she really bring the most feared *Jäger-Sucher* of them all down on these people's—and they *were* people, she knew that now—heads?

He'd kill them. Killing was what Edward did best. It had once been what Alex did best, too. It had once been what Alex lived for. But here, she'd found so much more to live for than death.

If she didn't tell Edward what he wanted to know, he'd either kill her or stick her in a cage for the rest of her very long and furry life.

What the hell was she going to do?

She could solve her problems by staying. Alex let her gaze wander over Barlowsville. She liked it here. She thought she could grow to love it.

Once the thought of being a werewolf had horrified her. She'd have eaten the last bullet in her gun to avoid losing her humanity. Now she understood—

She hadn't really been using it anyway.

A door opened. Alex's breath caught as she turned toward Julian's house. But the place remained silent, and her heart fluttered and stilled.

"Psst! Alex!" Cade hung out the back entrance of the lab. "You want to run with me tonight?"

Alex glanced once more at Julian's. They needed to talk, but it didn't have to be right now. Besides . . .

She turned toward Cade and waved. She could use a little cheering up.

Julian awoke to a pounding on the door. He reached for Alex, confused at first that she was there, then equally confused when she was not.

The moon poured into his bedroom, making him yearn. He'd find her, and they'd run together, just the two of them. But first he had to force whoever was at his door to shut up.

He found his pants in the corner with his shirt, but Alex's clothes were gone. He checked in the bathroom on the way past, the kitchen too, but she wasn't there. Considering he wasn't clasping his stomach and writhing in agony, she hadn't gone far.

Julian yanked open the front door. The man on the other side nearly knocked on his nose.

"Knut." Julian jerked his head back just in time to avoid the huge, ham-like fist.

"Neil," the man corrected with a scowl, lowering an arm the size of the logs in Julian's cabin walls.

Neil did not appreciate being called Knut, and Julian couldn't say that he blamed him. But it was difficult sometimes for Julian to remember. They'd grown up together, fought together, lived as werewolves together. He'd known Knut as long as he'd known Cade.

"Joe said you were searching for me."

Not actively. Not yet. But he would have. If he could keep his mind on the issue at hand and his hands out of Alex's pants.

"Where have you been?" Julian asked.

"Fishing."

"For two weeks?"

"I like fish." Neil drew himself up to his impressive height of six-five. It *did* take a lot of fish to fill up Neil. "Since when do you care what I do?"

"Since Inuit have been dying daily."

Neil's wind-burned face creased. "Why would that have anything to do with me?"

"Perhaps I should have said dying nightly."

Neil caught the innuendo right away. "One of us is doing it."

"Unless you've caught a whiff of an unknown werewolf in your travels."

"None." Neil's pale blue eyes narrowed. "You thought it was me."

Many had made the mistake of believing that Neil's calm demeanor and large stature meant he was slow, in both body and mind. They had died badly at the end of his sword.

"You *were* gone," Julian said, "and they *did* die."

Neil drew in a breath, glanced to the side, then back at Julian. "Who died first? Was it the wise woman?"

Julian blinked. "How did you know that?"

Neil's lips tightened, and he rubbed a big hand through his shorn dirty blond hair. No matter how many centuries he lived, no matter how short he cut his hair, or how many flannel shirts he collected, Neil would never look like anything but a Norse raider.

"I thought he'd gotten over that."

"Who got over what?"

"I'd have told you if he'd eaten a wise woman in the past two centuries." Neil's eyes met Julian's. "I swear."

"Who—" Julian began, then he knew.

He shoved Neil out of the way and raced barefoot and bare-chested across the snow.

Alex chased Cade through the moonlight. She wasn't enjoying this run at all. She'd thought when werewolves shared the moon, they bonded. That it was the equivalent of coffee with the girls, poker with the boys, maybe a couples' potluck.

Instead, she kept getting ice and snow kicked in her face as she followed his light brown tail on and on. No gamboling, no rolling and wrestling, no playing. No fun.

They weren't *too* far away from town at least. She didn't feel sick. But she did miss Julian. She wished she'd stayed home and run with him.

First she and Cade had loped around and around Barlowsville in larger and larger circles. Alex was a new wolf. She didn't know the procedure. It had seemed a little foolish to her, but Cade appeared to enjoy it. Every time she glanced at him, he was grinning.

Eventually they'd headed away from town, and the terrain had become rougher if that were possible. Even on wolf feet, Alex had stumbled, fallen, then slid all the way down a hill and into a hollow of water so cold she couldn't understand how it wasn't frozen.

Once she'd extricated herself, she looked around for Cade and huffed a surprised bit of air through her nose to discover that he'd disappeared into a fairly large grove of trees. She plunged in, too, managing to keep sight of his tail, even though the thickness of the branches nearly obscured the moon.

Eventually she popped out of the cover and into a clearing where a house stood, surrounded on all sides by trees and tall piles of snow—an oasis in a desert of ice.

Unlit, the building was but a shadow, not a wisp of smoke from the fireplace, no hint of a generator. Cade trotted past the huge monster truck parked to the side. How had that gotten there? She didn't see a road anywhere.

Alex made an anxious sound as Cade approached the door. What was he doing?

That became apparent an instant later when Cade straightened to his full height, naked skin gleaming silver. Then he reached out and opened the door.

Alex cocked her head, afraid she'd hear screams, shots, but there was nothing. Perhaps this was a place Cade kept apart from the lab where he could relax away from his weird science. She wouldn't blame him.

The thought of going inside, finding warmth, a towel, even clothes, appealed more and more as the water on her fur turned to ice, then began to crackle and break and rain around her paws like sleet.

The natural reticence of a wolf for a human abode made her hang back, paw the snow, pace. She wasn't going to be able to go in until she—

Alex closed her eyes and reached for human form. The shift took longer than Cade's had. Of course Cade was nearly as old, and therefore as powerful, as Julian.

Once she had two legs instead of four, Alex hurried inside.

"Close the door."

Cade's voice came from somewhere to her right. With the door closed and human eyes, she couldn't see much. The windows were covered. The moon could not spill in.

"This is yours?" she asked.

"It is now."

A light flared, so brilliant she was left blinking against the glare. When the black spots went away, she saw that Cade had set a portable lantern on the mantel. The room was so small and the lantern so bright, everything was illuminated.

The blood splotches on the floor, the basket of toys in the corner, and the hundreds of pictures of Alana Barlow that had been tacked over every inch of the walls.

Alex slowly tugged her gaze from the pictures to Cade, but before she even saw his face, she knew she was in trouble.

Julian managed to slow down long enough to avoid crashing through the door of the lab; he managed to calm down enough to keep from shouting his brother's name. Until he discovered the place was empty. Then he shouted a lot.

However when he found Alex's clothes, he couldn't speak at all.

A shadow fell over Julian where he knelt next to the neatly folded black slacks and white blouse. He had one of her ugly boots cradled in his arms like a baby.

"You've got it bad," Neil murmured.

Julian couldn't argue. He did have it bad. What he didn't have was her.

Apparently, his brother—the murdering, rogue werewolf—did.

"We have to find them," he said.

"Mmm," Neil agreed, moving around the room, glancing into drawers, closets, and the refrigerator. "They obviously went running together by choice." Neil gazed pointedly at the perfectly folded shirt. "He didn't tear her clothes from her body and force her to do anything. There'd be blood somewhere other than the refrigerator."

Julian growled.

"Calm down."

"How can I when I've just discovered my brother's been killing Inuit?" Julian set Alex's boot on the floor and got to his feet. "And why is that?"

Neil began to sort through a pile of papers on the desk. "I only know why he killed the wise women."

Neil calmly opened a folder and peered inside. When he didn't continue, Julian snapped, "Why?"

"I thought you knew."

"If I knew, *Neil*"—Julian drew out the name—"I wouldn't be asking you."

Neil frowned and glanced up. "Cade told me you knew, and that you were all right with it."

"With what?" Julian ground between clenched teeth. Several empty beakers rattled, one of them burst into shards.

"Don't get excited." Though Julian could incinerate him if he was of a mind to, Neil's voice and manner were nothing but calm. "You remember how Cade always had to talk to the local wise woman, shaman, whatever?"

"Yes. He wanted to know what they did."

Neil nodded. "Which is why he ate them. That way all their knowledge became his."

"That's nuts."

"That's Cade."

"And you thought I was okay with this?"

"Back in those days things were different. *We* were different. Besides, you never did anything about it."

"I didn't know!"

"That was probably why."

"What the hell was I doing when this was going on?"

"Leading a boatload of Vikings. You had a lot on your mind."

Julian ran a hand over his face.

"It wasn't as if people weren't dying, Julian. Back then, that was kind of what we did."

"I don't understand why he'd suddenly decide that killing someone, then eating them, gave him their knowledge. He was always talking to the local witch doctor types."

"And he was *always* killing and eating them. He didn't start when he became a werewolf."

Julian opened his mouth, then shut it again as he remembered Alex telling him her theory of the rogue.

A psychotic murderer in both forms.

How could Julian have been so blind?

"I have to find him."

"He has no reason to hurt her." Neil picked up another folder. "She's just some girl." He opened the cover. "Or not. What the hell, Julian?"

He slid the folder across the desk, and the contents spilled out. Photos of Alex. News clippings. Printouts of Internet searches. It all looked very familiar.

Because it was his.

Somehow Cade had gotten hold of the file Julian had made about Alexandra Trevalyn.

Werewolf hunter.

CHAPTER 26

"I loved her."

Alex pulled her gaze from that of Alana Barlow— on a merry-go-round, riding a horse, in the sandbox—all ages, all sizes, all Alana, all the time. There was even a collection of snow globes on the only table in the room, each one surrounding a different reflection of the beautiful, dead blonde.

Cade had pulled on a pair of sweatpants he no doubt kept in the house for the times he came here and . . . what? Beat off in the middle of her shrine?

"This is sick," Alex murmured.

A terry-cloth robe hit her in the face. "*You're* sick. You disgusting, filthy *Jäger-Sucher.*"

Since the room was cold and her goose bumps had goose bumps, Alex put on the robe. "I guess all the cats are out of their respective bags," she said.

Cade knew who she was—or close enough—and she had a pretty good idea who he was.

"Bet you were pissed when Julian took that bullet instead of me."

"Pissed isn't the word." With the speed she still hadn't quite gotten used to, he reached over and backhanded her so hard she not only flew off her feet but smashed into the wall.

Several of Alana's pictures tore free and skated through the air to join her on the floor.

"Bitch," he muttered. "See what you've done?"

A blow like that would have killed Alex if she'd been human. As it was, he'd merely knocked out a few of her teeth. She spat them on the floor and wondered if she'd live long enough to grow them back.

Alex gathered the photos and stood. "Where'd you get these?"

She was half afraid he'd say the place was Julian's; then she'd really be creeped out.

Instead he snatched the pictures from her hands. "Don't touch her," he said. "Never touch her."

Alex had to bite down on her lip to keep from saying that Alana was ashes, and they were a little hard to touch. She figured a comment like that would be the quickest way to lose another couple of teeth.

"I thought werewolves didn't show up on film?" she said instead.

Another great reason to become one. No more pictures. Alex had never been a fan. Smile for the camera. Look pretty. Be *on*.

Alana didn't appear to have any problem. From the number of photos, and the visible joy on her face in every one, she'd adored the camera as much as it had adored her.

"I asked for old photos from her Gramma, then made copies. Told her I was going to give them to Julian as a gift. Once he was ready." Cade tacked the fallen pictures in the exact places they'd fallen out of. "I never thought he would be."

"He isn't," she said. "Don't worry."

He rounded on her with a snarl. "He made you like *her*. Like us. Then brought you *here*. Why would he do that? He's lost his mind. He's lost his balls. He isn't fit to lead."

Alex didn't like the sound of that. *Not fit to lead* usually led to some kind of coup. And in werewolf land, that meant a challenge. Although why worry? She didn't think Cade could kill Julian.

Then again, she hadn't thought Cade could kill anyone.

There was a lot more to Cade than any of them had been aware of. She needed to discourage a coup—along with hatred of Julian. If she had a snowball's chance, she'd even have tried to convince him she wasn't evil incarnate—but she knew better.

"He wanted me to suffer," she blurted. "Killing me was too easy." His eyes narrowed, and she hurried to add, "Not that he won't eventually."

"I don't see you suffering. In fact, you fit right in with no trouble at all. And now you're his mate. He'll never kill you." He took a deep breath and slowly let it out. "So I have to."

Cade had planned this well. She was naked—or near enough. She didn't have a gun, a knife, a silver anything. And she'd returned to human form, where she was only a slightly faster, stronger woman, and from the speed with which he'd smacked her, not as fast or as strong as him. Shifting into a wolf would take too long, especially when he could do so in an instant.

Alex glanced at the windows; she couldn't help it. But they were shuttered and—

"No one knows where we are."

Her gaze met his, and she caught a trace of the madness he'd kept so well hidden lurking behind the eyes of a man she'd begun to think of as her friend.

"If they come to my place they'll think we went running

together. They'll wait until tomorrow to worry." He smiled, and the madness blossomed. "By then it'll be too late."

"Julian will know. He'll figure it out."

"He hasn't figured anything out so far. I have my brother as convinced of my peaceful nature as anyone."

"Love is blind," she said.

"And pretty damn dumb."

She had to keep him talking. If he was talking to her he wasn't killing her.

"You murdered my father."

Alex hadn't meant to say that. Bringing up death at all was probably a bad idea. But she'd opened her mouth, and out it had come.

Cade had been staring at a montage of Alana in a sky-blue dress, hair piled on top of her head and messily hanging about her ears. Kind of like Cade's.

She'd never gotten a look at his ears in this form but—

Alex frowned. She had seen his wolf ears, and they'd been as intact as hers.

"Charlie?" Cade turned away from the wall. "Never met the man."

Could Cade have found a way to heal silver? Who the hell knew?

"Why would you think that I'd killed Charlie?" he mused.

"If you didn't kill him, then how do you know who he is?"

"Julian has a dossier on you." His head cocked. "From your lack of surprise, you knew that." He lifted his gaze to the ceiling, tapped his finger against his lip. "You're searching for your father's killer. You think that he's here. Why would you think that?"

His head lowered, his eyes falsely wide, his mouth in a sarcastic *o*. "This has Edward written all over it."

Alex didn't comment, because it did.

"The old man pulled a fast one. He's been trying to find us for years. He never would have been able to." He clapped his hands. "But then Julian became obsessed with you and his revenge. So Edward lay in wait. He used Julian's pain to his advantage, let you become the perfect little spy." Cade began to grin. "I wouldn't put it past him to have leaked your identity to Julian in the first place."

Alex's eyes narrowed. She wouldn't put it past him, either.

"Then he tells you your father's killer is here, and the next thing you know you're volunteering."

Close enough.

"This is fantastic." He laughed. "I won't even have to deny killing you. You're a spy. They'll give me a goddamn medal."

"Julian won't."

Cade's laughter died, and he shrugged. "He's a fool. Lets Alana run off and be killed by you. Then tries to get cutesy, to punish you, and he ends up *mated* to you. Everything he touches turns to shit."

"He saved your life."

"And I thanked him. Am I supposed to be his slave until the end of time?"

"I think, yeah."

"I think not. He doesn't want to rule the world, well I do."

Uh-oh, Alex thought.

"I've been waiting and watching for a weakness." His gaze met hers, and he smiled. "Now he's got one. Once I kill you, he'll be writhing. I should be able to challenge him and win."

Alex blinked. Hell. The coup really was on.

She had to do something. She didn't want the village under

Cade's thumb. He was nuts. And what about the Inuits? They'd be nothing but a smorgasbord.

She needed to get outside, then to the trees where she could perhaps hide long enough to shape-shift, make her way back to Barlowsville, and blow the whistle on the wolf in their midst.

It wasn't much of a plan, but it was all she had. And it started with knocking Cade senseless enough for her to have a head start.

Before she could think too hard and too long about what she was about to do, Alex snatched up one of the glass globes full of water and snow and Alana, then she pitched it right at Cade's head.

It was a good throw—a great one, in fact. She put everything she'd ever learned from Charlie into it. All those years of instruction, of practice, combined with her increased strength, and she just knew that pitch was going to cause some damage.

Until Cade reached up with that surprising speed, snatching the thing out of the air an instant before it would have broken his nose.

Julian strode toward the back door, the change trickling over him like a winter wind. His jeans split at the seams, bursting open to allow his haunches free.

His fury at his brother for wrecking everything, combined with his fury at himself for not realizing it, allowing him to open the back door with hands on the end of paws before he shouted from a snout that should not have been able to form words, "Bring the others."

Then he hit the ground loping, following the scent of Cade and Alex down the street, out of town, then around and around and around. He knew she couldn't be far, but he also couldn't figure out in what direction they'd gone.

The scents overlapped; they went one way, then curled back the other. He was so angry, so upset, so—yes, he admitted it—scared his focus was shot to shit. He felt as if his brain would explode, so he plopped onto his haunches and lifted his nose to the moon.

"Oooowww-exxxxx!" he called, and the moon answered.

Julian, it whispered in a voice that rumbled through his blood. *Julian.*

His head whipped to the right. *There.*

He pulled on his power and the next instant . . .

He saw her.

Alex went for the door. Of course he'd had her close it. Not that its being wide open would have helped. Not when he was ancient, and she was so brand new. His speed was legend, and hers . . . Well, hers was not.

Her fingers had no more than brushed the doorknob, and he was there, slamming her head against it, making her as dazed as she'd wanted him to be.

She recovered quickly enough, which made her realize that her plan had been crappier than she'd thought. Cade would have recuperated from glass to the noggin before she'd run fifty yards from the house.

"Nice try," he said. "But I was kind of waiting for that. I read the dossier, remember? And there was that one article about you competing in a softball tournament."

Her neck burned; she hissed in a breath that smelled of scalded flesh, ashes, and silver. The knife glittered next to her face.

"Everyone was so amazed at your talent. How fast you

could pitch. How accurate and so darn hard. Where had you been? What had you been doing?" He chuckled. "I bet Edward loved that."

"Not so much," she managed through the pain. Was he going to hold that silver knife against her neck until she caught fire? And how could he hold silver anyway?

He lifted the blade from her skin, where he'd merely been resting it, though it had felt as if he'd plunged the weapon straight home, and she noted the thick iron hilt that kept the silver from touching him.

Edward had seen the article, too. Edward saw everything. Boy, had he let her have it.

Jäger-Suchers did not waste time; they did not play games. *Jäger-Suchers* did not allow their pictures to be taken; they definitely did not allow them to be printed in the paper. *Jäger-Suchers* did *not* draw attention.

Alex had never played in a softball tournament again.

"There was a follow-up article," Cade said. "About how you disappeared. How your name was false. How you paid in cash. They even tried to match your fingerprints, but huh— the entire hotel room had been wiped down. And your van had fake plates."

"Welcome to my world," Alex muttered.

Cade slammed her head against the door again, then leaned in close and whispered, "Welcome to mine."

In the distance the howl of a wolf lifted into the night. Alex realized how hard Cade had hit her when the howl began to sound like her name.

"Julian," she whispered, and Cade smacked her again. Strangely *he* didn't appear to hear that howl, or if he did he wasn't worried. Which scared her more than the knife had. He should be more afraid of Julian.

"You ruined him," Cade continued. "All he can think

about is you. He let the most beautiful woman in the world walk away. You *killed* her, and yet he trails after you panting." He yanked her upright. "Open the door."

Still a little woozy, Alex said, "Wha—? Why?"

"I'm not going to defile her place with your blood."

"Ashes." Alex managed to get her hand on the handle, but it wasn't easy. "Not blood."

"You think I'm going to kill you fast?" Cade asked, then he picked her up by the back of the neck and tossed her into the night.

Alex skidded across the ice, the robe riding up to her hips, the uneven surface dragging furrows in her skin. She scrambled to her feet, and Cade landed on her back, driving her face into the snow.

"You *killed* her," he said again, as if she didn't already know. "You're gonna pay in blood. Every last drop of it before you die." He stood, hauling her along, too. "I'd like to study it anyway." He turned the knife this way and that, considering the spark of moonlight across the blade. "For that I'll need the blood outside and not in."

He was stronger than she'd thought, quicker than he'd ever appeared as he dragged her to the rear of the monster truck and strapped her to the tailgate. The truck was so hopped up on its oversize tires that her feet barely touched the ground.

Alex fought, but Cade was no longer the lame little brother. She understood now that he never had been.

"You pretended to be a science geek—"

"I didn't have to pretend that." He slashed the knife through the air like Zorro. "I love playing with blood. You would not believe some of the things I've got cooking in my lab. Julian has no idea. He's all brawn. Always has been. I could make a whole new monster with what I've got in there. Once I'm in charge, I'm going to. Edward won't know what hit him."

Alex's eyes widened. Maybe Edward hadn't been lying about everything. Maybe it was just that the werewolf army he'd suspected was the brainchild of a different Barlow, and maybe the army wasn't even werewolves at all.

"Were you ever working on a serum to de-evil the other werewolves?"

"I wouldn't do that to them. Why be a werewolf if you can't enjoy killing people?"

"So you lied to your brother about the serum?"

Cade cocked his head, his gaze lowering to her chest. From the flare in his eyes, Alex figured the robe had drooped open.

She glanced down. She'd been right; the slight swell of her breasts was tipped by moonlight.

Another flash of silver and flames erupted from the four-inch slit Cade put in her chest. He'd obviously done this before, because he did it just right. If he cut too deeply she'd be doing a Joan of Arc imitation. Instead he just grazed the surface enough to cause blood to flow down her ribs like rain, putting out the tiny fire and leaving just a little bit of smoke.

"Honey," Cade murmured, licking his lips, "I lied to my brother about everything."

Boosted by his anger, Julian covered miles in an instant. He would have barreled right into Cade's back if he hadn't seen the flash of silver, caught the scent of flames and blood, then heard his brother's words.

The wolf's body sensed danger. Silver meant fire, and fire would kill. The human mind understood that Cade had a knife, and he was using it on Alex.

But he hadn't killed her yet. Right now he was just playing with her, as a cat might play with a mouse right before he ate it.

And just like a cat, if something bigger threatened to take away that mouse—

Gulp.

So Julian fed his anger with the scent of blood and fear—Who dared mark her but him? Who dared scare her at all?—and he threw up his invisibility cloak just as Cade turned around.

His brother's eyes narrowed. But there was nothing to see.

Cade spun back to Alex. "I've got all night. I can make this last. You'll beg to die. You'll wish you had."

"Eat me," Alex muttered.

"Oh, I plan to."

Cade drew a test tube out of the pocket of his loose sweatpants. "First things first, just in case I get carried away." He slid his fingers into the belt of the robe, then slid the flat of the knife along the smooth, flat expanse of her stomach. "Hmm," he said.

"Don't even think about it."

Cade laughed. "I'll think about what I want and do what I want. My days of listening to anyone are over."

Alex lifted her eyes and seemed to look right at Julian. But she couldn't know he was there. Except—

He sniffed. When he'd arrived he'd smelled her fear. He'd seen it in the stiff set of her body and the wariness in her eyes. Now . . .

He smelled blood but no fear. Flames but no panic. She seemed as relaxed as a woman-wolf could be while hanging from a monster truck with a psychotic werewolf running a silver blade over her abs.

"Whoops." Cade's wrist twitched, and a thin line of red appeared at Alex's waist. She didn't even flinch. Not when he cut her and not when the flames danced along the wound like a thousand tiny tongues.

Cade waited for the flicker of fire to die, then bent and licked the blood. As he straightened he stepped in and captured her mouth with his.

"Urgh," Alex said, twisting and turning as if she was in greater pain than when she'd been bleeding and burning.

Cade lifted the hand that wasn't holding the knife and cupped her breast, viciously tweaking the nipple until she gasped.

Julian erupted from the invisibility bubble, hands and feet sprouting from paws, even as his snout crunched inward to become both nose and mouth. If anyone had been watching it would have seemed as if he just appeared from thin air, a wolf pouring out of the ether and landing upon the earth as a man.

Before Julian could grasp his brother by the neck and wring it, Cade had danced to the side and the tip of the silver knife hovered just above Alex's jugular.

"That's what I thought," Cade murmured.

"You are so fucked now," Alex said.

Julian's eyes widened. She had that much confidence in him? He wasn't sure anyone else ever had.

"Let her go, Cade."

"I'm done listening to you. She deserves to die for what she did to Alana."

"Alana was never happy as a wolf."

"She would have been!" Cade shouted. "If she'd been with me."

"You were a werewolf, too, Cade," Julian said softly. "And in the end, she hated it."

"She would have grown to love it."

"That's what I thought, what I hoped. But the longer she was one of us—" Julian paused, then admitted the truth. "She was never one of us."

Alana had never embraced being a werewolf, and once she'd learned the truth that had been denied her—

"Alana wanted to die. If it hadn't been Alex, it would have been someone else."

"You lie!" Cade roared, and the knife nicked her skin.

Zzzt!

The tiny flame sounded like a bug zapper, but Alex's body jerked as if she'd been jolted by a cattle prod. Silver near a major artery appeared to be a very bad idea.

"Alana's gone," Julian said. "We can't bring her back. Hurting Alex won't change that."

"No," Cade agreed. "But it'll make *me* feel better. And you'll feel better, too, once she's dead. She won't be your mate anymore. You'll be free."

Julian's eyes met Alex's. Surprisingly, he didn't want to be free if it meant no more her.

"He doesn't care about you," she said. "He wants me dead so you'll be too sick to fight when he challenges you."

Cade's lips twitched. "I guess that cat's out of the bag." He tapped the tip against Alex's neck again, and again flames spurted as she jerked.

"Stop!" Julian shouted despite himself.

Cade ignored him. "Did you know that she's a spy?"

"Right." Julian's gaze was on Alex's face, concerned at the paleness of it. Which was the only reason he saw the shift in her eyes. He glanced at Cade, who smirked.

"Edward told her that the werewolf who killed her father was here."

"Is that true?" Julian asked.

Alex straightened her shoulders, the movement giving the impression of lifting her chin, even though she couldn't without risking another painful zap from the knife. "Yes."

"I could have told you that there was no murderer in my village."

"Except for him?" She switched her gaze from Julian to Cade.

"She's got you there, bro."

Julian ignored Cade, his eyes on Alex. "Why didn't you tell me about Edward?"

"I think she made an agreement, Julian. I think she's supposed to give him you."

He had to give her credit: She held his gaze, she didn't look away. "Is that true?" he repeated.

"No." She swallowed, the movement of her throat bringing her skin treacherously close to the knife. He barely had time for relief at her words before she continued, "I'm supposed to give him the whole damn village."

A chill passed over Julian that had nothing to do with his standing buck naked in the middle of the Arctic. "And in return?" he asked.

"I lose my tail."

Julian blew out a derisive breath. "Edward's not going to cure you. He's going to keep you. You're the perfect spy. Hell, *I* trusted you."

Her mouth trembled. "I know."

He wasn't sure if she was commenting on Edward's duplicity or Julian's trust, then decided it didn't matter.

"So," Cade said, "okay if I kill her now?"

"No."

Cade's eyebrows lifted. "You want to?"

Julian rubbed his forehead. "No."

"Well, I'm not going to fight you until she's dead."

"I'm not going to fight you at all."

"That'll make it easier."

"You can't let him win," Alex said urgently. "He'll treat the Inuit like animals, chase them through the wilderness and hunt them down like . . ."

"Prey," Cade murmured. "Great idea. I just figured I'd have my very own human farm. I could pick and choose what I'd like for dinner. But the werewolf version of 'The Most Dangerous Game' would be a lot more fun."

"You think my wolves will stand for that?" Julian asked. "No one likes to kill but you."

"They'll do what I say." He spread the fingers of the hand that wasn't holding the knife. "Once you're dead."

"Will they?" Julian murmured, and his wolves emerged like an army from the trees.

CHAPTER 27

Julian had felt them coming. He'd known they were there. He always did. They were a part of each other, between them a connection that only death would break.

The werewolves stood in a semicircle, human eyes peering at Cade from two hundred lupine faces.

Cade began to sweat. Killing Alex? No problem. Fighting Julian? Once Alex was dead and he was writhing, not much of a challenge, either. But facing two hundred werewolves?

"Not so easy now," Alex murmured.

Cade began to babble. "She's a spy. She'll tell the *Jäger-Suchers* where we are. And he—" Cade pointed at Julian with the knife. "He won't let you be what you were born to be. Werewolves kill. It's what we do best. You've never lived until you've scented their fear, then tasted their blood."

"Dumb-ass," Alex said.

Julian knew exactly what she was thinking—and when had that started? Cade had just admitted his crimes to the jury of his peers.

Every gaze swung to Julian, and when they did, Cade

made a break for it. He dropped the knife; he started to run. Before he'd gone ten yards, he was a wolf.

Julian didn't want to kill him, but rules were rules, and Cade had broken them. It didn't matter that he was Julian's brother. He was still a psychotic, murdering werewolf, which meant that he must die. Julian closed his eyes, and he reached for the change.

"Julian," Alex whispered, her voice full of wonder and fear.

He opened his eyes just as a ghastly, grisly howl cut through the night.

The two of them stood all alone beneath the moon.

The howl went on and on and on, then it stopped.

Alex wasn't certain which was worse—the howl itself or the silence that followed.

Julian stared into the distance, face as still as the night. His eyes glittered; he appeared carved from stone.

"They took care of it," she said. "So you wouldn't have to."

Julian's wolves understood what killing his brother would do to him. But they couldn't allow Cade to live. Not here. Not anywhere. Cade would never stop killing. He liked it too much.

Julian didn't answer. He didn't even move.

"A little help," she called.

She was half afraid he'd continue to stand there, leaving her exposed and vulnerable. She'd take her punishment; she wouldn't run. But she'd prefer to take it when she wasn't trussed to a monster truck half naked.

Julian leaned over and picked up the knife Cade had dropped when he changed. Then he crossed the short distance between them. Alex started to feel cold and not from the ice. Perhaps her judge was here and her punishment—

Julian lifted the knife, but all he did was cut the rope that bound her to the tailgate.

Alex crumpled to the snow. He could have reached out and kept her from falling. Instead he just turned away.

She climbed to her feet, adjusted the robe, thought about what she could say. "I got nothin'," she admitted.

She *was* a spy. She'd planned to send all of them to their deaths. That she didn't plan to anymore didn't change that she'd plotted mass murder in the first place.

But Julian had been right. His wolves were more like people than most people. Barlowsville was home.

And so was he.

She couldn't leave. They were bonded. Mated. Stuck.

Strangely that knowledge didn't make her feel trapped. It made her feel . . . loved.

When had she fallen in love with him? She really couldn't say. Was what she felt merely a by-product of their bond? Did it matter when the bond was real and true and forever? They were part of each other in a way she could never be part of anyone else.

She sensed the werewolves returning, the sensation of them getting closer and closer a tangible pulse deep within. They emerged from the gloom and took up the same positions as before—a semicircle facing Alex and Julian. Her time had come.

She didn't bother to defend herself. She had no defense. She could say she was sorry now, but really . . . why on earth would they believe her?

Julian took a breath, then let it out on a long, exhausted sigh. He turned and strode toward her, the set of his shoulders determined, even as his face remained oh, so still.

"This is going to hurt me more than it's going to hurt you," he murmured.

He was right. Her pain would only last until the flames died. Considering their mate bond, his could go on and on.

"It's all right," she said. "I understand."

She wanted to tell him that she loved him, but that would only make things worse.

He was two feet away from her when the sleek black wolf leaped between them.

"Ella," Alex said. "Let him go."

Ella snarled, and the hair on the back of her neck lifted.

"Really," Alex continued. "He's gotta do what he's gotta do."

A silver wolf with Rose's eyes joined the black one; another with hair like Joe's was right behind. Wolves drifted in from both sides, making a line of multicolored beasts between Alex and Julian.

He lifted his gaze. "I guess they've made their choice."

"No—" Alex began.

"They're right. My arrogance got people killed. My obsession with vengeance put us all at risk. I'm not fit to lead."

"Who is?"

Alex had meant the question to be rhetorical—really, who *was* fit to lead?—but Julian's smile had her heart clenching. "Oh, no. Uh-uh. You stay right—"

Julian threw back his head and howled. The agony in the sound—the fury and the pain—made her reach out. Her hand was only an inch away from touching him when he shimmered, shifted, and disappeared.

Alex had been right about the coup, just wrong about the new alpha.

That appeared to be her.

Julian left, and he didn't come back. Sure, she sent wolves out to look for him; she went to look for him, but if Julian didn't want to be found, he wasn't going to be. He had magic on his side.

Sometimes late at night she heard him howling, the sound a long wail of agony for the brother he'd lost.

But he didn't go far. Certainly she felt ill on and off, but it wasn't too bad, and it always passed.

She imagined him loping beneath the winter sun, breath streaming out of his snout in a white mist. He would run just a little too far, and he'd feel the pull in his gut, the bond with his mate, and he'd turn back. Then his stomach would ease, and so would hers.

In a few months the bouts of nausea subsided. Since this coincided with reports of "the master" being seen at the edge of the woods watching Barlowsville one day, Awanitok the next, she understood why.

She was lucky; the village practically ran itself. Alex didn't have any trouble at all. Once the wolves had chosen her, she was theirs just as she'd been his, and they listened to whatever she had to say.

Still, Alex's guilt ate at her. Her appetite faded, yet she seemed to be gaining weight. Finally she went to the café, found Rose, and asked, "Why didn't you kill me?"

"Kill you?" Rose patted her cheek. "Julian broke his own rules by forcing you."

Since they were in the center of the café during the lunch rush, Rose's words were greeted with a dozen nods and just as many murmurs of agreement.

"We should have killed him." Rose's sweet face folded into a vicious scowl. "I still might."

"I killed Alana. I didn't understand. Until he *made* me understand."

"*Made* being the operative word." This from Daniel, who occupied a nearby table with Josh. "We don't do that around here."

"I was going to turn all of you over to Edward," Alex announced to the room at large.

"No, you weren't," Rose said, and returned to work.

Alex still lived with Ella. She'd been told she could move into Julian's house, but the instant she'd set foot in the door, she'd started to cry. Without him, the place was too big, too cold, and too quiet

Ella didn't mind. She said she liked the company. Alex thought what the Frenchwoman liked was keeping an eye on her. Every time Alex turned around lately, there stood Ella.

"You're starting to give me the creeps," Alex said after it happened for the fourth time in as many days.

Ella had been frowning at Alex's stomach, which was pushing uncomfortably at the seams of Ella's best slacks. "We have to talk."

Julian stayed in the wild for six months. His guilt haunted him. Alex haunted him.

He didn't like the man he'd been, so he remained a wolf. He had plenty of residual anger at both Cade and himself to stay in his preferred form. But all that fury was exhausting.

He started sleeping each day, running each night. Eventually he started running to her.

They were mates for life, and thanks to him that life would be long. The least he could do was let her live without him. But he missed his home. It was the only one he'd ever had.

So he hung around the outskirts of civilization, and he caught a distant glimpse of Alex now and again, a flicker of her scent—ice, trees, and the faint drift of citrus—sometimes the sound of her voice, and that was enough.

Until it wasn't.

There came a night when he couldn't stand the separation any longer. He told himself he'd only watch her as she lay sleeping; then he'd leave. She'd never even know he was there.

Fool.

She'd been a *Jäger-Sucher*. There wasn't a werewolf in the world she wouldn't know was there.

She didn't run with the others most nights. She stayed alone at Ella's, and the lights went out very early. Not long after they did, he went in.

She wasn't in her bed; she wasn't in her room. He found her standing at the front window, staring at the moon.

"I wondered how long you'd stay away."

He tried to work up enough anger to turn invisible. He should have done it before, but he discovered that being near her made him so damn happy, he had no anger left.

"I'll go soon," she said.

"What? Where?"

She continued to stare at the sheen of the half-moon that coated the village in liquid silver ice.

"This is your place not mine." She lifted a hand, but she didn't turn around. "Don't worry. If you can hold on for a few days, I'm sure Edward—make that Elise—will concoct something to make this . . . connection go away."

"You won't go near him," Julian said, and the house shook just a little. "Not ever again."

"I won't tell him where you are. I know you didn't believe me, but now—" She took a breath, and it shook. "I'd never let him hurt—" Her voice broke.

Was she crying? No. Alexandra Trevalyn would never cry. So why could he smell her tears?

"I'll stay here until it comes. I'll let you keep it. You know that I'd never bring the *Jäger-Suchers* down on—"

What was she *talking* about?

She turned, and it was as if all the air had been sucked out of the room, his lungs, the universe.

"Our child," she finished, placing her palm on the full swell of her belly.

Julian did the only thing a man could do at a revelation like that.

He fainted.

Julian went down so fast and so hard, Alex would have thought he'd been shot if the night hadn't remained completely silent.

She went onto her knees. He was already coming around.

"Impossible," he said as he opened his eyes.

She took his hand and placed it on her stomach. The child, no doubt irritated at being awoken by the thunderous thumping of Alex's heart, took the opportunity to give her its usual vicious kick.

Julian gasped and lifted his gaze to hers. He didn't appear capable of further speech.

"That's kind of how I felt when I heard."

Ella had figured it out. Alex refused to believe her until her stomach began to expand, and the baby began to do the mambo.

"Impossible might be a good name," Alex murmured, keeping her hand on top of Julian's on top of her stomach. "It's your child, after all."

"But I can't— We can't—"

"You obviously can, and we *did*."

"How?"

His face was gaunt. He broke her heart. She wanted to kiss him, to touch him and pull him close. But that would only make what she had to do so much harder.

"You healed a silver bullet, Julian. Is there anything you can't do if you put your *mind* to it?"

His forehead creased. "A boy with my gold hair. A girl with your green eyes."

She stared at him for several seconds. "Did you hit your head?"

"I thought that once, when we were . . ." He sat up, but he didn't remove his hand from her stomach.

"Oh!" Suddenly everything became clear. Julian was magic, and when he thought of things, they happened. "We were having sex and you thought of kids?"

"I didn't mean to. I was thinking about—" He looked away.

"Alana." That he'd been thinking of his wife while he was doing Alex was kind of . . . yuck. Then again, had she really believed he'd been thinking of her?

"You were angry?" she asked.

"Back then, every time I looked at you I was angry." Julian twitched his shoulders, more of a wince than a shrug. "*Green* eyes. That was you. So I guess I wasn't really thinking of her at all."

But he always would be. Alex knew that now.

Julian sighed. "She died because I couldn't give her a child, but it seems that I could. I never considered—"

Alex squeezed his fingers, and he looked into her face. "I don't think you could have given her one. This mate bond seems to be the cause of a whole lot of—" She floundered for a word.

"Weirdness," Julian supplied.

"Yeah. Besides, would you ever have been able to work up enough fury at her to change the course of lycanthropy?"

His lips quirked. "Probably not."

Alex didn't say what else she was thinking. That Alana had taken the easy way out; that if Alana had truly loved Julian, she'd have chosen the hard way. As Alex had.

She lifted her hand from his and got up. He scrambled to follow, and she stepped away. She couldn't be near him and not want him.

"A life for a life," she said. "It's only fair."

"What are you talking about?"

"I took Alana, but I can give you this." Her palm skated over the fullness. "Once I have the baby, I'll leave him or her with you. I'll go to Edward. He'll have to do something to make this connection between us go away. If he wants me to be able to work for him without puking all day."

"Work for him," Julian repeated.

"There are still werewolves out there that need to be killed. But now I know that there are some who don't. I won't make the same mistake twice."

"That's—" Julian appeared to be searching for his words. Maybe he *had* hit his head. "The stupidest thing I've ever heard in all of my lifetimes."

Alex blinked. "I'm sorry?"

"You should be." He reached out and drew her to him— too fast, they bumped bellies. "You're my mate, Alex."

"You didn't choose me; you didn't choose this."

"I did." He touched her stomach again as if he had to just to make sure it was real. She did that several times a day herself. "I chose to make you like me. For all the wrong reasons, true, and I hope you'll forgive me. I was wrong. If you want to go back to the other world and be cured, I'll understand."

She laid her hand on top of his. "Why would anyone want to go back once they've found this?"

"It's a miracle," he said.

"No." Alex lifted her lips and kissed him; then she knew without a doubt that she was home. "It's magic."

EPILOGUE

Their son was born three months later. As soon as Alex held him in her arms, she understood why Julian had said her idea of leaving the child behind had been the stupidest thing he'd ever heard.

"I couldn't have done it," she said.

"I know," Julian murmured. Sound asleep, the baby still clutched at his finger.

"I don't think he should be able to do that yet." Alex leaned down and nuzzled the child's head. He smelled like the first snowfall of the season.

"I think there's going to be a lot of things he does that he isn't supposed to be able to."

They were treading new ground. As far as they knew, there'd never been a werewolf pregnancy, let alone a child born of two lycanthropes. Alex would have been lying if she said she hadn't spent a lot of sleepless nights worrying if the child would be all right. If it would actually *be* a child at all.

But now that he was here and he was "perfect," she whispered, all her fears seemed kind of foolish.

Julian had worried about who would take care of the child

on that single night when every inhabitant of Barlowsville ran beneath the moon. Alex had pointed out it wasn't as if the moon snuck up on them. They *knew* when it was coming. A few hours before it did, they would drop the baby off with an entire village of Inuit babysitters.

Julian also worried that Alex would someday feel the need to go out hunting for her father's killer. But the closer she got to her due date, the less she thought about anything but her child.

"Edward will find him," she said with a shrug.

For a while she'd been concerned that Edward would find her. She hadn't reported back. But neither had any of Edward's other toadies. He'd believe she was as dead as they were, and she'd let him. That part of her life, that other Alex, *was* dead.

Ella and Jorund appeared in the doorway. Ella had proved a huge help with all things baby, and Jorund . . . he went wherever she was.

The two had recently married, and Jorund now lived in Barlowsville. He'd left George in charge.

The day after he'd come home, Julian had given in to Ella's request to make Jorund a werewolf. Julian could no longer deny the power of true love. It crossed boundaries of age, of race, of species. True love made all things possible. Their child proved that.

"What are you going to name him?" Ella asked.

"Charlie," Julian said, and tugged his finger from his son's grasp.

In his sleep Charlie frowned; then he opened his tiny, perfect mouth and he—

"Was that a growl?" Alex asked.

Read on for an excerpt from Lori Handeland's next book

MOON CURSED

Coming in 2011 from St. Martin's Paperbacks

The first recorded sighting of the Loch Ness Monster was by Saint Columba in AD 565. The most recent occurred just last year.

"There'll be a sighting every year," Kristin Daniels muttered as she peered at her laptop. "Wouldn't want to screw with a multi-million-dollar tourist industry."

Unless, of course, you were the host of the public television show *Hoax Hunters*. Kris planned to screw with it a lot.

In fact she planned to end it.

Kris scribbled more notes on her already scribbled-upon yellow legal pad. This was going to be her biggest and best project to date. The debunking of the Loch Ness Monster would not only put *Hoax Hunters* on the national radar—hell, she'd probably get picked up for syndication—but would make her a star.

"Kris?"

She glanced up. Her boss, Theo Murdoch, stood in the doorway of her office. He didn't look happy. Theo rarely did.

Public television was a crapshoot. Sometimes you won; sometimes you lost. But you were always, always on the verge of disaster.

"Hey, Theo," she said brightly. "I was just planning our premiere show for next year. You're gonna love it and so—"

"*Hoax Hunters* is done."

Kris realized her mouth was still half open, and shut it. Then she opened it again and began to babble. She did that when she panicked. "For the season, sure. But next year is going to be great. It'll be our year, Theo. You'll see."

"There is no next year, Kris. You're cancelled."

"Why?"

"Ratings, kid. You don't have 'em."

Fury, with a tinge of dread, made Kris snap: "It's not like we were ever going to compete with *Friday Night Smackdown*."

"And we don't want to." Theo's thin chest barely moved despite the deep breath he drew. The man was cadaverous, yet he ate like a teenaged truck driver. Were there teenaged truck drivers? "Cable's killing me."

Or maybe it was just his high stress and two packs a day diet.

In Theo's youth, back when he still had hair, PBS had been the place for the intelligent, discriminating viewer. Now those viewers had eight hundred channels to choose from, and some of those even produced a show or two worth watching.

In the glory days *Planet Earth* would have been a PBS hit. Instead it had played on *The Discovery Channel*. Once *The Tudors*—sans nudity of course—would have been a *Masterpiece Theatre* staple. Now it was *Showtime*'s version of MTV history.

"Who would have thought that public radio would do better than us?" Theo mumbled.

To everyone's amazement, NPR was rocking, even as PBS sank like a stone.

"Not me," Kris agreed. And too bad, too. Not that she could ever have done *Hoax Hunters* for the radio even if she *had* possessed a crystal ball. The show's strength lay in the visual revelation that what so many believed the truth was in fact a lie.

Hoax Hunters, which Kris had originally called *Hoax Haters,* had come about after a tipsy night with her best friend and roommate Lola Kablonsky. Kris had always loathed liars—she had her reasons—and she'd been very good at spotting them. One could say she had a sixth sense, if a sixth sense weren't as much of a lie as all the rest.

Why not make your obsession with truth and lies into a show? Lola had asked.

And full of margaritas and a haunting ambition, Kris had thought: *Why not?*

She'd used her savings to fund a pilot, and she'd gotten that pilot onto the screen through sheer guts and brutal determination. She wasn't going to let something as erratic as ratings get her down.

"I'll make the show anyway," she said.

Theo's smile was sad. "It won't help. The powers that be were never very enthusiastic. I doubt they'd put you back on the air no matter what hoax you hunted."

Kris powered down her laptop and began to pack her things. "Who said I'd let them?"

"Scotland," Lola said. "Does anyone really go to Scotland on purpose?"

Kris tossed a few more sweaters into her suitcase. "Just me."

September was cold in the Highlands, or so she'd heard. Not that she wasn't used to the cold. She was from Chicago. Cold moved in about October and hung around until

June. There'd even been a few July days when the breeze off the lake was reminiscent of the chill that drifted out of her freezer when she went searching for double chocolate brownie yogurt in the middle of the night.

"Are you sure, Kris?" Worry tightened Lola's voice. "You'll be all alone over there."

Alone. Kris gave a mental eye roll. *Horrors!* Like that would be anything new.

Her mother had died, still promising she wouldn't, when Kris was fifteen. Her brother had left for college when she was seventeen, swearing he'd visit often. If "often" was once the following year and then never again, he hadn't been lying. Her father hung around until she turned eighteen. Then he'd taken a job in China—no lie. He hadn't been back either.

So Kris was used to alone, and she could take care of herself. "I'll be fine." She zipped her suitcase.

"I'd go with you—"

Kris snorted. Lola in Scotland? That would be like taking Paris Hilton to . . . well, Scotland. Kris could probably shoot a documentary about it. The film would no doubt receive better ratings that *Hoax Hunters.*

And wasn't that depressing?

"Aren't you getting ready for the season?" Kris asked.

Lola was a ballet dancer, and she looked like one. Tall and slim, with graceful arms and never-ending legs, her long, black, straight hair would fall to the middle of her well-defined back if she ever wore it down. However, Lola believed that that style made her already oval face appear too oval. As if that could happen.

Kris wasn't bland and average, unless she stood next to Lola. She also wasn't a washed-out, freckle-nosed, frizzy-headed blond unless compared with Lola's porcelain complexion and smooth ebony locks. The only thing they had in common were their brown eyes. However, Lola's were pale, with flecks of gold and green, while Kris's were just brown, the shade of mud she'd been told by a man who'd said he was a poet.

The two of them were still friends because Lola was as beautiful inside as out, as honest as a politician was not, and she loved Kris nearly as much as Kris loved her. In all her life, Kris had never trusted anyone the way she trusted Lola Kablonsky.

Lola set her long-fingered, smooth, graceful hand on Kris's arm. "If you needed me, I'd go. Screw the season."

Kris blinked back the sudden sting in her eyes. "Thanks."

The two had met while living in the same cheap apartment building—Kris attending Loyola University and Lola attending ballet classes on the way to her present stint with the Joffrey Ballet. On the basis of a few good conversations, and a shared desire to get the hell out of their crappy abode, the two had found a better one and become roommates.

Casual observers might think that Kris and Lola would fight like cats in a bag when shoved into a residence the size of Lady Gaga's walk-in closet. Instead they'd remained roomies ever since, earning the nickname the Spinal Sisters—because they were together so much they had to be attached at the spine.

Kris hugged Lola; Lola hugged back, but she clung. Lola had been raised in a large, loud, loving, pushy Polish family. Combine that with her appearance, and Lola had probably never been alone for five minutes in her entire life. A good thing since she didn't like it.

Kris felt guilty for leaving her, but she didn't have a choice. She couldn't start over again with another show. She believed in *Hoax Hunters*.

She also believed that the Loch Ness Monster was ripe for debunking, and she was just the woman to do it.

Kris gathered the backpack that contained her laptop, video camera, and purse. "I'll be fine," she assured her friend for the second time. "It's not like I'm going to Iraq or Columbia or even the Congo. It's Scotland. What could happen?"

Though it felt like a week, Kris arrived in Drumnadrochit, on the west shore of Loch Ness, a day later.

She'd been able to fly directly from Chicago to Heathrow; however, unlike the rest of the people on the plane, she hadn't been able to sleep. Instead, she'd read the books she'd picked up on both Scotland and Loch Ness.

Loch Ness was pretty interesting, even without the monster. The lake was actually a three-hundred-million-year-old crack in the earth's surface. Because of its extreme depth—nearly eight hundred feet—the loch contained more fresh water than all the other lakes in Britain and Wales combined, and never froze over, even during the coldest of Highland winters.

Since there had been over four thousand reported sightings of Nessie, which no doubt fueled the forty million dollars attributed to her by the Scottish tourism industry, it wasn't going to be easy to debunk this myth. Kris certainly wasn't going to get any help from the locals.

By the time London loomed below, Kris's eyes burned from too much reading and not enough sleeping. However, she couldn't drag her gaze from the view. She wished she had the money to tour the Tower and Buckingham Palace; she'd always dreamed of walking the same streets as Shakespeare. But she was traveling on her own dime, and she had precious few of them.

The city sped by the window of the bus taking her to Gatwick Airport where she boarded a flight to Inverness. A few hours later, she got her first glimpse of a fairly industrialized city. Why Kris had thought Inverness would be full of castles, she had no idea. According to her guidebook, it had nearly sixty thousand people and less than half a dozen castles. Still she was disappointed. Quaint would play very well on film.

She got what she was hoping for on the road south. The countryside was quaint squared, as was Drumnadrochit. White buildings backed by rolling green hills, the place should have been on a postcard—hell, it probably was—along with the long, gray expanse of Loch Ness.

The village was also tourist central, with a wealth of Nessie museums, shops and tours by both land and sea. Kris would check them out eventually. They'd make another excellent backdrop for her show. The charm of the town would highlight the archaic myth, illuminating how backward was a belief in fairy tales. The excessive glitter of tourism would underline why the locals still pretended to believe.

Kris had once adored fairy tales, listening avidly as her mother read them to her and her brother. In those tales, bad things happened, but eventually, everything worked out.

In real life, not so much.

Her driver, an elderly, stoic Scott who'd said nothing beyond an extremely low-voiced, "Aye," when she'd asked if he often drove to Drumnadrochit, continued through town without stopping. For an instant Kris became uneasy. What if the man had decided to take her into the countryside, bash her on the head, and toss her into the loch, making off with her laptop, video camera, and anything else she might possess? Sure, Lola would miss her eventually, but by then Kris would be monster bait.

A hysterical bubble of laughter caught in her throat. She didn't believe in monsters—unless they were human.

She lifted her gaze to the rear-view mirror and caught the driver watching her. He looked like anyone's favorite grampa—blue-eyed, red-cheeked, innocent.

And wasn't that what everyone said about the local serial killer?

The vehicle jolted to a stop, and Kris nearly tumbled off the shiny leather seat and onto the floor. Before she recovered, her driver leaped out, opened her door, and moved to retrieve her bag from the trunk.

Kris peered through the window. They'd arrived at Lakeside Cottage, which, while not exactly *lake*-side was damn close. Kris would have to cross the road to reach the loch, but she'd be able to see it from the house. The village of Drumnadrochit lay out of sight around a bend in the road.

"Idiot." Kris blew her bangs upward in a huff. "No one's going to bash you over the head. This isn't the south side of Chicago."

She stepped out of the car, then stood frozen like Dorothy opening the door on a new and colorful world. The grass was a river of green, the trees several shades darker against mountains the hue of the ocean at dawn. The air was chilly, but it smelled like fresh water and—

"Biscuit?"

A short, cherubic woman, with fluffy white hair and emerald eyes stood in the doorway of the cottage. For an instant Kris thought she was a Munchkin. She certainly had the voice for it.

"I made a batch of Empires to welcome ye." She held out a platter full of what appeared to be iced shortbread rounds topped with a cherry.

Since Kris hadn't eaten since the flight to Heathrow, she

took one, despite her belief that a biscuit should only be served warm, dripping with butter and honey.

At the first bite, her mouth watered painfully. Crisp and sweet—was that jelly in the middle?—she couldn't remember eating anything so fabulous in a very long time.

"It's a cookie," she managed after she swallowed the first and reached for a second.

The woman smiled, the expression causing her cheeks to round like apples beneath her sparkling eyes. "Call it whatever ye like, dearie." She lifted the platter. "Then take another."

Kris had to listen very hard to distinguish the English beneath the heavy brogue. She felt as if she were hearing everything through a time warp, one that allowed the meaning of the words to penetrate several seconds after they were said. She hoped that the longer she stayed, the easier it would get.

"Thanks." Kris took two cookies in each hand. "I'm Kris Daniels."

"Well, and don't I know that." The plump, cheery woman giggled. The sound resembled the Munchkin titters that had welcomed Dorothy to Oz. Kris glanced uneasily at the nearby shrubbery, expecting it to shake and burp out several more little people.

Then she heard what the woman had said, and a cold finger traced her spine. If they already knew her here, knew what she did, who she was, her cover was blown, and her story was crap before it had even begun. Why hadn't she used a false name?

Because she hadn't thought anyone in the Scottish Highlands would have seen a cable TV show filmed in Chicago. And how, exactly, would she present herself as Susie Smith, when her credit cards and passport read Kristin Daniels?

"You know me?" Kris repeated faintly.

"I spoke with ye on the phone. Rented ye the cottage. Who else would be arriving today bag and baggage?"

Kris let out the breath she'd taken. She was no good at cloak and dagger. She liked lying about as much as she liked liars, and was therefore pretty bad at it. She needed to get better and quick.

"You're Mrs. Cameron," Kris said.

"Effigenia," the woman agreed. "Everyone calls me Effy."

Effy's brilliant eyes cut to the driver, who was as thin and tall as she was short and round. "Ye'll be bringing that suitcase inside now, Rob, and be quicker about it than a slow-witted tortoise."

Kris glanced at the old man to see if he was offended, but he merely nodded and did as he'd been told.

Very slowly.

Kris's lips twitched. She'd have been tempted to do the same if Effy had ordered her around.

Rob came out of the cottage, and Effy shoved the plate in front of him. "Better eat a few, ye great lummox, or ye'll be starvin' long before supper."

He took several. "If ye didnae cook like me sainted mother, woman, I'd have drowned ye and yer devil's tongue in the loch years ago."

Looming over the diminutive Effy, deep voice rumbling like the growl of a vicious bear, Rob should have been intimidating. But there was no heat to his words, no anger on his face. He just stated his opinion as if he'd stated the same a hundred and one times before. Perhaps he had. The two did seem well acquainted.

Effy snorted and shoved the entire plate of biscuits into his huge, worn hands with a sharp, "Dinnae drop that, ye old fool," then she reached into the pocket of her voluminous gray skirt and pulled out a key, which she presented to Kris. "Here ye are, dearie. And what is it ye'll be doing in Drumnadrochit?"

"I'm . . . uh . . ." Kris glanced away from Effy's curious gaze, past Rob, whose cheeks had gone chipmunk with cookies, toward the rolling, gray expanse of the loch. "Writing."

"Letters?" Rob mumbled.

"Why would she need to travel all this way to write a letter?" Effy scoffed.

"Some do."

"I'm writing a book," Kris blurted.

There. That had even sounded like the truth. Maybe the key to lying was thinking less and talking fast. No wonder men were so good at it.

"A children's book?" Effy asked.

Kris said the first thing that popped into her head. "Sure."

Silence greeted the word. That *hadn't* sounded very truthful.

"Mmm." Rob gave a throaty, Scottish murmur, drawing Kris's attention away from the loch and back to him. Luckily for her, it also caught Effy's attention.

"Ye ate them all?" She snatched the empty plate from his hands.

"Ye said not to drop them. Ye didnae say not to eat them."

"And if I didnae tell ye *not* to drive into the water, would I find ye swimming with Nessie of an afternoon?"

Rob didn't answer. Really, what could he say?

"Nessie," Kris repeated, anxious to keep their attention off her inability to lie. "Have you seen her?"

"Mmm," Rob murmured again, this time the sound not one of skepticism but assent.

"If ye live in Drumnadrochit," Effy said, "ye've seen her."

Kris laughed. She couldn't help it. *"Everyone's* seen her?"

Effy lifted her chin to indicate the loch. "Ye have but to look."

Kris spun about. All she saw were waves and shadows and rocks.